THE SECRET IN YOUR HAND

Andrew Ame Aba

MINERVA PRESS
ATLANTA LONDON SYDNEY

THE SECRET IN YOUR HAND

ISBN 0 75410 550 4

First Published 1999 by
MINERVA PRESS
315–317 Regent Street
London W1R 7YB

Printed in Great Britain for Minerva Press

THE SECRET IN YOUR HAND

In memory of my late father and first teacher of English, Papa Paul Idu Aba, and dedicated to my dearest friend, sister and wife, Lulu Adoo Aba.

Part One

I hold a shell in my hand.
I open it.
Does it speak to me
Of drowned seamen
Shattered wrecks,
Miserable wanderers?
It only speaks to me.

The Secret, by an anonymous eight year old, from *Presenting Poetry*, ed. Thomas, Blackburn, 1966, p.64, with permission of the publishers.

Prelude

The auditorium was adorned with variegated bunting, potted plants, and fresh flowers in antique vases of a silver hue. Swathed in loops of cotton fabric in the university colours, the grand podium awaited the procession of the day's dignitaries. On either side of the high table was mounted the American Star and Stripes and the LCU flag, respectively. Handel's *Water Music* filled the air, as if wafting from the giant chandeliers of the state-of-the-art Graduate School Auditorium.

The functionaries began to file in – professors emeriti, regents, other professors, eminent friends, leading benefactors, the Lake City University president and the trustees. Even in their awe-inspiring gowns of academia, most of these men and women still came through as the simple, approachable persons that students knew them to be. So thought Dezmond Adama, as he drank in the sheer grandeur of the reception ceremony. There was none of that feeling of stiltedness, that sudden transmogrification into gods and goddesses, and that air of an annual carnival to which Dezmond had become accustomed back in his own country.

The students filed into their marked seats, each in formal business attire, a far cry from the quotidian scenarios of summer nakedness all over the campus, and everywhere else except inside church.

Dezmond was engrossed in his own distant world, only returning to himself when the auditorium broke into an applause. The president was giving his charge to the fresh graduate students.

'LCU is not a rest stop in your life's journey, though you are expected to live with all its challenges and thrills. You belong among the brightest bunch of candidates any college president can boast of, representing every continent. Congratulations for having been found worthy of LCU Graduate School, which is among the top of the pack in these United States of America.'

A loud cheer rent the air.

'In the same vein,' continued the president, 'you are assumed to have already succeeded in your various study programmes, unless, of course, you opt to flunk out; in which case, we are honour bound to rubber-stamp it for you...' A rumbling, chuckling reaction arose from among the students. 'Indeed,' resumed the president, 'a grade below "B" is a failure in LCU graduate courses.' Another wave of rumbling. 'I guess I'd better begin to conclude,' resumed the speaker, drawing some laughter. 'Always remember our motto; digest it; and make it your watchword in the challenges ahead. And now, shall we arise and declare it; one and all together: *Grow to become all that you can become!'* A loud prolonged applause followed.

'Distinguished guests, thank you for the generous response. But I'll make one more point; then it'll be time to shut up and sit down. Oh, somebody's reminded me here that I am professor of speech, after all!' Hearty laughter again punctuated his statement.

'On a serious note, this audience is the best bunch of guys I've ever been privileged to address. Nobody ever listened to old Charlie Fall this long without falling asleep!' The air of *joie de vivre* and laughter that now pervaded this gathering made the speech look like an after-dinner talk. However, the president was laying the plank to the punchline of his charge. Dezmond Adama enjoyed the humour, but even as he listened, his mind went back to some of the less humorous impressions which he had gathered during the 'candid talk' sessions of the orientation. Something told him that that humour was only a condiment, and a mere modicum at that, among the ingredients of the great melting pot called America. The speaker reminded him of a self-exiled Nigerian humorist who used to make his readers laugh, only to make them cry.

The president began to wind his speech up. 'Now, on a really serious note, I want to warn you young men and women looking so great and gorgeous in today's turnout. America, the beautiful, God's own country, yes indeed! This is veritably the best country on planet earth! God has truly put our boundary lines in the most glorious, most beautiful, and most pleasurable of places. Notwithstanding, ours is a problem-plagued, problem-oriented society. By the way, I'm glad you had Alvin Toffler's *Future Shock* as one of your orientation texts. It is not just another rave of the day but a serious book that tells it like it is.

'The late Albert Einstein, born German but naturalised American in 1940, spoke for our present-day society when he said, "The world that we have made as a result of the level of thinking we have done so far, creates problems that we cannot solve at the same level as they were created." You will have more than your fair share of these problems. Most will come on their own accord; a few will be wrought by your own very hands; and some will be engineered for you, perhaps, as a necessary throughput. Face your life walking tall! Never turn your back, for a good foot soldier wears no armour on his backside.'

The auditorium sat still to the last man.

'We look forward to harvesting and harnessing from among you, great thinkers, landmark researchers and new-century innovators, as we march into the last quarter of the twentieth century. Finally, having so successfully completed the rigorous four-week preparatory exposure, in two days' time, you will be launched into orbit, solo flight, so to speak. The sky is *not* your limit... You heard right: I said, the sky is not your limit. Mortal men like you have got to the moon. Alongside the LCU motto which I highlighted a little while ago, I recommend that you obey the law which our cybernetics colleagues call "the law of requisite variety". Requisite variety says that a system adapts to its environment to the degree that the system's internal controls incorporate variety. I believe that you and I are as much a system as any other. Go forth then, my beloved students, adapt fully, make your spirit and soul incorporate variety; strive boldly to become all that you can. Thank you!'

A spontaneous standing ovation followed. The key guests filed down from the podium amidst renewed exchanges of pleasantries and dignified backslappings. The tendrils of budding friendships began to break apart.

The sombre atmosphere was lightened somewhat, only by the rounds of hugs, kisses and handshakes. We'll meet now and again, in twos and threes, but in orbit, ruminated Dezmond, as he shook hands or hugged one friend after another. In the background one could hear an instrumental rendition of 'God be with you till we meet again'.

The words and spirit of the president's speech stuck indelibly in Dezmond's mind. That is my own head start, he told himself. The challenge comes so strongly, I can hardly wait to be launched into orbit. I will shut all doors and face tomorrow; let the problems come! I will overcome.

As he was staying on in Clement's Hall, perhaps, for the one month of grace before moving off-campus, he ranged from one scene or thought, to another, in the crowded terrain of his mind: Kano airport, with its endless *'Waiting for Godot'*... O'Hare airport, with its voluptuous black women borne on an awesome tide of human traffic... the minute-by-minute turbo-blast of computerised take-offs and landings... capricious tricks of the midsummer sun that confuse man's native sense of time; open-air square dancing with American girls! Goodbye to excursions, hospitality weekends, trauma clinics, church basement squash parties; get behind me, seductive green golf courses trampled by corpulent, self-pampering moneybags with their ever-black caddies! Get behind, Main Street of a million neon lights screaming to the madding crowd: Cinema: showing *Deep Throat*; Sizzling Crown Plaza; M&A's; Avant-Garde Movie; Pinball King; Tall Girls; irresistible Big Macs; Water Beds Inc; Beef 'n Ale; Fantasy Nite Close; a whole *embarras de choix*... get behind me!

Dear Father,

Our aeroplane landed safely at Lake City via London, Chicago, Indianapolis and Bloomington... even that cannot tell you how far away I am. White men took away my kola nuts. They do not know such objects of sacrifice here. And they said that bad Nigerians brought strange weeds here, saying it was for soup, only to make plantations of them. So, I now have nothing to hold and speak to our gods. About the amulet, tell the old shaman of Aroji that his juju did not work, maybe because I removed the five smooth stones of the stream at Kano in order to reduce the weight of my luggage. The only day I remembered the amulet and wore it has been my worst day here. Many terrible things happened to me. The worst was that a mad woman chased me with a knife and nearly killed me. As I write, the fear of what happened has not left me. Please, make sacrifices for me, though I have told you I am following mama's way of the church. I will not have time to write many letters, seeing how far and how long it takes. Just take it always that I am well. Life here is very fast and the books are many that I must read. I will try my best to catch aspects of life here and tell you all when I return home… Greet mama and all the children…

I am,
Your son,
Dezmond Adama
Lake City University, USA, 29th May, 1974

Chapter One

A rich watering hole! observed Dezmond to himself as his shoes clattered down the tall steps of the library block. I will saturate my brain in this fountain of knowledge. This is my own Library of Congress!

The LCU main library was indeed rich and mind-boggling in its capacity. Its stock of Africana alone surprised Dezmond. How could a North American library possess so many titles on Africa and African issues he had never even heard about in Nigeria? A mixture of envy and shame crept upon his soul as he remembered the Kashim Ibrahim library back home at Ahmadu Bello University, Zaria.

Dezmond's focus of the moment was, however, not the library but the office of his programme advisor. He had arrived there many minutes before his appointment, and in his determination to load every half-hour with action, strolled to the library.

The office secretary ushered him in. He hesitantly opened the door and bowed to the professor, more in nervousness than in obeisance. The professor's attention was yet fixed on a seemingly Faulknerian sentence which did not permit him the opportunity of making pleasanteries. The office was a small room crammed to the ceiling with books and journals. Its occupant crouched over his cherished book, with the aid of a table lamp.

As Dezmond was feasting his eyes on the book titles, Prof. Alvin Primate suddenly cleared his throat. 'Now, then!' he said. His voice boomed in the book-insulated space. 'You were rather early for this appointment.' The man sounded impressively Oxonian in his delivery. Swivelling his seat to face his visitor, Prof. Primate pulled a green dossier out of his drawer and signalled Dezmond to sit down.

'Yes, of course,' he muttered to himself, 'Dezmond A–d–a–m–a.' He sounded out the letters of the surname. 'Do I say it right?'

'Yes, sir; thanks, sir.'

'This one is easy enough,' he observed flipping through the dossier. 'In past years, I've had to insist that some Nigerian students of mine abbreviate their long tongue-twisters.' He grinned and Dezmond smiled.

'Point of interest; are you on the Nigerian or Biafran side regarding the war?'

'Nigeria, sir—'

'Listen,' interrupted the professor, 'you'll do well to cut out formalities, okay?'

'Yes, sir. Excuse me, please. I wanted to say that the Biafran War ended over four years ago.'

'Has it, indeed? Has it already become history?' pondered the professor, still thumbing the dossier. 'But the spirit of Biafra marches on somewhere out there. In the States it's still alive, I can tell you that much.'

'I've observed some of that, sir.' Dezmond's palm impulsively shot to his mouth as he slipped again.

'Now then,' intoned the professor, rising to his full, swarthy six feet six, 'call me Alvin, okay? But if you feel uncomfortable, like most of your countrymen, call me "Prof" but never "sir". Makes me feel like a crusty old fossil.' He then sat back.

'I'll try and adjust.'

'Very well. We are off to a good start,' responded the professor, rubbing his palms together. 'This folder says you were a straight-A student at your Bachelor's and Master's degree levels. If, frankly, these scores are genuine and have strong predictive value, I'd reckon you will crack through grad school in minimum time. I'll later talk about your waivers and the transferred credit hours.'

'Thanks, Prof,' responded Dezmond. The professor looked on as if expecting to hear something more. Dezmond followed through, 'I need not press the point, but my grades are genuine scores from certified transcripts at the University of Zaria.'

'Count yourself privileged to have Professor Alvin Primate as advisor!' announced his mentor, and gave Dezmond his hand.

'I'm privileged, Prof, and I mean it.'

'Then I have to ask you why you accept that you are privileged. You called for it. Your response is something more than the everyday polite type.'

'Well, if I may be permitted to say this, I've tried to find out a little about you... I was naturally anxious. I thought, since my fate is going to be in your hands, I should begin to know you even before now,' explained Dezmond. 'I must say, I'm very delighted with what I read in the *Who's Who* of the top ten universities.'

'Don't be intimidated,' quipped the professor. 'Alvin Primate is a commonplace name. Nobody has been able to separate the sheep among us from the goats. But, point of interest, where did you find that book?'

'Main library. I stumbled on it on the shelf of new arrivals. The Primate I saw has to be you, Prof.'

'Great! I'm glad you're befriending the library right away. But I'm not sure what you mean, putting your life in my hands or something. That's pretty heavy, don't you think?'

'Well, by way of speaking,' explained Dezmond. 'If you were advisor in a Nigerian university, you would understand. Back at home, most supervisors of higher degrees will brand it on their student's flesh that power of life and death is in their mighty hands. This is part of why I got frustrated in my doctorate work at the AB Research Institute. Thank God I am here at last. I don't want to reopen the past. Let sleeping dogs lie.'

'However, I'd like to know what kind of research you were doing,' said the professor.

'I undertook anthropological fieldwork on the old Nok culture.'

'Been published?'

'Mostly in local journals, and in monographs. A couple in international journals. Much of my materials got channelled into government documentaries and inter-cultural development programmes. UNESCO even used some. Other materials, I used in my undergraduate seminars or in my MA dissertation. The rest are stored up for the future.'

'Does that imply that you have a W.I.P.?' Prof. Primate's smile was pre-emptive.

'Work in progress? Not quite; maybe, a dream in the pipeline,' answered Dezmond, as if only thinking aloud. His eyes were set far away from his immediate surrounding. 'The doctorate degree is the ultimate; it means more to my life than I can tell...' He remained gazing for some moments into space, like a man trying to remember something, and his advisor waited, observing him.

'I'd say, it's all yours,' said Prof. Primate, a little abashed. Then, suddenly looking straight into Dezmond's gazing eyes, he coldly shot a question at him. 'I want your gut-level answer: do you reckon that my being a black man like you means anything in your assignation to me?'

The abruptness and deadpan tone of the question jolted Dezmond fully back to himself. He wondered whether in a moment's distraction, his mind had missed the trend of their otherwise genial interaction. He searched for an appropriate answer, but words failed him.

'Dezmond, I demand a frank response,' repeated the professor.

'Sir, I am incompetent to know how or why I got assigned to you. If there's any special consideration, frankly I'm not aware of it and never considered it. I suppose you should be telling me if there is anything I need to know.'

'Listen, I'm trying to get at the unspoken notions in the mind,' insisted Prof. Primate. 'What are your expectations? Are you excited? Do you hope for special treatment, for some special concessions, bending over backward, y'know, for the sake of a brother?'

'Well, if I have expectations, they are the normal, natural ones any advisee would have of his advisor. Nothing out of the ordinary. I do not take anybody or thing for granted, as a matter of principle. And whatever I've not worked for, whatever I've not merited, I don't want it. Prof, I wonder what made you ask that question. Have I betrayed some feeling of, em—?'

'Never mind,' muttered the professor, tossing the dossier back into his drawer. 'Point of interest. I remember at this moment an African proverb to the effect that it's not only yam that's eaten with oil.'

Dezmond was miffed by the unpredictable turn in the discussion. He had looked forward to a stereotyped advisor–advisee interview, a mutual sizing up, as it were, of the grounds of their working relationship, not a one-way sounding off. Or was this perhaps a test of his tolerance level? As far as he was concerned, this was the most important man in the whole world; he needed to understand him and his ways of thinking in order not to jeopardise his career.

'Everyone's got his own crazy style, Dezmond,' observed the professor, as if he was reading his student's mind. 'Don't get intimidated by anything or anybody, even your advisor. Welcome on board!' He arose and stretched out his hands, opening his palms. Dezmond quickly spotted the cue and slapped them, laughing.

'Been to East-side Lake City?' teased the professor. 'It's like going back home to Africa.'

'Yes. The excursion train even took us to Harlem, New York.'

'How did you feel?'

Dezmond hesitated. 'I could have cried. It's as you said. I felt as if I was back in a Lagos slum or something. You know, I felt like shedding tears. I'd take a good look at a man; or some women, with braided hair, wrapper, African blouse and all that; and then this strong feeling comes all over me that I *know* this person! I've seen that one ages ago, somewhere! I'd look another in the face and tell myself, this one was an Igbo man; or I'd watch the build and gesticulations of another, and say, she's surely from Yorubaland! I loved all of them, but I felt a sense of loss and guilt deep inside. I actually cried on the way back.'

'Well, I can figure that... didn't mean to draw you out that way, but that's a fine, positive feeling. You'll get over it for sure. When you begin to experience the good, the bad and the ugly, among our folks, as with every other group in the melting pot, everything will level up. You're right on track, man; cheer up!'

'I'm glad you asked me that question, but I was thinking I'd said too much. But then, what you've just said really speaks to my heart. Thanks a lot, Prof. I've taken more than our time.'

'No big deal. Just one more thing... umm... righ'! You could do worse than reduce your credit hours for this semester; too ambitious. It's good thinking as you put it, to tackle the big end of the fallen tree while it is yet morning, but you don't want to break your back. After all, you brought along a good many credit hours from ABU, plus the credit hours you won for your monographs. Sorry, I almost didn't tell you about that! We've got them all confirmed. Congratulations!'

'I'm grateful, Prof.'

'Welcome! I'd suggest you take, say, a maximum of eighteen or even fifteen credit hours this fall semester, with one elective, computer appreciation say, and progressively burrow your way towards your thesis. Righ', now you can walk in here any minute before you get into trouble. Don't wait until you land in a mess. Other than that, you're fit for much independent work. We'll review our regular contact sessions as we move along. Take care!'

Professor Alvin Primate gripped his arm, slapping his back even as Dezmond bowed down in reverence.

*

Dezmond Adama waded through the lunch-hour stream of students and sundry persons, flowing into the rallying point called The Rathskeller. Not having caught on to the American idea of the packed lunch, he proposed to buy himself a real hot meal at the union cafeteria. However, the sheer length of the service queue doused his appetite. He therefore opted for a beer which would also give him time to chew over the meeting he had just finished with his advisor.

He sat alone in an obscure corner of the bar, mulling over Prof. Primate's strange probings, with a six-can pack of Pabst beer to irrigate the process. His musing soon grew into a make-belief, in which he found himself re-enacting the drama of his visit to the advisor, filling in all the missing lines, reactions and postures he ought to have included in the critical encounter. Dezmond was not a habitual drinker. It did not, therefore, take long before he hit that mark when it no longer matters how many more pints the drinker pours into his limitless belly of dead waters.

He awoke from his daydream to find a half-empty can staring him in the face. The pressure of a big gulp cleared his hearing and he suddenly realised that he had been buried in the vortex of bedlam. He abandoned the can and made for the exit.

'Hey ma man! What gives?' A gangling fellow emerged from a smoke-filled corner of the Rath. 'How're you guys gettin' on, ma man?'

Dezmond's eyes were set on the exit. 'I've been busy with registration and house-hunting. Right now, I have a class,' he lied.

'No, man, quit jivin'! I know and you know you ain' got no damn classes.'

'Okay, okay. But who are you, by the bush? I don't remember meeting you,' questioned Dezmond, trying to bluff his way out. Until he had walked up to Dezmond, toe to toe, it did not seem clear to him that the man was after him. He now grabbed Dezmond's palm and whacked it with great flourish. His rolling baritone belied his slight frame.

'Ma name, Marcus G. Young, the Third. From PAID, part-time. Am a graduate assistan' in choreography and voice,' he virtually sang. 'Don' mean no hassle, bu' some guy s'pose t've hipped you on our organisation...'

About the same age as Dezmond, he sported a cream T-shirt on navy blue shorts, with PAID boldly printed across the torso. A two-tone Afrocomb with a moulded fist handle stuck out of his mountainous conked hair. He walked in the spring 'n' jerk manner of the inimitable black dude, characteristically punctuating his speech with flamboyant body movements.

'Sorry, there must be a mix-up somewhere,' protested Dezmond, turning round the man. He imagined that, like the members of one of those eastern sects who occupationally heckle students in the Union lobby, this PAID agent would be put off by a firm cold shoulder. But he was mistaken.

'I appreciate your cool, man,' responded Marcus G. Young, 'bu' you can save yo' time if you gave me a littl' attention, dig? I know you're Mr Dezmon' Adama from the home country. Single, twenty-five, AB, MA, LCU doctorate aspirant...' Dezmond stared at him, unable to utter a word. 'You got mailed an intro from PAID HQ a month ago, righ'?'

'I don't know what this is all about. Anybody can go get personal information from the dean's office, one way or the other, so I'm not impressed. I must leave now! If you hinder me, I'll really begin to yell!'

'Righ', go ahead now, an' embarrass us! Start yelling real loud! You won't ever like yo'sef if you get physical with me. If indeed you wanna scream, I know better how to package that act. I'll jes' plant a sachet of coke or some dreadful thing on you, and I'll hold you and holler so bad you'll regret startin' it up. How 'bout a deal, man? Play cool!'

'What deal?'

'I like this!' exclaimed Marcus G., doing a little dance to show it. 'Lemme jes' give you a five-minute low down from numero uno. PAID – y'know, Protect Afrika in Diaspora – is vit'l for the survival and sustainability of all blacks on planet earth! We're into reverse-racism, self-determination, group positivistic self-concept, equal opportunity; and all of that, and more, in these pluralistic but white-dominated Uni'red States of America! You needed PAID from day one or you gonna be nullified by White, Anglo-Saxon, Protestant bigotry! F'r example, you and I know you ain't gittin' no room on campus to lay your head. Why? 'Cos you're black!'

'Well, as for that, I know my application came late. I've explained things to your other guy.'

'Wale Jefferson?'

'Yes. We talked. I don't want to start all over again, but I have no hang-up whatsoever with Anglo-Saxons or anybody else.'

Hundreds of students and LCU tradesmen were preoccupied with quaffing tap beer and boasting fitfully into the air. The overhanging pall of smoke mixed with raucous rock music from the jukebox and the staccato exchange of cursings, each person straining to out-shout the other; in the midst of which were a few oddballs, seemingly reading or sketching portraits; the whole scenario looked like the market place of hell.

'You wanna split a pack?' offered Marcus G.

'No, thanks, I've had my drink.' They moved to a quieter spot where a small group of students of mixed races were discussing a team research project over drinks. Marcus strode to the bar counter and picked up two bottles of Molson's.

'Great! Jus' great!' he said, grinning broadly.

'What's great?' demanded the embattled Dezmond.

'We've come a long way, man,' explained Marcus. 'This is what we call give 'n' take. This dialogue.' He wrenched open a bottle by his teeth, took a long draught, and pulled his chair nose-to-nose with Dezmond. 'Protect Afrika has a database on all black students and professors in each major college, whether from Nigeria, Zaire, or Brazil – wherever! PAID runs a wire biznez that outstrips Watergate, but that's all classified, of course. Our computer network... well, le's jus' cut a long story short. Lemme jus' say, Protect Afrika needs y'all, jus' as y'all need Protect. I like for you to be wise and patriotic from this day forward.'

Marcus canvassed on, with well-rehearsed cadences, spicing his oratory with some emotion here, some historical fact there, including a few surprising details on Dezmond's background. If he had stopped at biodata alone, it could have been that he had tapped one of the countless forms which Dezmond had to complete at every stage of going to America. The man gloated when he shared some psychoanalytic snippets from Dezmond's medical history which was only obtainable in the ABU Medical Centre, back in Zaria, Nigeria. Those revelations, some dating back to his adolescence, and the very manner Marcus flaunted them, made Dezmond feel like a naked cadaver on a slab. Dezmond's perplexity was too much for words. He impulsively shifted further away from this would-be assailant.

'One mo' littl' thing,' continued Marcus, confident that he had at last caged his prized game. 'You don' know nuttin' until you hear this! Remember the honky broad that put a jackknife on yo' jugular on Main Street? She wuz commissioned by the KKK neo-Nazis to waste the nigger! And, jus'—'

'Why? And why me?' Dezmond interrupted. He had bottled up enough tension to burst.

'To scare yo' arse off honky women! White men don't wan' no nigger messin' around their broads,' explained Marcus G. 'I been telling Brother Jefferson 'bout my law of fixed notion! It states that all the experience of a black man are reducible to the black–white syndrome. Like, you became a victim of a conflict that took root the day the first slave ship docked in the US! It's on record that white man's scared of black blood 'ventually overthrowing the political, social, economic, plus military status quo—'

'For heaven's sake, I've had enough! I've not come all the way from Nigeria to involve myself in something that does not directly concern me!' Dezmond was now too agitated to remain sitting. 'I leave! And this is the last time any of you ever stops me!'

'Ma man, you need understanding! Our folks say, what a cat don' know, it jus' don' know. You're damn concerned, an' you better be, otherwise, you're a sitting duck for the honky machine.' Marcus G. Young emptied the second bottle of beer and stood up. 'So far, not bad! We've made progress. The gooks say, the journey of a thousand miles begins with one step,' he continued, striding abreast of Dezmond. 'PAID is never in a hurry. But PAID never gives up. Never gives in. It's like the saxifrage flower of the Colorado mountains. Its root thrives best in rocks. PAID is a rock-breaker; don' despise! Check it out, man! Adios! *A luta continua!*'

Chapter Two

The Union bulletin board was a hilariously refreshing oasis of its own type. Dezmond occasionally visited it for its guaranteed divertissement value. The fare on display ranged from side-splitting cartoons, through humour features, to fun adverts by which the LCU community conducted a handsome volume of business: 'Alsatian puppy for $1!' 'Math books, for peanuts: owner flunking out!' 'Efficiency for Rent: ten minutes' walk to campus!' 'Wanted: travel-mate to Apple City; blondes only!' 'Basement Boogie: Bring own Booze (Phone # XYZ).' 'Cosmos Soccer Club, NY, wants strikers!' Every week, fresh ones would go up.

One evening, the displays were so funny that Dezmond almost had his ribs cracked with unbroken laughter. That incident created the opportunity for his meeting with a younger man who was to play a key role in his life. Ironically, Dezmond at first gave him a stony response, fearing that he might be yet another canvasser for PAID.

'How did you figure out I'm a Nigerian?' Dezmond asked, having convinced himself that he was in safe company.

'Easy! The way you look, the way you laughed, and especially, your accent. I don't mean to be rude, but you're a CJC, am I right?'

'What's that?'

'Countryman Just Come!' laughed the man. 'I am Bro. Maazi of West Africa.'

'I'm Dezmond Adama. I'm excited to meet a fellow

Nigerian since leaving home eight weeks ago. Your Maazi has to be "Igbo", not so?'

'Well, until recently, we preferred the Biafran cover to Igbo because it drew more sympathy. Now the war is finished, we give glory to the Almighty God.'

The man fell in step, keeping up the conversation as they headed towards the car park. The warmth and spontaneity of their rapport was such that they seemed to have known each other for months.

'Man, you sure say, we never been meet for some place?' wondered Bro. Maazi in Nigerian pidgin English.

'*Na 'im-o!* Our people talk say, inside market sef, one broda fit smell anoda broda como't.'

'I 'gree bo!'

'Bro., how long you don' 'tay here?' asked the newcomer.

'Six, seven, years only.'

'What? You don' loss finish! How you manage stay so long? How you go return to Nigeria again? You no go know road now?' said Dezmond, teasing, as Bro. Maazi unlocked the passenger door for him.

'You see,' explained Bro. Maazi as he was fixing his seat belt. 'You know say Igbo wise. Why you no ask me wetin I mean by Maazi of West Africa? Na because, if I miss road, at least I fit land for dat kin' Liberia or Ghana!' They both laughed.

'But, truly, dem melting pot don' swallow you *kpata kpata*!' observed Dezmond.

'Ah, not Maazi! I will never become one with this modern wilderness.'

'You may be right. But look, your appearance. Even your way of talking ordinary pidgin don' dey affected.'

'Look deeper! Dis cake dey white only for outside. De inside dey original brown. You know how white man dey put snow-white icing for top of well-baked cake. Na so I be. De real me dey undercover. Dat icing sef, na only small small kids dey take am to be something great. Adults dey remove all dat coat of white sugar, go enjoy de real thing. You know what I mean?'

'I hear you! *Nna, gwam okwu n'America!'*

They exchanged exaggerated glances and laughed in unison. The Mustang throttled up to the intersection before Niagara Falls Boulevard. As the amber lights came on, the car heaved off the ground and sped towards the last overhanging traffic lights before turning off. Country music was booming from the car stereo set. The anchor intermittently identified the station as LCRJ–ONE.

'Man, you scared or something?' Maazi saw that Dezmond had his palms pressed on the dashboard, looking straight ahead.

'Sorry, I fear speed. That problem has always been with me. Only when I'm at the wheel myself do I feel confident.'

'You must have piloted the plane that brought you here from Kano!'

'That one was no problem at all. Once it went up, I didn't notice the speed. In fact, it was so smooth I thought it was not moving.'

'Na, CJC dey worry your head!'

'Maybe,' conceded Dezmond.

'Well, on a serious note, I don't consider myself to be a speedster. Maybe I'm just excited touching base! Y'know, seeing you is like seeing and touching the home country again. You know what I mean?'

'I understand.'

The Mustang slowed down even as the radio song was fading off the air. 'LCRJ–ONE! The station that feeds the total man, body, soul and spirit! Now, let's worship His Majesty!'

A solemn duet came forth so powerfully that it clearly

enraptured Maazi, even as he held the wheel. Soon they reached Niagara Falls Boulevard.

'Is this the street?'

'You no get eye? Na boulevard! Dat one mean say, na where big men dey live.'

'You really have touched base today. I doubt if pidgin will leave your mouth this day. I jus' hope you have no term paper to do, otherwise, you can't escape writing in some pidgin stuff! You can only imagine how confused your professor is going to be!'

'Na 'im, my broda! How for do? Na 'im Igbo may say, as for!'

The car pulled up at a one-storied building whose face was plastered over by yellowing ivy.

'Oh, glory be to Jesus!' exclaimed Maazi, as he jumped out. 'I am excited! I'm heavy! In quietness is my strength! I got joy like a river, peace like a fountain! Alleluia to Jesus!' He burst out singing, arms spread to the heavens. Dezmond Adama watched, wondering if this was all for having touched base, or was it a brainwave?

'C'mon, this is my humble pad.'

'Humble? This mansion?'

'No. Just a little corner of it, in the roof!' exclaimed Bro. Maazi, as each of them grabbed shopping bags.

'Living in the attic makes me feel special, and free like an eagle in flight.'

'Ehn, Maazi. What's LCRJ–ONE.'

'My choice station! Lake City Radio Jesus, Number One! I'm hooked in there, permanent. There's so much poisonous rubbish on the air, in the tube, and all over, I listen to nothing else.' They were on the steep staircase to the attic. Man, it is a matter of self-preservation,' continued Bro. Maazi. '"Whatsoever things are true, whatsoever things are honest, whatsoever things are just, whatsoever things are pure, whatsoever things are lovely, whatsoever things are of good report, if there be any virtue, if there be any praise, think on these things." My Bible tells me so, and boy, do I stick to it! That's what I call self-preservation! That's my daily secret of walking with God.'

The apartment looked impressive, with even the walls covered from ceiling to the floor. The set of living room seats were upholstered in olive green fabric embossed with patterns of cream. A tall room divider stood against a wall, stacked full with books, silver and glassware collections, a stereo set, and a small TV. A broad-leafed potted plant had weaved its course up the side of the room divider to the ceiling.

'This is what those adverts call an "efficiency" – a self-contained turnkey room. You just pay monthly lump sum for all the services, and forget it.'

'Na wa-o!' exclaimed Dezmond, as he sat down still admiring the room. 'Efficiency! Na real efficiency, bo!'

'Don't be over-impressed,' cautioned his host. 'All I need is a clean spot to read and to lay my head. If you wan' see proper splendour, settle down first. I'll take you places where you will see what is called vanity of vanities. Mark you, I'm talking about the homes of some Igbo men, Yoruba men plus women, Bendelities. I mean fellow-Nigerians!'

'From where did they get that kind of money?'

'Who knows? Only dem and dem gods know where dem get dat kin' dollars. As for me, I no envy dem. I no fit jealous thief. Destruction de wait for person wey de chop from devil 'im hand. Unless dem repent, dem jus' de feed dem sef for hellfire! De only tin' be say other Nigerians dey work hard for dem own money. Dose ones dey for different class.'

Maazi opened his fridge and asked his guest to make a choice.

'Any tin'! *Abi*, you get *tombo likwo*?' It was now Dezmond's turn to tease.

'What liquor?'

'Palm wine, if you please!'

'You're kidding yourself, CJC!' Maazi laughed. 'In this pad, all you'll get is palm-coke or plain OJ.' He handed Dezmond a can of orange juice. 'I'll put you some sound while I take a splash.'

He switched on the music and the plaintive voice of Johnny Denver took over the high Rocky Mountains of Colorado. Ten minutes later, Bro. Maazi emerged from the shower cubicle. 'Guess what's on for supper!'

'Sorry, I don't know the names of most stuff I've been grubbing since I left home. Mm... okay, rice and pork chops?'

'*Poundo* with standard *okra*!'

'I beg, Maazi, stop pulling my leg! How you manage get real food for dis kin' place. Please, no water my mout' for nothing!'

'Well, if you could dream of *tombo* liquor in Lake City, maybe pounded yam with okra is a lesser miracle. Me, I be man of God, and with God, all things are possible!'

'I can't believe until I see for myself!'

'When you wait to see first, which kin' believe be dat? No be so God talk am. Come, you mean dem never treat you to *poundo* since you land?' Maazi asked over his shoulder as he put water to the boil.

'For where? De only tin I see for dem caf way resemble food na smashed potato with gravy soup. De stuff be like... *kai*! Make I no spoil your appetite with small pickin' shit.'

'No, Dezmond Adama! Mashed potato is nothing of that sort. In fact, it tastes yummy. Maybe it was something else you grubbed.'

'Any way sha, I chop am. Hungry, ignorant CJC no get choice.'

The gas cooker was busy at three burning points.

'You can see, the taste of the pudding is in the cooking, right before your nose! Do you get the aroma of the stew with okra?'

'I see the magic coming up. But I will believe fully when my mouth confirms it.'

'Fine. You steer the okra,' ordered Maazi. 'Even if you imagine say I be your wife, for America, husband de help madam cook. Begin turn de okra. In ten minutes, you go see with your own mout'.'

The table was set with a steaming tray of okra 'n' stew and a molehill of white dough.

'Africa mus' survive!' exclaimed Maazi. 'This whiteman *poundo* is actually from bes' quick flour. The owners bake with it, but Africa man knows better. Let us pray...'

'Go ahead.'

'My Father, please, cleanse Dezmond and I by the blood of our Lord Jesus, so that our prayer can reach you... Thank you for giving me a new friend even from my country. Father, make it a lasting friendship which will help us to know you and glorify your name with our lives. Thank you for giving us this home cooking. We believe it is blessed and sanctified for us, so we accept it with thanks. As we eat, we also ask that you remember the many poor people even in this great city who are starving on two, three jobs in order to survive America. Provide for those ones too, Lord. Thank you for the fun we've had today, for journeying mercies, health and good appetite. Thank you for your loving kindness, in Jesus's name, Amen.'

Dezmond quietly made a sign of the cross before his face.

They ate with great relish, trading good-humoured small talk about events back home, and their experiences of life in America. The meal over, Dezmond sprawled on his chair, like a spent wrestler, leaving Maazi to clean up.

'Provided you don't doze off,' commented Maazi, 'you

may spread your limbs as wide as you wish. But having treated you to such a great meal, I deserve a payback. America is about give and take.'

'*Kai*, Maazi, that was some meal! The way I was hacking at that *poundo*, I didn't remember I was supposed to be behaving as a guest. Hunger drove away etiquette!'

'I don't blame you,' remarked Maazi at the kitchenette basin. 'I would have done the same thing if I were in your position. Better relax now. When I finish cleaning up, you'll give me a detailed account of the situation at home. That time, it will be my turn to scatter body for rug!'

★

Dezmond Adama woke from his nap to see Bro. Maazi poring over his Bible. He slouched back on the settee and left his host alone with his study. Sleep did not return to him. He just lay idling on a blank spot until he caught himself in it. He became uncomfortable. How can an adult mind stay barren for so long? he began to ponder. Yet, each minute comes laden with its own question, a new task, a fresh stimulus.

His wandering thoughts gravitated to his meeting with Bro. Maazi, and all the exciting experiences of that day. Dezmond had tried to argue that it was a fortuitous occurrence, but Maazi insisted that there was no such thing as happenstance. Maazi spoke about all things having a spiritual root; that events are first settled in the spirit realm, before they manifest in what men call reality. Dezmond could not understand the dynamics of Maazi's thoughts, though the combination of words made sense to his intellect. What did the man mean when he postulated that the things that the eyes see, are only temporal, the ones the eyes do not see, are the eternal and real? And didn't he insist it was not his puny self who was postulating, but that he was only speaking God's mind on the matter? Apart from singing birds, sun-painted cloud portraits in the sky, an endless expanse of ocean, a colossal ship suspended in space, does God speak in an audible language? How does a spirit speak? How does Maazi claim to have heard? And the way this man prayed! It was so real, so simple, it had to touch the soul. A man who can talk so effectively, must hear sometimes from the one being talked to, even if it is a spirit. Might it be that God is speaking to Maazi even now? Everything around him feels so still I am afraid to even clear my throat. I wonder which church he attends?

Maazi's eyes were shut. He had been praying in what he fondly described as the 'tongue of little ants'. When he finished, he sat up and saw Dezmond gazing at him.

'Well done,' greeted Dezmond. 'You caught me off guard. I didn't know it was your turn to watch me.'

'What were you doing?'

'Just wondering, and looking to see how you're doing.'

'Now wey your belly don' come down,' joked Bro. Maazi, 'knack me 'tory about Nigeria!'

'I will, but I first wanted to ask, which church you dey attend?'

'I belong in the church of Hebrews, 12:21–23, if I'm not confusing you. I will explain later. Right now, I'm waiting to hear home news. This is my first contact with somebody from Nigeria since the past three years. I have caught the spirit of Nehemiah. I'm burning to return... But I need as much correct information as I can get. Tell me, how are things back home? I am caught between the propaganda of Nigerian missions abroad and American Biafrans. We've heard about no victor, no vanquished. Thank God that General "Go-on" did not lose all what he had been taught by missionaries at Wusasa! But, tell me, are my kinsmen being well received into the Nigerian fold? Or is it so much propaganda?'

Dezmond narrated all that he knew, from mid-January, 1970, when hostilities ceased, to the latest major developments in post-war rehabilitation and reconciliation efforts which he had known about before leaving Nigeria. Maazi silently weighted every statement.

'It's incredible,' continued Dezmond, 'how fast the wounds are healing. I never believed Nigeria would come back together again. But they've put the war behind. East-Central State is as real now as any of the other eleven.'

'Man, I witnessed the pogrom! That wasn't propaganda! I saw it even at Otukpo railway station, just ninety minutes by road to Igboland.'

'Needless bringing it all back,' admonished Dezmond. 'What I know is that it is the Lord who put our country together, not Lord Lugard. That's why we didn't get frazzled into pieces.'

'I believe that. God surely loves Nigeria.'

'Go home and see how Igbo traders and artisans are moving back to the north. It is like a dream!'

'It took me almost a year after the war to get word about my immediate family. After that, blackout! Until some Igbo guy got into LCU. In between that, I was being bombarded with all kinds of newspaper and television stories and horror pictures.'

'I understand,' Dezmond said. 'I've fallen victim to some since coming, and this is four years after, so I can imagine. The ugliness of civil war and particularly those things that come with war, take time to go away. But believe me, it is a miracle! Igbo and Hausa–Fulani are living peacefully together in the same compound and getting on as one!'

'In any case, Igbos have no choice!' Maazi sighed. 'Biafra was so choked up with people that they had to move out at the earliest opportunity. It was like being caught between two evils. Except that home is home, no matter the odds.'

Bro. Maazi wanted to go on asking questions, but Dezmond was dropping hints of his own need to learn some more from Maazi's many years of experience in America. The conversation soon flowed in that direction, with Dezmond asking how Maazi was able to get to the USA in the first place. It took some persuasion for Bro. Maazi to narrate his adventure from the beleaguered Biafra, through Rome airport by a relief plane to the USA. He was among the earlier war victims to seek refuge abroad. So, with the wave of outrage the world over against the widely publicised genocide, Maazi found much sympathy.

'Individual families gave me great help,' continued Maazi. 'Some resident fellow-Biafrans too. Their good propaganda prepared ground for us, but many were busy scooping greenbacks for themselves. Anyway, I gained from their business. Their publicity about Biafra drew the Americans to my side. I thank God, they gave me the life support I badly needed. Some of them even took in Biafran refugees and sponsored them through college.'

For Bro. Maazi, providence was it, or so he understood it then; plus hard work. 'My late father used to tell us that hard work does not kill. They say Igbo people are born with diligence, but hey, my father's own was something else! I resemble him in that. I chose hard labour along with my full credit hours. You know the American system. When I qualified finally to take a proper degree, I thought I would read straight Business Admin. But for the first two years, I was forced to take English, Calculus, Psychology, TM, and all that. Beating about the bush, I used to call it, but it has helped me today, even the Transcendental Meditation.

'So, while I was struggling with calculus, I was also night guard, busboy, floor cleaner, dishwasher – you name it. Plus labouring on construction sites. But I have not really told you the main story, Dezmond. My sun began to shine only when I found how to stop struggling with my life.'

'You mean you needn't have done all those mean jobs?'

'I thought my life was in my own hands to make good by diligent work only. You know what I mean, using my hands and brains to become all I ever wanted in life. I need not tell you everything, including my woeful marriage and the rest of it. Then came the Lord Jesus, and he made all the difference! He got me to make a complete U-turn! That's the biggest story of my life, the only one worth telling.'

'Wait a minute,' interrupted Dezmond, 'I also know about Jesus.'

'Yes, that's the point! Everybody knows about Jesus. But that one is worlds apart from actually knowing him by direct personal encounter.'

'Left to me, that's a matter of semantics. But we've had a long day of fun together. Let's not start an argument on issues of private conviction. I can sense that it is your cup of tea. But we've met only today. Maybe, next time, we can compare notes.'

'Well, you're right. We won't argue. But you asked for my story. Jesus is the climax of it! When it comes to him, I get so excited, everything else is peanuts! I do not need to apologise about Jesus. You see, Dezmond, in the past, when I was a useless walkabout, I so misused my mouth that now, I'm in a hurry to make up for it. I promote Jesus anytime, anywhere!'

Dezmond hardly noticed when his host leapt into the air. The fervour that exuded out of him was so strong that he seemed not to be aware of his guest's presence. Now he watched Maazi's steps fearfully as he agitatedly pranced around the room even as he spoke on.

'I wish to make up for it,' said his host, 'but all the time on earth is not enough! We've had a long day – we've just met – yes! If I had the liberty, I would have fed your spirit, not your body. It was not by power or might that the great mountain became a plain and surrendered its headstone into the hand of Zerubabbel! It was by the Holy Spirit! The son of man spoke by his leading. So too, speaks his servant and friend! I promote Jesus likewise to whoever will listen. Also, to those who will not listen! It is said that they who are listening to the bell of death, hear nothing else... but the word of God is powerful. Jesus is Lord!'

Dezmond had crept out of his chair and was now leaning warily against the wall, confounded. This was not the man who had been laughing with him! His appearance was now strangely electrifying. His words flew out like a hail of hot stones. His very eyes emitted great energy or fire, as he flashed up and down in front of the figure standing utterly cowed by the wall. Mercifully, the pitch of his voice and the tempo of his movement soon began to come down. Dezmond's bewildered eyes again beheld the Maazi that he had met earlier that evening.

'I'm sorry,' was all that Dezmond could muster.

'No, you don't understand! But you will! *After many days*, says the Lord! I am not my own. I obey my master. I refuse to observe the wind or cloud when he gives me seed. The Lord says, even you will receive a seeing eye and a hearing ear. After many days! Only, may it not be as a thousand years, my Lord.'

'Amen,' responded Dezmond, absent-mindedly.

'I believe you know what you've just said. "Let it be so!"'

Maazi stepped in front of Dezmond and placed his palm on his shoulder. 'I'm taking you back to campus in a minute, but one last thing...'

This time, Dezmond was cajoled into perching on the edge of his seat.

'This may be strange to you. But those who really know him, must talk. Unless it is not Jesus, the Christ, who has touched them. Faith comes by hearing, and hearing comes by the word of God...'

Dezmond sprang up. 'Next time, please...'

'Fair enough!' conceded Maazi. 'Except that one never knows when there'll be a next time, if at all it ever comes. "Life is like a candle light,"' quoted Maazi, also rising to his feet.

Dezmond was heading for the door. 'Ol' boy, don't scare me-o!'

'I won't. If you had seen death as close as I have, you'd appreciate.'

As they paced towards the staircase, Maazi was still able to hold Dezmond's attention. 'Just months after I allowed Jesus to save me and take Lordship over my life, my heart was burning to share my transformation with Dike. He was a bosom friend who came here ahead of me. Each time I tried, the situation wasn't conducive, or he had a deadline to beat, or he wasn't in a good mood. One weekend, the guys went for a smorgasbord, y'know, buffet, at a place called Catch-Of-The-Night, and the devil caught him.'

'What?' Dezmond gripped the railing.

'A fish bone got stuck in his throat. He was too embarrassed to talk. Went home and kept swallowing big balls of *eba*. In six days, he was stone dead.'

'Fish bone?'

'It's many years now. But I've not gotten over it. That's why I grab every chance to tell it to whoever. Brother Paul called himself a debtor to the Greeks. I owe you this one duty of telling you now, that Jesus shed his blood for you, Dezmond Adama, that you also may overcome Satan and become God's own son for ever! Listen, even now, you are free to respond to him, y'know what I mean? Even on these steps here, you can pray to become a son of God. Dezmond, I'd be very happy to lead you in that prayer, now!'

'Maazi, *na wa-o*!' exclaimed Dezmond, as he stepped ahead to the exit. 'I am already a Christian. But your own brand is beyond limit. It's been a long day. Thanks for the home treat, and the discussion. We'll meet again soon.'

'By the grace of God. He is the owner of all souls. There is no ant that is crawling or dead, that He's not aware of. This is the God who told me, after many days. Nobody knows the length of His days. Only He and those He tells His secret. May you number your days aright!'

'Amen!' Dezmond had overheard yet another prayer.

'Amen, I say with you, Brother Dezmond Adama!'

Chapter Three

No. 19, Pine Avenue, a one-storey mansion with solid colonnades, looked like an Athenian model, from a distance. If, by any dream, it had been standing on an East-side street, it would have commanded great awe. But on this avenue of upper-class professionals, there were many of its kind, and others of even greater grandeur, all numinously grey, and impregnable from outside. The residents of the area must have sat down to agree on an architectural code; other neighbourhoods of the larger Erie County were not so uniform, so it could not have been a county specification. The buildings that lined the avenue were of same height, with similar basic features, each with its front lawn bordered by a cobbled driveway.

Fall was at its zenith, with her usual toll on foliage, strewn along the road and pavement. Every house had a fanciful sprinkler creating and breaking silvery rain patterns over the serene-looking green landscape.

Miss Frankwood unlocked the door with a practised smile on her lips. But only for moments. As her eyes fell on the visitor's face, she was slightly shaken. The visitor noticed it even as she tried to rearrange her visage.

'Mrs Frankwood?'

'Yes, yes. Pardon me,' she muttered.

'Dezmond Adama. Good afternoon, ma'am!' he greeted, disregarding her discomfiture.

'Yes, of course, Mr Adama. C'm right in!' she half-shouted, and ushered him across the living room, to the staircase. 'Just a little brainwave… a little distraction. Pardon me.'

She appeared as vivacious as her voice had sounded on the phone, what with blue denim jeans, and a tucked-in frock to match. She looked about ten years older than Mr Adama.

'Well!' Miss Frankwood gasped, as Dezmond caught up with her in front of the attic door. 'Here's the efficiency.'

She watched as the tenant-to-be inspected the room. It was spacious, with a panelled floor and built-in book-shelves, also wood panelled. The kitchenette was neatly fitted with a cabinet, gas stove, and fridgette. The roof was skilfully designed so that it did not slant sharply and create the menacing impression of bearing down on the room's occupant. Its walls were freshly coated with aquamarine wallpaper. One could still smell the native wood-scented glue that had been applied.

'How about the lock? Door lock?'

'I'll have it fixed. You can see, I only completed the wallpapering this morning. It's quite safe here, though,' explained Miss Frankwood. Then, smiling, she added, 'Aren't you a macho? A he-man?'

'Yes, I am a man. But frankly, I'm more of a human being! I sleep better behind locks!'

The lady looked at his face and laughed. 'Tomorrow, I promise! The Door Fixers' Union don't let members fix doors on Sundays,' she said. She paused, but Dezmond was satisfied. 'The rent is just one hundred bucks monthly,' she added.

'Fair enough,' said Dezmond, shrugging.

'Sure?'

'Sure.'

'It's a deal! I'll make out a receipt for your first down payment of a hundred dollars. You can move in any time this week. No refund if you change your mind. I need to emphasise that. Plus, I don't think we need a formal lease for this small transaction. Or do we?'

'No, if we're not required by law to do so.'

'When you're ready to move in, call me. Most evenings from five, I'm home. Come write your check downstairs while I get the receipt filled out.'

'Thank you, Mrs Frankwood.'

'You're welcome!'

Dezmond had his dollar bills counted and waiting, feasting his eyes on the portraits and other decorations on the living room walls and pelmets.

'Lovely family,' he observed, when his landlady handed him the receipt.

'Thank you.'

Dezmond moved in, and settled down the following week. He was determined to complete another speedy cycle of acculturation, this time in this predominantly white upper-class neighbourhood. Thanks to the daily increasing chill of late fall, outdoor life was diminishing.

Having put his coursework on an even keel, thanks to his advisor's strict guidance, he followed a routine of leaving for campus at dawn and returning at dusk. A few residents took notice of him. Despite his generous good-natured salutations to whoever passed by him, precious few cared even to glance in his direction. Particularly in the mornings, he found it very awkward to walk past a fellow human being and pretend that he or she was a statue.

Once in a while, a carload of youths would drive past and splash some dirty words at him. He would walk on as if he had not heard. On some Saturdays when there was plenty of sunshine, he used to have opportunity for a friendly chat with a neighbour tending lawn, fixing the family limousine, or just lazing in the sun. On one such fair-weather day, a charming old man accosted him and advised him to desist from saying hello to strangers on the street.

'I appreciate, sir. But sorry, I won't stop being myself. I'd even tell them my name if I had the chance.'

'Why the fuss?' asked the old man, switching off his lawnmower.

'That's our African manners. I'm used to it. If I drop it, by the time I get home, I'll have a problem readjusting. Besides, it is friendly. I love being friendly.'

'Well, makes some sense. How long have you been here?'

'Four months.'

'An' how long are you staying?'

'Two, maybe, three years, everything being equal.'

'Are you doing a degree or some'n?'

'Yes, sir.'

'Well, good luck!'

As the weeks rolled by, more neighbours began to take closer notice of Miss Frankwood's tenant. The enterprising ones even went the extra mile to respond to his unrelenting greetings or to chat. One old lady even revealed to Dezmond that the whole neighbourhood was agog with gossip about Miss Frankwood's live-in Negro, while individually they were pretending never to have had a glimpse of him.

'I must confess,' added the old lady that day, 'first time you walked past me, I became schizophrenic.'

'What!' exclaimed Dezmond.

'Scared, like. Upset.'

'Yes, I mean why? What did you see. A monster?'

'Tell you what, son, I'd never gone close to a knee-grow!' She giggled. 'But here I am, chatting away with you! And, what a pleasant surprise, my big Tory is friendly with you!' She tugged at the leash of her Labrador.

'That's the irony, isn't it, madam? Sometimes, dogs understand better than men.'

'Yes,' she giggled. 'Better continue our walk. Have a

good day, em, what's that name again?'

'Dezmond.'

As she turned, Dezmond called after her, 'Ma'am, d'you mind calling me African, instead of Negro, please?'

'Of course! I'm just too old-fashioned, that's all. No prejudice. Don't mean to patronise, but my littl' granddaughter tells me you're doing the *big* degree? What's that?' She stopped.

'The *doctorate*,' answered Dezmond with exaggerated panache, amused.

'You must've been around here for years.'

'No, just five months or so.'

'How come you're already talking about a doctorate of LCU? I should tell you I'm an alumna. AB class of 1920!'

'Great! It's an honour, ma'am, meeting you.'

'Thank you. Now, how about my question?'

'Oh, I did some of the work back in Nigeria,' explained Dezmond.

'Of course,' responded the old lady, thoughtfully, 'I'm such an old bigot, I am! Y'know something? Most Americans don't know zilch about anybody else! We are the world, and the world is us!'

'I don't blame them, ma'am,' conceded Dezmond, smiling at her genially as the old lady turned to go. 'Your country is so vast, it's a big enough hassle for Americans to know about it, not to talk of other places.'

'You're a kind young man,' she responded, giving a slight pull to the dog chain. 'Been nice talking to you, son.'

*

Success followed the efforts of Dezmond in his studies. He waxed stronger as the semester drew to an end, spurred on by the high quality of his grades and seminar inputs. Night after night, he would lie down to take stock of his work.

Often, the very words of the LCU president on the reception day would come back to him as if he was playing back its recording. He would then renew to himself his determination to overcome all obstacles that would confront him.

He decided, among his strategies, to take one day at a time; take each person and each situation as they appear, on individual merit. He vehemently eschewed all manner of stereotypes of human beings, and opinion polls; the non-empirical statistics bandied about in the press; and the daily astrological guides. He was convinced that they were among the subtle ways one's mind could be overrun by external forces. Equally, he decided to limit his interaction with Bro. Maazi until he understood his strange kind of religion. It was safer to stick to the time-tested and modest Mother Church Assembly into which he had been born. Even then, as there was no MCA nearby, his church attendances were few and far between.

Dezmond, therefore, had his life catalogued and systematically packaged in pigeon-holes, and he operated it like clockwork. He often recalled how his soccer coach in secondary school used to drum it into the players' heads that they must let the ball do the job. The team was drilled against exhausting energy by always running after the ball. The ball needed to be distributed. The player then plots a place of vantage for himself to drive home the shot. That was the way to reach the goal...

The old coaching lesson epitomised for Dezmond the mindset he needed to reach his objective – his doctorate. He would not run after life, dissipating valuable time and energy on mirage objects. If, for a mere leather football, men have taken pains to study and document how to win goals, how much more important it is, when the objective on the horizon is the golden fleece?

From day one of moving into 19, Pine Avenue, he set to

study his new home, and the ways of its occupants, in order to determine the best way to fit in his overall plan of life. Far be it for him to emerge from his attic hide-out and prejudge or prognosticate on his landlady, her family, or the neighbourhood, he resolved. Even the diviner, back in Aroji village, dared not hazard a word until he had garnered enough leads from his client. And according to his father on the eve of his departure, the white man is the most unpredictable creature on earth. The old man compared him to the silky-furred *oropi*, when cornered inside its tricky burrow. That rat is a master in feinting moves, warned the old man. When it senses an intrusion at the mouth of its hole, the cunning rodent waits and watches, then erupts right through the fresh earth between the digger's legs and escapes.

Two months after settling in, Dezmond had not met Mr Frankwood, but he kept his questions to himself. Only when Laura and Dave Junior, the adolescent children of the house, resumed their alternating fortnightly sojourn did Dezmond get clues that his landlady was not 'Mrs Frankwood', but the long-estranged, and now divorced wife of a Professor Gordon of LCU. She had deliberately introduced herself as Mrs Frankwood, using her maiden name, as was her habit in all arm's-length dealings.

Thus, the children's monthly visit oiled what would have been a clumsy breaking-in period for Miss Frankwood and Dezmond. Despite the liberty and exuberance of adolescence that prompted Laura and Dave Junior to break the tenant's bounds in the weeks to follow, Dezmond remained steadfast in his separation. His unspoken watchword was mutual respect and trust. For her part, Miss Frankwood was consistently formal and ultra-courteous in her posture, which suited Dezmond's purpose. Beyond the cursory greetings whenever their paths crossed in their daily coming and going, there was little opportunity for pleasantries.

Dezmond was bound to incur the respect of Miss Frankwood. She had never taken in a tenant until it became necessary to supplement her income for the mortgage payments on the house. She therefore did not even know what to expect in this venture, which she had taken to be a gamble. As a preamble to her tenant's do's and don'ts, she had shared that much detail with him, adding that the moment the experiment began to fail, she would make a refund and never venture into letting again. Little did she know that, on his part, her tenant had since worked out his own Draconian house rules.

He was always studying, never drank at home and never smoked openly. He went his own way with dignity, and rarely stayed out late, despite the fact that he had his own access key to the house. There were whole days in a stretch when he would remain upstairs working, and Miss Frankwood would not even be aware of him. His lifestyle proved completely contrary to the black stereotypes of 'rowdy, randy, and wrong-skulled'. Whenever he could, both in word and deed, he took pains to be seen to be different from such self-fulfilling generalisations about his race.

In seminar discussions, he was known for his clear-cut expressions on cross-cultural issues, which earned him regular appearances on TV talk shows in Lake City. One of the many campus quotes ascribed to him was, 'Any black African who allows himself or herself to fit into any black stereotype has walked wide-eyed into a wide-open trap.'

Dezmond's reputation soon spread around campus and beyond. The better the report, the more determined he was to sustain it. It was clear to him that the tall standards he had set were not a matter of slogans or psyching oneself up. He had since concluded that the only way to achieve his mission, the only way to contend with the pressures of the American environment as it unravelled itself by the day, would be by resolute self-determination. He would, therefore, not allow anybody to judge or pre-empt him, whether as another stud in massa's stable; as a statistic in failed black manhood; or as a pawn on the chessboard of life.

*

One month emptied fast into another as academic work continued in full swing, with forty thousand young people rolling up and down the campus like the waves of a great sea. Dezmond's coursework ticked on like a well-oiled clock. There was little room for idle banter, especially now that the chill of late fall had begun to tell on the favourite outdoor hang-outs and walkways. Indeed, many older people could be seen already donning their winter coats.

If you needed a bite or drink on the run, you could pick one from one of a row of vending machines, and plod to your next course venue. Lunch hour always centred around the ubiquitous brown bag or the vending machine.

On one of those rare fun days, Dezmond met one of his course teachers kicking a vending machine.

'Prof, you need help?' he shouted over the din. 'That one is a rogue vendor! You slot in a quarter and it gives you only a dime's worth of peanuts.'

'That's why I'm kicking the damn rogue to get my apple-pie!' The professor's joke drew applause from the queues of students and faculty alike, waiting for their turn. Dezmond clutched his cup of hot chocolate and cornered Prof. Peat.

'I'm glad to catch up with you today, Prof. Been long we saw.'

'Yer, been long. I'm glad you're getting more American by the day.'

'Am I?' said Dezmond, smiling.

'Talk of dimes and quarters, and peanuts – what can be more American? You're melting real good!'

'It's rubbing on, I guess! So, how about you? How're you getting along, ol' Prof?'

'Pretty good, I'd say. At least, better than most guys my age, downtown,' quipped Prof. Peat, a seventy-year-old teacher of Analytic Philosophy. 'I tell you, you've done very well in my course. Boy, I marvel at your great facility with my language. It's a shame most American kids cannot draw a line between colloquial and formal English. As for spellings, forget it! Hey, tell you some'n! Why don't you switch over, and take a Ph.D. in my course?'

'Get behind me, Prof!' exclaimed Dezmond playfully. The professor switched behind him and smacked his back. 'Frankly, I cannot leave Civilisations for Analytic Philosophy, though I've enjoyed the course.'

'Give me three cogent reasons why not,' insisted the silver-haired white man.

'I've done a reasonably advanced work on Civilisations. It has been my greatest area of interest and career prospects, and I'm beginning to appreciate my advisor. Frankly, I enjoyed the semester with you, but I can't leave now. I'd be losing eighteen months' worth of transferred credits. I can't afford that setback.'

'I thought as much!' conceded the professor. 'You'll do well to stick to your advisor. I know the damn fellow like the back of my hand. D'you know that up until 1952 he was a GI in the US Army? He's not totally recovered from the Korean War shells yet, I can tell you that! But he's a top-notch brain. Works like a horse. That's one Afro-American LCU is very proud of, and I ain't patronising. He's told me about you. Better not miss out on that, Dez!' He tapped Dezmond on the shoulder and ambled his way along.

Professor Alvin Primate was indeed a difficult man to understand, as Dezmond got to know. He was reputed as a scholar of esteem, and a workaholic who insisted on excellence in every endeavour one chose for oneself. To him, that was the essence of the American work ethic and achievement motivation: that by dint of excellence, any American, even from the backwoods of the Bronx, can grow to become the president of the most powerful country in the world. Yet others perceived him as parading an ego that was too strong for a black American; as being a threat to the dominant white psyche, and in the same vein, a judgement on black manhood. Over time, in a society where psychometrics and sociometrics die hard, underpinning every public opinion, the labels stuck to Prof. Primate.

Dezmond began to understand why his initial efforts at befriending this fellow black could not progress beyond the formal set-up. Through the black grapevine, he got more snatches of background information on his advisor.

Son of a veteran of the exclusively black, but since disbanded, 24th Regiment of the US Army, Alvin Primate imbibed a strong anti-racist trait from his late father. He grew up in the predominantly black city of Chicago, determined to excel in academics. Right from grade school, against the normal grain of expectations, he loathed sports, which he regarded as uncompetitive because they were dominated by Afro-Americans. After high school, he enrolled in the US Army from where he came back to take three degrees, in record time, at Cornell.

On a few rare occasions, Dezmond had the opportunity to draw Prof. Primate out of his well-fenced privacy. One particular day, not sure how to tread that turf, he began his probing with a rather shaky question. He had wondered aloud, to his advisor's hearing, why such a man as he was so misunderstood.

'Who by?' asked the professor, as a matter of course. He was going from his table to bookshelf, arranging some typed sheets. 'Who's misunderstanding Prof. Alvin Primate, you say?'

'Well, students, of course; your colleagues, and particularly, fellow graduate students who have had contact with you.'

'What contact?' questioned the professor, pausing. 'Who makes contact with who, in this menagerie of forty thousand, each in pursuit of his own?'

Dezmond wondered how to stoke the fire he had kindled. This was the closest he had got to his advisor in two semesters. At this particular time, he was helping out with documentation of data for one of his advisor's three journal or conference papers that were due for printing. The hour of Dezmond's breakthrough with the professor had not come, it was apparent.

'In any case,' continued Prof. Primate, 'I am a projectile in flight. How can any man understand a flying object?'

'Perhaps, by flying closely behind,' suggested Dezmond, tickled by his own humour, but still diffidently. Surprisingly, the professor laughed, his face aglow in this rare phenomenon. Dezmond felt awkward at this sudden change of mood. It came like late season savannah rain: now sunshine, now suddenly shower! But it was worth following up this opportunity.

'I'm trying to say that I appreciate you... what you want to do for me,' he continued ponderously. 'I've realised... you are the right person to be my advisor. I remember the question – you asked me one question which puzzled me. I kept wondering. For six months, I wondered why you asked me that question. We've come a long way, Prof. I'm aware that, sometimes, I've been like a pain. Sometimes, I've presented myself as if to trade wits with you. Or even to exchange words. But that's not my intention.'

The professor suspended his chores and sat down, looking rather puzzled. 'You surely have something on your chest you want to unload. Stop hedging around the issue and get on with it. Now, what's your problem with Alvin Primate?'

Dezmond's confidence increased strongly, now that he had engaged his listener's attention fully. 'Prof, thanks for this encouragement. Simply, I want to acknowledge that we have more things in common than I had realised. Like communication, for example. I mean, the ability to get across to the other person. This, of course, is an advantage for me as your student. However, if you permit me to say so, it could also put a kind of strain on our interaction.'

'Now, Dez, what exactly are you talking about? I'm trying hard to figure out what it is you're communicating this minute. What's the real problem? Certainly, this doesn't sound like you. You wanna hit the nail on the head, or what?'

'I expect more from my being attached to you. I want to know you more than just being advisor. To know you as a person, a friend. I wish you could open up to me a little more. I'm not talking about skin colour. If I have any racial hang-up, it is the motivation that racism gives me, to excel myself in my studies...'

'All righ',' interrupted Prof. Primate. 'I believe I got a notion of where you're heading. Looks like I've not listened very well to this other Dezmond that's been sitting inside you recently. Well, let's not get into all that now... I'll jus' try and tell you a littl' about me, and maybe we can move forward from there. Pull that chair closer and sit down.'

For the next hour, they engaged in an open-hearted sharing about one another in an atmosphere of good-natured give and take in which little was denied. Dezmond divulged personal details about his childhood; his travails with his higher degree studies in Nigeria; the great expectation awaiting him as a first-born of his father; and a whole lot more.

It was again Prof. Primate's turn. 'Well, I don't have

your kind of narrative skill… an' I won't attempt to follow your own pattern, 'cos you sure have a great way with words!' His openness made the conversation even more relaxed. He went on to sketch his life's story, from birth.

He continued, 'After the Korean War, in 1953, the US Army lemme go to college, a dream that had settled in my mind since I learnt of my granpa. At Cornell, I found I needed to prove myself at every turn. Sounds easy to talk about it now, but it was pretty tough, man! But it paid off. Still paying off!'

The phone tinkled and Prof. Primate buzzed it back to his secretary. Could she take the message, please? He chuckled meditatively and continued, 'It's been so with Alvin Primate ever since… oh, in fact, even before I was born.' He paused, shook his head, and continued. 'Y'know the meaning of my las' name?'

'I think… something to do with mammals?'

'Righ'! My granpa's slave name was Byron Loghorn, after his owner, Mr Manaseth Loghorn, you see? He was about twenty-one when Papa Linkum, as they called him then, signed the Emancipation Bill in 1863. An' boy, Granpa knew wha' he wan'ed! He escaped from Tennessee an' changed his name altogether to Gideon Primate. He was one of the ex-slaves who went to private Negro schools against the menace of racists who insisted that slavery was the natural estate of blacks. Granpa stumbled on "primate", and the word spoke what the young man saw in himself. That name reflected his dreams. "Primate" is *primus inter pares*. First among equals! Top bishop among bishops, literally. Even among animals, among mammals as you said, a primate is top of the pack! Granpa knew what he wan'ed! I believe he had a dream before Dr Martin Luther King, bless his gentle soul. Now you can see, I'm coming from a long way back there. Now you know what you're appreciating.

'Gideon, of course, you find in the Bible. Book of Judges someplace,' continued the professor, glowing with more pride, in the light of his worthy background. 'An ordinary homeboy, wheat thresher an' son of a peasant. Th' Almighty called him mighty man o'valour, an' so was he! He faced up to God's angel, asked all the right questions, an' wen' on to deal with those Amalekites an' the res' o' them!'

Dezmond himself was caught in the excitement, smiling as he chipped in a little comment. 'Granpa surely knew his Bible!'

'Oh sure! They all did! They had to. In slavery mo' than anywhere else, church provided the great elixir of life. You can see, I've come a long ways, baby!'

'I can appreciate that.'

Dezmond nodded now and then, as if to encourage this rare flow of personal history.

'It's been so with me all along,' continued the professor. 'D'you now figure out why I drive you guys so hard on the critical path? Because I'm driven by a history. Anyone else who has serious business with me, my wife, our three kids, my students... they have to fit into that regiment.'

Dezmond thanked his advisor profusely, overwhelmed by the unexpected bonus of in-depth knowledge of Prof. Primate's earlier life. His statement that he had much in common with him was even more accurate than he could have imagined. He was tempted to prove it further by matching the professor's intimate revelations with more of his own. However, he dissuaded himself in order not to overstretch his luck on that day. In any case, Prof. Primate was now giving him a cue by standing up abruptly.

As Dezmond walked out of the office, a weight was lifted off his back. He felt free and breathed more fully, and he strode away with a livelier spring to his steps. He stopped abruptly as a thought sneaked into his mind from the distant past. Like poles repel, unlike poles attract... He repeated the old axiom over and over, then resumed his sprightly walk. 'Like poles may repel all they want,' he soliloquised. 'That obtains in the realm of physics. Magnets and metals are not men!'

Chapter Four

Bro. Maazi picked up the phone.

'No. Dez! You don't need to lie. You've been avoiding me… Well, I know it beyond doubt…'

'I would like you to be there,' pleaded Dezmond. 'Not trouble as such, but I'm not sure what they're up to… Even to just sit down and observe? *Haba*, Bro. Maazi? But you do have me in mind, I believe?'

'Yes, I more than have you in mind, you should expect. But, let's keep in contact. Not only when there's trouble at your door… yes? Hello. D'you know how many times I called, and you were not there? And that's just in the last three weeks—'

'Bro. Maazi', Dezmond cut in, 'we'll sort it all out. There's a lot I want to tell you. Just that my work kept expanding, but we'll have some time during the Christmas break. So…'

'Okay, Dez. I'll table it and see what gives… yeah, you got it. If the Lord permits!'

*

The usual hubbub of the Rathskeller was at its lunch-hour peak. Dezmond Adama sat back, deflated and limp, like a tramp.

'I do not see your argument!' repeated Maazi, for the third time, as Wale Jefferson tore open yet another can. The words of the Afro-American student activist poured out like torrential rain.

'You say argument! I says bullshit! Ain't no point my making points! I got berra things to accomplish, dig? I gave y'all real case situations on blacks movin' into Caucasian settlements. You think I'm jes' jivin'? Now, guess who's gon' be busted, the next break-in 'n that neighbourhood! Say some broad gets raped? Who's the nearest scapegoat nigger gon' get busted? When the honky shit hits the fan, who's gon' take the can? Dez's in real mess, man! You jes' watch out, if you'all think I'm alarmist. Watch! The night Miss Frank-wha'rever gets on heat, forgerrit, man! Y'all think I'm jivin', righ'? I'm giving you the get-down facts of the now situation in Babylon. Stop looking at cosmetic tokenism an' gettin' deceived—'

'If you'll let somebody else say a word,' Maazi cut in. 'This man simply needed a place to lay his head. The only opening that came up was No. 19, Pine. He overstayed even his period of grace at Clement Hall and had to get packing. Dezmond wanted to avoid hassles. So, what's this quarrel all about?'

'Wale, what would you have done if you were in my shoes?' asked Dezmond. 'Even now, do you have any alternative as to where I can move? I'm willing to lose a month's rent in order to be free of hassles from you guys.'

'What kinda alternative you talking about? You ain't cut out for East-side LC! What with nightjars an' their pimps dodging yo' every step? How can you sleep amid the clanging and banging and whistling of an all-night boogie-down? East-side, where rodents and roaches'll eat up your bourgeois leather shoes! There's no place to hide, East-side Lake City. Not for Ph.D. candidates from Mother Africa!'

'Wale, this is totally uncalled for and unnecessary!' shouted Dezmond, rising. 'You had enough time to find me even a room to squat! You didn't care! Now, you're suddenly so concerned for my welfare! I'm challenging you again. Show me a place, any place, now! I'll move house!'

'You sho' stashed up some smackaroos, boy!' Wale teased, and shot his sixth can into a trash bag.

'I've had enough of this comedy, Wale,' intervened Bro. Maazi once more. 'I won't waste one minute more on such useless talk. Dezmond has settled down in No. 19, Pine. That's that! No point your crying crocodile tears now. You had your chance.'

Wale Jefferson went into a well-rehearsed mimicry of his imagined white landlady and black tenant, in a dialogue.

'I can imagine Mama Frankwood handing Sambo his bill of right conduct: "This efficiency's all yours, boy, here's the rules an' keys." "T'ank you, ma'am," says Sambo tenant. "You're welcome, darkie, but I don' wan' none o' your rowdy bongo drums in ma clean white precincts! An' no boogie parties either," says Mama Frankwood. "No, ma'am, no parties, no bongo drums," says Sambo tenant. "Good boy! One more importan' thing not written down. D'you have a pet?" asked Mama Frankwood, an' maybe, Sambo gets a littl' naughty an' smart-arsed, an' asks her, "Mama, which kin' o' pet y'mean, male or female?"'

From the moment Wale started this bit of planned mischief, Maazi and Dezmond did not wait to be further provoked. But Wale followed them with his lampoon, ending it with a fit of laughter.

Bro. Maazi would not leave Dezmond in a state of depression. As they drove to 19, Pine Avenue, he took the opportunity to cheer him up. 'You know one of my survival ways? The grace God gives me to see something noble even in a heap of rubbish. It reduces the effect of men's wickedness on my feelings.'

'What did you say?'

'Don't think too far about Wale's behaviour. Of course, he was drunk before he even descended on the six-pack. What do you expect from such a sponge? But then, I want to believe it is the brotherly love in the African blood that he is trying to express. Pity he's perverted it. He's carried it to a point of stupidity. The good aspect is that he is jealous that you moved into a white area; plus, you're living with a white woman.'

'Living with a white woman? Is that how you see it too?'

'No, Dez. Don't get me upside down, please. I'm trying to show you Wale's thinking. In any case, that's the way people see things. You and Frankwood are living under the same roof. Will you take *ogene* and go about announcing, "Hear-o! I am only a tenant-o! I am not sleeping with the landlady-o!" Even if you are mad enough to do that, who will believe you? Your best bet is to put Wale and his drunken talk out of your mind and face the thing that brought you to the States.'

Back in his room. Dezmond felt a strong sense of home, even of ownership. No matter what any detractor thought, this was his own turf. He had paid hard currency for it. He lay on his bed and his eyes began to survey the room afresh. It seemed that in the four months since moving in, he had been too engrossed in his books to admire his most intimate surrounding.

He felt cosy as his eyes absorbed the padded look of the room, carpeted wall-to-wall for better insulation against the winter. Even with the cold, on some afternoons he would pull up a shutter to admit rarified air from the tops of the pine trees. This produced a refreshing impact that was unique.

It suddenly dawned on him that an insect was crawling on his arm. He sprang up and grabbed the quilted bed-cover. The bedding had not been shaken out for days. A general house-cleaning ensued, after which he rearranged everything. The bed, his desk, the fridgette, the rocking chair, his settee, the bookshelf, dressing mirror, TV set – every item underwent relocation.

He held the electric heater and was amused when he recollected how it became part of his household. Miss Frankwood had agreed with him that the attic room would be colder, not on account of ice on the roof tiles, as he had imagined, but because the heating system would be overloaded during the imminent winter. Hence, she bought him the heater. Dezmond felt like a baron as he now slouched on the grandpa rocking chair, relaxing, letting his mind range far and near.

The overall picture of this place of abode which he presented to himself was one of beauty. But a beautiful picture is a question of what the mind tells the eyes to see. It may not be the complete view.

Dezmond saw in his abode a withdrawal into his person, away from pressures and masks. It was a cocoon, nay, another womb, a theatre of fantasy and realism, depending on the need of the hour.

But pressures can break down doors. They force themselves into a man's sleeping place, and the door cannot be slammed on them by human hands. The centre of a man's inner room is the very place where pressures love to hibernate. Like all other matter, every ordinary man expands under pressure. His protoplasm thins out. The cells begin to disintegrate and spirit, soul and body become disunited. That is when an embattled man puts masks on his face, even in his sleeping room. But masks and masquerades are for market places, theatres and Hallowe'en ghost-festivals. One's own sleeping room is a haven, a bare, unpretentious retreat. There, the naked man is free to stand and stare at his real self, transparent in his ugliness, with spots of beauty here and there.

There were times when Dezmond would stride about the room in a heroic modern-day re-enactment of Shaka Zulu. Other times, he spent hours indoors, completely naked, doing chores or just idling. To him, these acts of self-expression were saner than those of some white men, who would dash into the midst of a crowd of people stark naked, make bare their south end, and disappear like a fleeting arrow.

Sometimes, this strange liberty of Dezmond's would translate into streams of tears which would burst forth like the waters of a broken dam, ending up in mournful lyrics in his native tongue. Many of these intimate secrets were recorded in a private journal which he kept religiously and guarded like a treasure chest. But, as with all things under the sun, they were not to remain hidden for ever.

As for Miss Frankwood, she had from the beginning presented herself as a consistently proper, businesslike lady, not to be misunderstood or undermined in her need for extra cash for her mortgage and supporting her broken family.

Even Junior, her twelve-year old, received regular tutoring as to how to relate properly to the African tenant. For months, Junior watched him in the cold, calculating manner of a child. But the unencumbered innocence of childhood soon broke down the walls imposed by adulthood. It did not take long before he became Dezmond's exponent on American football, filling his ears with the exploits of O.J. Simpson and his other heroes of the day.

In return for touchdown runs, Dezmond spared some time to teach Junior soccer dribbles, teasing him that he could become a striker with the New York Cosmos and have Pelé as his coach. Some weekends, the two would romp around the grounds, practising set pieces against an imaginary defence wall. After that, they would jog two blocks down the road, to an ice cream bar or just lie on the lawn and tell each other fantastic boys' tales.

Miss Frankwood watched as the friendship grew. It would not pose any problem, she thought, provided it did not go beyond the occasional ball game and fabulous stories. Besides, she observed that only on weekends did Dezmond allow more than thirty minutes of leisure. By the second month of this friendship, Laura, aged fourteen, began to develop keen interest in soccer, often turning out in slacks, desiring to join in. However, the usual horseplay involved did not permit her to participate beyond the touchline. She was consoled with filling in as Junior's cheerer or ballgirl. The monthly two weeks' stay at Mummy's place became more and more exciting and the children looked forward to it more than ever before.

One evening, Junior grabbed Dezmond after a hectic day at LCU, and insisted he join in the dinner. Miss Frankwood and Laura were busy dishing the meal. Junior refused to be dissuaded. Miss Frankwood overheard the arguments, came out, watched the skirmish for a moment, and signalled Laura to set a third plate.

'I know my boy,' she explained, as Dezmond continued to protest. 'He ain't gonna give up. He could starve if you don't oblige him. And he means it. He's always a winner.'

Junior prayed victoriously and rapidly, and threw himself on the hot buns. Laura watched surreptitiously as the two adults tried to overcome a certain awkwardness. Broiled potatoes, roast beef, stewed tender corn, broccoli, and spiced gravy. The spread and its aroma provided ready subject for small talk. The coyness began to fade away when Dezmond joked that he had always thought that broccoli was some Italian in a grocery shop! Laura picked gingerly from her plate, smiling sheepishly or nodding in response.

After devouring three buns, Junior was ready to heighten the volume and tempo of civilised table talk. Each time he took a break from his worldwide contributions to the small talk, the coyness would creep back. Laura would urge him to try more beef, or taste the corn. Miss Frankwood would echo the same encouragement to Dezmond who kept manipulating his polite helping to no end.

Sometimes, Miss Frankwood looked altogether distant from the company, perched as her body was at the end of the table.

Must be the missing man at the head! Dezmond ruminated, recreating in his mind the feelings of his landlady, whom he had never before observed so closely and for so long. Now her guard was down. Building on the titbits which Junior had fed him about his dad, Dezmond slipped into his own mind game, and began to piece together his portrait of a brain-charged assistant professor of nuclear physics… There would sit, Dr Gordon, elbow dug frenetically into the hard wood, uttering an occasional grunt to his chattering boy, who'd be all too keen to tell the day's adventures to an ever-busy, ever-distracted daddy…

Dezmond imagined Dr Gordon throwing glances at his wife without really taking cognisance of her. He was seeing with only the eyes while the mind was fixated on the high-mounted cyclotron in his nuclear physics project. Dr Gordon would probably harpoon some stubborn string beans and systematically chew until his bare molars were left with nothing to grind than abstraction. Perhaps, at that very instance, sonny would shoot his eleventh question, or Mrs Gordon would let out a quaint prompting cough; then Dr Gordon would be awakened for his next performance.

Dezmond visualised him gazing at the blank wall over his wife's freshly retouched coiffure – daddy, husband, head of table, spirited into the airless incubus of the latest black hole hypothesis following that other visionary, Galileo, who was imprisoned for his ingenuity. Assistant Professor Gordon would, perhaps, contemplate over his plate for a while more, then drop his fork. A final grunt, then he would trudge his way upstairs to suck at the stale stub of a Henry Stevens cigar…

Miss Frankwood kept her gaze on the empty seat at the far end of table. She might indeed have been conjuring up her husband, even as the guest indulged himself in his own recreation. In between dainty morsels, Dezmond was drawn out by a teaser from Laura, or a silly quip from Junior's repertoire of school jokes.

Finally noticing his mother, Junior drew nearer and asked, 'Mum, are you all right?'

'Sure honey,' she intoned, as casually as she could manage. 'Guess this is one of those lousy dumb days! Dezmond, I appreciate your company at dinner. I should thank Junior for it! Sorry, I felt kinda dumb at table.'

'No problem, Miss Frankwood.'

'Well,' she retorted calmly, rising, 'you don't have to say anything, Dezmond.'

⋆

Christmas time in Lake City turned out to be the season of tinsels, carols, and heady commercials which Dezmond had experienced all his adult life. The LCU had gone on break mid-December, to allow faculty and staff to join in the Yuletide fray. If any student needed and deserved a vacation, it was Dezmond Adama. Spurred on by the ever-increasing attention of his advisor, he had worked very hard throughout the semester, and had recorded mostly As.

However, to him, Christmas meant an opportunity for advance work on future courses, a time to do 'a general recce' as he called it, toward his doctorate proposal. In this regard, the notorious heavy snowfalls of the eastern coast of America helped him to remain indoors. Sometimes, for days in a row, Lake City would be buried in a mountain of snow, often leading to multiple vehicle accidents, and crippling socio-economic life. It looked as dreary as it was comical to Dezmond, seeing rotund, winter-clad figures scurry past one another in the deep freeze, headed for the next heated shelter. At such times of heavy snow, even his one-hour TV indulgence was depressing to him, as if the massive overburden of ice and snow would slough off the screen unto his floor.

Only occasionally did he call Maazi or some course mate, to chat or compare notes. Distraction aside, he was afraid of Ma Bell's monthly bills. His phone usage was, therefore, limited to what he considered very necessary calls. Even his advisor he called rarely, preferring to consult him face to face, which seemed to him more respectful. Miss Frankwood noted this fine inclination towards prudence and offered to absorb his phone bills, but Dezmond politely objected. He would foot his own bills, since there was no telephone in the efficiency package. That way, he would keep himself under discipline regarding friendships and use of time.

He continued to win his landlady's respect. She was so impressed by his consistently genuine and simple manners that she was compelled to begin to question her lifelong prejudices regarding the black race. On the few occasions Dezmond was cajoled into having dinner with the family, he proved to be a well-bred gentleman, without putting on airs in order to impress anybody. As usual, table talk was mainly between himself and the two. And, what a way he had with the adolescents! Their mother would only chip in now and then, by way of rekindling the fire of conversation while she listened. She enjoyed what she called the elegant British flavour in the man's style of English, which made her desire to hear him talk and talk whenever the opportunity arose.

Perhaps, racial stereotypes do not really cut across continental boundaries, thought Miss Frankwood. Or perhaps the pressures which undermine black American men are different from those that obtain among African aborigines. Even then, considered Miss Frankwood, there are always exceptions to the rule. Dezmond must be one exceptional specimen.

On thinking back, Miss Frankwood felt very satisfied that her gamble was paying off. Before taking in the tenant, she had resolved, despite her mortgage needs, that she would tolerate only those who would submit to stringent house rules. She stated it in her advert. When, unexpectedly, a black man turned up, she could typically have played him off with one excuse or the other, but she found herself yielding to nobler impulse. As Dezmond moved in, she told herself that having admitted him, the only way to be fair to herself and to him would be to at least discard, if not altogether bury, her preconceptions of a lifetime of living in all-white communities. She told herself that she owed it to her sound American upbringing to now demonstrate her belief in the much-touted equal opportunities, and in the inalienable rights of all men, regardless of race, religion or gender. She also trusted herself to be able to keep control of her life and property, and take the best possible decision in any given situation.

This was the secret of her quiet strength against the ridicules and taunts of the neighbourhood, right from the first week Dezmond moved in. These 'Fascist bigots', as Miss Frankwood called them, gave up after about nine weeks of fruitless harassment. She took quiet note then of the humour and dignity with which her tenant surmounted the barrage of racist intimidation. Indeed, that was when she began to pay closer attention to him. Little did she know that he was facing a different kind of flak from his own black brothers in the name of a group called Protect Afrika in Diaspora.

A silent evolution in her mindset was going on, from a stand-offish, businesslike detachment to a deep personal respect and unspoken admiration.

Ironically, however, Dezmond became increasingly wary and shy of even the occasional treat with Miss Frankwood and her children. No doubt he sensed a growing warmth as a result of the closeness of shared meals, but he felt he was overexposing himself at a vulnerable point. Such liberties also added up to a lingering distraction which he could ill afford in the face of his private study targets during the Christmas vacation. He therefore programmed his movements to avoid dinner time. Junior, with whom he had logged many man-hours in horseplay, he kept at bay. Seeing the demands of graduate work even in the relatively free-flowing American academic setup, he knew that in the third semester, his cup would be full enough without his widening new avenues for social divertissement. Sometimes, for a whole working week, he would not set eyes on the three other residents of No. 19, Pine, leaving for campus at twilight and returning to roost at dusk.

This avoidance plan worked smoothly for Dezmond as he diligently pursued his studies, not taking cognisance of all the Christmas bustle in the air.

On her part, Miss Frankwood's Home Medicare for Veterans kept her sufficiently busy. Junior had already left for his daddy's and Laura was to later join him for a skiing camp which their dad had previously promised them. Everything fitted well into place at No. 19, Pine Avenue, until the spirit of Christmas set to work.

One morning as Dezmond was preparing to leave his room, he heard a gentle tap on the door. There stood Miss Frankwood, smiling.

'Miss Frankwood!' exclaimed Dezmond, fidgeting with the door handle. 'Must be serious.'

Both of them stood face to face at the doorway.

'Nothing serious, Dezmond.'

'But you've never come up here since you showed me the place. What's the matter?'

'No big deal,' she answered, with a wave of hand.

'Oh, please, come inside,' Dezmond said, finally remembering his manners.

'I need to catch up with you this morning before you fly off again. In a word, Dez, I've come to apologise—'

'What on earth for?' he interrupted.

'Well, it's a bit stale now, but I guess in a way, it's still fresh. I embarrassed you at dinner. I'm really sorry. Please…'

'For heaven's sake,' protested Dezmond yet again, 'I can't even remember what you're talking about, frankly! So, why this now?'

'I got bothered, Dez. Plus, I should tell you, it was a case of displaced reaction. My annoyance was meant for somebody else, not you at all.'

The more she explained, the more confused and embarrassed Dezmond looked.

'I ain't got no problem with you,' she pressed on. 'So, don't continue this hiding game you've been on for weeks now. You belong here, okay?'

Dezmond was at sea as to what to say, but it would look worse if he said nothing. 'Well, thanks, Miss Frankwood, I really don't know… Well, whatever it was, I do not have the slightest memory of it. Please, believe me. Really, I have no problem with you or your children.'

'Listen, I'd like you to know I care. I had to get this little matter off my chest.'

Dezmond was still holding onto the door even as Miss Frankwood was climbing down the stairway. Over the tall pines, the winter sun was tantalising the landscape, now bathing the rooftops in its pale light, now shielding its face behind the grey clouds from the distant factories of the Tonawanda area of Lake City.

The day was particularly chilly. Dezmond had no real business on the sleeping campus, but all the same he did a leisurely round of the bulletin boards, picked up his mail and some belated seminar papers. He was in high spirits, having received news of home from Maazi and a Nigerian student who had recently arrived. This cheerful atmosphere prevailed as he swaggered on his way home at nightfall.

Miss Frankwood and Laura were lazing together in the lounge when the man walked in, evidently in very good spirits.

'Hi, ma'am! Hi, Laura!' he called.

'Hi, Dez! Back home just in time!' chorused mother and daughter.

'The table's set for three! There's a surprise treat tonight!'

'Oh no!' exclaimed Dezmond, stopping in his track.

'No? You can't refuse this one!' urged Miss Frankwood as she got up from the giant pouf on which she had been watching TV and conversing with her daughter. On her part, Laura engaged herself in rearranging the table-mats and cutlery. For a girl of only fourteen, she was already showing the typical sensitivity of womanhood. She had the taciturn traits of her father, but whenever she spoke, she sounded more mature than her years. Often, her calculated silence communicated more than words.

'Dezmond, it's too late to cop out,' remarked Miss Laura Gordon. 'Table is laid for three, and you know how expensive groceries are these days. Mummy's cooking is not for the waste bag. Besides, hear this: Mummy tried a black recipe for the first time! Pork chops with corn bread and Mexican tomato sauce over venison!'

The spread looked enticing even by mere presentation, not to include the seductive aroma of well-spiced meat. Laura reverently whispered through the prayer before meals and the three settled to dinner.

'So, Laura, Junior went ahead of you, then?'

'Yea, I wanna cheer Mummy up a littl' bit,' she explained. 'A day or two more, an' I'm gone again. Then I'll be back again! Like a yo-yo!'

'Dear sweetheart, that's what the song calls making the best of a bad situation,' her mother all but sang.

'Makes some sense in this situation,' added Dezmond, as he broke off a portion of his corn bread.

'Like it?' asked Laura expectantly.

'Sure! Corn bread reminds me of home. It is very similar to a corn dish that I've enjoyed from childhood. Tastes good. The last I ate something so yummy was at Maazi's place.'

'Thanks to Mummy!' Laura rhymed in, smiling.

'Yes, indeed,' echoed Dezmond. 'But you've taken much trouble preparing this. Y'know, these days, even we Africans don't take food for granted.'

'What does that mean?' wondered Miss Frankwood.

'Really, madam, you're overgenerous to me. I know how expensive it is to fix a posh meal like this one.'

'Oh, now I know where you're going. After all, it was me who said food is expensive, but this is just—'

'No, Mummy, I did,' interrupted Laura, 'But Mum, I hope we aren't doing something wrong – arguing at table, and with a guest sitting right there!'

'Oh dear! Let's enjoy the meal.'

They quietly relished their helpings for a while and then Laura, smiling over her plate, threw in a joker. 'I have an idea! Dezmond could chip in a coupla dollars a week for a hot meal in the evenings. Especially now that it's winter vacation and you'll be staying in most days.'

'Great idea! Dezmond, what d'you think?' echoed Miss Frankwood. 'A hot meal each winter night. Sounds just great!' Dezmond took his time to consider this surprise package. 'I'd grab it if I were you,' added Laura's mother.

'I guess I can't escape your constant invitations to free food. I think it feels better with Laura's suggestion. Why not? I'd be more comfortable chipping in than freeloading so often!'

'So, we're in business!' exclaimed Miss Frankwood jokingly. 'We'll get the contract details drawn up later. No small print, I can assure you!'

The dinner proper over, Miss Frankwood was mixing her own cup of Sanka coffee when the phone rang. Dezmond, who sat nearest, impulsively picked up the receiver but almost immediately dropped it in the outstretched palm of his landlady. She held it to her ear only for a minute and gently replaced it.

'It's the bad guys, Mum!' exclaimed Laura, drawing up to her mother's side.

'Laura dear, clean up and go upstairs,' instructed her mother.

Miss Frankwood and Dezmond sipped their coffee in silence. Laura took her time to do an extra-thorough cleaning and finally had to bid them goodnight. If the prolonged hush had raised any suspicion in her mind, she did not betray it.

'Poor Dezmond!' declared Miss Frankwood, as she heard the banging of Laura's door. 'Remember, you're not to help me with these calls. You have enough hassles just being my tenant, don't you think?'

Dezmond silently studied the spiral of steam ascending from his cup. His face looked, every pore, the image of his intrepid ancestors in the daunting African jungle. A pattern of heroic images floated across his mind's eye. 'It was about me, wasn't it?' he asked.

'No. You've been here just months. They've been at it for two years, since Dave and I broke apart, y'know.'

She cut herself short. Gripping her cup tightly in both hands, she held it close to her face. The steam settled on her visage, shrouding it in apparent pain. Without a further sip, she gently lowered it to the table-mat and rose to her feet, suddenly assuming a more authoritative, matronly appearance.

'This situation does not really concern you, Dezmond,' she went on. 'I have the right to take in any tenant. And you're free to live here for as long as you continue to keep our house rules. Period!'

Notwithstanding the commanding tone, she looked miles away from that sure-footed, straight-bargaining landlady whom Dezmond had met five months earlier in her rugged denim jeans.

'Good night, Dezmond,' she said, as she again picked up the cup. 'Another busy day is here already. Tomorrow comes all too soon. We'll get to know each other. And trust one another more. Then we'll sit up together to watch late-night movies. Y'know, some nights I let the kids stay up with me until Junior's enemy appears on the screen to ask us parents of the eastern sea coast, "Do you know where your children are?"' Her attempt at mimicking the TV announcer made both of them laugh.

That night, Dezmond fought a battle. Only when he woke up and found himself soaked in sweat, and his bedding in shambles, did he realise it had happened in dreamland. Cold fear filled his chest as he sat up recalling the nightmare, his bare arms suddenly invaded by goose-flesh. He pulled the quilt over his head and struggled to reconstruct the encounter.

The attack was so real that he wondered if indeed he had not actually experienced it some years back. He could not regain his sleep. At dawn, he came downstairs to phone but halted his steps on seeing Miss Frankwood using her living-room extension.

'Are you all right?' she asked, cupping the mouthpiece.

'Yes,' lied Dezmond. 'Good morning.'

'If you wanna make a call, I'll be done in a minute.'

*

Maazi arrived at No. 19, Pine, looking cool and unruffled by Dezmond's alarming call. He pulled the back chair close to the bed and sat down. 'Man, you look beat up!' he commented.

'That's why I had to call you.' Dezmond sat up on the bed.

'Somehow, I am glad you thought of me. What exactly happened?'

'I had a nightmare. It shook me up very badly. In fact, I'm not sure it was just a dream. I need your help, Maazi.'

He had gone jogging at dusk. They had taken him by surprise. There was a broken-down vehicle by the pavement, covered by light snowflakes. Dezmond heard his name and looked over his shoulder. Nobody. He slowed down to a trot and kept his eyes and ears on full alert. A voice said, 'C'mon, Bro. Dezmond,' slowly and coldly. From the ground, as it were, emerged a gaunt figure, blocking his way. 'Take it easy. We're PAID hands,' he said, just loudly enough. The man flicked his cigarette stub into the hedgerow and the headlights of the vehicle flooded the street, blinding Dezmond. That seemed to be the agreed signal.

'I turned and tried to split,' continued Dezmond. 'Just then, I felt this tight grip on my nape. There must have been two of them because I couldn't move my right hand either. "Keep floatin', man! We don' mean no harm," one of them muttered into my face. "Don' let this honky neighbourhood get mixed up with this situation. Keep floatin'!"

'When I saw that I was going to be thrown into that truck, I knew I had to do or die. I began to kick and shout anyhow. It was then I heard a big bang in my ears. I thought I had been blown up or something. Look, Maazi, I can't even describe what I went through. This is just the bit I can recollect. My eyes have remained open like this for over thirty hours.'

Dezmond finally relieved himself of the memory of this strange experience, to which his friend had listened, intermittently praying silently for insight, and for what to say.

'You are really exhausted. You must catch some sleep. I've heard you. God knows you would call me. I believe He will help us even now. Jesus is the answer. Always. My Father has already spoken concerning you. It is not His intention that you live in harassment from demons. Frankly, Dez, I don't know how to comfort you. Other than this, I really don't know what to be telling you right now. Quit running your own life. Hand it over to Jesus and see the difference. This is the only way to peace and joy that I can offer you.'

'I hear you, Maazi. Maybe one day God will answer our prayers. Please pray for me. I badly need some sleep. It's like pebbles are running inside my eye sockets.'

'I will, of course. Thank God for that much. But that one is like Sunday–Sunday tonic.'

'That's what I need now. Tonic.'

'Well, I don't want to just pray for you now and then. I want you to get to the point where you pray for yourself. Then we shall be praying together in agreement. Praying for you all the time is like loaning you my winter coat when you can jolly well grab your own, and for free too.'

'Someday, I will. Please pray for me,' pleaded Dezmond, as he lay back, exhausted and dispirited.

Maazi stood up and raised his right hand over Dezmond, his eyes shut. He remained silent for minutes, as if waiting for a divine direction, then raised his voice. 'My Father, God Almighty! Your mercy endureth for ever. I come by the blood of our Lord Jesus Christ who has made it possible for me to call you father. Let the words of my mouth, even the meditations of my heart, be acceptable in your sight this day. In Jesus's name! Father, I stand for my sake and for my friend, Dezmond Adama. Your word is that all souls belong to you. And Jesus has died for all men. Therefore, Satan has legally no claim over this life. Satan, Jesus has paid fully for whatever debt is owed you concerning all men, including Dezmond. I bring the precious blood of Jesus in judgement against you! On the ground of the finished work of our Saviour, I break your chains of bondage upon Dezmond's life. I pull down your wicked veil over his eyes of understanding, and cast it underfoot. Let them cease to operate, in Jesus's name!'

'Amen!' responded Dezmond.

'Dezmond Adama, your heart will receive the understanding of these truths. By your very mouth, you will confess the salvation and lordship of Jesus Christ over your life. You will not die but live to glorify the name of our Lord Jesus. Thank you, Father, for your kindness and mercy. Thank you for always proving yourself true to your word, for always proving yourself strong on behalf of your sons. Let your wonderful name be exalted above all the earth and heavens! As I leave, I commit Dezmond into your hands. You are God, and the choice is yours, to have mercy on whoever you wish. You know, Father, that I have staked your name for this man. Answer me speedily, Father, that the devil may be shamed once again. In Jesus's name!'

'Amen.'

'As for sleep, I command you demons who stole his sleep, by the power in the blood of Jesus, on the authority of the word of God, surrender it now! Sleep, I command you to return and overwhelm his eyes now, in Jesus's name!'

'Amen.'

'As I go, I move under the banner of heavenly hosts. Lift up your standard over me Lord, against any plan of the enemy. Thank you, Father, in the mighty name of Jesus!'

Dezmond muttered the last 'Amen' and propped his arms pensively under his head. Maazi moved the chair to its original position and sat meditatively at Dezmond's study table. He continued to pray in a muffled tone, repeatedly nodding his head in punctuation of whatever he was transmitting unto the heavens. For some moments he would freeze as if decoding some divine feedback. When he was done, he picked a piece of paper and scribbled a message for Dezmond.

Study Hosea, chapter 6:1–3. Ask the Holy Spirit to help. Faith cometh by hearing, and hearing by the word of God. Call me whenever you wake up. Any hour. Jesus loves you very much!

Chapter Five

'What gives, ma man!' said the voice on the telephone line.

'Who?' demanded Dezmond in a sleepy voice. 'Y'know what time this is?'

'Early dawn. Still snoozin'?'

'That's my business! Who are you, anyway?'

''Course you know! I'm calling to remind you for the las' time. Go meet PAID. Give peace a chance! And give yo'sef a break. Protect Afrika in Diaspora don' bite, man! An' em… if you wan' my opinion, they've done pretty good by you. Never seen them guys so long-suffering with nobody.'

'What's that s'posed to mean?'

'You got a pretty long rope, Dez. But it's run to the penultimate, that's what!'

'Well, Wale Jefferson, I told you, I have no business with them. I wasn't sent here to defend or protect anything else except the doctorate. That's my focus. I won't be stampeded into Diaspora or any such thing—'

'Listen, Dez,' Wale cut in, lowering his voice, 'you'd be a fool to go on messing with PAID. You sure don' know who you're dealing with. Now, you've made yo'sef such a big issue, the senior guys of Protect Afrika wanna try convincing you themselves. Anyways, if you persist in yo' donkey stubbornness, they'll find you. They're not into kid stuff, watch out!'

'What exactly do you mean?'

'I mean, you stop playing smart! Go to PAID, Saturday!

Don't allow a noble cause to get sour in your month before you learn your lesson. I'm done. Take it or leave it!' The phone clicked.

*

The headquarters of Protect Afrika in Diaspora towered nine levels over its whole surroundings in downtown Lake City. Its service gate swung open, and as a hatchback sedan slipped through, the gate automatically shut back. One of the two men who flanked Dezmond on the back seat untied him and nodded towards the back door which had swung open as the car screeched to a stop.

The entrance lobby was carpeted in crimson, furnished with sturdy-looking upholstered seats clustered in crescent shapes. The receptionist smiled at the escorts as they led their captive up a short flight of steps to the service elevator. One of the two had introduced himself to Dezmond as Germini Jones, but the other man had not spoken one word. It was he who had gagged and strapped Dezmond when he walked into their trap that evening, two blocks from Maazi's place.

On the last floor, the men marched into a crescent-shaped office with an imposing masonia-wood desk placed centre back. A purple flag hung in great furls from a chrome mast. Dezmond could glimpse part of the crossed fists insignia of PAID. Beside it was the striped and star-spangled USA flag. Portraits of historic men and women were arranged on the pelmets, with bold captions pasted below each of them. Dezmond was able to recognise President Abraham Lincoln, Marcus Garvey, Frederick Douglas, Martin Luther King Jnr, Louis Armstrong and Mohammed Ali. Among them was the portrait of an elegant mulatto of exquisite beauty, by the name of Mrs Elizabeth Keckley.

'Relax!' ordered Germini. 'You'll have better company in a moment.'

Then the two men marched out.

'Ekurole, Broda!' came the greeting in Yoruba, mellowed with Afro-American intonation. The soft and cultured female voice seemed to come from hidden receivers. There was a little creaking sound, and Dezmond turned to see an ebony-skinned lady of Amazonian stature shutting the door behind her.

'Please, sit down. Feel at home. This is Afrika in Diaspora!' she declared in her soothing voice. 'In a moment, you'll have the privilege of the long-awaited audience with Dr Olongo Abdios and Baba-Kekere Batunga. Oh, Bro. Germini says you're charmed by the portrait of Mrs Keckley! She sho' was a head turner! She was the chief dressmaker of Papa Abe Linkum; she was the most influential black person in the White House of the time. She's my role model! Except that I'm going to the White House at least as a vice-president! Meanwhile, may I offer you a drink? Corn beer, cocoa cocktail, or palm wine?'

'Nothing. Thanks.'

'Take water then, the drink of peace. Pure water gives life.'

'Nothing, please.'

'You'll understand, Brother Adama. It is great honour to be co-opted into the noble cause of PAID. This is not another Black Panther situation. We're unique in vision and mission, and methods. I've been involved in this business for three years, so I can tell you. I didn't understand it at first. Nobody does from outside.'

'Were you abducted, gagged and dragged into it? This is plain criminal!'

'PAID enlists by persuasion,' retorted the lady, with a knowing gleam in her eyes.

'Persuasion, you say?' Dezmond asked, staring bold

facedly at her.

'Relatively speaking, yes. There are different degrees of persuasion. The order you make is the order you get!'

'What do you mean?'

'Listen, Brother Adama. I quit a twenty-one grand pay pack at Rank Xerox to take up a PAID job. The dough is less but I just feel great. Fulfilled! It feels really wholesome here.'

'Well, *I* came to America for the doctorate,' recited Dezmond, as if to reassure himself. 'I have enough trouble already, trying to do just that...'

A green light was now blipping over the door through which the lady had entered. She responded by taking Dezmond by the hand and ushering him into a large circular hall. Its high walls were painted in olive green, and the ceiling had the creamy look of unsullied pearl. Its floor was solid marble, cast in bold squares. At the centre of the floor lay a circular Persian rug of beige colour, with poufs of varying sizes all around it. Apart from two divans between which the PAID and American flags were mounted, and an exhibition shelf lining a wall, there was no other furniture. Three men sat on the rug in lotus postures, mumbling in triune monotone.

On the walls were displayed the bones and skins of big game animals. The skin of a gigantic cobra, with its head intact, stood out amidst a circular arrangement of *adire* tie-and-dye, with portions of batik. The masonia shelf displayed antique carvings from West Africa; intricately worked elephant tusks and ivory bangles; a replica of the Bini Head; a huge tortoise shell; and other sundry curios of black Africa. The ends of the long shelf were supported by ceramic sculptures which were modelled after the obelisks of the ancient Egyptian pyramids.

Dezmond's apparent resistance began to melt under a blanket of fear that suddenly overcame him. He had seen similar objects before in museums, but they did not emit any such eeriness. As he glanced from one thing to the other, he noticed camera shutters jutting out of the far corner of the high ceiling, like the eyeballs of an owl.

'You have come. *Salaam!* Be one with the brothers,' greeted Dr Olongo Abdios, who squatted in the middle of the three. He wore *danshiki* of fine Kente weaving. His bare scalp was well oiled, and his face and forearms were covered with thick white hair. 'As our ancestors say, take the fire from your chest and kindle it on the ground,' he instructed. 'Do not fear. Do not want to fight. For this is our place of peace.' He nodded at the lady and she bowed and left.

His slow manner of delivery sounded like another incantation. As Dezmond listened, he felt a spell creeping all over his body. His impulse was to resist by way of an outburst or by feigning sudden madness, or simply to frustrate them by adopting a completely mute and motionless posture. But the more the old man gazed at him, the more he waned in body and soul.

'My son, honour your fathers and mothers. Sit in your own place. The elders tell us, you may not refuse a call but what is behind the call. Is that not said?'

Dezmond perched on one of the smaller poufs.

'Now, to the method of your arrival here,' continued Dr Abdios laboriously, 'I instructed the same. I have no apology. But explanation, yes. You also know. This edifice is head office, Protect Afrika in Di–as–pra in all North America. PAID is founded on love, common dignity, and respect for brotherhood of man. In particular, black. In Brasilia also, we have. Also, Lagos your country. Of Lagos, you must know, perhaps. I forget to warn you. My English is not supreme. Not perfect, I mean. Please, ask question if not comprehended. I will repeat. Only when I voyage from Brazil I must speak English.'

The halting manner of his expression, with its languid tempo, made him sound unsure of his direction. However, this soon proved deceptive. Whenever he got to his punchline, he left no doubt that he had registered his desired impact. His demeanour became more and more casual, apparently in an attempt to make the atmosphere more convivial. The old man would pause intermittently but Dezmond remained glum. However, the anger which was in his bosom on his arrival was being eroded. Baba-Kekere whispered to Dr Abdios in Swahili, apparently to prompt him.

'You must come to Brazil,' continued Dr Abdios. 'We have much in common, your nation and our nation. The Abuja idea is from our Brasilia capital city. Surely you know the foundation of Brazil is on the sweat of black men? Like USA. Next to Nigeria, the greatest demography of blacks is Brazil. Over fifty million now. But no voice. I need not tell you of Azania, Namibia, and the rest. Soon, they will be free. PAID is contributing.'

Dr Abdios' face radiated a mysterious awe. His eyes rarely left Dezmond as he spoke. On his part, the latter had perched so long on the pouf that it was beginning to feel as if he was suspended in the air. He knew that he had not been abducted to PAID HQ just to hear nice talk. The man's languorous style must be a smokescreen for a bitter pill that was yet to come. He comforted himself, however, that he knew the intention of his captors. He was sure they would not hurt him, he concluded, and he soon began to consider shifting his defence tactics. From a position of uncommunicating silence, he decided to yield a little ground. He began to rehearse the argument in his head. As if he was tracking Dezmond's mind, Baba-Kekere cleared his throat.

'What did you say to Big Queen?' he suddenly asked him.

'Who's Big Queen?'

'The mama who showed you in here.'

'Nothing that I remember.'

'Nothing?'

'Well, she offered me drinks, and I didn't want,' responded Dezmond, hedging.

'You said something about terrorism,' insisted Baba-Kekere Batunga.

'This is an abduction! It is a serious abuse of my basic amendment rights.'

'What amendment?' asked the old man, raising his voice. 'Did you call Bro. Jones – Germini Jones – a terrorist when you were accosted?'

'They looked so. They acted so,' retorted Dezmond defiantly. 'What do you call someone who grabs a free, law-abiding person on the street, gags him, ties him up, and abducts him?'

'Now, Tunga,' intervened the old man as tempers began to rise, 'let me talk now. Son, we must contribute, all of us, to PAID. Man, child, woman, everybody! Student and everybody! Sometimes what you call terrorism is a mandate. The elders of Africa say, the gun booms loudest in the ears of those who live next to the battleground. You have not seen racism truly. So you talk amendment. What amendment? We cannot be meek and gentle like the Eck Master. We cannot afford his patience. We do not have his spirit nature. You must understand your role.'

The meeting endured into the night. The old sage proved to be a deadly and tireless tactician. He brought the full weight of his wisdom, his knowledge of African proverbs, and mysticism, to bear on Dezmond. As persistent and hard-nosed as Oriana Fallaci, he probed provocatively into every detail of the young man's defence. Yet, as he pried so intently into his captive's life, he was able to avoid antagonising him.

'That is why I call you,' concluded Dr Olongo Abdios.

'I still don't understand why you people went to the extent of almost killing me first. Why all this trouble? What differences does it make if—'

'Grave!' interrupted Dr Abdios. 'Grave difference! I quote the Eck Master. Whoever is not with us is against us. You especially, I need not tell. I regret very much, you do not appreciate PAID. Our elders say, you caution a small boy against the night and he says, but the moon is shining. Think of the danger of racism. Even your life is in danger. You must comprehend. Ph.D. is good, but not between life and death. It must help your people. And then your life.'

A lady brought in another round of drinks. This time, there were three glasses of red wine and an additional empty glass for Dezmond who, under pressure, had settled for mineral water. Batunga went behind a divan, picked up an embroidered bag, and handed it to the third man who had remained quiet all along. The man brought out a big tobacco pipe and a golden box and announced, 'It is ready.'

He took time to fill the pipe, tamped it and lit it. Puffing meditatively at it, he passed it to Baba-Kekere Batunga who savoured it awhile and in turn handed it to Dr Abdios. The old man held the pipe with an air of sacredness and sucked at it until the acrid smoke engulfed his face. Dezmond, all keyed up as he watched them, was quite nauseated by the pungent smell of half-dried leaves.

'Do not fear,' admonished Dr Abdios, cupping the pipe in the crook of his palms. 'Among brothers, there must be agreement, unity. This is communion for us,' he added, raising the pipe as he sent up another billow. 'In ancient Egyptian oracle, the same. To create one spirit, to make flow the utterance. The Greeks copy from ancient Africa. Dezmond Adama, take in the token and pass on!'

The ritual was building up. The spell that had fallen

from the beginning when the old man set eyes on Dezmond came down with greater impact. He sheepishly took the pipe with both hands and waited for instructions. At last, he put it to his lips and drew in the draught of hot smoke.

'You may now drop the pipe on the earth,' concluded Baba-Kekere. 'The final charge comes from our elder, Dr Olongo Abdios. The lips of elders are lips of wisdom and light.'

'Thank you, Baba. You have spoken like the son of your father! Dezmond, my boy, listen well. I repeat again, the law of PAID loyalty. You should not abandon ship. You should not betray secret. If you run again, that's your last run. No more effort from PAID to reach you. You run at your own regret. Enforcement after this day is not for human ability, but spiritual.'

As he arose, the quiet man whispered something to him. The old man added, 'Yes. Against involving police department. It is not good to bring police into the union of brothers. A word is enough. We release you to the Queen. The rest, routine administration.'

At the press of a bell, Big Queen came in, bobbed a curtsy, and offered her hand to Dezmond. She led him to her own office.

'For now, it's all over,' she explained, folding her arms. 'Just remember all that wen' on with the elders. Each week for the next month, PAID will require you to file your write-ups. We normally microfilm them to the branches. As you've been told, your contribution is basically in the propaganda department. Your next appointment is precisely one month from today. You may now go down by the main lift up front. Someone's waiting to take you back. He'll identify you.'

*

Dezmond was dropped off at the junction of Main Street and Pine Avenue. He therefore had enough space and time to work out a way to hide his traumatic state from whoever might begin to ask questions. The dark winter night gave him the needed cover. The cold winds revived him as he trudged along. On arriving home, he slipped in and quickly disappeared upstairs. Miss Frankwood must have gone to sleep, thank God!

It was not until ten o'clock the next morning that he got out of bed and found his way downstairs. Unknown to him, Miss Frankwood was still indoors.

'Dezmond, I don't mean to patronise but you've become a recluse,' she remarked casually as he was stepping down the stairs.

'Good morning, my landlady. Please, patronise me all you want.' He leant against the wooden handrail, his arms folded. 'I'm waiting.'

'Give yourself a break, swot! This is vacation time. I'd say you've done pretty good, despite all the hassles. "There's a time for everything." I bet you've never listened to that beautiful song.'

'No. I've never. D'you have a recording for me?'

'Would you have time for it if I did? Give yourself some rest and get back strong for next semester. That's what vacations are all about.'

'You're ever so kind, Miss Frankwood,' he responded. Then, smiling broadly, he added, 'You know, I've just realised what a rare name you have! Strange, isn't it?'

The lady just stood there studying him from afar. Was the man teasing her?

'Well, I cannot afford a holiday,' he continued. 'There's work ahead of me and life seems ever so short.'

'I know about hard work, Dezmond. Come and sit down. Let's discuss hard work!' Chuckling, she plonked her full weight onto the pouf and pointed to the second one for Dezmond. 'Talk of hard work – it's me that'll tell you!'

As Dezmond was adjusting himself on top of the giant pouf, Miss Frankwood got back to her feet and made for the kitchen. 'Care for a cup of coffee?'

'Coffee is good. Except when it turns my brain,' he mumbled. Miss Frankwood who had since switched on the coffee maker, filled a cup for him and took a wicker chair by his side. After two or three pensive sips she cleared her throat.

'The Christmas craze is all over me! This is the time to tell it,' she announced.

'What?'

'You're a dear, genuine person!' Dezmond seemed not to have heard that. 'Well, looks like we've both been playing games. Y'know, "I'm okay – you're okay" kind of stuff. Haven't we been hiding something?'

His mind automatically went to the PAID encounter of the previous night. Miss Frankwood felt he was perhaps embarrassed by the sweet and sour feeling that may sometimes be generated from a lady's unexpected attention.

'Do you know something I'm hiding?' asked Dezmond.

'Maybe I'm not as strong as you imagine,' continued Miss Frankwood, giggling a little between sips. 'I'm not sure, but... okay, I want to say, you're a great guy! You're a genuine guy, Dez. I really, really like you! How about that for a confession?'

'Thank you,' he responded with diffidence. After that, he ran out of words for a long while. He then regained his composure and added, 'But I'm somewhat – I don't know what to say, Miss Frankwood.'

'Well, for a start, do me one favour, Dezmond,' she went on, with an air of childlike abandon all over her. 'We're friends, okay?'

'Sure.'

'From now on, call me Penny. After all, who else addresses me Miss Frankwood except—'

'The mailman!' Dezmond chipped in. They laughed together, more for the mutual relief than for the aptness of the humour. As if energised by his joke, Dezmond turned squarely to her and looked her straight in the eyes. 'Miss Frankwood. I'm not a kid any more although you're making me feel like one. I think we've done very well. Let's stay with that. Let's not start something, please. You know, it is one small spark that engulfs the whole bush. Let's cut out this big joke while we can.'

'Now you're talking! Y'know, I love it when you talk. You say we've done well. I guess I know what you mean. We've done well for other people. The truth is, you and I have been damn unfair to ourselves. I've decided to quit pretending! And right now, I have a wacky idea!'

Dezmond stared at her, mouth agape. She looked both serious and funny in the same breath.

'How wacky?' came the question after a long silence of eye fighting, it seemed. 'And what does wacky mean, anyway?'

'Let's go to Palmyra!'

'I see you're not kidding.'

'It takes two to tango, two to trust,' she all but sang.

'Palmyra... where is Palmyra?'

'A cute suburban town in New Jersey! Even now, it won't cost a life's saving to have a treat there. You'd love the indoor heated swimming pool at The Palm Motel, called Swan Lake... Stop hesitating, Dez! What d'you say? I'll let you chip in a coupla dollars so you won't quite lose your macho. How 'bout that for Christmas?'

'Really! Never seen you like this! I'm just surprised.'

'It's a deal, then!'

'Well, it takes two!' responded Dezmond, awkwardly raising his cup in the gesture of a toast, and spilling some coffee on his thigh. He rose and clinked his enamel cup with Miss Frankwood's. 'You've called me friend. I know you mean well. I accept. But, Miss Frankwood, this is coming all too fast. Have we had time to consider the implications? The cost?'

'What implications beyond what we're already going through? Of course, friendship, worthwhile friendship, has costs. But, we can't fix that right now, can we? We'll just play it by ear and see what gives, okay?'

In his mind, Dezmond had a response which, however, had not matured enough for expression. He looked at Miss Frankwood, wishing to say something to her counter-challenge, but the words failed him. How so simple, even vulnerable, the lady appeared that moment! And what a candid departure from that sure-footed portrait of the landlady who had welcomed him into No. 19, Pine!

*

The duo drove into Palmyra Palm Motel on Christmas Eve. By the time they were turning off the interstate into the long drive to the hotel lobby, they had not settled the debate as to what code or contract of behaviour would guide their tryst. They finally arrived at a truce. They would let it ride, as suggested by Miss Frankwood. No hard and fast rules. It would be more fun, they agreed, to expect anything and nothing. However, they would surely indulge themselves in snowball fights and in swimming. The salad bar at the smorgasbord would be kosher feeding for the period. They would talk a whole lot, and discover one another as both of them always enjoyed good conversation.

The weatherman had feared that the eastern coast of America might not have a white Christmas due to the vagaries of winter. By midnight on Christmas Eve, however, the snow began its surprise descent. Silently, the face of the earth was being clothed in subliminal white. Dezmond braved the cold to watch the fluffy flakes take over. He had never experienced this glorious vista of winter, only the bitter cold winds and dirty clods of ice on pavements. As far as his eyes could reach, the earth appeared so pristine in her white covering that, as he stepped on it, he felt like a tramp desecrating a virgin. He stooped low and scooped a handful of the manna, as it were, throwing it up like a sacrifice back to the heavens.

As he was searching the dark sky, a fresh release of snow cascaded from the invisible dark mountains in the night sky, enveloping him in his housecoat. He seemed to be kissing the flakes, with his arms spread out as if in expectation of a lover's embrace.

'Better get back in now!' shouted Miss Frankwood from the balcony of her room. Unknown to Dezmond, she had been watching him with much amusement. 'If you wanna see next year's snow, better get out of the cold fast! Pneumonia ain't much fun!' She had to clap her hands for Dezmond to realise that someone was out there.

'Merry Christmas, Dez!' she greeted as he hopped over the balustrade.

'Happy Christmas, Penny!' replied Dezmond, giving her a non-committal peck on the cheek.

A surprise stage had since been set for a twosome Christmas Eve party in Miss Frankwood's chalet. A bottle of white Burgundy was chilling in a wine bucket, amid two candle lights. A sassy version of Labelle's raunchy song was playing, flooding the chilly night with its vibrant percussion and the teasing refrain, *'Voulez-vous coucher avec moi, ce soir?'*

'Don't say anything, Dez!' ordered Miss Frankwood, picking out the wine. 'I'm gonna make a toast. Can you guess?'

'To the Christmas Eve!'

'Close! But only close! I'll give you one tip, smart dummy!'

'Go ahead!' Dezmond squeezed his eyebrows in mock concentration regarding his next shot.

'Did you realise how much you thrilled me a littl' while ago? You've just made a bit of history!'

'Oh, now I know! Penny! Penny!'

They embraced, wine bottle and all, and did a spirited jumble dance around the lights. Miss Frankwood handed Dezmond the wine, which he opened and served. As they lifted their glasses, she toasted, 'To the first night you called me by my name! To the eve in which we dropped our defences!'

'To Penny! And our eve of a white Christmas!'

They each did a savouring of the drink, and spontaneously drew close to each other. Face to face, they entwined their arms and drank from one another's exchanged glasses. As they searched into each other's eyes, it seemed that the naked reality of life was staring back at them. All the considerations, principles and resolutions which had been uppermost in the past months seemed to have vaporised into this one airy, starry moment.

'Dez, dear, we've tried to be decent, self-controlled and all that. No matter what, nobody believes we've not been making love. Now, tell me something... something far-out and raw... something spaced out! There's nothing binding us. Thank goodness dearest... Dez!'

'Penny.'

'Yes, Dez,' she whispered, giggling into his face.

'There's a question you've never asked me.'

They broke free from one another's arms; Dezmond poured a fresh round of wine.

'Of course, I know you're not married,' she said.

'You guessed right. But you've never wondered. At least, not to my knowledge,' pressed Dezmond.

'When a woman begins to fall in love, some thoughts don't come until much later.'

'I guess so. But at the age of twenty-six almost, I should be married. D'you know why I'm still a bachelor?'

'Really, I didn't think of it at all,' Penny explained, rolling the wine glass in her hand. 'For American guys, marriage is not late at twenty-six, for all I figure.' She gingerly set down her glass by the flower vase, and cupped Dezmond's face in her palms. 'Listen, Dez, I know two things, okay? You're not yet married. And you're as man as they come! There's time for everything, righ'? For now… let's explore! They say, there's nothing new under the sun. But maybe, there's something new in the winter night!'

*

Dezmond kissed Penny's forehead and tried to flick open her eyelids. She rolled over and feigned deep sleep. Grabbing her by the hips, he tickled her until she burst into frothy laughter, raining his face with a splatter of playful slaps.

'Penny, keep those lovely big eyes open! I want to tell you something.' She widened her eyes the more into a grotesque expression as she rolled up her frame and placed her back against the bedhead. Dezmond sat up and took her hand in his. 'I appreciate you. Sounds somehow funny, but I appreciate your trust.'

'I simply love you, Dez,' she responded, looking very grave, almost mournful.

'You're worth a fight, Penny. But that's not the problem. All these six months, you probably thought I was Mr Clean Guy or some kind of freak. But that wasn't it. I have been afraid. I've been battling quietly with myself.'

'You sound pretty serious,' observed Penny, readjusting herself. 'Why are you saying all this?'

'I have an old fear. I don't know when to stop anything once I've started. This thing goes beyond you and me.

Maybe it's much too soon to worry, but do you know what we've got ourselves into?'

'We've come a long way, Dez! It's not as if we're moon-struck college kids out on a joy-ride. We're adults! I'm almost a grandmother. We can run our lives, can't we?'

'Nothing is ever going to be the same again for you or me. Do you know that? You should expect great opposition from the—'

'Any worse than we've been going through all this time?'

'Worse! Much worse! When they get to know.'

'Who's gonna tell them?'

'Love never hides, Penny. It always shows! Always! The neighbours will begin to sniff around all over again. Then of course, we're now going to get the real hassles from the black guys. I tell you, nothing will remain the same.'

'I know where you're at, Dez, dear,' responded Penny. 'I'm trying to think along. But this same song keeps coming back to me.' He gazed at her incredulously. '"For everything, time... for every season, time..."' she sang in a solemn tone, gazing back at him.

*

'It's funny sitting here so comfortably with you,' said Miss Penny Frankwood. The other guests had begun to leave soon after she and Dezmond dived into the swimming pool. Now, it was time to get cuddled up in giant towels, and talk by the side of the Swan Lake.

'Yes. Those folks who were eyeing us would never know we weren't this close even three days ago! They probably think we're married.'

'That's true. But it's funnier than you know. You're the second black man I've spoken with in my whole life! The first time was sixteen years ago, when I was already nineteen. Can you imagine the kind of American I was growing up to be?'

'What! I'm surprised. Where was that? Did you just talk with him, or you shook hands or something?'

'Oh, get off, Dez! Don't be funny!'

'No, for real, I'm curious. Tell me more about it. In fact, tell me everything about yourself.'

'Everything? Who can do that? Who knows everything about herself? If I did I'd tell you.'

'Really?'

'Why not? After the other night, what's there to hide? Except that you're gonna be a jealous, possessive man!'

'Like all true lovers!'

'I can figure you being jealous,' volunteered Penny, dipping her feet in the warm waters. 'But I can't stand possessiveness. Seems terribly kid stuff to me. When a man's possessive, it's the little baby inside him that's crying.'

'In that case, count me out!' joked Dezmond, splashing his feet in the pool. 'I'll stick with just being jealous!'

'It's getting chilly in this towel, Dez. How about getting back to the chalet? Don't forget you're playing host tonight. One good turn—'

'Deserves two rounds!' concluded Dezmond, loosening his towel.

'Your humour can be a littl' weird. I know of dirty old men. Never heard of dirty *young* men, but there's one right here.'

'Hey, jump in! Let's have the last lap. The whole pool now belongs to Penny Frankwood and me. C'mon in!' he shouted, bobbing out of the foaming surf.

Later, Penny lay prone across Dezmond's bed, with a pillow under her nape. Dezmond sat by her, listening intensely. Every once in a while, he would lift her up by the shoulders and put the shared coffee mug to her lips. Then, she would lie back again and resume her story.

'Like I told you, I was a prudish nineteen year old in the finals of medical nursing. They had this gorgeous smasher, a lieutenant from Fort Wayne, come give us a career talk. He was just a genius! But Penny Frankwood wasn't listening.'

'What was wrong with—'

'Just listen, Dezmond!' she interrupted. 'I'm telling you something serious.'

'Sorry. Please, go on,' he urged her, drawing nearer and stroking her long brown hair. 'After all, I asked for it, right?'

'Righ'!' echoed Penny, as she brushed aside his hand. 'I wasn't listening,' she continued. 'I found myself swooning. Couldn't wait to shake hands with that guy. Never came so close to such a well-made handsome man! Except in paintings.'

'First crush only at nineteen?' teased Dezmond. 'Where had your parents been hiding the beautiful queenette?'

'That was the only chance I had even to get infatuated! I was destined to begin and end with a very Anglo-Saxon American called Dave Gordon.'

Dezmond straightened himself and concentrated more intently.

'It started as a boy-next-door kind of kids' game, with candies, silly love notes, and stuff. Well, we got married when I was twenty-one. I was happy. Put in all I knew. Plus some of mum's old tricks! Dave and I were complementary. Y'know, what we lacked, we made up for each other, and let sleeping dogs lie. We had a weird saying then whenever a littl' fight was coming… oh, what were those quaint words again, I wonder?'

'Live and let live?' suggested Dezmond.

Penny was startled. 'Who's been telling?' she shouted in consternation.

'Nobody,' answered Dezmond, in a matter-of-fact manner. 'Just guessed.'

'Guessed! How on earth could you have guessed?'

'The hint came from your own mouth,' explained Dezmond in a disarmingly gallant style, to dispel the air of mystery and suspicion. 'When you were struggling with your memory, trying to recollect what you called your weird saying, "Live and let live", came to my mind. Remember, you had just mentioned how you used to let sleeping dogs lie?'

'Great! Dezmond, I think you're a genius!'

'What do I say?' joked Dezmond, throwing up his hands in mock chivalry. 'I'm about to blush!'

'Stop flattering yourself! Just accept the compliment and shut up.'

'Thanks for the compliment! And the advice. But, before I shut up, let me say I'm glad your lieutenant and I are a match at least on the score of genius!'

'Dezmond! How jealous can you get! Now, d'you really want to hear my story, or…'

'Please, go on. I'm listening. No more interruptions, I promise.'

'Oh, that reminds me!' She excitedly drew up to Dezmond, caressing one of his pyjama buttons. 'D'you remember the first time we met? The day you came to check out No. 19, Pine?'

'Sure.'

'If you'd looked well, you'd've noticed how nervous I was the moment our eyes met.'

'Actually, I noticed it.'

'You did?'

'I kind of understood. I knew you were uneasy that a nigger had showed up. You did a good job of it, though, the way you wiped out the uneasiness within seconds. For my part, I was sure you were only being polite in showing me the place. I knew it wasn't going to be mine.'

'Oh no! How very wrong!' said Penny, laughing. 'You can never guess this one! Listen. When I opened the door, it was like I'd set eyes on a long-lost friend. I thought it was that lieutenant I'm telling you about. You looked so like him, I just couldn't believe my eyes! It was like I was hallucinating. Until you spoke and moved. I'd never seen such a lookalike!'

'You've done very well keeping it to yourself all this time!'

'Have I? It's been a physical and emotional strain for me. All the time I was showing you round the room, I was in great conflict. Suddenly, I couldn't trust myself any more to hold out. I felt sick, weak. Later, I thought of returning your deposit. But my mind grew weaker by the day. I kept asking myself, How could you do such a dishonourable thing? The day you moved in, it was like teenage butterflies all over again. But I beat them down gradually. What I went through is something else.'

'Poor Penny! If only you knew! I too was going through hell, for moving into a white neighbourhood, and a white woman's house. But you really kept things under control.'

'You could say that. The truth is, you've ended up being a help to me. You can never guess how much help you've been.'

'By just being there?'

'More than that! You settled in, and within weeks you cured me of almost all prejudices regarding blacks. In a way, it helped me that you were such a perfect guy, minding your business, keeping the rules, working hard and all that. That helped me to stay high 'n' dry and dignified, no matter how terrible and lonely I felt. Oh, some nights, I'd stay awake, fighting my emotions. Next morning, I'd meet you downstairs, and your conduct would check me. It was like this man doesn't even care whether Penny exists! Why should I make a nuisance of myself? He's okay! But then came Christmas, and I melted. Couldn't keep the secret any longer!'

She wrapped her arms around Dezmond and laid her head on his bare chest. 'I don't know about Nigeria, but Christmas here is about family reunion, love, family and togetherness. After four years of divorce, I thought I'd got used to empty, lonely Christmases. Until Palmyra came on my mind. And now, here we are!'

'It begins to figure out,' commented Dezmond, after a prolonged and pregnant lull. 'You've braved a whole lot, Penny. I could never have dreamt that you ever thought of me in that way. Apart from the hassles of Protect Afrika, it's been okay for me living with you. But for all you may say, I wasn't playing superman, a strong character of exemplary conduct, and so on. It was simply that I had no illusions. So it was very convenient and easy for me to carry on the way I was doing. We'll get to my own story by and by,' he concluded. 'For now, let's finish yours.'

'Yes, indeed! I'd almost forgotten. Where was I?'

'How it was with Prof. Gordon…'

'Yes, I put in all that I knew… I said that already, I think. Well, our marriage was super, so gorgeous his friends envied us, made a big fuss about our closeness. I didn't thing it was a situation for me to be overly self-conscious or fussy about. I knew that marriage is about love, accord and friendship. Anyway, I soon learnt better. There's something that hates marriage continuing in love, agreement, and laughter.'

Penny paused to hear the TV weather forecast. 'Along the eastern seaboard, prolonged snow, most of tomorrow morning. Temperature, below five degrees Celsius.'

'Dave and I got on,' she resumed, 'until Junior was born. Then also, the LCU chair of physics was offered him. I looked forward to moving to New York State. That was the beginning of our drift! Naively, I'd expected his new job meant a break, a fresh start. But Dave got more and more swallowed up in the quicksand of his nuclear physics. His lab became the centre of life. The drift widened. He became increasingly alienated from the children. As for me, I was an all-time put-off for him. His alienation from me was something else!

'I visualised Laura and littl' Dave growing up to swell the common statistics of single-parent American kids. Over time, I convinced him to submit to psychiatry. One shrink or the other brought help – unknown to the LCU authorities, for obvious reasons. Things only got worse with the family. Eventually, it snapped. We first said, "Okay, let's separate and see if time will heal the cracks." I've found now that time has no intrinsic means of healing! At last, we divorced altogether. Even then, I never had the guts to go through it. It was Dave Gordon who hired the attorney that handled it all. I felt terrible for the kids when Dave turned out raising hell about custody. For once, I couldn't look him in the face! I began to pop barbiturates of all kinds until I became hooked. Then I graduated from sleeping pills to the real McCoy, chlorpromazine. My shrink soon diagnosed a whole bag of phobias. I had nowhere to run. Daddy had died the year before... I still can't quit the thought that our failing marriage worsened his heart condition. Well, I had no choice but to go into a psychiatric centre back home in Bloomington where my brother lives. Soon after I got out, I quit Veterans' Hospital, got a mortgage on 19, Pine, and got involved in Home Medicare... Now, you've heard all there is about Peninnah Frankwood! One good turn...' she concluded, quickly placing her fourth finger on Dezmond's lip, 'deserves another. Your turn!'

Chapter Six

The Pinto was checked and scraped clean of crusted ice under fresh snow. Dezmond tipped the bellboy and made for the front passenger seat when Penny promptly blocked his way with her body, pressing the car key into his palm.

'Your turn to drive!' she announced, and wheeled her way to the other side.

The car spluttered through the grime of stale snow and icy puddles, steadily churning its way towards the interstate. Dezmond concentrated fully on the unpredictable road surface.

'Feel bad?'

'No. Why?' demanded Dezmond, glancing quickly at her. She was smiling. 'Do you?'

'No. Just that you're looking dreadful at the wheel.'

'Caught up in three first-time experiences all at once! Never driven an automatic, to start with. But here I am, stuck with it, and I'm trying my best on an iceberg, with snow still falling. Can you beat that!'

'My sympathy! But how was Palmyra? Any other first-time experience?' She smiled teasingly.

'Depends on who's asking!' replied Dezmond, chuckling.

'Who's gonna be asking?'

'Y'never know!'

'How the mind works!' sighed Penny. 'On our way to Palmyra, I tried to guess your thinking but I got no clue. But what turned out was simply wow! How about you?

What d'you say?'

Dezmond slowed down and changed to the right lane. 'You got fixated with the image of one Saint Dezmond of Pine Avenue! On my part, I guess I was observing my survival principles, not knowing what was coming. Well, I'm delighted it worked out the way it did. But frankly, I never dreamt we could ever get so close. Never!'

'Ever heard of a tall, handsome debonair guy and a thirty-six year old ex-cheerleader drive in one car to a motel, spend two nights in adjoining rooms, and come out high 'n' dry?'

'Eh? Now I know you set me up!' joked Dezmond.

'What were you doing in a lady's room after midnight, on a Christmas Eve? I only hollered for you to get out of the cold. Next thing, I saw a lanky knight hop over my balustrade!'

'Peninnah!'

'Hey, that's how my pop always called me!'

'How did anyone dare, reduce his little queenette down to a miserable British Penny!' They laughed together, with Dezmond not flinching one jot from the wheel. 'On a serious note,' he concluded, 'now that we're returning to where we rightly belong, my fear is, can we survive this adventure? Can we really fathom what we're getting into?'

Dialogue gave way to the ever-swelling Boxing Day vacation traffic. Penny reclined her seat and lay back as Dezmond pressed harder on the pedal and swerved back into the fast lane. The endless run of the eight-lane highway was separated by a strip of brush. Dezmond imagined how like the savannah grass of his Aroji hometown the place would look in the coming spring. He maintained a steady cruising speed without further strain. Now and then, a faster vehicle would emerge on his rear mirror and he would go over to the slower lane. Although he had a firm grip of the steering wheel, his thoughts went thousands of miles across the Atlantic.

Five days to the year's end... The season of the ingathering of all descendants of Aroji for the yearly *ej'-alekwu* ancestral feast. His father would now be cleaning up his ancient shrine, dusting down the aged totems which stood for his direct lineage: Odod' Ilolo, Ilol'Onu', On' Ojobo, Ojob' Ododo, Odod' Ojo, Oj' Aada, Aad' Aroji. As with Aroji children of every generation, Dezmond had to be able to name his fathers backward for seven generations at least.

Name by name, Dezmond's father, Adam' Ododo, would present each of his seven children before his pantheon of gods. He would call to their remembrance dedications made years ago for each of his children. He would then slaughter a black he-goat on an altar consisting of a stone slab, to reinforce the now crusted blood offerings of past festivals.

The New Year's Eve was a crossroads at which a man could seek the favour of his ancestors for his children, wherever they were. Dezmond had never sat at the shrine, even when he happened to be at home during a ritual. However, he never despised it, seeing that it was the only real anchor to life which his father understood, having inherited it in his turn. And it worked for him more evidently and dramatically than the foreign gods of the hapless churchgoers...

As he sped along, having gained more confidence with the automatic transmission, reminiscences of the rustic place of his birth and breeding flooded his soul. After just nine months, the nostalgia for home was so overwhelming that he would sometimes shed tears in the confines of his room. It seemed that those places and people he had taken for granted all his life suddenly became glorified by virtue of their distance and inaccessibility.

Aroji felt so far away that even his native tongue began to forsake him. There was no Nigerian in the whole of

Lake City who had even heard of a minority people by the name of Aroji. Therefore, the pressure of homesickness and loneliness sometimes drove him into a world of make-belief. He would create a scenario and conduct a one-man dialogue in his native tongue. Sometimes, the outcome was so hilarious or so tearful that he would tape his one-man skits and play them back to himself in the secrecy of his room.

Dezmond's reminiscing widened like eddies, recoiling strangely to the spot where his grandfather had ceremonially buried his umbilical cord. What a mysterious hold the umbilical cord has had over the life of an Aroji, Dezmond wondered, even after having rotted into the earth's womb! Severed at birth, it persists as a vital link to the very earth of one's ancestors. No wonder the umbilical must be sent home to the very origin of their fathers, no matter where an Aroji offshoot is born! Just as it is an abomination for the corpse of an Aroji to be interred in any other earth! The corpse of their married daughters too, must be brought home, no matter how far away or how long their marriage had endured. Home is Aroji and every other land is bush land...

It baffled Dezmond, then, that many of his fellow Africans had no intention of returning home. Some had completed their studies but chose to take two menial jobs in tandem, while suffering running battles with the immigration watchdogs. He saw how truly great America was, and that there were ample opportunities there for hard-working, lawful residents, despite the vestiges of racism. Notwithstanding, Dezmond reasoned that it still remained somebody else's land. Borrowed robes remain borrowed robes. The borrower wears a perpetual reminder on his back.

Dezmond recalled a concluding statement at one of his talks on the African students' forum.

'If any country can be said to be endowed with every good thing, among bad things, America is it. Thus she easily seduces the best brains from all over the globe... I consider it immoral, even treacherous, to complete one's studies and remain here, serving oneself.'

Since then, he had become popular as 'Countryman', to which he would give a thumbs-up salute and say, 'Straight for Aroji!'

Dezmond's reminiscences, like the ripples of a suddenly stirred lake, ranged back and forth, far and wide, even as the highway flew between the car wheels, like the racing white waters of an Appalachian river.

⋆

Only two weeks of the winter vacation was left when Dezmond realised he still had a great backlog of study preparation to accomplish. He purposed to busy himself in work in order to compensate for all the hours lost to what he usually regarded as idle pastime.

The heavy snow of Christmas persisted to the month's end, as if to freeze out the old passing year. Outdoor life again became almost impossible, except for a few derring-do neighbourhood addicts of winter sports. Even for Dezmond who had cultivated a love for snow, the unrelenting cold had begun to chill his excitement. He now understood why an acquaintance had once teased him for having opted to live in the armpit of the US, out of all the beautiful areas he could have chosen in God's own country.

Winter favoured him in his long hours of study, unlike the festering heat of the tropics which generates raw exhaustion. And so Dezmond fell on his books with a vengeance. He would settle for the maximum allowable credit hours in spring! Furthermore, he would update his personal journal, to which he ordinarily devoted three quality hours every other day, as he once explained to Miss Penny Frankwood when she chided him for overworking himself.

Since Palmyra, Miss Frankwood, for her part, carried on her business and house chores as one who had overindulged herself in a long vacation and, on returning to base, had to make up for it. The two had had the opportunity, all on their own, to relive their Christmas escapade. When Laura and Junior resumed their ding-dong routine of domiciliation, they had a bagful of authentic adventures to impart to whoever was available to hear. They had no inkling that Mummy had even left the house, except that they and Daddy had phoned at midnight on Christmas Eve. Mummy had simply gone to The Beef 'n' Ale for a drink with the old girls, explained Miss Frankwood.

Thus, Penny and Dezmond were relieved of any possible suspicions. They cut down their level of interaction for fear of letting out hints which might raise the kind of sticky questions adolescents often ask their enamoured single mothers. More so that lately, Dezmond had caught Junior eyeing him rather jealously as if to say, My friend and playmate seems not to have time for me these days.

The dinner arrangement still stood. However, on many evenings, Dezmond would find a pretext to stay away from the table. During such successive days and nights of abstention, he was popping so-called protein tabs, one of which was nutritious enough to sustain him for even two days. Other times, he would depend on fruit snacks or TV dinners from his fridgette.

Miss Frankwood, of course, saw that Dezmond was overworking. In spite of his disguises, the strains were becoming evident. One particular day, she felt so compelled to warn him that she could not wait for her children to complete the week before she broached the matter in hand.

Penny's visit again took Dezmond completely unawares as he undid the latch and found her standing before him.

'You're slowly killing yourself,' she warned, as she stepped in and shut the door behind her. Dezmond took down a tall pile of books from the bed and signalled her to sit. She ignored the gesture.

'For crying out aloud, what the hell are you doing to yourself?' she demanded.

'Jus' let me capture this present idea,' he pleaded, returning to his Olympia typewriter. 'If I stop abruptly, it may dry up.'

She stood, gazing quizzically at him, and asked, 'What's all this stuff?' But Dezmond would not be distracted. Penny stooped, prying into the sheaves of paper littered all over the bed and across the floor. Several academic journals were heaped face down on the quilt, while books lay tucked into each other, awaiting the next onset of marathon page-turning.

'How many of them can you handle at one time?' she asked.

Dezmond lifted his face as if only now aware that somebody was still standing beside his table. 'I'm sorry,' he muttered, turning to Penny.

'This is simply weird, Dez!'

'What is?' he enquired, looking around himself.

'You hardly even care that I'm here. You just keep banging at those keys, then you'd stop and just gaze at the wall for many minutes.'

'Oh, the gaps...' he tried to explain, gesticulating. 'Those are the spots in my stream of consciousness. There must be dry patches of ground from where to watch the flow. Of course, all the currents later merge along the line and eventually submerge the spots.'

'Dezmond, what are you talking about? You sound like a book! Are you all right?'

'Of course. Except that you've broken our rule. Why are you here? I can still hear the voices of Junior and Laura downstairs.'

'Never mind! We may be carrying it to such a perfect point that they begin to suspect something. In any case, they might as well begin to get wind of it. But that's not what's bugging me this moment.'

'Penny, this is stress, I know. But it's only for a couple of days before resumption. I need to beat time. I need to impress the doctorate proposals panel. I must convince them that I mean business. Once I get them to approve my abstract, I know the work is virtually all wrapped up. After that, I'll slow down. The writing of the actual dissertation will be like putting on the finishing touches.'

Miss Frankwood was not convinced. Indeed, the unusual zeal with which he spoke, raised her anxiety all the more over his state of health. As a nurse of considerable experience, who had herself suffered stress, she knew that a concentration of plasmodia could well catalyse manic self-exaction in a full-blooded tropical native such as Dezmond.

'You're only wrecking your health in a hurry. Graduate school's supposed to be fun.'

'Seems my only way of excelling. I want to impress Prof. Primate, especially.'

'Y'know, Dez, you should get on pretty good with that guy. Are you sure you've not misunderstood him, seeing as you often bring home bad reports about him? Ain't he a brother, after all?'

'I know what you mean. He's black. I'm black. Or should I say he *looks* black. Maybe that's why we don't gel. I believe you've read about some blacks who love to hate fellow blacks. Even themselves.'

'Dezmond, you've really got a hang-up! Maybe the guy's trying to help you and you've misunderstood. I remember Jod Gordon – Dave's kid brother. He bombed out of

Dave's freshman physics. His weekly grouch was that his own brother was after breaking his back. Jod was a 3.7-grade-point average achiever, but Dave was hell-bent on the full four points. But that's another kettle of fish from yours. In this case, you're really your own slave-master, Dez. At this frenzied rate, you'd have burnt up all your strength before you even get halfway.'

Penny's eyes scanned all around the room like a searchlight, even as Dezmond attempted to distract her with fresh conversation. Close to Dezmond's feet under the table was an enamel saucer which caught her eye. She went under and picked it out. It was half-full of ash and tiny coils of partially burnt paper, with little wooden spikes jaggedly stuck in the cold ashes. Her face was ablaze with shock.

'You've kept this secret pretty well, Dez! How come you never told me you're hooked on pot?'

'I'm very sorry, Penny,' he pleaded, standing up. 'I don't indulge as such. Only occasionally. To clear my head when I'm stuck.' He fidgeted like a child caught with his hand in the soup pot, a shrunken image of himself. Penny kept gazing at him with pity and concern, lost as to how to express her disappointment.

'Dez!'

'Frankly, I've already kicked it. I've not touched it since—'

'Who're you trying to kid?' screamed Miss Frankwood. 'You need urgent help, an' I'm gonna call for it right away!'

'No, please!' pleaded Dezmond desperately, holding Penny's hand and falling on his knees. 'I'm off ganja already. I've not touched the stuff since we vacated. Believe me, I'm ready to clean up for good.'

'For God's sake, Dezmond, stop this! Get on your feet. You're meddling with brain damage! You bet, I won't let you take chances with marijuana addiction. Listen, I'll pick up the bill for your therapy, if that's what bothers you, okay?'

'No. You know my health insurance is intact. I just don't want to get mixed up with rehab processes or anti-narc agents. I'll be all right. I'm determined not to enter any hospital. I will return to Aroji the same way I came here. On my own feet, and strong! Stronger, with my doctorate!'

'Dezmond, you must listen to me!' shouted Penny, gripping him by the shoulders. 'You're in serious trouble already! With every word you speak, I'm more convinced you need help before you crack up.'

'Penny, you won't throw me out, will you?' He sounded genuinely desperate.

'No, Dez. You know I won't. This remains your home. But you must co-operate. Let's get help to kill the habit before it eats you up and gets you into harder drugs, okay?'

He seemed to consider her words for some moments.

'You won't call in the anti-narc people, will you?' Again, this stalwart specimen of well-built manhood was looking like a cowed caricature of himself.

'Oh, what a pity! I feel awfully guilty that I'm looking in on you only now. I wish I'd been more sensitive. But I hadn't the slightest clue! You kept your tracks so clean, I never smelt a thing!' She was downcast, muttering on darkly about her predicament. 'We're wasting valuable time talking, when I know exactly what you need! But I can't drag you there. Are you gonna co-operate! Or do I call anti-narc?'

'Penny, I have enough trouble already with grad school. And the black guys. What...'

'What's your own suggestion?' she snapped, plonking herself on the edge of the bed and crossing her legs.

'Take my promise, Peninnah. I know the words I just spoke to you. I mean every one of them. I want you to believe this. It happens that my recent thoughts of you are what made me decide to quit smoking grass. I should've since thrown those old roaches down the drain, but I forgot. If only I had done so! You don't know, but when you found it, I wanted the ground to open and swallow me up. Please, believe this. I don't want to be so exposed. Whatever help you can give at home, I will submit to it.'

Miss Frankwood sat still as if slain by those words. Her determination melted under the heat of Dez's open-hearted confession. From pity, her feelings began to warm up to empathy and an uncanny love.

Dezmond pulled out his chair in the discomfort of the ensuing silence and sat down, quite unsure of himself. His sense of betrayal and guilt so overwhelmed him in the wordless communication of the moment, that he could not look at Penny.

On her part, she was seeing a positively proud man who had suddenly gone down in his own self-image, even in the face of a lady who had only recently sold out to him. She was paradoxically relieved and revived by the same words that had so weakened her body and mind. They showed this man to be someone who knew how to quickly pull himself together and get up, should he fall down. She turned the whole matter round and round in her mind even as Dezmond was eclipsed in his own thoughts. At last an idea occurred to her, and brought badly needed relief to both of them.

'Where's the rest of the stuff you've got left?' she asked suddenly, bracing up.

Dezmond pulled out a crumpled leather pouch from under his mattress. There were three untouched wraps in it, each half as fat as a Havana cigar, and as long. Their irregular shape proved that they had been hand-rolled.

'How long have you been smoking?' she asked. Her whole attitude now was evidently soft and sympathetic, thanks perhaps to the compassionate milk she had as a true nurse… and lover.

'I'd just been going over all that,' answered Dezmond, a trifle surprised at the timing of the question. 'I'd never touched this stuff before. Never even saw it back home, though the civil war made it common.'

'And you didn't smoke pot even then?'

'No! Maybe, I might lie to you some day, but I can't imagine now what situation would make me do that.'

'I'm sorry, Dez. I believe you.'

'When I was in Clement Hall, almost every student was wrapping ganja and doping. Nobody did a thing about the nuisance.'

'I know. But outside the campus walls the law won't look the other way. Y'know, Dez, there's a thin line between habit and addiction. What's your own experience like?'

He rose to his full height and began to pace the room, his back to Miss Frankwood.

'Many times the guys urged me on. I bluntly refused. They would come back from rock parties and tease me, call me square, and things. They kept doing that for a month until I decided I'd give back their bluff. That's how I landed in the soup.

'But then, y'know what? The first time I held a joint, I remained the same old me. All the others got stoned. They looked surprised, even foolish. I thought I'd really damned them. I said to myself, now they'll leave me alone, I'm impervious to their dope! They became all the more determined to break me. Pride had set in. One funny guy suggested it must be that the portion that was lit for me was tempered with dried paw-paw leaves. You know, some bad guys… I should say, badder guys actually… mix it that way to cheat on the street market.

'They kept hassling me. "How come you pretend, when the baddest stuff comes from Nigeria? We hear your folks make tea of ganja. You've been so stoned, seen so many highs it don' make no more difference in yo' system." One evening I got mad enough and I again tried it. This time the thing blew my brains into the seventh heaven! I burned like pure flame and my thinking soared above the here and now. I was restless and sleepless; so energised, I saw myself traversing infinity. Imagine, Penny! Infinity! Nothing seemed undoable! I guess, to diffuse the energy, I fell on my Olympia and pounded it until I passed out right there. I woke up in the ICU with a drip in my veins. I remember what a demonic urge I had, to fill the terrible emptiness in my tummy. They call it the "munchies"...'

'What happened on discharge from the unit? You must've got counselling. Did somebody follow up?'

'To be fair, they made referrals. Well, I quit smoking right away. Or so I thought. When the scare left me, I again craved for more. This time, I didn't need any drum beaters. I danced the *kpanlogo* all by myself. Once in a while, I'd go some place and burn a joint. But it's all over since the end of last semester.'

'Who exactly was supplying?'

'Oh, it's all over campus. The real stuff and the mixed. Any student can afford one or the other.'

'Dez, d'you know something? Imagine those winos out on the streets of downtown and East-side, Lake City. D'you imagine they turned winos and junkies just overnight? It was just one drag for a start, then one wrap, then finally the whole bag of addiction. I believe you when you repeatedly assure me you've quit. Unless you truly kick the habit back to hellfire where it belongs, you're gonna be no more than a burnt-out potential.'

'I'll appreciate this, for ever, Penny,' he said, taking her hands in his.

'I know you will. And I'm sure glad,' she responded, standing up.

'I've no regret, after all, that you came up here and

found me out! That helps me stick by the pledge I already made. My guilt and shame are over! I owe all this to you, Peninnah. And more. What if I wasn't living here? I don't know who would've helped me.'

'Dez, I'm even happier than you that it is all over! I can't bear to think what would've happened if anti-narcotic guys picked you up.'

'God forbid!'

'It's all over. We'll never have to remember this again. Take it you never touched the stuff, okay? I'm gonna flush down all this and we'll put it all behind us. My last word on it is this: Peninnah Frankwood is not ever again going to monitor you for drugs or anything. You be your own watchdog. You be your own rehab. You be your own counsellor and conscience. Okay, Dez?'

'Sure! Thank you for ever, Penny!'

She stood up and opened her arms to a coy, penitent Dezmond. Overwhelmed by the unfathomable power of forgiveness, tears welled up in his eyes even as he tardily embraced Penny and kissed her.

Chapter Seven

Spring…

Season of regeneration and growth! A good time for hoping, and renewing! The name, even the connotation, of spring bears on its petals, a divine example of fulfilment for man in his natural pursuit of the produce of seed-time.

The barren earth of winter was miraculously transformed into a vast haven of plush greenery, clothed with blooms of rich coloration. Well was the Maker and owner of times and seasons moved by Noah Lamech to vow that, as long as the old earth existed, there would be no cessation of seed-time and harvest time, summer and winter, day and night, cold and hot. What an age-old relief! From the barrelled-in, bundled-up incarceration of winter, renewed foliage and blooms were now joyfully beckoning men to the raptures of perfect gardening!

So it was that the spring semester gave a new fillip to the person and work of Dezmond Adama. He convinced himself that, with such an impetus, the season would determine whether he would make or mar his mission. Like a foot soldier on the final onslaught of a protracted battle, he threw in all his efforts with a single-minded focus on his target. He meditated on his dissertation well in advance of himself, breathed it, dreamed it – of course – and even visualised its title on library shelves.

At Dezmond's request, PAID HQ had his assignments shelved, excepting some light enquiries on African culture which he always disposed of at his leisure. The leadership of PAID had been so impressed with his documentary work and especially with his flair for black community mobilisation jingles that he was promptly granted a partial leave of absence.

They went further to identify with his doctorate programme and expressed a readiness to even facilitate his research by setting up a small Tactical Resource Team, as they called it, to back him up. Dezmond dissuaded them, fearing that the methods of PAID were not amenable to the academic work situation. He preferred to keep hidden from his advisor this more or less forced relationship with the black movement. In any case, he pleaded, he had no problem in his pursuit of the doctorate that warranted any intervention from outsiders. Even the offer of dollars to augment his ABU fellowship grant was politely turned down for fear of his being bonded or obliged to two organisations at the same time. He vehemently argued that such funds be dedicated to the recently launched inner-city adult literacy campaign.

As far as he could during his weeks of active involvement with Protect Afrika in Diaspora, Dezmond kept his lips sealed about it, to both Miss Frankwood and Maazi. Whenever a suspicion arose, either from his long hours of engagement outside his college schedules or from the occasional hush-hush phone conversation, he would give the impression that it was something to do with the African Students' Association. The nearest his secret came to being uncovered was when Miss Frankwood overheard a rather hot telephone exchange one night, between him and someone she perceived to be from a black cultural group. Apparently, the person was inviting Dezmond to a function, but this was still in his earlier days of resistance to the over-zealous moves of PAID scouts. Dezmond recollected how, on that occasion, Penny picked up the gauntlet on behalf of the adversary, without her knowing it. She had innocently urged her tenant to honour the black brothers for his own safety, but he unequivocally told the caller and Miss Frankwood that he would have nothing to do with the black movement. Thereafter, the lady only expressed a fear of possible repercussions from the group. At least for that period, she wiped off her mind, any notion of Dezmond ever getting drawn into Protect Afrika in Diaspora.

Thus, with PAID pressure put behind him, Dezmond's work progressed in leaps and bounds. He maintained his track record of high scores in his main courses, mopping up all the dividends from the modular courses and electives alike. Spring motivated him greatly beyond his own expectation of his prowess.

Towards the end of the semester, he was summoned by his advisor for a meeting, well outside the agreed schedule of consultations. As soon as he entered the office, Prof. Primate pulled out his folder, and pored over his own appraisal comment on Dezmond's research proposal.

'Again, this is strictly a minority position,' he observed, looking Dezmond straight in the eyes. 'If you insist, you may go ahead and develop this thesis. However, there are doctorates and there are doctorates. Think about that...'

'Might it be the lacuna in my—' Dezmond asked by way of explanation.

'Lacu-*what*?'

'A blank area. There must be a missing link somewhere in the proposal. I don't know, maybe I had a brainwave or something, when I was writing down the stuff. Otherwise, the whole thing came to me in one unbroken package.'

'So then where did you lose the focus?'

'Prof, I'm not yet sure where the problem really is. But, if I may ask, how about examining a subject from a totally new, independent viewpoint?'

'What about it?' echoed the professor, slouching on his swivel chair.

'Is it allowed? Would you permit one to take an avant-garde position in a research work of this nature? I'm just wondering... I don't mean to be cheeky, or anything.'

'Listen, Mr Adama,' retorted Prof. Primate, sitting back up and drawing his face as close as he could to Dezmond's own across the table. 'What you're attempting to do here is a crazy redefinition of historical thought. You wanna rewrite an age-old concept to fit your hypothesis? You're getting muddled up with a new wave bloomer called reconstructionism! It's simply crap! You must've been reading a lot of academic bull!'

'No, I've never heard of such a thing. I don't know how you classify it, but I guess you're talking about the counterfactual issues I want to argue in my dissertation. Prof, is there no division between science and cultural politics?'

Exasperated, Prof. Primate flung himself on the back of his chair, his large arms, dangling in despair. 'Damn it! I don't believe this! You're not the same guy I've had in my seminars. Something's gone real wacky with you, man!'

'What can be so wrong, Prof? Is it altogether impossible to develop a so-called crazy, theoretical idea? Should we be always predictable in our hypotheses? This could be one of those challenges in which the end justifies the means. I can prove it, if you let me!'

Prof. Primate slowly stood up and beckoned Dezmond to a settee by the only window in his office with a garden view. Sitting down, he patted the space next to him and Dezmond obeyed. He had never sat that close to his advisor, so he perched half-heartedly on the edge, as if overwhelmed by Primate's bulky presence. But then, the professor wore a warm, comradely expression, addressing the issue in a low, gentle tone, almost counting his words.

'Dezmond,' he began, looking at him with kindness on his face, 'it's not a question of classification. It's a matter of validity! What's valid knowledge? What's a relevant, applicable research work? This should be of serious concern to you, especially. Coming all the way from Nigeria, what's the use of... well, wasting your time and ABU dollars if your doctorate makes no impact on the development of your people, one way or other? Why d'you reckon you got sent out here on study fellowship? You surely can't afford the kind of study you've proposed. A colleague of mine calls it "ivory tower luxury suite". You can't afford it; you don' need it!'

Dezmond was thinking along, as it were, his head bowed in deep concentration. Encouraged that his counselling was cutting into his student's heart, Prof. Primate pressed home his point.

'Point of int'res': history has its innate make-up which makes it history. Sometimes, it's not even recorded. Or it's recorded with a slant or outright bias. But it's still history, by definition. The event happened but nobody recorded it, or somebody took note of it inaccurately or wrongly... for whatever reason. D'you follow what I'm getting at?'

'Maybe one or two illustrations might clarify it for me,' responded Dezmond, looking up. 'Somehow, my brain feels like sawdust this morning.'

The professor paused, then continued.

'Hmm... take the case of President Lincoln. Historically, he's one of the greatest, if not in fact, *the* greatest of American heroes of all time, right? He fought and won the Union War. He was Papa Linkum to the niggers, having signed the great Bill of Emancipation from slavery, and all of that, right?'

'Right.'

'But, d'you know that a lesser-known but equally valid history shows he had some really obnoxious notions about blacks? He believed in freedom for slaves but not with franchise, equal pay or with social equality. He was among those who considered blacks intellectually inferior to whites. That's the main reason he played cool over War Office requests for the commissioning of black super-feds whose bravery in the war earned them commendation even from their white commanders. In fairness, and with due honour to President Lincoln, I guess you could say he was genuinely ignorant in his views about this aspect, and had no malice at heart. But the fact still remains that he was, and is, wrong in this matter. Now, in how many records would you find this historical fact on Abraham Lincoln? Rather, the Negro of his time deified him, and oh, you dared not speak bad of Papa Linkum and go scot-free! D'you get some insight into what I'm trying to get across?'

'I'm beginning to grasp something... but, if I may observe, it seems to me your illustration fits more into my own argument than—'

'Good fun! Show me just how!'

'Only what is captured or recorded is history.'

'Nope! Count one, you're on a wrong premise, logically.'

'Just a minute, Prof! Say, something took place, and nobody recorded it. We don't know it took place, do we? In that case, where's the history?'

'Dezmond! Depends on what y'mean, recorded! You forget the very primary source of history... oral accounts of participators, eyewitnesses and all the stuff passed down through generations of "earwitnesses", if you like—'

'How authentic—?'

'C'mon man!' Prof. Primate interrupted him again, in return. 'That's another kettle of fish you're introducing. If push comes to shove, how authentic is written history? What's its origin in the firs' instance? Those same oral accounts, of course! And, as you very well know, even if it were possible for the primary actors or makers of history to all perish over time, the archaeologists are there to go dig them all up! History's more dynamic than you think...'

Dezmond was now sprawled on the settee, smiling broadly to himself, his hands thrown behind his head in leisurely fashion. The professor paused, looked at him, and waited for an explanation. Had he perhaps seen the light of his teaching?

'What you just said simply speaks for me! I wonder how that word escaped me all along. Dynamic! *Dynamic!* Precisely what I've tried to express: the dynamic nature of history,' Dezmond began to explain.

'Listen, man! You're treading the way of some neo-babelian cabal on the west coast who call themselves analytic philosophers. Those fellows imagine they can rephrase history to suit their present-day notion of past events... Are you listening, Dezmond? Remembered our seminar on Arnold Toynbee? What did he come up with after toiling over the history of civilisations? Just a phoney conclusion that the chiefest religion of man is self-worship! That was his bottom line, *finito!* For goodness' sake, Arnold Toynbee shouldn't be your model! Don't mess around, either, with the devolution or revolution framework of Spengler, whichever you call it. If you must research civilisation, approach it from a wholly different direction. Hey, listen, I'd put my God-given grey matter someplace else if I were you... y'know, an area that would address the socio-political problems of a developing economy. You have more resources here to give it a better crack than in your country. Take full advantage of this...

'Yes, you talk of a dividing line between what you call *scientia* and politics. Well, there's no such line, my man, and surely not for you, as far as I'm concerned. As far as I remain your advisor, we cannot allow you such a luxury, even if you can knock up an argument for delineating them.'

He paused, expecting a response; but Dezmond remained gloomily reclining, as distant as a lone star. The

Professor lunged across the room to his clothes tree. Even as he donned his spring jacket, he studiously lingered on, in the hope that his student would say something in return. Like a distraught straggler aroused to his right senses, Dezmond suddenly came to himself. As he stood up, his facial expression signalled that he was about to say something. 'One last question, sir.'

'Well?'

'How come that, out of five faculty members, my own advisor is among the minority of two professors who turned down my research pro—'

Prof. Primate wheeled round on his heels, strode to the door and flung it open, waving Dezmond out into the noontime sun.

Chapter Eight

'I'm glad you called, Mazee. I wish I knew, myself, where he's gone.' Miss Frankwood spoke calmly but her voice was trembling. That was Maazi's third call in a span of four hours. 'No. I'm not aware of any trip. He left as usual, in the morning, with his college bag. If he meant to travel or something, he didn't say... I had no such hint... No, I don' think so.'

Although this was the first time Dezmond had been absent from No. 19, Pine Avenue all night, Miss Frankwood did not initially consider it a thing of great concern. A few other times, he had stayed out very late into the night, but would return no matter how late and quietly slip into his room without rousing the whole house. But it was different this time. Even by noon the next day, there was neither any sign of Dezmond, nor did anyone send word of his whereabouts.

Miss Frankwood was growing nervous by the minute, practically hindered from making any engagements, and even from her house chores. All she could do was to sit by the phone, expecting a call. Still each peal of the phone startled her out of her wits. She would first hesitate, then grab the receiver, only to flinch again, for fear of the message that might come through. By the morning of the third day, she was a wholly confused wreck. The intense anxiety aside, she managed a little sleep only with the help of Valium. Her nervousness grew to a point that she was hardly able to co-ordinate her thoughts.

Over and over, she had called the few phone numbers she knew, from where she could get word: the Graduate School, the African Students' Club, the Rathskeller, County Library… all to no avail. The one number not available to her was that of Maazi, but she nursed a hope that he would be calling her any moment. Surely, he would have a lead as to Dezmond's whereabouts! The outcome of this expected last hope would, therefore, determine her next move. With Maazi now calling only to enquire, her worst fears surfaced and her already febrile imagination began to run riot. Whatever had befallen Dezmond? Should she not call the police? But, how incredibly calm Maazi remained even when she was narrating to him the details of her three-day ordeal, searching for a missing man by telephone! Did Maazi perhaps know something that she did not?

She had occasionally met him at close quarters, although his visits to Dezmond were few and far between. Indeed, Maazi did not approve of what he called 'a sin-prone situation', and had, therefore, explained that he would not be visiting him as often as he would have liked to. Each time she heard Maazi talk she was left with an impression of a naive, cut-and-nail man, very unlike his friend. He sounded to her like an unbalanced personality, whose fixed and rigid response to all the hard realities of life was the flat, 'Jesus is the answer'.

The last time she had met him in conversation with Dezmond over coffee, she remembered teasing him about what, in the first instance, the question was, to which Jesus is the answer. She had watched him launch into what sounded to her like an excited monologue on the primordial sin in the nature of man… the grandmother of all woes and wickedness… the all-conquering blood of Jesus… the sweet sleep of the saints which men call death, from which the saints will arise and ascend into eternal glory… the eternal, second death which is the verdict of those who reject the gospel of salvation through Jesus Christ...

Miss Frankwood recalled those words. The man had spoken like a possessed person, completely consumed in his own utterances, not minding that he was only an acquaintance and a guest. She had then asked him what kind of religion he practised, even as he was calling the name of Jesus. And why talk with so much violence, when the Jesus she knew had been a meek and humble man? A seemingly strange quotation promptly rolled out of Maazi's mouth, which both Penny and Dezmond did not accept as coming from the Christian Bible:

'From the time of John, the kingdom of heaven suffereth violence, and the violent take it by force!'

Yet, ordinarily, Maazi was a very docile and withdrawn character when workaday issues were being discussed. He would listen a lot, nodding occasionally, if in agreement, but hardly opening his mouth. Unlike his fellow countryman, he remained unmoved by the things that excited other students. That often made Penny wonder how two such contrary personalities could be friends. How she wished, in her anxiety, that Dezmond had other friends with whom she was more comfortable and could freely discuss her present predicament!

'For crying out aloud!' shouted Miss Frankwood. 'I'm sure bothered, buddy! Dezmond's more than just a tenant. He's become family... Laura and Beaver are bothered too, of course! I'm bothered nuts! Nobody is able to give me the slightest clue where he might be, or if he's okay. What? Of course, it scares me... Don't you think I should call the MPID?'

'Sorry, call who?'

'Missing Persons Information Desk.'

'Oh! Well... why don't we wait through today? Maybe... if by tomorrow there's still no news, then... Be calm, Miss Frankwood.'

'I wish I could take your advice. I don't know what's going on! Dezmond might be in trouble someplace! And there you are out there, all very cool and well-behaved. How come you're not alarmed?'

'I could be, but I've got somebody who handles such things. And I've been unloading it all on him. Jesus is able! Without doubt... I can say that Dezmond's safe wherever he is...'

'There you go again, even now!' She held on to the receiver, not knowing what else to do. Crazy as Maazi's words sounded to her, she got a strange assurance from them. Suddenly realising she was holding the wire between her fingers, she shouted, 'Hello! Hello!'

'Hello! Now I can hear you very clearly. Your voice kinda went off, or something.'

'Mazee, d'you have the number of any of those PAID guys? That's the only link I've not been able to call,' she shouted hysterically.

'Yeah, I thought of that. Each time I've called you, I've tried the guy called Wale Jefferson, but he's not been in. What?... Yes. I'll try him again.'

'Mazee, I suspect those PAID guys,' she said, lowering her voice. 'They know what's going on. Didn't Dez tell you of their threat calls?'

'He mentioned it. I didn't think much of it.'

'You didn't?' shouted Miss Frankwood in disbelief. 'Y'mean you took them for gran'ed?'

'Strange... y'know? Even when I was calling Jefferson, I didn't imagine that angle of it... well, yes... I don't doubt that possibility. Even that the guy himself hasn't been in all this time, is suspicious. Well, we must hang up now. I'm speaking from a coin box... don't bother about that just now. I'll be leaving... somebody's getting beserk, waiting. Remember, worry won't better the situation. Me, I will not give my eyes sleep until I receive definite word on Dezmond.'

'Call me back the moment somebody sends word. Any time… I'm keeping vigil with Sanka coffee and the telephone, anyway… Y'know, Mazee, I have this weird feeling that—'

'Please, shut it out the best you can… no… no harm will befall your tenant, in Jesus's name! Bye for now!'

Miss Frankwood held the phone handle to her bosom, whispering a deeply felt 'amen' into a vacuous mouthpiece.

*

'Protect Afrika in Diaspora!' repeated Maazi with each stride. An ominous aura surrounding that name had just struck him. For about three hours, he had shut himself in, on his knees.

His voice was loud, his case persuasive, but as he went on, he became gradually weakened. His quiet worship was distracted and soon after, a drowsiness began to overshadow him. Suddenly, his heart was lifted and he received an insight into the name, Protect Afrika in Diaspora. He jumped to his feet and began to stride up and down his room. He could not recollect his last utterances by the time sleep began to overtake him. He entreated the heavens to help him pray in line with God's will, not according to his human sentiments.

'I am the temple of the Holy Spirit!' he proclaimed, as he strode about the room like a warring soldier. 'Unto Jesus, by whom and for whom all things were made, belong my members! He is also your head, you powers and principalities, according to the mysteries of God's plan concerning all things. Satan – you cannot, therefore, borrow or misappropriate my mouth to speak contrary spirits! Hear you, the word of the Lord! The Holy Spirit helps my infirmities even now! Cover me, Lord, with your full armour as you again lead me into battle alongside all the saints that are praying this very hour. And I know that all things work together for good to those that love you, and are called according to your will.'

Maazi burst into songs of praise in Igbo language, lifting his hands and waving into the heavens. As if saturated with the presence of God, he fell prostrate and worshipped Him in diverse utterances, songs, and silences. He lay still in that position as if asleep, but when he was done, he sat up with his back to the wall, and again went on verbalising his petition.

'His soul belongs to you, Lord. The devil created nothing except wickedness. His is to kill, steal, and destroy your perfect works. But he has no ground except that he is a liar and thief. My Lord Jesus has paid in full by his shed blood. Satan, you have no right over Dezmond's life, whether he knows it or not! In Jesus's name, I command you to loosen your hold on him, now! I break all your chains of bondage on him, and I declare that he shall live to receive his own share of the completed work of our Lord Jesus Christ.'

He arose and resumed pacing the room slowly, like a man reasoning out a thought. Then, as if suddenly prompted, he again broke into words. After some time, he began to pour forth a stream of seemingly foreign indecipherable sounds.

He then gave thanks to God for revealing the secrets of the enemy and for being made worthy to share in some of those secrets. Protect Afrika in Diaspora! What a simple, obvious name of noble intentions! But, he had received a revelation into some of the secrets behind this attractive slogan of a name. A book should not, indeed, be judged by its cover, Maazi recalled.

He sat down again, to contemplate on the vision of PAID which had been granted him in prayer. He had seen, as it were, a giant billboard of exquisite artwork. Upon it was displayed in glittering letters, a highly attractive list of projects and programmes: *Cultural Advancement*; *Inter-Continental Exchange Scheme*; *Open University on Africa*; *Long-Distance Black Learning*; *Black Mortgage Plan*; *Quarterly Black Convention*; *Roots and Herbs Research*... In between the items on this menu were inscriptions such as, '*Accredited by Government*; *Alpha-rated, Approved NGO*' and so on.

Maazi moved around the massive board to admire these offers more closely, as they appeared to him, but a whirl-wind arose and blew him some metres backward. Before his eyes, the board suddenly shifted and, without a sound, became a concrete platform whose ends he could not fathom from where he was standing. In a twinkle of an eye, he saw this stage-like set, peopled by men and women, mostly blacks, physically engaged in one activity or another, along the lines of the earlier inscriptions.

As he watched this instant transformation from still pictures to animation, an ultra-brilliant light flooded the scene at centre stage. He could now see, behind the busy activities, a translucent sheet right across the middle of the stage. Equally, strips of the same airy material dropped down both wings of the massive stage.

The foreground of this strange animation suddenly be-came blurred, and Maazi's attention was fixed on the happenings behind the screen. He saw groups of people, all shaved to the scalp, sitting on the bare floor, each in utter concentration on someone whose presence was not visible in the scene. As he wondered what those persons were doing, an invisible hand began to inscribe racy captions for each of the groups: *Black Insurance Power*; *Help from Herbs*; *Egyptian Pyramid Fast*; *Black Roots Defence*; *Vital Force Cultiva-tion and Sustenance*; *Night Flying*... and others he could not capture. After some time, an undulating stream of smoke emerged from the left of the stage and ran through the captions, swallowing them up in its track. The stage lights went off. And when Maazi's eyes readjusted to their normal focus, only a silent void was left of this whole vision.

He prayerfully meditated on the strange spectacle, asking for the spirit of wisdom and understanding. A little later, some scriptures in his heart came into remembrance, pointing out how God reveals some of his secrets to his sons.

What a veil! thought Maazi. How did this escape exposure all along, except that men are spiritually born blind, even born dead? He knelt down and began to address the vision. 'Lord, prosper all genuine efforts to advance the lives of our people. Thank you for exposing those of them that serve the devil. By the power in the blood of Jesus, I paralyse the demons behind the smokescreen! All you chieftains backing satanic groups, I bring you to judgement! Expose them, Lord, and make a public show of their shame as you did, their father, two thousand years ago! I plead the all-conquering blood of Jesus for Dezmond. Grant us favour for him. Remember your word, Lord, that you are God, who gives mercy to whomsoever you please. Show us mercy, thou Lord of the harvest, in Jesus's name!'

He was practically on all fours, pounding the floor as he travailed with all the compassion he could muster. At a point, he was groaning and choking with tears, for he had been granted a vision of Dezmond's predicament. He saw him bound in fetters and gagged with a bar of iron. In the midst of four bare-bodied men, he sat as if under judgement. Yet none of the men was talking or moving. Bro. Maazi remained on his knees until his crying virtually choked him and made him dumb and breathless. He felt as faint as an autumn leaf, not having tasted food or water for three days and nights of continuous total fasting.

At last, he got a prompting to look up a verse from the Bible. He opened to Psalm 29 and, shutting his eyes, asked the Holy Spirit to direct the action that was needed for that moment. He then lay aside the Bible and rose to his feet, saying aloud, 'The word of God is that they that wait upon him shall not faint. Therefore, you body called Maazi, obey the word, receive strength now, in the name of Jesus! The enemy shall not find your ears to whisper his lies.' He prayed, standing still: 'Jesus and Moses were in every detail men like me, when they fasted forty days and nights. Silence, therefore, thou body! Hear the word of God and renew your strength! The Lord gives power to the faint and increases strength to the weak. I shall mount up with wings like an eagle! I shall both run and walk without fainting!'

He picked up the Bible again and opened it, held it high up, and launched into a thunderous declaration. 'Hear, oh you territorial spirits of the north, south, east and west! You powers, principalities, and rulers of the world's darkness; demons and foul spirits of the second heavens and of the waters! Your counsels concerning Dezmond shall not stand! They shall not come to pass! All your speakings shall never prosper! They shall be drowned by the awesome voice of the Almighty God who has since spoken concerning that soul. So be it, in the mighty name of our Lord, Jesus Christ!'

He shut the Bible slowly, and bent double as a crabby pain clutched his bowels like that of a woman in childbirth. So did he remain, grunting in pains, now sobbing inaudibly, now shouting out an anguished phrase or simply gasping for breath... until a sense of let-up and peace settled upon his soul, and he lay down and fell asleep.

Chapter Nine

An unusual rap on the door interrupted Professor Primate's work. He quickly adjusted himself and shouted out a response. Two men entered the office sporting very dark glasses. The leader had a reporter's tape recorder bulging out of his shirt pocket. They rendered their salutations and in the same breath apologised for not having booked an appointment.

'Help you?'

The men glanced at each other and, as if automated, both of them recited what must have been their routine in such situations. 'Mind if we sat down?' Without waiting for an answer, they positioned themselves across the table from the professor.

'Righ', what's this all about?' demanded Prof. Primate, straightening himself.

'We've come to share some'n with you, responded the leader. 'Jus' listen.' He then pulled out the mini-recorder and placed it on the table, pressing a button.

The first part, a lady's voice, gave a run-through of the landmarks in the life of Dezmond Adama, up to his enrolment for study fellowship at LCU. It was followed by portions of dialogue between Dezmond and sundry unidentified voices, then snippets of remarks by Prof. Dave Frankwood, Maazi and Prof. Alvin Primate, in various informal and private situations. Then came on a flotsam of chatter about PAID, 'white supremacy', 'counter-racism', 'cultural relativism, and black affirmative ultimatum', interspersed with applause.

If any coherent message came out of the recordings, it was that Dezmond Adama was a well-endowed asset. He came to take a doctorate, determined, unlike many Africans, to return home. But he got trapped in a racist conspiracy which sought to block his access to the redemptive influence of his black kindred. A voice came on, vehemently talking about 'some smart-arsed nigger who wan'ed to clinch two firsts', but its context was unclear, and the speaker not identifiable.

In Prof. Primate's portion, which was distinctive and emphatic, he was responding to a female questioner, probably a white journalist. It was to the effect that he was the genuine champion of the black cause for insisting that blacks excel. He insisted that he loathed 'tokenism' and other kinds of 'coloured concessions', and did not subscribe to any of the mushroom groups claiming to be champions of black deliverance... They were mostly 'phony, occult self-seekers and daydreamers'. As an academic counsellor, he had no business with his student's 'private preferences'. Dezmond could be top-class material, but he had wrong-headed notions, and needed to be protected against himself... There was no 'black–white dichotomy' in intellect, therefore, the same standards of excellence must apply to black, white, or Chicano endeavours in academics, commerce, or sports...

The leader then stopped the tape and put it back in his pocket.

Prof. Primate cleared his throat. 'I stumbled on an African proverb somewhere, which says a man shouldn't run away from his own toga because it's become tattered rags. That's the only wisdom in my letting you guys enjoy the liberty of sitting in my office this long.'

The men braced up spontaneously like twin serpents about to strike.

'The las' part of your stuff is surely Professor Alvin Primate, in word and spirit. I don't care one nickel how you guys got it, but I stand by all that and more, of course! Now, tell me. What's the game plan?'

'Easy, men! Just hip us on the res' o' the crap the honkies been laying on Bro. Dezmon'.'

'Gen'lemen, my time for jivin's over! Can't help you! I suggest you try harder on your electronic eavesdropping.' He stood ramrod straight on his side of the table, head erect, his fiery eyes trained straight on the men.

'Pr'fess',' shouted the leader menacingly, 'we're here on serious biznez. PAID assignment ain't no joking matt'r! Y'wanna play ball or play tough?'

'What ball?' shouted the professor. 'You guys just walk in my door, an' I reckon, well, must be some'n important. The next thing I know, you're placing this piece of crap on my table. What's the big deal? Any kid can tap a conversation! Wha're you wasting my precious time for?'

The men sprang up like zombies, shouting at random. 'What's your big problem with Protect Afrika in Diaspora? Why put yo'sef on the firing line? Who the hell d'you count yourself to be?'

'I ain't got no business with your group or any other. You know it! I don't meddle with propaganda stuff. Whatever the firing line you're talking about is best known to you!'

'Why then are you sitting on Bro. Dez's jugular? You got that guy cracking up, man!'

'Who told you we got a problem? Dezmon' tell you?' The professor was now pacing up and down his side of the table. The men's eyes followed him whenever he turned, gesticulating agitatedly as he spoke. 'Damn! You guys are really great at time-wasting. Tell you what, I gotta leave righ' now!' He reached his clothes tree and picked up his blazer. He brusquely adjusted his tie and turned to the two men, who were busy consulting each other in whispers and signs. 'I'm the LCU-acknowledged advisor of Dezmond Adama! I don't even know who you are! If there is anything to discuss, I ain't discussing with two strangers who just gatecrashed on me!'

The professor kept his dauntless expression as he strode to the door. He wondered, however, what exactly was their intention in not budging, even with all his hints that they should depart. Two granite-cast faces with the pockmarks of the ghetto! He knew that genre of his kinsmen too well! Still he was determined not to yield his ground or betray any trace of fear. They are probably armed, reasoned Prof. Primate, but a man only dies once. He studied their every movement as he held the door. He could now see that beneath their rough-cut mugger-in-dark-alley personas lay a polished, gentlemanly mien. As if to reinforce that impression, the second man suddenly switched his style of speech, cutting out all the sing-song cadences and flowery images that characterise the idiom of the native Afro-American.

'With due respect, Professor Primate, bear with us. We'll be done in five minutes. All we want is that you begin to appreciate PAID, even for yourself, how it impacts on your own life. If you'd close that door, we'd appreciate. Can you give us a littl' something to take away?'

'Like?' interrupted the professor, unflinching in his angry stare.

'An insider input on Mr Adama. What exactly is his predicament? Of whose engineering? What do they want of him? We'd appreciate a concrete statement to take away because PAID needs your viewpoint into Bro. Dezmond's situation.'

'Listen. Like I said, he is my student. That means he is my problem, kind of. I'm more concerned about him than anybody else. If there's any predicament at all, it's me who's facing two righ' now, on account of one graduate student. I'm of course referring to both o' you guys who're like sitting in on me this moment. For crying out aloud, in my fifteen damn years of tenure professorship, am I suddenly unfit to convince a student to rethink his research topic? I've no bloomy idea where the guy's gone! Since PAID cares so much, maybe you should make a concrete comment on that one!' He banged the door and stood by it, waiting for their answer.

'Lemme say some'n,' the second man launched out. 'My personal opinion... You remind me of them sadistic, slave-driving graduate advisors back in Dezmond's country. The guy's so smart, you can't stand him!' He stood up and yelled, 'That's a black brother, man!'

'You're flat-out wrong!' yelled back the professor standing right up to him. 'Your opinion is so cheap it stinks! You don't need no third-grade wire-tapping to get to know who I am. I'm black, yes! But I need no apologia! Incidentally, your Bro. Dezmond doesn't either! I don't believe in sloganeering. I don't need to advocate blackism of any sort!'

'Say man, what d'you do then?' retorted the man. 'Where d'you belong? What can you die for?' His neck veins were bulging with rage.

'But you had it taped already! Well, for avoidance of doubt I believe that blacks must stand on their own feet, and strive at least *alongside* whites, not hollering for special head starts and all kinds of junk concessions!'

Both men stood toe-to-toe, eyeing each other, primed to pull punches.

'Leader, let's get outa here! This dude's completely sold out to his self-opinionated ideology,' the man called out.

In reply, the leader drew closer to him and whispered, 'Stop shooting crap man. He sure ain't a dixie! That guy's making a point. I'd say that's the spirit of PAID. Talk later.'

'Well, gen'lmen, I'd say, for an unscheduled visit, I've

done pretty well by you. Good evening!' said the professor. He stretched for the doorknob and turned it. Even in the man's pocket, the clicking of the tape recorder was audible enough.

As they headed for the door, the leader offered the professor a handshake. 'One las' word…'

'Please yourself.'

'You've done real good, haven't you?' He had a wry grin on his lips. It did not look like just a last word, after all. Not keen on taking chances, the professor bid them yet another good evening and stepped right out of his office into the long corridor. Several faculty members, janitors and groundsmen were still milling around. The sweet scent of spring out in the corridor added to Prof. Primate's feeling of relief and well-being.

'The las' word is that PAID has put a big stake on a couple of Afro-Americans of your calibre. Can we make a pact? Privileged info, of course.'

The professor paused, jolted by this curious turn in communication. It was too late in the last round to dither, he considered, even in the face of a veiled threat. What pact, anyway? Or was this a subtle blackmail? He cleared his throat, pointing his finger at the men.

'Lemme tell you guys! When PAID and all the rest are set to really fight the black cause, they're free to come join me!' That punch hit home like a cold pack. 'Poin' of int'res',' the professor added, 'what's the big stake?'

'We'll get in touch!' retorted the leader, as they scuttled down the corridor.

*

Prof. Primate drove home by a different route from his usual one. Just in case, he reasoned, as he pulled into Bailey Street, replaying the episode in his mind. What did they think of him? If, indeed, there was a conflict, what was his role in it? What wrong had he done in all of this? Perhaps, Dezmond Adama had been cornered into pitching camp with PAID. He was ever so visionary, inclined to rebellion, and anti-establishment. But would he abandon his cherished studies, just for an adventure? Must have been lured into it! Even then, what would be the nature of his involvement?

As the Chevrolet approached an intersection, the professor slowed down. The more he tried to distract himself from thinking of the encounter, the more the questions cropped up. However, he was very satisfied with how he handled the confrontation. The cheek of it! He had given those bums something to chew. He remembered the line about Dezmond cracking up. Well, not too far-fetched a possibility. He would not put it beyond a maverick of Dezmond's type, especially in the face of pressures. Now, what's an advisor's role supposed to be in such a situation...? Thank God for Wyvonia! The nearer he got to his home, the faster he moved.

A professional psychologist in an inner-city college, Mrs Wyvonia Primate always scheduled her work in such a way as to be available most times her husband was returning home. Their three children were undergraduates at Stanford on the west coast, so they had only each other to keep the home warm. The man began to unload his day's pressures right on the threshold of their duplex, after his wife had hugged him.

'You done well, Alvee,' she affirmed, as she began to set the table. 'But how long you gonna wait for Dezmond to show up with some explanation? I feel you oughta file a formal statement on his absence. In fact, that's adult truancy. And, come to think of it, from all you've told me of that guy's character, something may be going wrong with him. He probably needs help...

'As for this weird visit to your office, both the LCU and the Police Department should have a report! We don't take no chances, Alvee.'

As her husband sat down, she bent over his shoulder and kissed him.

Chapter Ten

The last three days of the Programme Evaluation Week of PAID were devoted to a closed-door session between PAID leadership in Erie County, and the Brains Trust group, among whom was Dezmond Adama. For tactical reasons, explained Dr Abdios in his introductory speech, participants had not been privileged to know the details of the week. All twelve of them had arrived at the PAID headquarters, believing they would spend a half-day of the usual monthly meeting of PAID associates and linkages. To their chagrin, they found themselves spending three days that were full of surprises.

The meeting took off like a well-packaged holiday, each person supplied with a functional wardrobe, right down to underclothes, swimming trunks and pyjamas. Provisions were made for indoor and outdoor relaxation, including mini-golf courses and horseback riding even for debutantes such as Dezmond.

Curiously enough, the participants were not at liberty to enjoy these facilities beyond the one-hour recreation of the first day. They were all required to undertake a preparatory regime of three days' fasting which, according to Dr Olongo Abdios, was designed to inculcate in them, self-sacrifice, human suffering and discipline. By the last day of the throughput, Dezmond, who had never imagined himself forsaking food for one day, discovered that he had begun to enjoy it. He was particularly intrigued by a simple observation from the pep talk of Dr Abdios on the first day, that among the vital needs of man, food ranked fourth after air, water, and sleep. He had never considered how men generally take air and sleep for granted, often behaving as if the chief purpose of life is food.

On the last day, Dr Abdios' talk focused on the widening scope of PAID projects and the need for the chosen twelve to renew their commitment toward involvement at a deeper level. Thereafter, the participants broke up into teams, according to their areas of operational specialisation. Dr Olongo Abdios then withdrew to the inner chambers on the ninth floor, having handed Dezmond over to those in charge of his own team.

'That's how much pain our men take to train rookies,' explained Batunga. 'Your own ceremony takes place at the foot of the pyramid.'

Big Queen was the first to arrive at the venue with her protégé in tow, followed by two other men. Each of them took a position on the mat. At the appointed moment, Big Queen jangled her giant brass bangles, which was followed by a bell tinkling from an unseen source. Baba-Kekere emerged from behind the made-up pyramid, wearing the customary *danshiki*. Behind him was the Keeper of the Shrine, Onimole, the acolyte of the day. He held high a soot-covered shard in his palms, which was half-filled with palm oil. In the centre of the oil, was a coil of burning wicker which emitted scented smoke.

Baba-Kekere took his position and the acolyte squatted in the centre of the fetish cabal. As he lay the potsherd before Baba, he intoned an Arabic mantra in a trembling voice which sent chills all over Dezmond. Big Queen disappeared from his side as the others took up the refrain of the incantation. The atmosphere was so charged that the heavens capriciously responded with continual flashes of lightning.

'Brother Dezmond Adama Ododo!' Onimole called out.

It was evident from his facial marks and accent that he was a Yoruba import.

'Wait!' ordered Baba-Kekere. 'We must clear a little doubt in the air. It has been revealed. Bro. Dezmond, you have seen and judged for yourself what PAID stands for, in the cause of the black race. This is not the hour to permit doubts. Cast off every lie of our detractors. This is not an occult ritual. Throughout history, every civilisation has used its science to advance its cause. We use black science to instil loyalty and to cook our operatives against all kinds of risk. This is only to remind you of what you have already been told. You have been found deserving of higher work. We cannot expose you at that level without properly equipping you. Are you ready or not?

'Bro. Dezmond Adama Ododo, answer your own name!' continued the Yoruba man. 'It is I, Onimole, calling you.' Dezmond nodded three times. 'You are indeed a man of favour. Our elders say that he who fights the cause of *upi* tree licks *upi* soup. Otherwise, you should not yet be here. Confirm that you have finally surrendered all doubt.'

'Yes.' He looked so still, squatting there, that you would think he was a statue.

'If yes, why are you afraid?'

'I can't tell if this is a dream, or whether, at this moment, I am a man or a spirit.' But for his lips that moved, he looked as frozen as a corpse. The men chuckled at his dilemma.

'But all men are spirits first, before they are men,' offered Onimole. 'Fear no more. Understanding will soon come to overtake you. Then you will see that our real concern is the overall advancement of the black race. Now, I stand as your blood father. I submit you for the necessary cooking! Are you ready?'

Jolted, Dezmond jumped to his feet, his calf muscles swollen and set to explode. The acolyte kicked his ankle and he crumpled to his knees.

'Son, endeavour to use your spiritual eyes! Only a child sees his shadow and tells himself he's now a grown-up. You need power to survive. This process is to put power in your body against danger. Even if you personally do not want it, you need it for the sake of PAID investment on your life. For the third and last time, are you ready?'

At that, the two men arose, bowed, and processed solemnly a talking distance away, leaving behind the acolyte, Baba-Kekere, and Dezmond. They soon returned in Indian file with two cast-iron pans and a small bundle of root cuttings. One of the pans was half-filled with water; the other with lumps of charcoal. These items were placed down reverently, and as they returned to their positions, the acolyte stood up and repeated the exact motions of the two men. He slowly walked in the same direction and returned with an axe and a contraption that looked like a pair of bellows. He then set the coals on fire, keeping the flames alive above the nozzle of the bellows. Meanwhile, Baba-Kekere was peeling the meaty fibre of the roots and soaking them in the pan of water. Within minutes, the content was transformed into blood-red hue. The other men engaged themselves in staccato incantations with their eyes set on Dezmond who was now positioned in their midst.

The incantations ceased as Onimole disengaged the axe head from its wooden handle and planted it in the red coals. Baba-Kekere then began to explain the proceedings to Dezmond.

'It is the day in which a pot is moulded that its lip is shaped. This is another circumcision for the real manhood. Put forward your right arm!' he ordered. 'Your hands shall take up arms. They must now be placed under black insurance.'

He took Dezmond's hand, made a short, incision with a

razor blade on his wrist, and held it horizontally until three drops of blood fell into the solution. He then inserted a tiny round object into the incision and gripped the spot with his thumbs until it became sealed by coagulated blood.

Meanwhile, the axe head had become one with the flaming coals so that you could not easily notice any difference. To Dezmond's utter shock, Baba ordered him to stoop low and, with his teeth, pluck the axe out of the fire. The young man did not believe his ears. It was either that he had not heard well, or the old man had momentarily lost his senses, he told himself.

'The act must be tested. The axe is your token of power. Pick it out by your teeth,' repeated Baba-Kekere, his tone cold and grave. Everyone waited. Dezmond also waited.

Suddenly, the old man stooped, and going on all fours, lowered his bearded face into the fire and, in a flash, stood erect with the glowing axe head between his teeth. This has to be a nightmare, Dezmond assured himself. Baba stood still for a couple of minutes, bent low, and let the red-hot axe drop into the red waters which immediately began to bubble. The incantations resumed while the axe was sizzling in the liquid. When it was cool enough, Onimole picked it out and replanted it among the hot coals. Again he set the bellows to work. This time, Dezmond felt a strong bond springing up between the old Baba and himself. He began to grow more courageous. When the axe had blended with the blazing coals, he knew that, indeed, it was his turn to eat fire.

'Our elders say, palm kernel tells the mouth that proper food is on the way,' said Baba-Kekere, tapping Dezmond on the shoulder. 'This is a token of a great future.' There was no further persuasion needed before the young man bent over the fire and bit the red-hot axe head...

*

Weary and forlorn, Miss Frankwood rallied herself on hearing the accustomed raps on her front door. Dezmond Adama stepped in from the night, a ghoulish version of himself.

'It's the PAID guys, isn't it?'

He nodded, slinking into the living room. Under light, his eyes looked sunken and strained, his lips dry and cracked. As Miss Frankwood relocked the door, he rested his back on the wall and gazed at her like a caged animal.

'Well, at least you're alive,' she gasped, surveying him all over. Drained down to his very bone marrow, the man slid down the wall, crumpling on the spot where he had stood. Penny hurried to the kitchen and managed to pour out a mug of steaming chocolate.

'I'm awfully sorry,' was all that Dezmond could muster as he was handed the drink.

'Take your time,' replied Penny, wondering how terribly wasted Dezmond had become within three days of his disappearance. What an ordeal the poor man must have been put through! But she was not in a hurry to have him talk. He needed to recover himself, even as she herself had been terribly exhausted in the three days of tortuous waiting and wondering.

Looking at every angle of Dezmond's narration, which was as strange as it was long, Penny was convinced that he needed to see a psychiatrist. She could already observe signs of advanced trauma setting in on him.

'I can guess what you're thinking,' he volunteered as she sat watching him. 'But my doctorate! What will I do… if I'm exposed? I may need help. But no one can be dedicated to two different gods, at the same time.' He stopped abruptly, gathered some energy and clambered upstairs. Penny stood looking speechlessly at him. When he reached his door, he searched in his bag, keeping up a stream of monologue until he rummaged his way to his keys.

The next day, against Penny's plea, Dezmond left for the campus, anxious to see Prof. Primate. On arrival at the Union, he was caught in the whirlpool of a springtime campus gossip. The story was that two men had attempted to abduct an Afro-American professor to avenge an African student of his, whom he hated so much he had vowed to block him out of LCU. The grapevine news sounded familiar. But Dezmond did not realise that he was the student in the eye of this whirlpool.

It was, however, not long before it all began to dawn on him. The numerous glances cast at him and the undue attention he was being given heightened to a bizarre dimension as he approached his advisor's office.

The professor received Dezmond calmly, as usual, signalling him to a chair in front of his table. As he was rounding off what he had been writing, Dezmond stood behind the chair, studying his advisor's mood, gauging how best to explain his long absence. He gripped the chair even more tightly as his advisor seemed far from finishing with the job at hand.

At long last, Prof. Primate dropped his pen and tapped the table. 'Now then! Sit down and just listen to this…'

'It's hard for me to prove what I've told you,' concluded Dezmond, when it was his turn to speak. 'I really don't know how I can defend myself but please, believe me. If you don't, this day will be the end of the road for me…' He went on to narrate his travails under PAID right up to the more recent three-day ordeal, the impact of which only God could tell. Prof. Primate sat back and judged every statement from Dezmond's mouth. Throughout his emotion-drenched account Prof. Alvin Primate did not so much as cough, leaving Dezmond in doubt as to how his defence was being taken.

'Dezmond, I have good news for you!' announced the advisor. 'I accept you're innocent of that dastardly visit. I know you got involved in PAID only by way of duress. I'm aware how traumatised you are, even now. What you need is sympathy, not doubt or rejection. I am still your advisor.'

Those words fell on Dezmond's ears as soothing balm. And, like a festering boil, a ball of pressure burst inside his bowels. Hot tears streamed down his cheeks as he covered his face, awash with relief. On his own part, Prof. Primate was visibly embarrassed, seeing Dezmond in such a sorry state. Not knowing what to do, he kept urging him to take courage. At last, Dezmond quietened himself and sat up again.

The professor continued, 'More than ever, I'm determined that you earn your doctorate. I've given serious thought to the whole matter. I need not go over all of that with you. But, three things you must do! Quit No. 19, Pine Avenue, soon as possible! Frankly, I've tried to keep my nose out of it all along, but now, it's got to a point I must advise against your continued stay in there. I don't care whether you're getting under the quilt with Dave's ex-wife or not, but it's time you moved. And quickly too. Secondly, make a clean break with those bad guys! Duress or no duress, go denounce their claims on you. It won't cost much to take out an ad in the campus paper and possibly two slots on air. Of course, in your own interest, you'd have to get close to the Police Department, jus' in case. Finally, and here's where I come in: choose another topic for your dissertation! We've been on that this whole spring semester so, that's not a new issue…'

Dezmond did not hear the rest of Prof. Primate's wise counsel. Each of the must-do instructions hit him like a thunderbolt, particularly the last one. As he listened, a bout of dizziness and numbness struck him and he slumped, collapsing over the table.

*

'Why are you so hard to convince?' asked Miss Frankwood for the second time since Dezmond had left her and Maazi in the living room. 'Seems I'm not communicating.'

'Madam, I agree he needs help. But I believe he's under spiritual attack. His situation requires a spiritual solution, not a psychiatrist.'

'Listen, Mazee! I'm a professional. It is very clear to me I'm wasting my time trying to make you understand. Don't be deceived the way you see him looking and sounding okay. I owe Dezmond a duty, no matter what you say! He needs reconstructive therapy, if you care to know, not more voodoo! Since leaving the ICU three days ago, his anger and distress have been persistent. I called you because I believe you're his friend. If I can't have your support, I'll handle it alone. You know I care. I'm not gonna sit back and let him crack up when I know too well what to do!'

'I'm sorry, madam,' responded Maazi. 'I didn't come to your house to upset you. I'm not here to challenge you. I'm only saying what I believe. If he's able to agree with you, well, by all means take him to a psychiatrist... That's him coming. He's not altogether out of his mind, after all. If he consents, go right ahead.'

'Do I hear something about consenting?' asked Dezmond, descending the stairs. 'A man at the crossroads! What consent can he give? It doesn't look as if he even exists. Primate has spoken. Now, it's your turn. But the real bombshell is what Primate released that day. When was this now...? Those drugs have so disoriented me I'm losing my sense of days. Penny, when was it I left the Intensive Care Unit?'

'Three days ago.' She watched him come down, every step a slow, calculated action, until he lowered himself into his seat.

'Thanks, Penny,' he said, looking endearingly at her. 'They gave me a credential for my three days at the ICU!

See? ICU? Sounds like some university!'

'What credential is that?' prompted Penny as Maazi sat, observing their interaction.

'PTS.D.! I got awarded a PTS doctorate. After just three days!'

'That's not a pleasant thing, Dez.'

'What's that, anyway?' asked Maazi, feeling left out.

'I'll tell you,' whispered Miss Frankwood.

'Go ahead and tell me now. I'd like to know. Some mental situation, isn't it?' demanded Dezmond, searching Penny's eyes with suspicion.

She hesitated then shrugged. 'It's one of these new medical terms: post-traumatic stress disorder. Just a big name for a simple condition. A little therapy and your present vision will be quickly revised, then you'll bounce back to life. That's all.'

'Life is not that simple,' Dezmond began to enunciate.

'Why d'you say that?' Penny wondered.

'It is not as clear-cut as the Prof makes it sound,' continued Dezmond, not taking notice of Penny's question, or even of the presence of the two people in the room. He seemed to be addressing a faraway situation. 'The joker is in the man's hand. A lone man cannot take the whole credit of killing a big game. But he must be recognised very well for my PTS doctorate. That's something at least! PTS.D.! Our people can reckon with that! A farmer with only water-yam in hand calls it proper yam, because that's his own yam proper. A bird in the hand is worth two in the bush! I must obey what I can among his tall orders. The simplest of them first. One more day and the psychiatrists and spiritists can come together for ecumenism...'

On and on he spoke, waxing more strongly the longer he spoke, oblivious of the two who quietly sat back and let him talk. Maazi's head was bowed in prayer. Penny concentrated on every utterance of Dezmond's, trying to tie up the many loose ends. Suddenly, the man's gaze dropped to normal eye level and he again showed an awareness of the presence of Penny and Maazi.

'Ol' boy, which one be de tallest building for dis town?' he asked Maazi, while still facing Penny.

'Beg your pardon?' asked Penny who could not figure out Dezmond's pidgin.

'The tallest building! What is the tallest building or tower in town? I know of the Empire State Building, but New York City's too far for me.'

Penny was as startled as Maazi, who was staring at Dezmond in fear and disbelief. 'Why on earth do you ask for the tallest building?' Penny cried out, alarmed.

'Not as you think!' exclaimed Dezmond with a boyish smile on his face. 'Only cowards commit suicide. I told you both I will not return home in a coffin. I only need to make a loud announcement. I need a tower and a giant gong. One more day, and I will be ready for everything... I have three bridges to cross, then Ph.D. will be added to my PTS.D.!'

There was seemingly no end to the man's rantings. As Maazi continued in silent intercession, Penny withdrew to make phone calls upstairs. After a while, she came down and prepared chocolate drinks for the three. Dezmond brushed aside her offer, accusing her of having poured a dosage of Morton's powder in his cup.

For the first time, Maazi was compelled to spend a night in 19, Pine Avenue. He prevailed upon Miss Frankwood to retire to bed only after both of them had taken turns persuading Dezmond to go upstairs. Little did Maazi sleep that night.

Chapter Eleven

Penny Frankwood, true to her promise, followed her treatment plan with compassion and discretion. She did not want questions raised about Dezmond's continued fitness for advance studies.

For his part, in order to get official backing for his prolonged absence from graduate school, Dezmond had asked for a two-week break to sort out some pressing personal problems. The most bitter of the prescriptions from his advisor was that he had to forsake all the materials gathered up for his dissertation, and begin afresh. 'The Spenglerian wheel of history: from Egypt to Egypt.' That topic had held together for him a rich collection of thoughts and gleanings from a whole year of reading towards his doctorate. That was the title of his dissertation. It had become ingrained into his brain cells and even lined his very veins, much like a terminal disease. All his efforts at divorcing himself from it only generated nightmares which drained his energies by the day.

Midway into the semester, Dezmond had not resumed his studies. As the hot summer was returning, this once vivacious young man was worsening in health. His life degenerated into one of mere existence, swinging on a pendulum of moribund depression and spasmodic bouts of hyper-activity. In the grip of death-like seizures, the man could remain frozen for hours, looking as impregnable as Aso Rock. The moment that incubus left him, he would burst into any self-exerting action which suited his immediate impulse. He would jump out of bed at dead of night, and take on a wholesale scrubbing of the house, until the crack of dawn; or he would disappear into the cold night in pyjama, jogging at random until his heart began to catch fire.

One particular weekend, as if to compensate himself for the cumulus of depression overhanging his life, he sat up for nearly twenty hours writing volumes of words which nobody else was allowed to peruse. If no activity readily came to his agitated mind, he would alight on the telephone directory and keep the unsuspecting residents of Lake City busy with strange calls. Miss Frankwood was not careful enough to notice the unusually bloated phone bill of that period. But one morning, she woke up to discover Dezmond decked in an improvised apron, furtively washing a heap of clean crockery, and cutlery. Her kitchen looked as if a gang of famished hunters had made a night-long foray into its pantry. From then on, she knew better.

*

Miss Frankwood supplemented the therapy of her visiting psychiatrist by supervising Dezmond's six-hourly medication. She also sacrificed hours of her work to engage him in sessions of psychoanalytic dialogue, which Dezmond took as normal conversation. Penny found herself sometimes delving into areas of the man's life which had been buried in the subconscious over the years. The bond between them grew as she convinced herself that she had an obligation to restore the man to stability and see him through to his cherished objective.

His manic-depressive swings aside, Dezmond's generally irritable demeanour did not deter Miss Frankwood. In the place where she used to behold a charming, handsome face full of manliness, now hung a scowling mask. Still, she bore it all, certain that his endless nightmares and irascibility were being caused by a traumatic experience which must have been inflicted on him by his black associates, compounded by the hardline attitude of Prof. Primate. Once in a while, in renewed effort to further plumb Dezmond's state of mind Penny would lead him on and on, as he sat, yielded like a lamb. Then an abrupt banging of a door, or a crashing of chinaware, and he would be completely thrown off his momentary balance. For a long time thereafter, he would remain there, only staring at every object suspiciously until it was time for another round of drugs.

Even at this stage, Laura and Junior did not know that Dezmond had such a problem. During their visits, they knew he was upstairs, most times, but was no longer available to rough-house with Junior or even share in dinner. All the same, there were enough indications in their attitudes to show that they were aware of the special attention which Mummy was now paying to Dezmond. They got hints that the rapport between Mummy and tenant had gone beyond the good-natured hospitality which was taught them in their civics lessons.

The two kids discussed their suspicions very often, and soon began to nurture a secret siblings' burden. Their behaviour began to change in the same measure. Traits of stubbornness, withdrawal tantrums, and general gruffness began to manifest themselves. Sometimes, they would cut visits without bothering to call their mother. It did not take long before their grievances ripened to a bursting point, in a rather unexpected place and time.

One evening after dinner, having just returned from the week's visit to No. 19, Pine Avenue, Laura and Dave Junior confronted their father. Though their vexation had been festering like a sore over time, they introduced the matter as abruptly as kids are wont to burst open even the most serious of their concerns. Prof. Gordon sensed that his children were up to something more than the usual tolerable mischief.

'Daddy,' started Laura haltingly, flashing a glance at Junior who was dragging his chair closer.

'Hmm.'

'Dad, could you stop reading your stuff jus' a minute, please?' insisted Laura. Junior waited patiently for his cue. Prof. Gordon lifted his face from the journal, peered frostily over his horn-rimmed glasses, and resumed his reading.

'Dad, we wanna ask you a question!' Junior announced emphatically.

'Yes.' he responded, his face still glued to his journal.

'It's a serious matter, Daddy,' Laura pressed on.

'Go ahead, Laura! My ears are right here.'

'Well then, Daddy, we wanna know when you're gonna bring mum back home!'

Slowly, Prof. Gordon put down his journal, cursing under his breath as he removed his glasses. 'Laura, dear, who are "we" who wanna raise this question?' Thrown off balance, he was stalling for time.

'Junior and I, of course,' responded Laura. Then both of them added in chorus, 'The two kids of Dr and Mrs Gordon!'

'And Penny, too, perhaps? Isn't she in on this?'

'Dad, Laura told you already.'

'Yes, of course,' came the glib response of a distracted father.

'Stop kidding, Dad!' screamed Laura, highly agitated. 'We're not babies any more! We want your answer!'

Prof. Gordon had to reckon that he had been caught in some trap. His mind set to working out how to escape. He gazed at Laura intently, trying to gauge her thoughts. How quickly she had grown! He suddenly realised he had really not been paying attention to his children, Laura particularly. It now occurred to the beleaguered father that her seemingly emotional outburst may be only the tip of an iceberg of resentment. This situation needed a cold, calculated handling.

'What did your mum say when you asked her this question?' Prof. Gordon asked tactically.

'We didn't ask her yet,' Junior queued in.

'Why not?'

'We've got to start someplace, Dad! And it happens we're starting with you.'

'You're the dad, so we picked you first,' added Junior, smiling. Prof. Gordon did not see anything to smile about as he turned on his chair to squarely face the challenge.

'Now, listen, Laura, Junior, Penny and I are divorced! You surely understand that, don't you? We're not merely separated. We're plain divorced, okay? There's no question of any one taking any one back. You've got to appreciate that. You're no more the little kids you were when it all started.'

'That's exactly the point, Dad! Whatever you say, whether you're separated or divorced, or whatever, Dave and I were not party to it. We're part of the family as much as either of you. Yet none of you asked if we wan'ed any divorce or not. We—'

'Well, it's too late, kids! Too late in the day for any smart arguments. No going back. Never! And I can tell you, Penny'll say the same thing when you ask her. She oughta.'

'How d'you know that?' The question was prompt and sharp.

'What d'you know, my littl' Laura Gordon?'

'Dad, d'you love Mum?' asked Junior, jumping down from his chair, to his father's side. 'Did you really love Mum?'

'Oh, come off it, son! Of course, I did!' he drawled, cuddling his son. 'We loved one another, I guess. Then things began to get sour… Well, you could say I had my own faults. Guess I could've tried harder. Never gave her enough time, perhaps… Didn't notice how tender and kind she could be. Until it got too late…' He went on, talking more to himself than to the children. Then, abruptly realising he was divulging too much, raised his voice. 'Now, why the deuce have you kids suddenly brought this up?'

'We want Mum home, that's why!' Junior retorted in a clear, unequivocal voice.

'We're sure you can make it up again to each other. Forgive one another. And start afresh,' Laura added, her tone now mellow with kindness. 'Daddy, y'know something?'

'What?'

'I know Mummy's missing you badly. Your marriage will work again, if you're willing to give it another chance. She cares for you. Honest, she does!'

'How d'you know that? She tell you?'

'Mummy's not the problem, Daddy dear…' She seemed poised to say more, but somehow swallowed the rest of her words. The three remained silent for a long while, as if they were reviewing their earlier utterances and thoughts. Laura and Dave expected something more from their father. On his part, he considered the whole encounter and felt he had given away too much, not knowing what other card was up their sleeves.

At last, Prof. Gordon stood up, clutching his journal. 'Laura, Junior, I understand how you feel. But, believe me, it's too late in the day. I'm free. Penny too is free to do whatever she wants with her life.'

He drew Junior nearer and kissed his head. Laura stormed away from the table but he caught her by the shoulder, kissed her on the cheek and said, 'Good night, my littl' Laura!'

Laura said not a word. Junior, however, grabbed his

father's hand and walked with him to the foot of the staircase, saying, 'Goodnight, Dad!'

'Night, son!'

'And Dad, think of Laura and me. You and Mum are free to do as you wish. But we're not free to do as we wish. Let Mum come back home, Dad!'

It was a particularly heavy-footed Dave Gordon who plodded his way up those stairs that night. He looked instantly twice his age. After a hard day's labour comes sweet sleep, says the Preacher. But not for Prof. Gordon. He tossed and turned all night long, with every word of the night's unexpected confrontation, ringing in his ears.

Dave Junior had kept his own side of his agreement with Laura that Mummy was not to be immediately told of their dinner-hour encounter with Dad. Suddenly, Laura felt she should no longer involve her brother in such a complicated adult matter which might eventually turn out to hurt him. Besides, a feeling of gender loyalty now seemed to set in. She went on to narrate that night's experience to her mother, and in turn confronted her.

'Tell me the truth, Mum,' she said. 'D'you have any love left for Dad?'

Miss Frankwood resisted this inroad into her private life, and assumed a deaf-and-dumb posture. But Laura would not let her. 'I won't answer such a question,' her mother explained, at last. 'Not even from you, sweetheart. Some things get too complex when you have to talk about them with your own kid. In some ways, it's unfair. You may be a big girl now, Laura, but you're still my baby. You'll never be big enough to be let into certain areas of your mum's life.'

'Mum, you know I'm not gonna accept that for a put-off! I'll let go for now but when you're in a better mood perhaps, we'll get back to it.'

*

It took about eight weeks of intensive medication and close care before Dezmond began to recover. In place of the harassed-looking, stony-faced ghost of himself, he gradually regained his usual form and agility. Caring for him in the circumstances in which both of them found themselves brought out the very best of the nurse in Miss Frankwood. Like Florence Nightingale, she was as hard-working as she was strong willed. And below her unruffled face hid a heart of great compassion. She had of course, known and appreciated Dezmond at his most personable and most admirable, so she did not count it a burden to nurse him back to stability so painstakingly.

The deadening effects of chlorpromazine gradually faded away, and Dezmond's bony frame, weak and shaky at first, was subjected to routine physiotherapy. On his own, he would log an extra hour, jogging on the spot in his room and up and down the stairs, building and toning up his muscles. Miss Frankwood had promptly emptied his room of books, blocking him against further stress. But, like a prisoner reduced to the stark nakedness of his cell, he resorted to painting invisible images in the vast canvas of his fertile mind.

One evening, when Miss Frankwood arrived in his room for the now reduced medication, it was a well-groomed, fresh-smelling gentleman who received her.

Two weeks before, Dezmond was hardly aware if there had been a door where he now stood. Yet, all those days of his breakdown, that was the same passage through which Miss Frankwood came and went. Often, she met him in a dreadfully doleful state, coiled up in the corner of his room, or in bed, quaking with high fever, endlessly muttering in delirium. She remembered once pulling him up and several times repeating to him a Yiddish saying, as she called it, which she wanted him to memorise: 'A joyful heart brings about good healing but a broken spirit dries up the bones.'

Now, there he stood, dressed in slacks and tee-shirt. Disconcerted, Miss Frankwood stepped back but Dezmond urged her in, excitedly announcing that he had just finished rehearsing a poem he had composed for her. Without hesitation, he began to recite it:

Spring's mine for a season
But my Penny's most fair!
Spring's the reason
Of nature's care.
Let's dare to pair
Never to despair!

The seriousness with which he rendered his poem belied the apparent triteness of its content. This was Dezmond's own way of expressing his gratitude to his nurse and lover. Childish as the words were, Miss Frankwood understood where they were coming from. She was hearing a message that lay well beyond those puerile lyrics.

Chapter Twelve

The spring semester was winding up before it began to dawn on Dezmond Adama that his mission to America was slowly beginning to slip through his fingers. His advisor's three-legged prescription, since ratified by a formal letter from the dean's office, hung over him like a verdict of death.

As for moving house, though he had not mustered enough courage to disclose his plan to Miss Frankwood, he had made up his mind to do so on a minute's notice. Bro. Maazi was zealously house-hunting for him on Niagara Falls Boulevard, nearer campus. However, as to the core problem of change of research topic, he had made no headway. All his attempts to reason out a new proposal was like kicking against a brick. Pain and frustration stalked him at every turn.

Mercifully enough, PAID froze its demands on him until such time as he had recovered and got back on stream. In the midst of so many trials, this little gesture was very significant to him as a source of respite and hope. But not for long. When he emerged virtually in the last week of semester, Prof. Primate served him a summons from the LCU Medical Board. He needed to clear himself as to his 'current psychological status'.

Meanwhile, Prof. Gordon had finally been granted a court injunction against the continued co-parenting of Laura and Dave Jnr by his ex-wife. His attorney's argument was that 'under the erstwhile custody plan, the two minors were overexposed to morally and emotionally dysfunctional influences capable of traumatising them, and subsequently endangering their well-being in the pluralistic American society.'

In the same period, Penny's brother in Bloomington, the only other family she had left, wrote her a rare one-sentence note, dissociating himself from her, for reasons which he said were obvious to every sane person.

Thus, the two occupants of No. 19, Pine Avenue were like quarantined animals, with little or no outside contact except for Bro. Maazi who called once in a blue moon to ask after Dezmond. Even then, he had curtailed his contacts, having concluded that his friend's situation called for a direct, divine visitation. When Bro. Maazi last fasted and prayed concerning him and Miss Frankwood, he came away with a clear understanding that he had dared to help the Holy Spirit convict a man of sinfulness. His zeal had made him try too hard in his own efforts to persuade Dezmond to forsake the way he was going.

Despite his regular prayers for his friend's soul, he indeed found himself to have become all too eloquent in preaching to him. Bro. Maazi repented of his sin of presumption, and asked for help never again to project his own arguments and anxieties whenever a soul was placed within his evangelising reach. He remembered how even the erudite Paul of Tarsus restrained himself from preaching to the Corinthians with the wisdom and eloquence of words, in order not to undermine the impact of the Cross of Christ. What, indeed, could be as sharp as the word of God, for cutting into the most stubborn of spirits? This Bro. Maazi had asked himself as he meditated on the matter. When next the opportunity came, he would depend only on the Spirit of truth to wield His sword of the gospel through his mouth. So it was that the next time Dezmond called to unload more of his mounting burdens, he was surprised that Maazi conversed like any other normal person, without stuffing his ears with preachy talk. No wonder that this time, when Bro. Maazi invited him to visit, he accepted without hesitation.

During that visit, Dezmond was put at ease by the seemingly ordinary kind of things that dominated their interaction. His host found a valuable way of discussing the topics that were comfortable for him, without dragging in his Jesus. It was only as he was seeing Dezmond off to the Pinto that some Bible treasures long hidden in his heart for himself, effortlessly began to flow into the conversation.

'Without Christ, we can do nothing worth anything,' he heard himself saying. 'This sounds foolish in the face of what may be seen as the real issues of life. But it pleases God to save those who believe, by the foolishness of the gospel. Yet, the foolishness of the Almighty is wiser than the wisest wisdom of men…'

Dezmond unlocked the car door, throwing himself unto the Pinto seat. His brusque motion was a far cry from the tremors of anxiety inside his heart. Even with his hands on the steering wheel, he began to pour out his soul, confessing how he had reached the end of his tether; how he would be presented to the Medical Board only to be rubber-stamped out of graduate school; how even his people back home had cut off communication; perhaps, because they had been misinformed that he had taken a white woman for wife; yet, every hour, he was discovering what exquisite, deep-seated gem that woman was made of… He thanked Maazi for his efforts at house-hunting, but wondered aloud when he would get the guts to tell Penny of his ultimatum to move.

'At this stage,' Bro. Maazi advised him, 'I don't think it's just a question of moving house. Your problem will also move with you. Jesus has been knocking at your door, saying, "If any man hear my voice, and open the door, I will come in to him, and will dine with him and he with me." Why not let Him move in and occupy the whole room of your heart? You want peace, contentment, success, and all that... But that's like climbing an iroko tree from the top. The intention of God, who alone gives these things, is that we seek first His kingdom, and its righteousness, and all other benefits will be added.'

Dezmond's hands were still resting on the wheel, his eyes peering vaguely into the void ahead of him. He cranked the engine, glanced at Bro. Maazi's calm face, and shifted the transmission lever.

'Better get going!' responded Bro. Maazi, patting his arm. 'When you get back, look up Proverbs 23:26. Think upon it, and ask God how a man can give Him his heart. I promise to keep backing you up. Ride on in Jesus's name!'

*

Dezmond was to cut off Bro. Maazi soon after. Somehow, he began to fear that the man's preaching had taken a subtle turn that rendered him restless and even more confounded in his unexplainable resistance. It was worse when he was in some predicament, and resorted to Maazi's advice to read a particular verse or passage of the Bible. Such references spoke so directly to him that each time he read them, it felt as if a hot knife was cutting through his diaphragm.

By the beginning of the long summer semester, his crises were gathering even greater momentum. His student status, under the provisions of 1–20 visa had become invalidated by his continuous absence from his study programme. There was no place to hide, no room for rest, except the same old No. 19, Pine Avenue. It was like being holed up for the day of reckoning. His only hope of revalidation lay in the outcome of the Medical Board. For weeks he waited in silent apprehension. If he scaled through, his prolonged absence would automatically be counted as a valid sick leave. In this condition, Dezmond saw himself as an endangered species of rat which had one more trap lurking somewhere within the maze, through which it must manoeuvre in its passage to the open field.

Penny became all sorts of crutches to him, looming larger than life in his disoriented state. Now, she was the fulcrum of his existence, the very compass of his floundering ship. Another time, she became his own 'clean, well-lighted spot' in the dark jungle of his American adventure.

She, in turn, began to appreciate Dezmond as a veritable anchor, forsaken as she was by every other person who meant something in her life. She discovered that beyond her noble involvement of nursing a sick friend, fate had thrown her a sacred challenge: to remould a life. She saw in it, a trust, into which vortex she had been drawn by the mysterious hand of providence. Man being such a complex entity, in her characteristic devotion to the task at hand, she found that a second life was being simultaneously remoulded and rejuvenated: her very own. Like beached stragglers in an ocean convoy, they became inseparably bonded to one another, recreating an island haven that progressively became all their own. Within the fence of their small world, all other personae, props and effects in their swelling drama quickly faded into oblivion. Peninnah and Dezmond took centre stage. Even with the violent waves of life's many storms battering them, these co-travellers moored their rugged bark to their own new-found-land. Their numerous escapades in this lovers' nest unfolded like a soap opera in which the grave and the whimsical, illusion and reality, the tragic and the melodramatic, fantasy and fact, all alike, rolled along in the white waters of their confluence. And there was no particular pattern in the flotsam...

*

'I'm losing grip on you, Dez.'

'Losing grip on myself, y'mean?'

'How d'you mean?' asked Penny, sitting up. Dezmond was lying on his bare back, not minding the lawn and the itchy sweat it was causing him.

'I wish I knew.'

Doubt was etched on Penny's face as she watched Dezmond, his skin glowing under the summer sun. 'You never let me into all those screwy things that wen' on at the Diaspora. Those guys put you on oath?'

'Remember: live 'n' let live, okay?'

When she had had her fill of the evening sun, she stood up and tried to drag along Dezmond. 'Let's go back inside, man! Maybe you can then tell me how you're losing grip on yourself.'

'I'll talk with you even here, Penny. It's a straight-line issue, really. For all we're going through, your husband hasn't exactly—'

'Ex-husband, y'mean.'

'He hasn't really forgotten you. And—' He stopped abruptly, springing to his feet. He drew closer and held her by the shoulders. 'Penny, you're so real in and around me, and yet so unreal. You're all I've got left – and, perhaps, my breath! And I'm in danger of losing even that! You're my only hold on meaning, at this very moment. D'you appreciate what I'm saying?'

Penny held his hand and gently pulled at it as she lay back on the lawn. 'Let's lie right back here. Lay your head on my tummy and try forgetting whatever you heard the kids discussing. I'm gonna lull you to sleep. I want you to be so relaxed you'll dream. And if you do, tell me. Remember, I'm your psychoanalyst, okay?'

And he did dream…

In the dream, he had gone shopping with Miss Frankwood and the children. As the foursome jostled out of the mall, each heaving a pack of purchases, Dezmond exclaimed, 'I feel like family!'

'But you are *family!' retorted Laura nudging him with her bag of groceries. 'What else is family?'*

'That's quite right, Laura,' affirmed Miss Frankwood. 'Look how we all get along together! I bet some Saturday shoppers are admiring us and thinking, Oh, what a cute family!'

'Not with Laura and Junior looking all-American like this,' argued Dezmond.

'Oh, that!' quipped Miss Frankwood. 'Just walking past, you can't be sure who's black and who's not. Ever met any octoroons?'

Dezmond looked surprised. 'Octo-what?'

'Mummy's getting very funny,' chipped in Junior, equally at sea.

'No, I'm not. Octoroon is not my creation. That's a mulatto who's only one-eighth black,' explained Miss Frankwood, smiling.

'How does that work out?' wondered Dezmond. 'I sure need a calculator!'

'I'll tell ya!' volunteered Laura. 'Say, Mummy had a white granddad and a black grandma, and I was born to she and Dad? I'd be an octoroon!'

'That's what I'd call "genematics",' joked Junior, 'Please, rattle it out once again.'

'Y'know, Dez? Some white folks out there may indeed be black but you never know by mere looks,' explained Miss Frankwood. 'They pass for white.'

'Blood's thicker than skin!' remarked Laura.

'Quite so! That's being black, technically. Says a whole lot about black blood, doesn't it?' Dezmond responded.

Suddenly, Dezmond felt many hands tapping his cheeks. He opened his eyes only to find that he had been dreaming.

⋆

Summer had overtaken Lake City suddenly. It felt rather

unnatural to have an air-conditioner whizzing gently in the room. But the temperature was so high that sleep was unbearable without it.

'This place suddenly feels like the tropics!' exclaimed Dezmond from the blues.

'Let's talk less now,' whispered Penny. 'Too much talk kills—'

'Kills what?' teased Dezmond.

'Int'rest. Creative fun. We're completely free now! We need not fear stereotypes any more, do we?'

He took a long draught of his Campari and passed her the glass.

'Dez, d'you remember when last we were like this?' she whispered.

'A whole week ago! Can't believe it! Whatever else have we been doing?'

'Have you noticed? It feels every time like the first time all over again. How about you?'

'Oh! What a brute I've been! Please, coach me on how to say such sweet things.'

'Dez, I almost heard you saying, sweet nothings! Did you mean to say that?'

'No. But if you ask me, sweet nothings have their own part in life… So will you now coach me?

'No. I'll tell you something else, this time, right in your ears because walls can hear.'

Dezmond clapped his ear to her lips and she gave him a little bite on the lobe, promptly soothing it with her fingers as she went on.

'I'm not kidding just now, Dez. But I've kept something funny to share with you… almost a year now. I wan'ed to save it for our Palmyra anniversary but I can't keep it any more.'

'Well? I'm dying of suspense!'

Dezmond waited, but she was not about to say it after

all. She just lay across his lap, gazing serenely on the ceiling. A tear fell rapidly down the side of her face but before he knew it, she had wiped it away with a stroke of her finger.

'Must be quite serious. You're looking so tense. I'm getting worried,' observed Dezmond.

'It feels funny telling you this but I think I should. D'ya know my first real taste of womanhood was at Palmyra? I'd read all about it... known all about it... but I'd never really got there. I even had shrinks and countless obs and gynaes take me apart to put me together on that count, but no luck! Oh, you should've guessed when I came, that g–l–o–r–i–o–u–s Christmas Eve!'

'Sorry, I wasn't watching. I had my own earthquake to manage. Been pent up nine months! Was like everyone to himself!'

'How come you're so exact? You keep a dirty diary?'

'No. Clean, by and large! No cancellations. No smudges or secret codes! But, come, why didn't you share this good news all along?'

'I said I'd kept it for our first anniversary. Plus, I wasn't sure if you'd understand. It might sound like stereotyping... An' that would spoil the whole fun.'

'Well, Penny, I understand. This is not one of those... So, it's been fun ever since?'

'You bet!' answered Penny, bursting into a laughter of relief. 'Each and every time since!'

'I guess that's a great aspect of compatibility that's not talked about. Some partners are outright compatible. Others have to work it out.' He shifted her off his lap and gave her a full-mouthed kiss. 'We're far-out compatible, we are!'

'You better say it loud! However, for me, it's far more than any of your big words. You made me a woman. In a way, you gave me life. You gave me expression... I love you, Dez...'

'I love you too, Penny...'

★

'Look what trouble we're in, but it doesn't seem to matter any more,' resumed Dezmond as they lay, far apart, each engaged with his or her own thoughts.

'There'll always be problems, Dez,' responded Penny in a distracted tone. 'And problems often have a way of taking care of themselves... Can you guess what my dream was?'

'How come? I'm the one who's supposed to be dreaming for you,' protested Dezmond jokingly.

'Everyone dreams sometimes. I have one this moment. Call it a daydream if you like, but I wanna be with you for as long as I'm able! How about you?'

'But we already live together! Who knows how much longer we have to wait for LCU? Only, if I should die suddenly, please have my remains boxed home. That way, my ghost will not haunt my kinsmen. Then for my memorial, plant a river birch tree on your lawn.'

'My dream's not about dying and memorials. I wanna live with you for ever; that's what.'

'Maazi tells me the oldest man ever still died at nine hundred and sixty-nine years, and was buried in his father's land.'

'Dez, talking of planting a tree, d'you remember the day I found the wilting twig of some plant hanging over my door at the Palm Motel?'

'Oh, the day I accused you of doing white fetish, and you flipped over?'

'Even then, you said you were sorry, and I forgave you. But if you wanna start it all over again, you're calling for a fight.' Getting to her feet, she stood astride, fists raised in readiness. She moved in on him as he lay defenceless and bare-bodied on the floor, and placed her bare foot on his stomach, her fists still held menacingly in readiness.

'No, I don't wanna fight. Not when you made sure you drained all my strength.'

'What?'

'No, no! Peace! No fights today, please! Just lie down beside me, and let's talk. Remember all the stuff we ever wanted to talk about? Now we have time on our hands to bring them back again, and exhaust everything,'

'Just a minute!' She dashed to the place where she kept potted plants and reappeared with a fresh sprig of mistletoe. 'Now, this is the love plant I tried to show you in winter.'

'Love plant?' he asked, sitting up to examine it closely. 'Where's the flower that says it?'

'No flower. You're supposed to kiss the damsel you find under this plant. I think a Palm Motel housekeeper was pulling a practical joke on us, hanging a dead mistletoe on my door-way.'

'What an ignoramus I was!'

'Don't you have mistletoe in Nigeria?' She sat on the floor beside him.

'Maybe it's wasting in forests all over the place. But we have our own Arcadian trick. More direct than hanging leaves around hotel rooms!'

'Dez, you're talking like a book again! What's "Arcadian"?' She was now lying prone across him. When she turned her head, she pressed her ear hard on his stomach, creating a titillating suction sound.

'I thought you were Anglo-Saxon…' said Dezmond, teasing.

'Yes. That's why I know when not to sound like a book. Where d'you get such a weird old word from any way?'

'Old school vocab. We used to cram exercise books full with new words for every situation. Sometimes, just for showing off!'

'So, what's "Arcadian"? I know an arcade, but I can't see

the link.'

'Means simple, get-down, countryside stuff.'

'All righ'!' she exclaimed, giggling. 'If I should ever have to plant a river birch for you, I'll also remember it was you who taught me Arcadian!'

'Another memorial!'

'Hey! Why d'you keep thinking memorial? D'you expect you'll die soon?'

'No. I don't know, rather... Anyone can die, soon. We should all be thinking that way more often, if you ask me.' He looked dead serious.

'Let's leave that one alone for now. Tell me, what's the Nigerian substitute for mistletoe?' she asked, switching the subject.

Bent on teasing, Dezmond cleared his throat and grinned. 'Again, it's a question of cultural relativism!'

'You can jolly well say that all over again! In spoken English!' Penny protested, boxing him lightly on the lips. 'Really, Dez! Since you're quite clear in your thinking what you wanna say, and I'm sure you are, why d'you have to use such jaw-breakers? Mischief, isn't it? Listen, arcade or Arcadian's enough for one night. So what simple thing were you trying to Arcadianise this time?'

'Oh, wow! You're coming on pretty strong!' exclaimed Dezmond, as they slapped each other's hands and laughed together. 'All right! We don't substitute anything for mistletoe. But we have our own equivalent that's just as good. Maybe even better from our point of view! But that's really not it. So long as the equivalent serves the same purpose, that's it. I'm trying to explain cultural blah-blah. That's my area of bull-shootin', if you like!'

'Dez, I demand decency!'

'Oh, my apology, Lady Peninnah! As I was trying to explain, the white lover has his mistletoe. Back home, the boys simply stick a fresh green stick of broom in a juicy piece of fruit and offer it to the girl of their heart! Not the cutest, but says a whole lot!'

'What stops girls from doing just that?'

'Well, it would be very odd indeed. Beside, they don't chase openly. Not like here where a broad can walk up to a dude and declare her crush, point-blank. Even in that, we're yet a third-world people!'

'Well, you watch out for me! I'm taking notes. Some day, I'm gonna lead a women's revolution in Africa!'

That night, Penny presented Dezmond with a plum apple with three dental picks stuck in its top.

Chapter Thirteen

In six weeks of being practically ostracised, Miss Frankwood limited her services to clients who called to request special or urgent attention. She had informed them that she was on a prolonged holiday to make up for a backlog of annual leave. As for Dezmond, once a week he made pilgrimage to the Graduate School, or called Prof. Primate, to no avail. Apparently there was no decision yet to communicate. He kept hoping that, with the spirited defence he had put up before the board, he would be cleared of all blame, and be set free to complete his study programme. He took the time of waiting as a grace period for attempting a new research proposal that would satisfy his advisor and every other member of the dissertation panel.

Penny had been going to the grocery shop alone during that time, but one evening she asked Dezmond to accompany her. The liberty of the summer air loosened their spirits from the inwardness of the withdrawal which had been imposed on them by a combination of forces. This outing provided opportune time to digress from themselves for a change.

'Remember that evening Dave came for the kids?' asked Penny as she sat in the car outside McDonald's. Both she and Dezmond were having double-decker sandwiches and a shared cup of vanilla milk shake for a treat.

'Yeah. What happened?'

'You should tell me, Dez. Junior was darn sure there was some kind of face-off.'

'Who with? Me?'

Penny nodded.

'Really, I see... Was that what your son was calling a cockfight or something? As for as I know, it didn't really go to the extent of being called a face-off.'

'You saw Dave anyway. How did it go?' asked Penny, taking another bite and trying to snatch the plastic cup from Dezmond.

'Well, when he rang the bell, I was right there. So I opened the door and lo, there was your husband!'

'Ex-husband, Dezmond!'

'Your ex-husband, sorry again! He was a bit surprised, naturally. I couldn't pretend I'd not seen his face somewhere before. Our eyes certainly jammed, as we say back home. He looked me over, y'know, like a slave on the block—'

'Dez!' scolded Penny, 'that's not nice!'

'Okay, looked me over like, and said, "hi!". I too said, "hi!" and stepped back in without turning.'

'Did you imagine he had a pistol or something?'

'You kiddin'? Could've brought a whole sub-machine gun or a jackknife, if you ask me! Men have been blasted for mere peanuts! The guy's motive would be pretty obvious, should he blow out my brains. But God forbid it!'

'Yuk, Dez! I can't imagine it!' she exclaimed, shuddering.

'Anyway, thank goodness! Laura appeared quickly enough. In a minute – what a relief – they were gone!'

'Now, here's why I brought back the story,' explained Penny, placing the drink on the dash-board. 'The drama was only just beginning the time Dave drove off.'

'Oh yeah?'

'Now, you bite your hamburger. I'll give you a lowdown on it... On their way to Williamson, Laura opened up a discussion with her father. I don't know the whole detail but it wen' on till dinner. At table, the kids ganged up and demanded from Dave, if he loved me, if he ever loved me, and stuff. He said he wasn't sure where they were coming from, an' he fenced a whole lot. Laura looked him in the face and asked if he had any love left for Mum and all that. Know what he said? Laura quoted his exact words to me. Something like, "Maybe, it's just human… I'm a little jealous, but, only for the sake of you kids… Never reckoned Penny could be so kind and tender. Guess I didn't care enough… Strange, but I'm happy for her, believe me. Only we couldn't get on that well…"'

Dezmond had since stopped chewing. 'I kind of feel really sorry, even guilty,' he said. 'Penny, why are you telling me all this? I kind of feel, well, bad…'

'What about? How about me? And you? Who cares about my own side of the story? D'you notice that since his goddam court order, none of the kids has even called? I know he jus' won' let them! So, here's Peninnah Frankwood, mother of two adolescents! Dave's making it look like it's another womb that bore them. Imagine Professor David Gordon talking of protecting anybody! I think it's time I turned the hose on him! I'm gonna see my attorney! It was I who said I hated legal hassles, but righ' now, I'm ready to rock the boat real good! Dave Gordon isn't gonna take away my children on some spooky grounds of his goddam protection against God knows what!'

'No need, Penny,' Dezmond cautioned, his eyes gazing thoughtfully at the windscreen. 'Just, don't you worry. After the storm comes a clear sky. Don't overwork your emotions.' They abandoned their snacks altogether. Their eyes roved all over the parking lot but their thoughts centred on their situation. Who could fathom the nature of the imminent storm when the clouds had only just begun to gather? From the look on his face, this was what Dezmond seemed to be asking himself after all.

'I have every cause to worry, you understand? I worry about you and Penny Frankwood. I worry particularly about my boy,' remarked Penny, looking vaguely into space.

'Junior? Why?'

'That kid's got too much of his father in him. He's developing a resentment. Hateful when it manifests. And now, being that close to Dave can only worsen his little temper.'

'Poor Junior! I miss my main man! Been long we shot basket together. Las' time they came, I could hardly move a limb.'

*

The months flew quickly past. Summer ended. Autumn came and went. Then came another winter, the season of hibernation of seed life. With winter emerged a forest of potted plants in a corner of the living room of No. 19, Pine Avenue. One day, Dezmond trundled in under the weight of his winter gear, and saw Penny fixing up a large wooden cupboard. A thick sheet of cellophane was spread on the floor, covered with debris.

'Another part of the real Penny, eh?'

'What?' she asked, without looking up.

'How did a forest surface in our living room?'

She pushed her pliers back into her apron's kangaroo pocket.

'Meet some more members of the family,' she chanted with girlish relish. 'Oh, I'd love the tropics, I'm sure! Over there, there's real sunlight. Poor Janice, ever-wandering,' she scolded, separating two plants whose tendrils had got entwined. 'This one's the most jealous of them all!'

'Really? Is that possible?' asked Dezmond, striving to cultivate instant interest. 'I see you're very devoted to plants as well. They must have a way of loving you back, I imagine?'

'Janice'll soon bloom,' she continued, ignoring Dezmond's teasing. 'If she's not petted and talked to for even two days she gets schizophrenic! Flora and fauna are pretty close in nature, y'know?'

'Amazing!' observed Dezmond as he treaded her steps around the pots and plants. 'But where would men run to, if these shrubs should suddenly turn into little nagging women, for instance.'

'Worse, if they suddenly turned into snarling little men! Come round this side,' she directed. 'See these cuttings? They're Mexican. They're called Aztec Queens. Now, this one… you'll love her! Tessy of Harlem! Pinched her shoot from a rip-off plant shop three years ago! It's my souvenir of our first and only weekend in Big Apple. I got Dave to engage the shop-keeper in a chat while I went snipping. That's about the only little adventure we ever had together! Tessy's much happier here, though, than in crazy New York City.'

Dezmond followed resignedly, hands folded behind as Penny carried on her inspection and roll-call: Lazy Lizzy, Wandering Jew, Spring Dew, the Begum's Fan… As they meandered between the plants, Penny would nip off a yellowing leaf here or realign a climber there, while narrating a background story or a bit of joke concerning one or the other. How can this woman have a soft spot left in her bosom for anything else on earth? Dezmond wondered. Penny looked up and somehow read something in the pinched contours of his face. 'Say it out, whatever you're thinking,' she ordered.

Dezmond was a little embarrassed. 'How come? I never knew you're a mind-reader?' he asked.

'A hurting heart hears even what's not spoken. Don't you understand the power of emotional injury?'

Miss Frankwood suddenly weaved her steps out of the thicket of plants, and began to twist and wiggle seductively round and round the living room, like a Brazilian belle possessed by the nymphs of the samba. 'Once the mortgage's cleared,' she chanted, as she swirled round Dezmond, slowing down to a more graceful tempo, 'we'll be free! Free to fly to Florida! Or sell this place and elope to Arojee. I'd love to take wings with a man who asks questions! A man who talks... a man whose face shows the inside of his heart! Fly with me, Dez dear!'

She kept up that languid tempo with a silent song, intermittently glancing over her shoulder, as if soliciting some response.

'How about the children?' mumbled Dezmond barely audibly. Penny froze on a step and searched his face.

'I know your fear!' she sang, resuming her waltzing as abruptly as she had stopped it. 'I've borne children. And, if you wish, there's more to bear! Neither black nor white! Nor octoroon! But *café-au-lait* and winsome! Let's fly to Florida! And dream fresh dreams together! Let's dare to pair, remember? Never to despair!'

The waltzing died down and Penny bobbed to Dezmond who stood there helplessly, perhaps trying to decipher this new bout of ballet.

'Now, what's on your mind?' Penny quizzed as she stepped right up to Dezmond, standing gingerly on her toes to better reach up to him.

'Nothing. Just turning one thought round and round... An adult mind should never just be blank, should it?'

'Stop jivin', Dez! As far as I'm concerned, I've got no pride left to protect! We've got nothing left! Except one another! How much longer can we go on like this?'

She stood there highly agitated, her bosom heaving under her folded arms, waiting for Dezmond...

*

For the first anniversary of Palmyra, Penny and Dezmond booked the very same chalets they had used the previous year and set out to re-enact their former tryst.

'Well, Dez, two weeks ago I said Florida,' explained Penny over their Christmas Eve drinks. 'Now it doesn't have to be exactly Florida. That's just my own idea how to begin to get used to the tropics! I've read quite a bit about Nigeria, the equatorial rainforest, the people's culture, and stuff.'

'Which of the people, Penny? You're still daydreaming, dear. You don't know what you're talking about!'

'Now look who's talking!' she exclaimed as she all but dropped her half-empty wineglass on the table. 'I don't know what I'm talking about? Someone's white-mailing perhaps, as you'd say?'

'No, no, Penny. I know when you're not joking.'

'Then what are you talking about? We've never had one glass too many, have we?' she asked sneeringly.

'Listen, Peninnah!' Dezmond breathed firmly through his teeth as he sprang up from his seat and grabbed her shoulders. 'I love you! You know I do! I even dreamed of marriage. Because I love you! Plus, the way things are… Indeed, what else is left for you and me? But then, I reconsidered the whole thing afterwards. Penny, when push comes to shove, you'll find it's not another safari! I'm telling you, when you get closer, when the nitty-gritty of all this catches up with us, it's going to be something else.'

Dezmond let go of Peninnah, turned his back, and paced to the window overlooking the wide lawns. Exactly a year ago, he had stood out there amidst adorable snowflakes. Instinctively, he drew the curtain railings aside and stood watching the interplay of tinsel and lights. The candlelight behind distorted his silhouette on the glass window which, in the absence of snow, presented him with a bare, steel-faced earth. Snowflakes were nowhere in sight, but what did it matter? He suddenly felt foolish to have ever imagined that he could become one with the phenomenon called winter. Worse still, with Peninnah Frankwood... As he stood reordering his thoughts, he felt Penny's closeness behind him and gently turned.

'Listen, Dez, the pressure's telling, isn't it? On both of us, that is. I'm sorry the way I spoke. Let's forget it for now. We'll know how to cross the river when we get there.'

'No, Penny. We've got to that river already. I've got to be crazy to imagine we could get married.'

'Oh! You just realised that? How much crazier can anybody get? We might as well go gung-ho into it, and damn it! Whoever sang that song may be a rock, but I ain't! I'm in love, Dezmond! And the best thing I ever heard was when you told me you love Peninnah Frankwood.'

'Penny, I meant it. But ever since, I've not had any peace.'

'How d'you mean, may I ask?' she blurted out, emphasising each word as she stood, her arms akimbo.

'Penny, I love you too much to take you home. You must try and understand this. I don't know how to get you to see what I mean.'

'I sure didn't get that!' remarked Penny turning round him and peering closely into his eyes. 'You wanna say that again?'

'All of last week, I couldn't sleep. The whole implication of marrying you, taking you to Nigeria. It's simply crazy! You don't know what it means, Penny. I cannot stand the thought of what you'll suffer. Oh no! More so, as Aroji will hold you responsible for whatever happens to their son...'

She allowed him to let off steam, then gently took his hand and led him back to his seat. It was almost midnight.

'Happy Christmas!' she said, smiling.

'Happy Christmas!' he responded, lifting his glass. 'To Penny and our reality!' She lifted her glass and put it on her lips but did not respond to the toast. She rather mumbled something and quickly turned her face away from Dezmond's gaze as a teardrop rolled into her wine.

'You didn't hear my toast.'

'I did. But I'd taken a sip that went the wrong way.' She cleared her throat and added, 'How did you want me to respond to that kind of toast, anyway?'

They sat speechless for over a quarter of an hour, as if they had exhausted their conversation.

'Been a long day!' sighed Penny finally as she stood up, stretching her lithe frame. 'You're hosting, Dez. And I'm all yours! Let's leave the future and live one day at a time!'

'Live and let live!' added Dezmond taking her hand.

*

'What came over you, Penny?' he asked later.

'Why? Some'n gone wrong? I'm having a swell time, as ever!' she said, snuggling even more closely.

'Is that why you were shedding tears? Never seen someone drink wine diluted with tears.' The joke fell flat.

'Didn't know you noticed,' replied Penny, not a bit amused.

'Sorry. I didn't know how to handle it,' said Dezmond, soberly. 'There's no way we can survive!'

'Well, it's not exactly that. I sure felt bad. I felt sick,' Penny told him. 'I wan'ed to throw up, the way you went about it. Still feel bad. But you know I have a good fighting spirit. I'll respond yet... That tear rolled down when the words of a Sunday school drama suddenly came to my lips... Well, you're not a great Bible buff, same as I, but you must've heard the beautiful story of Naomi and her sons' widows?'

'Oh, em... sounds familiar,' lied Dezmond.

'Well, I acted the part of Ruth... It's amazing that I spoke those wonderful lines twenty some'n years ago... "Don't plead with me to leave you, or return to Moab. I will follow wherever you go, and live wherever you live... Your people shall be my people, and your God, my God... Where you die, will I too die, and there will I be buried."'

Her voice faded off as she re-enacted those lines much in the same childlike tone of innocence in which she had spoken them those many years past. She shuddered violently in Dezmond's arms like someone struck suddenly by a fit of fever. She barely got to the last word before she burst into an uncontrollable flood of tears, even as she broke off and rushed into the wash-room.

Chapter Fourteen

'Gillepsie's Take Away, East-side Lake City,' read the signboard, hanging by chain above the entrance. The place was filled with blacks, Latinos, Chicanos, and a coterie of whites. A cluster of hamburgers sizzled on the grill, filling even the customer's hall with a lot of smoke. As Dezmond stepped in, an oily-faced man of baronial dimensions emerged, pointing aggressively in his direction.

'Watch out! The nigger's nuts!' shouted the man. 'Maybe searching for some white broad out here! Big deal for blackie!'

'One submarine, please, without onion rings,' ordered Dezmond, disregarding the many eyes that were trained on him. 'For takeaway.'

'What? This carcajou wanna tuck in a dollar fifty worth of sub? Who's gon' slave for Sambo here, sucker?' raged the fat man, his stomach quaking above his tight belt.

'Easy, Gary! You're really at your worst today,' shouted a female voice behind the counter.

'Cut the crap, woman! I ain't talking to you! That guy stinks! An' if a he-goat stinks regular time, how much more when he's on heat?' The crowd just stood watching from the queue as big Gary shook all over with laughter. A foot-long sandwich was speedily wrapped and passed over the counter.

'One sub here, to go! Dollar fifty, please!'

As Dezmond reached out to the white lady at the cash register, big Gary grabbed the wrap from her and stuck it out. 'Come 'n' geddit, Boy Sambo!' he shouted with a mean sneer on his fat face.

'Who's he talking to, lady? Where I come from, I'm nobody's boy. Just refund me my money!'

As Dezmond stretched out his palm for his money, in place of the foot-long that Gary had stuck at his face, there mysteriously appeared the nozzle of a pistol! To Dezmond's shock and utter confusion, the white man who stood feet astride, behind that gun, undeniably turned into Dave Junior, larger than life-size! For a hazy moment, it looked clear to Dezmond that his friend, Junior was about to throw him a basketball. But, before Dezmond could shout his name, a shot exploded, throwing the packed hall into stampede...

Dezmond shuddered violently on the bed to which he had been strapped. Panting, he opened his eyes and glanced all round him. One side of his face was covered with gauze and plaster. The bullet had grazed his maxillary, leading to much blood loss before the first-aid people got to him. He had been in shock ever since he was rushed to the Erie County Hospital, and intermittently, for three days, he kept shuddering and screaming in his nightmares.

Bro. Maazi had stuck by his side, having fought a running battle with the nurses who insisted that their patient be left alone. At last, thanks to his importunate pleadings, he was permitted to talk to him the day he was taken out of the emergency room.

'Where am I?' demanded Dezmond, trying in vain to turn.

'Erie County. No cause for alarm,' Maazi assured him. 'You're okay now. God took charge. Just take it easy.'

Dezmond slowly lifted his right hand and felt round his head. Was this one of those nightmares?

'Man, we have reason to praise God for evermore! It was a miracle!' Maazi suddenly lowered his voice to a whisper as the next patient stirred restively to signal that he was being disturbed. 'The bullet just missed your brains.' He put a small mirror before Dezmond's face while looking out for the nurses. 'Just a stitch or to two settled it. Praise God for his mercies!'

'Amen!... Maazi.'

'Hmm?'

'Was my face stitched?'

'Just a little tear or something. The nurses wouldn't answer my questions. But you're all right.'

'I thought I'd died... Incredible! I saw how I was covered up on a stretcher. They were taking me to the morgue.'

'No, I guess you were in a state of shock.'

Dezmond looked wan, his lips pale and caked up. Even tea he would not drink, until Bro. Maazi scolded and cajoled him into taking a few sips. He did not have enough strength to talk. But he knew that Maazi would not be allowed to keep him company for long. Yet nobody else would clear his confusion as to what exactly had happened. He therefore summoned all the strength he could, in between splitting head pains, to interview his friend.

'Was it really Junior?'

'Am afraid, yes.'

'Oh, my God! Oooh!' moaned Dezmond, squirming under throbbing pain. Maazi turned his back and let him relieve himself.

'Maazi,' whispered Dezmond when he had calmed down. 'They found him?'

'He didn't run. Too shocked himself. Seems he fell down in shock, right there.'

'Where did it happen?'

'Oh, right there in the house. Nineteen, Pine.'

'Nineteen, Pine? But—'

'You'd only been dreaming all kinds, I guess. The nurse told me you think it happened at a restaurant some place... Well, some neighbours immediately called the police. That time, Miss Frankwood wasn't home.'

'Yes, how's she?'

'She is okay now. At first, she was devastated.'

'Where's she?'

'She and Prof. Gordon are helping the law enforcement guys.'

'Poor Penny! What a mess!'

'Bo, just thank God for His mercies-o!'

'I do, Maazi. But, pity her too… She'll be worse off than myself,' said Dezmond, his chest heaving. 'That woman loves me. She saw me at my best… and at my worst. See? Yet she stood by me. What else is love, Maazi?'

'I beg you, Dezmond. Don't overstretch yourself.'

'How's Junior?'

'He was in the LCU clinic initially, but his mum phoned to say he's to see a child psychologist.'

'Where on earth did he get that gun?'

'Dez, don't bother yourself about all that just now. Get strong first of all. Then you may ask all the questions you want. All the pieces will fit together. For now, just rest… Try and put your mind off the whole thing. Be thanking God for preserving you. Now, here comes the nurse! She won't let me stay another minute. So, let's pray…'

From real life to dream and back to life, whatever is deemed to be real life! Who can draw the dividing line? Maazi hesitantly made his way out of the ward.

*

Preliminary investigations were quickly concluded, pointing to the obvious: Dave Junior and Prof. Gordon, owner of the .45 calibre pistol, would be facing charges. Miss Laura Gordon, Miss Frankwood, and Mr Dezmond Adama, would be key witnesses. Meanwhile, Junior and Prof. Gordon were granted bail, awaiting the full recovery of the lead witness from advanced trauma. On its own part, the African Students' Association staged a peaceful sit-in on the Graduate School grounds, in solidarity with Dezmond.

Similarly, Protect Afrika in Diaspora issued a press release in protest against 'the white system's well-orchestrated plot to break, and ultimately eliminate a present-time asset, and a future leader of the African nation.'

★

On his next visit three days later, Maazi was delighted to see a much brighter Dezmond propped up in bed and browsing through a magazine. The whole atmosphere around him was spick and span, with his personal effects neatly stacked up on the bedside locker. The nurses too, showed greater warmth and looked ready to allow the visitor all the time he wanted to stay with his friend.

'Ol' boy!' greeted Maazi offering a handshake. 'You look clean 'n' cool today!'

'I just t'ank God, Bro! T'ank you too, my broda!'

'Me? Wetin I do for you? I beg, don't give me what belongs to God. His other name is "Jealous", you no know?'

'God? How can?' demanded Dezmond, shifting his body. 'Any way, dis place na hospital. Let's leave dan one for now.'

'Well, as you want. But I'm not about to preach,' explained Maazi. 'Your blood pressure is high enough without me worsening it!'

'Boh! Sit down and gist me. What's happening, man?' asked Dezmond, tapping the bed. 'What's going on? Any bombshell from Primate an' 'im people? Any CJC with news of Nigeria? And, how about Penny? You see am for me?'

'*Haba*, Dezmond!' reacted Maazi, almost shouting. 'Which is which? Which one d'you want me to answer? After all, you've been away only ten days, not so?'

'Ol' boy kookoo, try understan' now,' pleaded Dezmond.

'But I understand! That's why I'm here.'

'Okay. How every tin?'

'Every tin fine, believe me!' retorted Maazi.

'Not to worry, you hear? All will be well with you,' he added, placing his palm on Dezmond's shoulder. 'The most important thing now is, get strong and get out of here. Okay?'

'Yeah...' sighed Dezmond absent-mindedly. 'That's my real fear right now. Getting out to face the truth...'

'I guess you're right. But what can you—? Will you kill yourself because of a Ph.D.?'

'Not that, Maazi,' explained Dezmond, lifting up his head. 'It's something else now.' He gasped, and letting his body drop back onto the bed, added, 'Well, you've said it all. I won't kill myself for any Ph.D.... That's past and gone for ever, I tell you.'

'Dezmond, What exactly d'you mean?'

'I'm up against something else... Another ugly reality's confronting me right now. But this one I will overcome!'

'What're you talking about?'

'This is the end of my road, Maazi,' pleaded Dezmond. 'Thank God, you've stood by me though we sometimes differed. But it's now I need you, more than ever. Somehow, I know you've been praying for me. Please, stay by me... don't stop praying.'

He sat up on the bed, tucking the pillow between the wall and his lower back. After ten days of dedicated regimen, he was fast regaining his stability. It would not be long before he would be discharged.

'Bro. Maazi,' continued Dezmond, 'can you count how many times you've heard me boast that I would not leave America a dead man?'

'Well, Dez, you won't die! You will live to glorify the name of the living God.'

'Amen! But listen. Now, I'd rather die in this land than

stand in court to testify against Junior and his Dad! I can never imagine doing that to Penny. She has suffered everything for my sake, and stood by me all through.'

'You may be right. But how will you escape it?'

'I've thought about it, and sorted it all out. But I need your help, Maazi. I've decided to, well, that's right. Escape!'

'Escape to where?'

'Back home to Nigeria! Soonest! And that's where you come in. Aroji elders say that shame does not chase a man right into his home. Bro. Maazi, I hope I'm not making you sin… Please, do me this one last duty as a friend and countryman.'

'What exactly are you up to?'

Dezmond pulled Maazi nearer himself and, in pidgin, took time to let him into his master plan. 'I t'ink you see am?' he concluded at last. 'Bro., help me, for God sake!'

★

Three days later, County Immigrations Office received a computer printout from an informant, exposing the illegal status of some foreigners, among them, one Dezmond Adama…

Meanwhile, Dezmond had taken leave from ECH, giving Clement's Hostel as his new address, although all his belongings had been moved to Maazi's place. On the second day of his parole, two men, ostensibly immigration officers, one white, the other Afro-American, found their way to Maazi's place without forewarning, dressed in slacks.

The paleness of early winter pervaded Niagara Falls Boulevard.

For obvious reasons, and so as not to attract the curiosity of student neighbours, the only luggage Dezmond wanted to take along were a briefcase and his Olympia portable typewriter.

To Bro. Maazi, the action reel was rolling all too fast. Regardless of his foreknowledge, there had not been time enough to readjust his mind to the reality of his friend's decision.

Impulsively, he raised a fist-full salute, his head bowed solemnly as Dezmond was being led to an unmarked car. Gloom overhung the whole house while he stood on the steps watching, as if he was not sure how real the scene was.

Bailey Street off Main... the car slowed down as it approached the overhead sign, pointing to Lake City International Airport.

'Here we are!' announced the driver.

'Yeah, baby!' affirmed the black officer. Then, turning to his colleague, added in whisper. 'Far as we're concerned, this is for real!'

*

The two officers shoved Dezmond rather briskly along, to the check-in desk of Pan Am Airlines.

'Why those strange glances?' Dezmond asked them aloud, not having spoken since he entered the car.

'Who's glancing?' asked the Afro-American officer.

'Do I appear that weird?'

'Keep movin''!' ordered the white officer.

'Why all this? Am I nuts?'

'Dunno!' replied the white officer, gently nudging him forward. 'You make sense to me.'

'But once you're said to be nuts, who can unsay it?' reasoned Dezmond.

'Right!' agreed the black officer. 'Yo' word 'gainst everybody else!'

'More likely, you get thrown into some loony house... Far as I'm concerned, you're okay, guy. But, right now, you're a non-legit resident under deportation order. You're being quit on account of your expired 1–20, remember? Got your letter of deportation?'

'Oh sure! This one's the best you ever did,' whispered Dezmond.

A lanky six foot two, with a well-carved goatee with moustache, and exuding an aura of command, Dezmond stood out among the milling crowd. He moved on calmly with an air of gravity stamped on his matinée idol face. His black trousers, with his crew-cut hair, added mystique to his presence. He seemed to float through space as he walked thoughtfully through the exit tube to the departure lounge.

Just before take-off, the two officers walked into the cabin and led their man to his seat. They hung around without arousing any curiosity, leaving seconds before the door was slammed.

Dezmond would place his valuable luggage nowhere else except on his lap. His eyes moved from one type of co-traveller to another, with his ever-bubbling imagination generating images and sounds deep within him.

Occasionally, through the window, his eyes would pan the sky and focus on the bleak horizon of industrial Lake City in winter. When he gazed long enough, he would spot a plane emerging from where the sky seemingly touched ground, now looking like a pinball, now burgeoning in size, and finally nosing toward the very window through which he was viewing.

Thirty-five minutes after boarding, the Boeing 737 took wing, piercing through the air as the wan sun flirted with amoeboid clouds. It soon stabilised to the smooth level at which the intercom crackled to herald the next announcement: lunch would shortly be served, and thereafter, passengers would be treated to a film show entitled, *Bwana's Odyssey*. Stereophones were available for hire at three dollars apiece.

Something about a lissom lady across the aisle from his seat suddenly caught Dezmond's attention.

'Doreen, of course!' he burst out, after desperately racking his memory. Impulsively, the lady turned, and her face flushed red with embarrassment. It seemed she had long noticed him, but kept her face inclined away from that side.

'Doreen, remember Clark's Gym, the night of the African Stars soccer binge?' Doreen could have been a cast-iron statue in spite of all the attention from Dezmond. 'Not even a glance! Is this Doreen?' he exclaimed.

He undid his seat belt and sprang into the aisle. 'It's you all right! Why d'you pretend so? Where's Okelo's boy, Doreen? Who told you Big Daddy Idiot eats mulattos? Okelo said you're scared of leopards and hyenas? But they're no more in Africa! Go look in your parks and nature museums...'

It took a cabin steward and a man in the lady's row to prevail on Dezmond to return to his seat.

Lunch was served and cleared, and the earlier atmosphere of stillness became increasingly boisterous, with some passengers chatting; others were heading to the washrooms; and there were trolley loads of ostensibly duty-free drinks, cigarettes and perfume for interested buyers. In the midst of the traffic, the promised film was showing on screens suspended from the aeroplane's roof, at intervals all the way down the fuselage. The spectacular scenes soon caught Dezmond's eyes, though he had not previously shown interest. Without a stereophone to monitor the soundtrack, he found sport in observing the pictures, decoding body movements and reading lips.

Evidently, the background to *Bwana's Odyssey* was an exotic saga about an East African safari. On the screen, a hoard of jaunty-looking Masai would emerge, with their inevitable weapons of manhood resting on blanket-draped shoulders. They were showing their ivory-coloured teeth to the lone bwana, who was costumed like old Stanley in white shorts, white shirt, and a white peaked helmet to boot.

'May I have your attention, please!' announced Dezmond at the top of his big voice. The passengers within reach of his voice turned to his direction, and immediately turned back to their various concerns. A few amused ones gave him some attention, for what it was worth.

'There was once an era of shining enamel which was proof positive of the pacification of problem natives by *Pax Britannica*...' he recited, periodically pausing for breath and inspiration, as it were. 'To the simple subjects of a declining empire, archives and museums boost morale. A senile patriarch never stops reminding everyone of the dead days of his own virile manhood. White man needs to animate, rather, to immortal-animate his colonisation prowess. His great motivator is celluloid technology, which transforms heady natives into modern men! The mirror, the pinhole, the Polaroid, and the screen... they line the road from native self-assertion to serfdom... But Britannia is over! This is the era of *Pax Americana*! The wheel will turn right back to Egypt, where it started.'

He paused to study the screen. A group of people, adults and adolescents alike, was herding around a blonde tourist in a local market place. As if provoked by their wild, fawning behaviour, Dezmond turned away. Stretching across the passenger by the window, he pushed up the window shade. The wing of the plane was shining its path serenely through the clear heavens. When the dance of the sun's rays on metal became too dazzling for his eyes, he excused himself, and pulled down the shade.

On a fresh impulse, he suddenly got up, and launched into a headcount of the passengers, turning round and round where he stood, craning his neck to get the furthest possible view.

'My straying eyes see you passengers even as luggage,' he muttered to himself. 'In the underbelly of this ship, each of you has an identity strapped to a piece of ownership. Identity and ownership, I… my… mine… cupidity… a straining toward territory, promotion, doctorate. We all have babies sitting inside… Imagine eighteen adults in an elevator, erect as celery stalks, facing the exit, decidedly dumb, and each minding his or her own body odour…'

For the second time, the purser approached Dezmond and again persuaded him to sit down and allow others to enjoy their flight. He swallowed the purser's winsome look, and quietly complied. He then reclined his seat, apologised to each of the passengers on his row, and pulled a blanket over himself for a much-needed sleep…

The plane continued to cruise, as if completely suspended on a keel of foam. Steadily it swished through the firmament, with intermittent tremors and ripplings. Now it seemed to waver slightly, then tip a little… The descent had started, down through the clouds, with pressure building. The lights flicked on, flooding the cabin with life. Then the tinkling intercom again, announcing the final approach to Ikeja International Airport. As the undercarriage dropped with a thudding noise, Dezmond awoke, startled. The pressure of his seat belt jolted him back to himself as he attempted to jump up.

The window by his side was not, after all, the sky-view attic window of No. 19, Pine Avenue he had been dreaming about. This was flight WT094, from Lake City via J.F. Kennedy Airport, New York City, to Lagos. He excitedly pulled up the plastic shutter, sticking his nose to the window as if in a hurry to catch the scent of his fatherland. In the available light, all he could recognise in the Lagos night were the brackish waters of the lagoon, looking like a colossal raft run aground.

After his continuous self-exertion in flight, for the last three hours he had been over-powered by an other-worldly slumber, in which he found himself treading again the long, rugged sea-shore of his life's voyage.

Part Two

When a thing goes bad,
it goes bad unto its owner.

An Idoma proverb

Chapter Fifteen

Once upon a time in the whole district of Aroji, there was not a soul who could decode the written language of the white man. The nearest barely literate letter-writer-cum-translator was the same old sole teacher at Adupi Village School, ten miles' trekking distance away.

Modern times crawled in, and the blind eyes of Aroji people began to open. Thanks to their God-given palm produce, Aroji adults taxed themselves and handed the proceeds over to the Holy Ghost Fathers to establish St Joseph's Church and School. Soon, some families were able to boast of boys who could write and interpret letters received from far and near. The pilgrimage of letter-writers to Adupi gradually came to an end.

However, telegrams remained a dreadful phenomenon to handle, much the same as mail written in red ink. They were both harbingers of calamity. On the rare occasions when they did not bear news of death, they were scripted in language which only a few of even the literate could decipher. Such *telegra*, as the villagers called it, caused shocks that sometimes even resulted in deaths. That way, they fulfilled their own prophecy as carriers of calamity.

A telegram postmarked LC NYS USA11276, arrived at St Joseph's in December, 1976, addressed via Mam'Uteriza Adama, to Mr Adama Ododo. Apart from its unfamiliar appearance, this was the first time Aroji would be witnessing a telegram addressed via the name of a woman. It therefore threw the whole village into great consternation and communal tongue-wagging. The headmaster was careful not to entrust such a bombshell to a schoolboy so he elected to deliver it himself. On getting to the house of Adama Ododo, he would also volunteer to read it for the family. That way, as an informed community leader, he himself would not need to depend on the market place to fill in on the newest story in Aroji.

On seeing the HM a short distance from her grinding mill, Mam'Uteriza emerged from under the eaves, looking all keyed up for a fight. She instantly fell into a frenzy of agitated questionings, recriminations and rejections of imminent woe. This was not her telegram! She indeed would never be sent any! St Joseph and the gods of her fathers would not let calamity fall on her or upon her husband's household! St Joseph and his wife, the eternal Virgin Mary, would take good care of her son in America! 'Echem!' she called, turning to the headmaster, 'should I thank you for that thing you are holding? Not me! They say my name is on it. How can that be? It is not my own Teriza Adama, I beg!'

The HM was transfixed with embarrassment. There he stood, in the middle of Adama's compound, holding the telegram lamely in his hand. *Inee* Enewa Ogo, matriarch of the larger Odod' Ojo clan, soon came by, on her noontime routine of asking after everyone's well being.

'Echem, you should have known!' scolded the matriarch. 'I know you are a stranger in this place. But your own Igbo is nearby in Amra village, where our girls fetch firewood. Tell me in your own place, can you walk to somebody's wife and break bad news to her behind her husband?'

'*Inee*, am sorry,' pleaded the HM in passable Idoma tongue. 'I will never try it again. I have learnt my lesson.'

'Give me that fearful paper, son! I outgrew the name of woman long ago! When my brother, Adama, returns from farm, we will know what is inside it. Even if it be death, it will not be the first or last. Corpses can never fill the earth's belly.'

Except for some patches of grey hair, Adama Ododo, a stalwart in stature and repute, was untouched by his sixty-odd years of age. Well before dawn, when other householders were yet making ablution toward offering the day's sacrifice to the gods, Adama was already sweating on his big farm. Each morning he either went to his big farm, or weeded the backyard garden; tended his palm saplings; or mended the fence around his wife's prized reservoir of run-off rain-water. Even for leisure, he found light labour within the compound or right inside his hut.

Like a dry season bush fire, the rumour of death by telegram reached his ears as he trudged home at sundown. At last, he turned into the path that led directly to his house. From that distance, he could see much of his compound. A small crowd had gathered in the centre hut. This gathering is not for me or any of my own! was his prompt reaction from afar. He shrugged his shoulders to emphasise his rejection of foreboding. When he got closer, he stopped and cursorily greeted some of those gathered as befitted their names and titles.

Except in the compelling circumstance of death, rarely did his Aroji kindred have cause to gather in appreciable number on Adama's account. He was reputed to be a lone ranger, whose queer mode of behaviour showed him to be an unreachable, self-sufficient man. He was strong in physique and in the hidden ways of his ancestors. To him, one of the simple safeguards against witchcraft was personal secrecy, and frontal verbal attacks on those he suspected to be fly-by-nights.

The people were getting impatient, waiting for Adama to clean up and present himself.

'What is he washing for this long?' queried one of the

elders. 'Even a new wife will not spend so much time in the place of bathing.'

'Maybe he thinks we are gathered here for his palm wine,' protested a younger householder. 'If that is so, I have a whole keg of masculine wine in my own house, begging for mouth. What is the food that has ever entered man's belly which saw the end of hunger? He better come out now, or I leave!'

'You speak well,' added another man of the same age as Adama. 'The man is a strong tree that stands the winds alone! I think it is the blood of his Amra mother working in him! If it were for him alone, I would have left this house already. Our people say that one finger cannot pick a louse from the hair, but not with Adama Ododo! Now, I must tell you all: I forced myself to come, for love of Aroji and for fear of you people refusing to assemble on the day my own trouble will come.'

The woman of the home, Mam'Uteriza Adama, stepped into the midst of the men, promptly falling on her knees in plea. 'Elders, mothers, and men of Aroji, you are the hands that own me. I know I am just an ordinary woman, but please, allow me to explain—'

'Who speaks for me there?' exclaimed her husband, emerging from his main hut. 'Don't you know that the insider who knows your footmark is the one who can trace your movements? Leave this to me!'

'In any case, it is good that you have now come out,' *Inee* Enewa quickly spoke out, in order to pre-empt any possible uproar. 'It is I, Enewa Ogo, who is speaking. Adam' Odod'Ilolo, sit down!' She rose, an amazon at seventy-two, whose presence commanded respect throughout Aroji district. 'There is no need wasting more time! It is said that the iron that has been brought to the smith's forge has a purpose. So, let us go into the matter that has gathered us here.'

'We agree, *Inee* Enewa!' chorused the men. Others objected, shouting, 'The man has not even greeted!'

'Adama,' continued *Inee* Enewa, raising her voice above the protests. 'Our people say, he who owns a wandering dog never stops whistling. Do you know why it is so?'

'*Inee*, I am listening.'

'It was your own brother, from the same penis with you, Otetebrete; the bird which sees the moon from inside a hut! He it was, who went out spreading alarm that one of our own has died somewhere—'

'That is not so, *Inee*!' Adama shouted, with his face set high up in defiance.

'That is good. If, for the first time, this *telegra* is a good one, then we thank Imaachi and the God in the sky. But—'

'*Inee* Enewa,' Otetebrete cut in, squatting with his palms cast down in the dust, penitent. 'You elders say that when a crab catches hold of one finger, let the whole hand be dipped back in the crab's water; it may then release the finger. I accept that I did wrong. But only that I meant to do good. Aroji, kill me if you will. But I feared that something evil happened in my brother's house.'

'That is enough!' shouted several men. 'You will learn your lesson one day!'

Others sat glum, while yet others were screaming for the head of Adama as the real offender. 'Enough of him! Adama is the person who should be begging!'

'He will talk,' responded the matriarch, 'if you sit down and listen to him. Adama, indeed, it is you who has committed the greater offence. Are you blaming Aroji for gathering here? Should we not have come when we heard this alarm of death?'

'Not so, Enewa, mother-of-many,' responded Adama.

'First, since we came, nobody has greeted us, not to talk of offering us even one lobe of kola nut,' continued *Inee* Enewa, not giving regard to his nephew. 'We were sitting here when, like a white man, you walked into your room, ignoring all of us! I do not blame the good woman of the home. I know you would have dealt with her if she had given us common drinking water. Aroji, am I lying?'

'No!' responded some of the men.

'Aroji, let me ask you. Has any of you come here because he is dying to wet his dry gullet?'

'Not at all, *Inee*!' chorused the men and women alike.

'Enewa, you have spoken my mind,' responded the most elderly man who had been quietly taking tobacco snuff in his corner. 'When she speaks, no person, man or woman, can add! Now I will only tie up the ends of this matter. It is not how long you stay on top of a wife that brings about a male child. Let us bury this thing quickly. Night is coming, when we should be at home to welcome to dinner, the spirits of our ancestors. Otetebrete! Next time a thing hides its head, do not say to yourself, I must see its face. Do you know why it is said that only an unwise outsider would ever roast the head of a hare? Answer me!'

The tale-bearer had no answer.

'I want someone of his age to tell this young man the meaning of that proverb!'

No one volunteered.

'Gbaa!' exclaimed the old man, disgusted. 'I am ashamed of all of you! Is there not even one of you who grew up under an elder? Young men of these days! They grow fast and tall as the paw-paw tree. There is very little inside them... Otetebrete, stand up! You have shown sorrow enough for your wrong. Next time, be careful! An outsider who thinks to roast the head of a hare, will be made to produce its horns. But, does a hare have horns? Sons and daughters of Aroji, this matter is finished.'

'Finished? It is not!' shouted a group of men. 'How about—?'

'Be calm yet!' ordered the old man. 'I know where I am

going… Adama will speak when the time comes. He himself knows that he has something to mend. Does one mouth send another mouth on errand? If not, why should anyone have to tell him what to do?' He paused to see who might want to challenge his wisdom. They all kept their peace, so he continued, rising as he rearranged his *achi* loincloth over his left shoulder. 'The whole trouble was caused by this thing called *telegra*. While some of you were making noise there, a little *uja* bird whispered to me. This is the *telegra*! I will now open it before all of us. Let us see whatever is inside it.'

He brought out the telegram which *Inee* Enewa had since slipped into his hand, and dropped it on the floor in front of them. 'Where is Akawo, somebody?' he asked.

Adama stood up. 'Before Akawo steps forward… I greet you, elders, men, and women of Aroji. You have all spoken wisely. *Inee* Enewa, I cannot doubt your word. Even if I was carved out of an iroko tree as some people think I am, you are still my mother, and the mother of many. Our eldest here has spoken well. When those of you who love to hear me talk, were calling for my head, our eldest said, I will speak. This is the time. *Inee* said something which touched me. Let me say this: a day before I begin to behave to you like a white man, let our ancestors take my life! I never meant to ignore you. Why it looked like I ignored you was that I needed to wash the farm dust off my skin. As for some of the things I said which offended your ears, our elders have a saying. If you know a man to be a blacksmith, you greet him by the title, "Omerigwe". When I see a broad daylight witch sitting among men, under my own roof, I cannot keep my mouth closed! That is why I talked the way I did. I ask for your forgiveness, Aroji. As for this *telegra*, it is as our eldest has told you. There is no death or calamity in my home. Instead, this is a day of singing and dancing, not sorrowing. I ask you all to sit down and rejoice with me.

Palm wine is on the way! Teriza, bring the kola nuts! I will soon tell you all about it.'

It was well that it all ended in a celebration. Dusk was beginning to grow into dark night. This was the hour of homecoming for ancestral spirits, after their wandering through groves, over distant hills, and through many waters far and near. This was late dusk, when foul words must not be spoken; when whistling is forbidden, in order that a dog is not unwittingly summoned from its confines; late dusk, when it is taboo to directly mention the mangy canine because the ancients abhor its eating of human waste; and worst of all, its uncanny insight into their spirit world.

*

Aroji was overshadowed with expectations for many days in succession. In Adama's house only the children slept. The adults had their eyes and ears transfixed on the trunk 'A' highway.

And yet, telegrams had never been known to equivocate, except during the Biafran War when they told common-place lies to force the Nigerian Army into granting furlough to the soldiering sons of Aroji.

Adama lay prone, his nape propped up by a leather-bound headrest of silk cotton wool. His mind was crowded with interweaving emotions, recollections, and sheer imaginings. Was that paper really a telegram or a trick of an enemy? Which of the enemies? Whoever was this person, Maazi, who called himself a 'Brother', and had signed the telegram? Why was it not Dezmond himself who sent it?

Adama replayed in his memory the drama of that after-noon when the telegram arrived. It delighted him greatly that he had spoken his mind against men such as Inancha and Ochohe, who occupationally terrorised the village with their witchcraft. After all, he thought, since all lizards appear with their soft underbelly to the ground, it cannot be known which of them has stomach ulcer until such afflicted ones are turned face up. From Aroji folk records, Adama recalled some accounts of bloodthirsty witches who, in the final throes of divine judgement, died torturous deaths, wracked with pain, screaming and yielding up the names of several of their victims.

As a young man, he had desired an early fruit of manhood, a son, to grow up alongside him, to attend school, and lift him up in the evening phase of a hard life. How could his ancestors now allow any shame to come upon his house, and let his enemies laugh at him in scorn?

On one of those fitful nights, burdened with forebodings, he lit his lantern and pulled the telegram from under his headrest. He then opened it out before the light and began to contemplate the typescript. The brownish offcut paper, now crinkly from much handling, yielded nothing. The typescript bore no resemblance to his son's handwriting which the old man had since imprinted on the very tablet of his heart, an indelible token of the literacy which his gods had forever denied him. From the time Dezmond went to Kuru Government College and began to write letters home, his father had become even more enchanted by the mystery and power of these flimsy-looking *igrigi* symbols that can speak as loudly as a man.

Adama Ododo became accustomed to his son's hand, always marvelling at the mystery of those ever-consistent strokes and curves. Each mail from Dezmond was a treasure, and a compensation to him. He, therefore, had them all fish-lined on an old bicycle spoke, proudly displayed for his continual adoration in the recess of his sleeping place. This cherished trophy of over a decade of his son's schooling was indeed his own way of identifying with the great magic of writing which his son once told him, was invented by fellow Africans in an ancient land called *Ijippti*...

The cocks of Aroji were now out-crowing one another, heralding another chilly harmattan dawn. Able sons of landed men were already afield with their *ukpaka* palm climbing gear, for the twilight rounds of wine tapping. The children of Adama Ododo's house awoke to a sudden sense of hollowness. It was like dreaming that next morning would be Christmas again, season of dancing masquerades and new apparel; a time of sweet rice and rare meats; presents and parties; only to wake up and find Papa sharpening not the slaughter knife, but the same old farm cutlass! Vacuity hung thick in the air.

After those three days of waiting, Adama called out his grand court of totems and emblems of ancestral power, arrayed them on his mud altar, and began to clang his giant gong to the second heavens. Having waited in vain for the news of Dezmond's triumphant return, it was verily time to stir the gods into action. As he struck the bloodied gong with all his might, he raised his voice in petition.

'Spirits of my fathers, Odod'llolo, llol'Onu, On'Ojobo, Ojob'Ododo, Odod'Ojo, Oj'Aad'Aroji. As you stand in your order, I offer kola nut and cockerel, the same way you fathers taught us. Accept my sacrifice! Protect me and my house, father of all fathers, Aad'Aroji! Whoever brings evil, let that very evil turn against him. Whether man or woman, young or old, whoever puts a curse on my own, let a greater curse fall on such a one! Whatever belongs to such, let it be scattered! But for those who seek our good, let the same good follow them. Left to me, let the hawk fly and perch, and in the same way let the kite fly and perch. As the sheep chew their own grass, let the goats equally chew their own. And the cows too. Let one not deny the other his own. Whoever thinks otherwise, let him not taste good! Let his teeth break in his mouth. Whoever casts evil on my children, you who produced me, Odod'llolo, let all his own seeds perish! All the witches that seek my downfall, break their wings for me; blind their right eyes! Make them vomit the blood they have drunk…'

Adama went on and on as he continued to hit the gong to the rhythm of his utterances. At one point, he dropped the gong and in turn picked up a calabash of water, then oil, which he then poured on the ground in front of the altar, saying, 'This is water. It is for peace. Your servant pours it out for you. Drink it, O earth! This is palm oil which I now pour for mercy.' He then got hold of the cockerel, slashed its throat and sprinkled its blood on the altar, the gong, the other shrine implements and his assemblage of gods, naming them one by one. 'Spirit of my fathers, eat this sacrifice which I make on behalf of your son, Deshmon. Have mercy on us! Guide his steps home, and open his way as he returns from the land of the white man. I now lay before you this *telegra* that has brought us confusion of days. Deshmon is in your hand. Bring him home! Let the sun pass over him, and also the night…'

With that, he pulled out a drum from the shrine and went into a prolonged session of chanting and gyrations until the sun began to peep through the evergreen forest of palm trees.

His wife took her own petition to morning mass at St Joseph's. While the bidding prayers were going on, she concentrated only on what she desired for her son. 'My God, do as you want concerning him,' she prayed. 'You gave him to me as the first-born of my womb. I accept whatever you want. But, Almighty, you alone are God. I am but an ordinary woman. I am crying to you. Forgive me all my sins. God, let your hand upon my son be a good hand. I believe you have heard my begging. In the name of the Father…'

On her way back home, she saw five of her other children prattling as they warmed their bodies over the harmattan-borne fire. From where she was, their exchanges sounded agitated and amusing. But when they noticed that an adult was approaching, the drama would freeze. Mam'Uteriza Adama, therefore, decided to hide behind a tree and eavesdrop on the little ones.

Said her five-year old girl, 'I was very happy last night. But when I woke up in the morning, my happiness went away. I wonder, why was I so happy?'

Akawo, her brother, explained that it must have been the good news about their big brother that made her happy.

'Dezmond is on his way home from America!' he reminded them all.

'*Ehen!* That is how it was said yesterday. And the other yesterday also,' grumbled the little girl. 'But he did not come. Will he come back today!'

'Do not worry,' said Akawo, falsely reassuring her. 'When you were sleeping, the radio said that Dezmond Adama Ododo will return tomorrow. That must be our brother! There cannot be two Dezmond Adamas coming from America at the same time! The radio called even the number of the sky train which brought him to Lagos. He will be taken in another one to Enugu Airport. Then a motor will drive him home to Aroji!'

The little ones burst into a shouting contest about who should first give account of his or her expectations and dreams of what Dezmond would bring each of them from America.

'Me, I grew so tall he may not even know it is the same me!' shouted one of the smallest urchins.

'Hmm! How tall?' teased a bigger one. 'How won't he know you after only two years of leaving home?'

'I told Papa to send him my picture,' said another.

'Which picture?' asked the only girl there. 'When did you take a picture?'

'My class picture of last year. I marked my head with an

arrow to show him where I stood. If Papa did not send it, then the trouser Dezmond will buy me will not be my waist size.'

'Now you have said your own, who can tell me what Dezmond will bring me?' shouted the girl, giggling with excitement.

Mrs Adama having heard an earful, picked up a whip and went at them. 'I heard you, little owls!' she shouted, brandishing her cudgel. 'What you have in your little mouths are the seeds of witchcraft, if you don't know! That is how witchcraft begins. But I will flog it out of every one of you! Now, go get your cutlasses and brooms, all five of you! Go!'

'It is good you went for your *morny mash* this morning,' remarked Adama from his shrine. 'We need help from your gods of *Sen Josef* and the gods of Aad' Aroji. Together, they will blow away any evil wind that may be heading our way.'

'The God in the sky, he is strong. He needs no help,' Mam'Uteriza declared as she stood behind the thatched fence to hear her husband through.

'Since first cockcrow, I have also been talking to my fathers about my first-born. They demanded meat, that the earth of Aroji be appeased with blood, oil, and water. If not, they said Deshmon's feet will be turned to the paths that lead to forests and many market places... Teriza, are you hearing me?'

'I am still here.'

'I gave them a cockerel. But even as the giver, I am not satisfied with that. No matter how lean an elephant gets, he cannot be mistaken for a rabbit. I know what our fathers expect of me even at these times of drought. I want to be sure they accept the sacrifice.'

'Have they asked for a goat? Doesn't your cock have enough blood?'

'Thank you! But I have decided to give them a goat. So,

hurry back in and ready yourself for Ukpoju's house. They say he still has some four-legged beasts.'

'My husband, if you will agree, I desire that my hands will never again touch your shrine things. It is said that the water one cannot drink, one should not wash one's face with it.'

'Teriza, daughter of Odoko, this goat is for the sake of your own son, the one who opened your womb! It is for clearing the way for his homecoming,' retorted Adama Ododo. 'It is a pity and shame for me and you that I have no other wife. My sweet-smelling only wife, Teriza, tell me, have you ever seen scrotum sitting on top of penis? If you have, or if you have ever heard of such a wonder, tell me, I will climb down from my manhood and become your wife today, now!'

'I have never seen or heard of it, my husband!' she answered light-heartedly, laughing. 'Even if someone's scrotum is sitting like that, how can I get to see such a thing? Only the man and his wife will know! That is, if such a strange man can have a woman!'

'Well spoken! When you finish teaching me book, come and collect ten pounds and hurry to Ukpoju's house! Do not waste time until he leaves for Ukwo. The goats will cost more once they enter that fence of those useless *Natif Otority* tax people.'

'My sweet husband, I have heard,' replied Mama Teriza as she moved on. 'Has the hawk ever liked anything concerning the chick? But Jehova knows that I am only being your wife!'

'You speak well!' shouted her husband, noticing that she had started moving to her hut. 'Now that your own mouth has said it, don't force me to remind you whose wife you are!' He raised himself off his ritual stool and strained his neck over the fence. 'And, listen! When next you want to crack a proverb over your husband's head, remember it was this same shrine worshipper who showed you the way to *Sen Josef*. If they are turning you into a man like the one who took his money and married you, built that hut and put you in it, then, it is time to stop all this churchgoing!'

'Thank you very much, my husband! The hand that owns me, thank you for opening my eyes-o! I will do what you say! And I will at once forget all the proverbs that I ever knew!'

Another day of waiting was unfolding, with the harmattan sun creeping along a tardy line from its eastern hideout.

Chapter Sixteen

Flight WT 094 had not yet taxied to a stop before the passengers began to fill up the aisle, apparently in reaction to nine hours of airborne claustrophobia. Dezmond was among the first to unbuckle his seat belt. Travelling so light, he found it easy to hop into the choked traffic on the aisle. Jostling his way right up to the main exit, he stood there with his nose virtually glued to the back of one of the cabin staff.

When the door was finally flung open, he flew into the exit tube. With his luggage held high in the air, he sped ahead like a hurricane. 'I'm home! Home! Home at last!' he shouted, swinging his briefcase wildly over his head as he stormed his way through the long tunnel-like hall.

Once through with Immigration, he joined the multitude of fellow passengers crowding towards the passenger terminal. In sheer excitement, he broke through a chain of security men and press who were trooping after a team of government dignitaries, to the VIP lounge. As a plain-clothes agent elbowed him aside, he flung his case at his head, barking at him, 'Back already, aren't we? The home treat already! We've hardly stepped on Nigerian soil! What a shame!'

An enterprising news photographer quickly snapped the imbroglio and scurried on to his main target. The carry-on of grand speechifying and orchestrated applause indicated that some newsworthy person was enjoying a field day with journalists and onlookers.

'Sycophants!' volunteered Dezmond, pouting at the crowd. 'Ask him questions! Challenge him instead of smiling fangy smiles for PR peanuts!' As he noticed the plain-clothes agent approaching, he turned and strode into the arrivals hall, which was teeming with passengers from several flights. He then threw his luggage on a chair, walked over to the news-stand, and picked a copy of *National Focus*, flipping it round. A back-page headline caught his attention.

'Look at this!' he exclaimed.

'Na wot, sir?' asked the news vendor. 'Sontin happen?'

Dezmond held out the paper, '*Chief Executive Admits Zombie Role!* D'you know what this means to your daily bread?'

'*Oga*, I beg, pay money! Nuttin' concern me for dat one.'

'Crumbs!' cursed Dezmond as he dropped a ten kobo coin at the vendor's feet. He then approached a police constable at the stand, and waved him a salute. 'Hey, PC! Lemme use your ballpoin' a minute.'

'Ballpoin'?'

'Ballpoint... biro pen!' explained Dezmond. 'I wanna draft a *baad* something!'

'Quite excuse, sah!'

'Those sharks who've swallowed our nation! Someone's got to begin to stop them!'

Dezmond raged on until the crowd began to drift towards the news-stand, ready for another entertainment.

'You're all the same,' he shouted at them as they formed a circle around him. 'CEOs, boardmen, policemen, newsmen, customs men, night-soil men – you're in the same mess!... Listen, plain-clothes men! Stop your follow-follow! You're paid tax dollars to protect, not to misuse state power on people... Where's all the oil money going, while others are wearing out their arses after degrees? Where are all those tons of confiscated laces and lorry-loads of hardware?'

The larger the crowd grew, the more worked up he got, lashing out at every imaginable group. At that point, a car pulled up at the entrance to the hall, its strobe light flicking, reflecting the urgency of its mission. Its doors flung open and out jumped four security officers and a lady in white overalls. They marched up to Dezmond and quickly closed in on him.

'Excuse me, sir,' said one of the airport security officers. 'Could I have a look at your passport, please?'

'Why?' demanded Dezmond, looking over the crowd towards where he had dropped his briefcase.

'Occasional random check,' replied the officer, cool as a cucumber, with his eyes levelled on Dezmond.

'No, man, I don't buy it,' replied Dezmond, backing off. 'Why pick on me? What's the big deal? I'm just another Nigerian, come back home!'

'Well—' began the second man.

'Well,' Dezmond interrupted, 'who're you, anyway? Lagos crooks come in all covers. Go do your act someplace else!' He spoke louder, still backing off, bumping into people. Stumbling, he regained his balance, and zipped away zigzagging through the crowd. The men gave hot pursuit. On crashing into a row of seats he braked abruptly, certain that that was where he had dropped his luggage. The spot was as bare as air. Dezmond slapped his hands in anguish and let out a long shrill wail. His cherished briefcase and his close companion, the portable typewriter, had disappeared! In the briefcase were contained his valuables: an international passport; a volume of thoughts from his readings; portions of his aborted doctorate material; a few hundred dollars, courtesy PAID; and above all, his omnibus notebook in which were captured his visions, fantasies, dreams, and might-have-been gems of creativity.

Before the Nigerian Airport Authority officers caught up with him, Dezmond recovered somewhat, and burst into a jazzy run, this way, then that, then back where he was certain his luggage should be. He paused to think for some moments, then broke into another bout of furtive searching, darting up and down the rows of seats, and peeping round corners. He stopped short now and then in his tracks, checking suspiciously round and about the flood of travellers who were surging in and out of the massive building.

A futile, desperate search it was! His face was contorted with anguish as he finally gave it up and headed for the information desk. Half blind from rage and poor lighting, he bumped into a distraught group of newly arrived passengers, who were clambering over a jumble of luggage beside a broken-down baggage carousel. Promptly, he threw himself into the scramble, pulling, elbowing and tugging, until a free-for-all fight broke out.

The NAA Officers, now reinforced by some intrepid operatives, caught up with him before much havoc was done.

'Let go! Leave me alone!' screamed Dezmond, kicking and flailing his long limbs. But the men's arms were knotted in his in such a way that, with a heave, he was lifted off the ground and propelled all the way to the waiting car.

★

'Your name again, sir?' asked the police desk sergeant.

'Dezmond Adama, for crying out aloud! That's the umpteenth time you're asking!'

'*Oga*, this *Americana* is getting too much! Do you know you could be charged with conduct likely to?'

'Meaning what?' asked Dezmond over the counter, sneering at the desk sergeant and his other ranks. 'What bull is that? I'm back home to my own beloved country. I'm excited! I hug and kiss the arrival hall, and… and, I'm just excited! What's the crime in that, man? Never been back home after two years?'

'*Oga*, sir, dat is what we call conduct likely to cause breach of peace and constituting yourself into public nuisance,' explained a rather sympathetic constable.

'What do you want me to enter against you?' asked the sergeant, his pen already set over the station diary.

'What you say?'

'De tin you just say, is dat your statement? Is dat de statement you wan' make?'

'If you will. I'm fed up to here with all your crap. Just get done with it, lemme get outa here. I must find my stuff!'

'Come-o! Dis man no understand why he was brought here-o! Sarge, sir, we should stop playing with him. He tinks we are just here to be hearing big *Americana* for nuttin'.'

'Okay, Mr Dezmond Adama, declare your personal effects. Remove your watch, and your goggles, the shoes, the belt…'

'What on earth for?' shouted Dezmond, banging the counter. 'What the hell's goin' on here? I've lost all my belongings! Isn't that enough trouble for one day?'

'You're even lucky, you're only staying behind counter,' said the sergeant. 'That's our instruction. If not…!'

'If not, what? D'you guys realise what I'm passing through? Think what it means to lose your valuable belongings. Dishwasher, deep-freezer, A-C, VTR, colour TV, stereo set, name it!'

'Na waa for dis man!' exclaimed the constable, impressed by the array of possessions.

'Put all that together, the content of my briefcase is far more valuable! That's what I'm talking about.'

'I see,' said the sergeant, beaming. 'How much dollar is that? And did you declare same on re-entry, on statutory prescribe format?'

'Listen, man if you're thinking I'm gonna bribe, forget it! I'm not talking about dollars, okay? Now, you better do your worst now! And get over with it this minute! I've run outa gas, okay? Look how you're wasting my precious time. The arrival hall is where the real confusion's going on right now. But y'all are sitting doing nuttin'! Lemme outa here! Now!'

His hollering was so loud that it forced the ASP in charge of the station out of hiding. As he emerged, the sergeant barked out an order and half a dozen policemen sprang to attention at their various nooks. The superintendent waved to them in acknowledgement as he strode to the counter.

'I am Mr Jinadu, OC APP. Please, come to my office,' he said to Dezmond in a very amiable tone. On entering the office, the officer offered him a seat and tried to engage him in conversation, even offering tea into the bargain. Dezmond became visibly suspicious.

'Never mind the embarrassment, Mr Adama. It's one of those things,' continued the ASP, still courting Dezmond's friendship. 'We'll need this form completed, however. Just for our records,' he added, placing a pen and a half-blank form before him. 'Under "Statement" there, just write two or three sentences as to what happened, and that settles it.'

Dezmond gazed at Mr Jinadu, not sure what to make of his totally different approach. Is this not perhaps a booby trap? he wondered. And for a police officer to offer a man tea in his office! But then, he thought, it sounded as if all he needed to do to be released was simply, fill their form. He stared at the blank space, chewing meditatively at the butt of the ballpoint pen, glancing continually at the officer. When he turned his stare to the sagging rain-soaked ceiling of Mr Jinadu's office, he recalled the routine warning of the American police the moment one was under arrest, that any utterance made then could be used as evidence against the person arrested.

'But I'm not under arrest, am I?' he asked Mr Jinadu.

'Take your time,' advised the OC APP, seeing that Dezmond seemed to be having a problem writing something. 'Maybe I should excuse you,' he added, leaving the room. 'Feel free!'

Minutes later, Dezmond began to write his statement. His thoughts flowed coherently, but the words came as heavy as lead, with his mind blanking out for stretches in between. The zeal of some hours ago had been replaced by deadening doldrums which came from within. Even the pen in his hand began to feel like an iron dumbbell as he struggled with his consciousness.

Suddenly, he felt a new surge of energy, and within minutes he had filled the statement form, only for the old incubus to overcast him shortly afterwards. At that stage, he simply held dumb-bell to paper, crouching over the table until, like a wilting leaf, his head dropped. Instant sleep, it seemed, overtook him.

On returning an hour later, Mr Jinadu removed the form from under the arm of Dezmond who was now wheezing in his slumber. Its contents intrigued the officer, coming from a man he had mistaken for one of those cases of impressively dressed, fluent English speakers, who cannot read or write. However, the statement read like an enigma:

> *Home, yet not home. Incarcerated by NPF, NAA, winter of '76. Planes plummet through snow smut, into the sea. Mine landed tonight! History has been denied happening. Another made, on one hand. Here I am, expressing angst on a blank sheet of statement. Two intersecting circles intersect at two*

> *points. A mother orbit, like a kangaroo, contains other orbits. The theme is perfect roundness or ellipsis with a charcoal chip. Cerebral debris fermentation equals epiphany or oblivion. For doctoral enquiry in analytic philosophy! Semantics. Same antics. Police detectives crack. To be continued to conclusion.*

Mr Jinadu immediately filed his report to the medical director of the NAA who was already privy to the other reports of the chief purser of Flight 094 and that of the chief security officer. The required line of action was obvious.

Chapter Seventeen

Island Neuro-Psychiatric Centre, Lagos.

As if incensed by the reflective purple colour of the unmistakable signpost, Dezmond suddenly broke into a rage of vituperation. So wild and noisy was he, that he brought to a stand-still the normal activities of the centre. The Nigeria Airport Authority ambulance drew up at the reception lobby, and a scuffle ensued, which drew workers, visitors and inmates alike to the scene.

Another kind of argument soon followed between the police officer and the Duty Medical Officer. Frustrated by the failure of his persuasive effort, the former resorted to muscling his way through the centre's new admission procedures. He raised his voice above the din, vigorously explaining why yet another government patient should be accepted. However, the centre's experience with police referrals was one of unpaid bills, inadequate documentation, lean funding for the welfare of patients, and in some cases, abandonment. Worse still, there was no vacant bed for a new patient since the facilities had been overstretched.

The timely intervention of Dr Nwosu, a senior consultant, brought an end to the argument between the two officers, both of whom were bent on carrying out their lawful orders.

It took a fresh battle to get Dezmond out of the ambulance. He presented as a textbook psychiatric case, what with his extreme hostility and his dishevelled, wild and disoriented appearance. He was outright aggressive when the DMO put some routine questions to him. Having forced his way through, the police officer submitted to the DMO a sealed envelope containing confidential information on the patient, right from his boarding the flight to his overnight custody at the airport police station.

About twenty-four hours later, the crisis had greatly subsided, Dezmond having been continually dosed with chlorpromazine. When he first woke up, he was persuaded to bathe and take a bowl of hot *acha* cereal with *akara* bean cakes. For the next three days, he was to be holed up in a makeshift bed in the ward, growing more anxious by the hour about his missing luggage. He became increasingly resentful and inimical to his surroundings, despite the many comical scenes and verbal humour that abounded in the ward. Three days of limbo, thought Dezmond, yet no word about his cherished belongings! By this time, he had altogether run out of patience. He began to raise many worrisome questions to which answers were not forthcoming. On the fourth day, he embarked on a full-scale resistance: no more talking, no more voluntary taking of drugs, tacit abstention from food. Since he kept his peace and his condition even looked stable, the authorities left him to himself, only monitoring him from a distance.

Another wave of agitation, however, set in on the fifth day, when Dezmond became aware of the inmate's uniform on his back. This discovery threw him into an endless quarrel with no particular person. From then on, he settled for Hausa as his only acceptable language of communication. When he got tired, he stopped talking altogether, and sat on his makeshift bed for hours, or moped around looking as dense as mercury. Within those few days, despite his scanty meals, he grew fatter, becoming all too rounded, tender to the touch, and almost lifeless in his reflexes.

Up to that fifth day, true to prophecy, neither the NAA nor the police authorities had visited or phoned. When the authorities of the centre contacted them, they were dutifully reminded of the comprehensive documentation which had been delivered with their patient. Having, however, established that Dezmond's case had no criminal aspect to it, being purely psychiatric, the centre decided to contact the Ahmadu Bello University, Zaria, with a view to transferring him home to his employers. One of the consultants knew of a doctor from Zaria who was attending a seminar in Lagos University Teaching Hospital, Idi-Araba, who might be able to facilitate the necessary arrangements.

★

'I am Shaban,' smiled the visitor, offering his hand.

Dezmond gazed stonily on as he stepped slowly and hesitantly into the visitors' lounge. He stopped an arm's length from the visitor, ignoring his self-introduction.

'I am Shaban,' he repeated more loudly, returning a kind look for the man's hard countenance. 'Can we sit down?'

'What is Shaban?' asked Dezmond abruptly. 'Shaban... Nathan... Which one are you? Maazi told me of Nathan, the prophet.'

Then came a long, uneasy pause, as if to let pass the mounting waves of tumultuous cheering from the inmates' soccer match. Dezmond eased himself into a chair some spaces away from his unexpected guest.

'My name is Shaban Mshelia,' repeated the visitor, sitting down. 'From Zaria.'

'Friend or foe?'

'Friend!'

'Have you found my missing luggage?'

'Sorry. I didn't know about that.'

'Why are you here? You don't belong here!'

'Well, Dr Nwosu—'

'Who's Nwosu?' Dezmond enquired yet again, his eyelids flicking restlessly as he examined Shaban's face.

'He works here. We're attending a seminar together. He told me there's someone on admission here who's from ABU, Zaria. So I decided to check. May be I could be of some help.'

'Are you from ABU?' For once, a wan smile appeared on Dezmond's lips.

'Yes. Fellow in medical research... Now that you smile, I think we've met somewhere before. I'll get to remember as we chat along. That is, if you'll smile a little more.'

Another stormy wave of applause from the football game swept over the reception room. No rules, no referee! Just one massive riot over a practically invisible ball, thanks to the numberless players in the pursuit. Dezmond glanced at Shaban, then in the direction of the games field. He smiled to himself.

'Where's your dangling emblem?' he asked unexpectedly.

'What's that?' asked Shaban.

Dezmond raised his eyes and, in an exaggerated body movement, peered into the front pocket of Shaban's kaftan. 'You're rather different. You don't dangle about your own emblem of power.'

'Oh, that!' exclaimed Shaban, laughing with great abandon. 'I don't need a stethoscope at a conference. In fact, for my kind of work now, I need not dangle anything.'

Dezmond laughed heartily with Shaban.

'How's Zaria?' he enquired after some minutes, moving nearer. Shaban, however, preferred that the conversation centre on Dezmond.

'Still surviving. But foreign grants are getting thin... I hear you've just returned from the US. Were you on Fulbright fellowship or something? How lucky you are!'

No response. The pandemonium from outside swelled

in volume, a signal that their mass travesty of soccer had at last broken up. The hubbub of the players and spectators apart, whistles of varying decibels rent the air as sweat-soaked inmates, some of them barely clothed, surged past the reception hall into their communal bathroom. Dezmond seemed totally absorbed by something in this stream of men, and appeared lost in his contemplation on the scene.

'So, what's your department?' resumed Shaban, noticing how distracted he had become.

'What?' interjected Dezmond, as if he had been jabbed with a needle.

'We were talking about ABU. Wha—'

'Oh, yes. My department... Funny! Research fellow, Culture Research Institute.'

'Now, wait a minute!' Shaban interrupted in excitement. 'Now I'm sure we've met before! It was you who gave that public lecture!... I remember, during one of those Historical Society weeks, wasn't it? A very strange topic it was, if my memory is right!'

'I don't know. Maybe.' The response was deadpan, distant.

'You were saying a whole lot about the hypothesis of... erm... who was that, now? Yes, Ibn Kahdun! Yes, I believe that was the name! I remember it well because my fiancée was then doing one of your courses. She actually dragged me to that lecture but I ended up enjoying it. I still remember how you threw the whole hall into a heated debate. That was about five years ago! No wonder your name rang a bell when Dr Nwosu mentioned it! And on seeing your face, I had the feeling I'd seen you before!'

'I'm stuck with it,' lamented Dezmond, looking away from Shaban. 'Ibn Kahdun's hypothesis followed me. Now, I'm in a lunatic asylum... I know you are sent to get me. I'm not returning to Zaria, anyway. I'm tired... my body is weak… too much sedative. I just wanna go home, man. My nerves have gone dead… I am cold right inside my bones…' Dezmond spoke laboriously, his voice laced with pain and barely audible. 'First thing, they shoot syringe,' he rumbled, stretching out his needle-riddled hands, his fingers shaking. 'See? Hundreds of jabs. They're no good with my luggage stolen. I accepted asylum only while waiting for my missing stuff.'

'Oh, my! Your whole luggage!' That note of concern acted on Dezmond very much like a shot of adrenaline.

'That's the real McCoy problem they should be after! That's all I've got to show for it! They stole my briefcase and my Olympia! I get pissed off. Next thing, I'm in police jail! They're asking for my passport! They wanna know my history… How many letters I got in the US… Did I ever wrap a weed?… Did my mother's father ever have a son who went nuts… When did I last have sex?… Did a white woman ever turn me on?… Did some mugger hit me on the skull before? Damn! I quit talking!' he concluded, exhausted.

'Why?' asked Shaban seemingly upset. 'We're friends,' he said, having misunderstood Dezmond's last statement.

'Why talk? I can prove nothing! Unless they return my things, I'm walking a thin thread.' He stopped abruptly, took a long look at Dr Mshelia and continued, 'I like you though… I can tell you: my sanity is locked in there. My proof is in there! Everything that matters is in there!'

A long stretch of silence set between them, the more silent because the few other inmates and their guests who were in the lounge had left. On his part, Shaban had done enough talking to draw Dezmond out. He needed to listen as the man unveiled both his conscious and sub-conscious selves. Silence did not serve any good purpose in that situation. So, seeing how drained he looked, Shaban tactically primed him back into talking.

'Do you know Dr Nwosu?'

'That's the guy who ordered me put in this prisoner's jumper! He's never talked to me. He hates my face. I know. Why d'you ask?'

'Nothing, really. Just that he made me know you're here. It is funny you think bad of him. He's in charge here, actually. He's making the contacts for ABU to take you home. That's really why I'm here. And I'm glad I came. We're both research fellows of ABU. You're my wife's old teacher! How much closer can we be?'

'You wanna leave now?' Dezmond asked suddenly in a forlorn tone. 'You're ready! We're ready – set – go! That's it!' he shouted. 'That's it! Everybody is so kind! So sweet! So concerned! You'd think we're all little day-old chicks! You're not different after all, friend?'

'Oh yes, I'm different! Very! You'll see,' explained Shaban calmly, unmoved by Dezmond's outburst. 'When I tell you I'm your friend, I mean it in every sense. You'll see. Now, let me speak for Dr Nwosu and the others who are working here. They have to do some things and say some things in order to reduce the effects of this job on their own feelings. It's a hard job y'know?'

'What job?' asked Dezmond, looking totally lost.

'Psychiatry. These guys face much antagonism and resentment; even personal risks, on a daily basis,' explained Shaban. 'Some of them try to play down those pressures by behaving in all kinds of funny, funny ways. That's why they easily get misunderstood.'

'I'd like us to talk a lot more, Dr Shaban.'

'Who told you I'm a doctor, by the way?'

'Guessed,' replied Dezmond, amused. He too now stood up.

'However, don't be deceived. For all I'm saying about them, I'm not a psychiatrist! But let's not get into that now. I'll be back here in two days' time. Then we'll talk some more. I'll see Dr Nwosu. If he concludes his arrangement, you and I may even leave here together when our seminar is over.'

An intractable bond was developing between the two, fired not simply by a fortuitous crossing of paths, but by a mutual liking which was kindled by the unusual circumstance of their meeting. Like a child under pressure to gratify himself, Dezmond could hardly wait for the two days before he would again talk with his new-found friend.

*

Dr Shaban Mshelia kept his appointment on the dot of the minute. It was not a regular visiting day, so a special permission was granted for him and Dezmond to use the office of one of the associate fellows for greater liberty in conversation. The Centre encouraged these visits and, this time, facilitated it with extra hospitality. Through Dr Mshelia's interaction with their patient, they hoped to get a better insight into his problem, and be in a good position to make a cogent referral to the ABU Psychiatric Centre at the Teaching Hospital, Kaduna.

Dezmond Adama walked into the office, looking so drawn and discomfited that Dr Mshelia was unsure of how to reopen the much-awaited chat. One strategy he had learnt in his long-standing association with psychiatrists was to face every case as it presented itself, not scheming ahead about what questions to ask or what teasers or baits to apply in impasse situations. Over several years of research and teaching of medical sociology, he had undertaken what he called 'participant observation' in which he had often posed as a mentally deranged man himself, and actually lived in asylums, to gain knowledge and direct experience of various forms of psychosis. A general practitioner in medicine, he had developed an enthusiasm for the less lucrative field of psychiatry, just as he preferred to specialise in teaching the sociology of medicine to premed students. In his pursuit of scholarship in the sociology of medicine, he had spent over two years gathering data from orthodox institutions such as the Aro Psychiatric Hospital, Abeokuta, and from traditional mental homes. He had observed that psychosis was prevalent among academics, but from his sociological point of interest, Dezmond Adama's case presented him with an unusual opportunity, having originated in a multi-racial environment.

Dezmond sat on the only other chair in the room, placed in front of the office desk at which Dr Shaban Mshelia had been waiting. After quietly examining Shaban's face for a long time, he shot him a question 'What do you know already?'

'About what?' asked Shaban, not betraying any unease.

'About who!'

'About who?' echoed Shaban, accepting correction.

'Me.'

'Precious little.'

'What?'

'Not much. Just the bit in your statement to the police. And now, something about your stuff that's missing.'

'How do you know if you do not have my luggage? You've looked in my records!'

'You told the police about the nature of your luggage and some of the things in your diary or notebook. You'll remember, when you're well rested. But what does it matter what anybody gets to know?'

'No,' he answered, laughing. 'I smoked grass! The sergeant did not understand exorcism. I needed paper to exorcise. They refused me pen and paper. Okay, I had a pen. I needed only a plain sheet—'

'What do you need to exorcise?' Shaban cut in.

'My mind.'

'What things needed exorcising?

'Dreams. Big dreams… pain… death… no, not fear. Fear of what? You don't know what I lost! Years of notes written as I went about. That night, I filled four sheets of Kalamazoo. I urinated on them one by one.'

'Now, I don't believe you.'

'But I did, I tell you. I urinated on their Kalamazoo.'

'Dezmond, I want to listen to you, okay? You're not exactly putting me off. I'm listening.'

'A rare gift, I tell you.'

'What?'

'Nobody listens around here. They holler at people.'

'How come? Who are "they"? The doctors or the patients?'

'All the same. They're all in the same boat.'

'But psychiatrists do listen. They're trained to listen patiently,' Shaban prompted him.

'Maybe,' answered Dezmond. Then, after a long pause, he went on more enthusiastically, 'Your friends listen too much. Is that natural? When you're talking to them, they're not listening to you. They're hearing the people inside your belly who are using your mouth. Look how I talk, and you listen. And you talk, I listen. I'm not hearing other voices… D'you write things? D'you keep a scrapbook, kind of?'

'I write,' replied Shaban, highly amused. 'Everyone writes.'

'No! What d'you write?'

'Great! Seminar papers, reports, project proposals, stuff like that!'

'How modest! What else?'

'If you insist, I do poems when I've had a glass of good wine,' confessed Shaban, laughing. 'Luckily, only one critic has seen them: your former student! She thinks they're a disaster!'

Dezmond chuckled thoughtfully, and asked, 'What

makes you write poems? Apart from Bacchus?'

'Bacchus? Wine?' questioned Shaban.

'The god of wine... and fertility,' replied Dezmond and they both laughed.

'Jokes aside, I see a lot in life that I want to pin down, to record,' explained Shaban. 'I took to the camera. But it was draining my pocket... Y'know, everybody, take my picture! Take my picture! Poems are less costly. I can do a bit at a time. My own time. Its gestation and delivery are packed into one intense hour, if you get me.'

'I can't imagine how a man can string together the many things that must happen in a long story. Even the energy to sit down and write! Count me out!'

The duo became carried away with one another's interests and ideologies, sharing freely one another's adventures through life. They spent over two hours in dialogue, comparing experiences, exchanging jokes and laughing together.

Dr Mshelia was even able to persuade his friend to touch on some of his experiences in the United States. However, when the probing turned sensitive Dezmond recoiled. Suddenly, the old incubus overtook him, and he turned frigid and impervious to his friend's continued overtures. It was as if a demonic time-keeper had struck an ordinarily inaudible bell in his ears, to signal that he had spoken more than enough. No one could decipher what went on in his mind, as he sat frozen at the desk with no discernible focus in his eyes. Having tried all the cajoling, provocational and motivational art he had learnt in his years of borrowing the mantle of madness or that of a curer of madmen, Shaban gave up.

Without one word of farewell, Dezmond walked away, clutching his packet of biscuits and jar of apple juice. Dr Mshelia sat back watching as he disappeared into the inmates' ward. He then locked the office, and went in search of the Duty Medical Officer. Since his seminar would end in two days' time, he would return the next day for Dr Nwosu and himself to conclude arrangements for linking Dezmond Adama with ABU in Zaria. He hoped to meet him in a livelier mood, and perhaps travel north with him.

Chapter Eighteen

Dr Shaban Mshelia waited for an hour at his last rendezvous with Dezmond, but in vain. He finally gave up, locked the office, and headed for the staff club where he might get a clue as to his friend's whereabouts.

Three men in white overalls and a staff nurse at lunch greeted him in the Yoruba language. He nodded and asked in English where he could find Dr Nwosu. The lady pointed to a closed door just ahead to the right, with 'Brain Games' labelled on it. Dr Shaban hurried his way in, and found Dr Nwosu and a colleague bent over a Scrabble board. The third man in the room was busy apparently working at a crossword puzzle.

'Hausaman! How's the going?' Dr Nwosu called, as Shaban shut the door behind him. Despite the visitor's previous protestations, Dr Nwosu was certain that whoever came from the north of Nigeria had to be a Hausa man. Not able to convince the Igbo man that he wasn't Hausa by ethnic grouping, he had since resigned himself to this ascribed identity.

'You've been very lucky with him, haven't you?' observed Dr Nwosu.

'Perhaps. But not today. He's not even showed up! Nobody seems to know where he is!' The two men simultaneously shoved aside their Scrabble board and stood up, a little surprised.

'We spoke heart-to-heart two days ago. This is my last visit. I even hinted him on your plan for his referral. I don't know why he should suddenly shy away from me at this point.'

'Are you not a professional nutcracker like the rest of us?' shot in the lone player at the word puzzle. 'I read your seminar paper, anyway. I'm looking forward to the marriage!' He then promptly returned to his puzzle.

Dr Shaban Mshelia gave the man a bland stare, and looked back at Dr Nwosu, possibly for an explanation. The man was already deep into his puzzle, having completed his bit of nose-poking.

'My friend, what marriage is that?' asked Shaban, smiling at the yet unintroduced man.

'Your symbiosis, as you called it, between orthodox psychiatry and the traditional approach to psychosomatic disorders… Wasn't that your seminar paper?'

'Yes,' answered Shaban lamely, taking closer interest in the tense-looking man.

'Now you know what marriage I'm talking about!'

'Yes,' affirmed Dr Mshelia rather hesitantly.

'Well, that's Dr Jamabo,' explained Nwosu, at last. 'Cuts the picture of a spy, doesn't he? You'd think he's monitoring everything that's going on in this club.' Then, drawing closer to Shaban's side, he whispered, 'He's a colleague, but also a patient. Convalescing on brain games.'

Dr Nwosu's Scrabble companion, noticing that Dr Jamabo was about to unleash one more broadside, decided to distract him by jumping into the conversation. 'I'd suggest you don't worry about him,' he said aloud. Shaban glanced at Dr Jamabo's direction. 'Not that one. I mean, your man from America. He may be bogged down somewhere with depression. For all I know, you could have alienated him without knowing. I mean, your friendship; here today, gone tomorrow.'

'Possibly,' added Nwosu. 'He might even be suspecting that you'll ditch him after you've become such good friends.'

'What are the chances that we can travel together? I could not get you yesterday to find out about that. You know I'm leaving tomorrow.'

'Well, you could...' Dr Nwosu began hesitantly, punctuating his doubt with a sideways rocking of his head.

'Well?'

'Well, I'm considering his condition... the swings. He needs to be well managed on that long drive to the north. I would have liked him to go by air, but with visibility that bad even in Lagos, there's no way a plane can land safely in your Kaduna harmattan.'

'Indeed, I say no!' shouted Jamabo, jumping up. 'That young man is not a textbook case of manic-depressive psychosis! A guy trips off on good Afro-American grass and the rest of us sweat over his management. After all, marijuana is child's play when you're considering the inducers of cortical insult. It does not even cause psychasthenia!'

'Dr Jam!' called Nwosu playfully, trying to stop him before he could get to his usual point of 'auto-flight', as his colleagues called it: a violent outpouring of words which nothing could staunch except a strong dose of sedative on the spot. Dr Jam paid little heed to the moment's distraction.

'Grass does little harm, I say!' continued Dr Jamabo. 'And, let's tell the truth and shame Satan! Half of us nutcrackers do smoke grass. Well, as for me, I won't lie, because I have learnt that all liars will go to hell! Me, that's the only drug that has kept me sane since I returned to this crazy country...'

Dr Nwosu hurriedly disengaged from Dr Shaban and switched over to attend to his colleague.

Shaban left the centre a sad man, wondering whether he should not, perhaps, alter his travel plan. How could he leave without a parting word to his friend, more so now that he had even given him hope of both of them travelling together to Zaria? He felt an extra burden of guilt having learnt that Dezmond's last-minute withdrawal syndrome might have been triggered off by his sudden doubt about their newly blooming friendship.

A strong psychic bond had indeed begun to develop between Shaban and Dezmond, apart from the ordinary historical and working linkage which they had discovered. From his long intimate conversations with Dezmond, he was beginning to gain insight into his condition. Basing his judgement on a combination of his general medical practice, his live-in study of a wide spectrum of mental cases, his long interaction with experts in psychiatry, and above all, his deep probings into Dezmond's life, he began to work on the notion that Dezmond's sickness required a unique eclectic management. Perhaps, this would be the breakthrough he had been waiting for, to prove his pet thesis on the need for symbiosis between conventional Western psychiatry and African traditional mental healing.

Yet, he did not think of Dezmond in terms of having found a guinea pig. Rather, his budding commitment was being fostered by the strong bond which had sprouted between them. Not known for any strongly consistent spiritual or religious leaning, Dr Shaban Mshelia found himself philosophically examining the circumstances which culminated in his getting so involved with Dezmond. How was it that this specific seminar was timed to coincide with Dezmond's admission at the centre? If he had not met Dr Nwosu at that seminar, how would he have come to meet Dezmond? How was it that he had indeed seen and heard Dezmond talk five years before? Was it another mindless coincidence that this same man had taught a history course in which his fiancée had participated? These, and other questions and pre-existing drives in Dr Shaban Mshelia, led him to see Dezmond's case as an assignment of fate. He resolved that on returning to Zaria, he would think through it all, and develop a proposal towards getting involved in the management of Dezmond's case. He even considered it advantageous now to disengage physically from him and thus be able to set down his argument in as detached a manner as possible. He would leave Lagos next day, hoping to rendezvous with Dezmond a week later at the ABU Teaching Hospital, Kaduna. Before his departure, he would send him a note through Dr Nwosu.

Even then, on his way out of the INC, seeing the inmates pouring out of their wards for the evening's game, Shaban stopped. Assiduously, he watched the men walk into the pitch, individually and in groups. Perhaps, Dezmond Adama would surface the next minute... But it was a futile, last-minute fantasy.

Twenty hours later, and at an altitude of twenty-five thousand feet, one of the cabin staff on Nigeria Airways Flight WT 301 to Kaduna walked to Dr Mshelia's seat.

'A note for you, sir,' she said, in the typical la-di-da style of a Nigerian airline hostess. 'Sorry, one of our ground staff gave it to me just before take-off.'

The enveloped note was simply addressed, 'Shaban'. He ripped it open, his eyes flashing down through the page, to the bottom. 'Dezmond,' of course, he muttered, as he skimmed through the Kalamazoo sheet, his eyes flashing. He went back to the beginning of the page, browsing quickly through its contents. The orthography looked shaky and the lettering irregular, but it made sense:

Dezmond to Shaban.
I ran away. I know you will come
as appointed. My book is gone! *Tired*
of waiting. I need a hold on my mind. I
dreamed last night. It may happen. Do
not search. No prison sweater on my back.

Carries a crazy number. Smells suspicious.
You said to write again. I started. If not stolen also, I can trust you. Watch the blank sheets.
Look well. There are no blanks but pregnant voids. Bye.
Dezmond, PSTD, ICU, INC
No. 03 Neurosidekick Hostel

Shaban read the note slowly, several times over. Many feelings of guilt and regret about what he should or could have done were running through his mind. By intuition, or perhaps wishful thinking, he tried to convince himself that, for all his threats, Dezmond, even in his most agitated moods, would be unable to beat the security measures at INC, what with its indomitable fence and mighty halogen lamps all around.

Dr Shaban Mshelia arrived home a restless man, increasingly disturbed about Dezmond. He had scarcely sat down before he began to make phone contacts with the Culture Institute, ABU Hospital, Kaduna, and anywhere and anybody he imagined could be of help. The next day, he booked an appointment with the director of the Culture Institute to brief him and solicit his help. After a half-day of dialling, he finally got through to the Island Neuro-Psychiatric Centre, Lagos. His fears were confirmed. Dezmond Adama had disappeared from his bed, two nights before. A search team had since been sent combing all of Lagos, with the police assisting. All the relevant agencies had been put on alert.

Thanks to Dr Mshelia's efforts, after three days the Institute and the Aroji Development Union in Zaria sent out two separate teams in search of Dezmond Adama. To wear away his mounting anxiety, Shaban spent time gathering information on Dezmond, from his colleagues, from students, and through access to some files. After a week, an official search team to Lagos returned only with a formal confirmation of the patient's disappearance. Every effort, said the letter of regret, was being made with the co-operation of law enforcement agents and the Fire Department to find him. An administrative enquiry had also been set up to probe the circumstances of Dezmond's escape, achieved in spite of the stringent security arrangements of the asylum. Similarly, after a week of snooping around Aroji and neighbourhood areas without divulging their mission, the two other teams returned without a hint as to Dezmond's whereabouts.

Shaban began to slip from hope to despair and fear that the man might have died somewhere in the wilderness of Lagos, unknown, unannounced, buried by council sanitary operatives, like the carcass of a stray dog. The morbid image of a bloated, smelly carcass on the highway plagued him relentlessly, every night. Some nights he would be startled in his sleep, with his heart palpitating at an alarming rate. He could not bear the thought of Dezmond dying because it would mean the loss of so many opportunities. Besides, he feared that his visits to him in Lagos would very likely come up in any enquiry into Dezmond's vanishing act. He was bound to be linked with the incident, given the circumstances of his interaction with him.

Two weeks after his return, he took a casual leave and flew back to Lagos to start his own independent enquiries. From The Federal Palace Hotel where he lodged, he trekked to the INC, checking every likely place where men gather or where the idle or mentally unbalanced men and women of Lagos hang about. From INC he hired a taxi for the day and widened the coverage of his search. He ordered the taxi to drive gently through the heart of Lagos Island, from Keffi Street in Obalende through Igbosere to the hub of activities at Tinubu Square. There he spent an hour hovering around, drifting from one cluster of men to another, asking a question here, striking up a little conversation there. All to no effect!

From Tinubu he went to the all comers' Campos Square, where all cadres of men gather, waiting for life. Shaban did not find any clue about Dezmond. Although he was dressed in a manner that cut him out as a typical Lagos 'street smart', he did not find it easy to get his message across. Lagos hoodlums and ragamuffins know their own. Someone who does not belong stands out like an apple among rotten mangoes.

Every day, for three days, he repeated this same routine, taking different routes to the same places and adding more hang-outs of this sort to his lists. Only when he got to the Iddo Railway Terminus did he get a glimmer of hope.

An old news-vendor at the station confirmed that he had seen a man of Dezmond's description about two weeks previously. He had been the first customer to have asked for papers that morning as early as 5.30 a.m. Only a stranger would ask for newspapers that early at Iddo. The old man guessed that Dezmond must have slept in one of the many shacks or kiosks scattered on the passengers' platform, judging by his crumpled appearance. On hard reflection, the vendor who said he had operated at that same news-stand for almost thirty years, recalled that Dezmond had on a blue pyjama suit. That a man was clad in night wear in a public place did not surprise him, he said. That feature was common enough, since simple, ordinary folk could never understand the wisdom of dressing up in gorgeous apparel only to go and lie down. What surprised him, however, was what he described as the 'super perfect' English which came out of the man's mouth. Dezmond had settled for a back issue of *Time International*, which he sat down on the vendor's bench to devour, page by page.

The more the old man talked, the more he remembered, spurred by Shaban's unusual attention. He narrated how, as Dezmond avidly went through the magazine, he was glancing every so often around himself, like a wanted man. That was when the old vendor started sensing that all could not be well with this man. At this point, Shaban gave him a long hard look with his teeth clenched, as if to strike him. The old vendor chuckled with understanding and sympathy.

'My son, dem plenty for dis Lagos,' he explained. 'No way I for take know say na runaway inmate. Sorry… as for dat, who dey normal for Lagos? Me sef, I dey normal? I no know who normal for dis our jungle!'

Shaban understood. But that moment, he could not contain the bitterness, frustration and sheer physical strain of the days of fruitless searching up and down so many far-flung places.

Speechless, he paced away from the news-stand, not sure of his destination. He soon found his feet at the edge of the steep platform at a point where its protective railing had collapsed. He checked his blind steps just short of the sharp drop to the railway siding. Pacing along the edge, he studied the gridiron network of the rail lines. Two locomotive engines were shunting, puffing coal dust around the yard. The one passenger train he saw stood far off, forlorn and dormant, its carriages like a row of long-deserted blocks, their frosty-looking windows all pulled down.

No, no, thought Shaban, dissuading himself against the idea that then began to well up in him. No need… if my few hours with him are anything to go by, he wouldn't be lying low in a dirty coach, wasting away. He's probably jumped onto a train or lorry, bound for freedom, as he would see it… anywhere!' But where could that be, among ten thousand possible places?

Dr Mshelia gave up. He could not find any taxi for whatever money he offered, because the traffic was flowing in the opposite direction to his hotel on Victoria Island. He manoeuvred himself into the flood of pedestrians and began to walk...

The next day, seven days after his abortive search project, he flew back. He met some relief on getting to his house, however.

The chairman of Aroji Development Union had stuck a note under his door three days previously, saying that Dezmond had surfaced at Aroji! The details would be given him when he got in touch.

Shaban pulled back his door, wrenched the key back to 'lock' position, then began to run. He took three quick steps, then came back to his right mind. He was barely conscious that he was trying to run ten miles when his Ford Escort was securely parked in his carport. He again unlocked the door and dashed into his bedroom to get his car key.

In another fifteen minutes, he was heading towards Angwan Bako quarter.

After the longish greetings and pleasantries, Shaban could not wait any longer. 'Well, Mr Okpe, I'm waiting to hear something. Did you see Dezmond with your own very eyes?'

'In fact, I send one of our *brodas*,' explained Mr Okpe, a retired army sergeant. 'He bring message dat Dezmond is in chain. Dem tie 'im leg wit heavy wood.'

Dezmond had blazed into Aroji on Ukwo day when the market was at its peak. With the speed of an arrow, he made a beeline through stalls, skipping and jumping over wares and breaking through groups of bargainers without uttering a word. He then disappeared into space. Many saw him for what he obviously looked like: another madman drawn by the intoxicating spirit of the market place. The few who were able to recognise him as the long-expected son of Adama Ododo became petrified at the sight. They were certain that the fleeting ghost who flashed past was a sign that the young man had died in earnest in the land of the white man. From ancient times, Ukwo market was the rallying point of all sorts of devil-possessed men and women, but never had Aroji people seen such a phantom phenomenon.

That same night, however, a team of young men found an exhausted flesh-and-blood Dezmond Adama in a cassava farm where he had dug in to rest, having filled his bowels with sweet fresh tubers from the earth. They dutifully dragged him to the palace.

His family flocked to the palace of Och-Aroji to plead for their son to be released to them, but the chief would not hear it, sympathetic as he was that their anxious vigils had ended up in such a heartbreaking situation. Dezmond, he explained, being a high 'government' person, would remain under his official custody until the government came to take him away for government treatment. So it was that, in order not to risk anything and by so doing, put his throne in jeopardy, Och'Aroji had Dezmond duly bound in fetters, having sent his report to the divisional police officer, and the paramount king of Idomaland at Otukpo, awaiting further directives.

*

'Let's have your proposal in more professional terms,' Professor Gavel finally suggested. 'Something shorter, more scientific, and more realistic. Just for the files, actually, if you care to know!'

The surprise change of mind on the part of his boss brought radiance to Dr Mshelia's face.

'Thanks, Prof, for giving me the chance!'

'It takes a hard-nosed fighter such as you, to get this old Briton to budge. One exception though,' added the director of the Medical Research Centre quickly, swinging his swivel chair gently as his round eyes keenly observed this visionary old student of his. 'The witch doctor's patient must be formally referred. The centre will not bear any costs—'

'But…' Shaban cut in vainly.

'We've not done yet… If you must go, your best shot is to take a weekend. We can ill afford to allow you three whole working days, when you've already taken a whole week. You're on your own, Dr Mshelia. The centre cannot afford the expenses of this new adventure.'

Dr Mshelia's face twitched out of anger and a feeling of betrayal.

'Then, sir, you might as well keep your so-called approval!' he shouted, cracking under pressure of the past weeks. 'I ask for your support as an old friend, but look how you're now trying to kill off a noble project!'

He sprang up, and in a flash, was at the door. Prof. Gavel knew what a single-minded, focused chap Dr Mshelia had been in his clinical student days. But he would not tolerate insubordination. Before Shaban could reach the door, he was firmly ordered back.

'You are losing your head, young man,' admonished the professor. 'You mean to hoodwink me, do you?'

'I don't, sir,' replied Shaban from where he stood, midway between the door and Prof Gavel's desk. 'But it was you who taught us about perseverance, about guts and going after big dreams, and not fearing to stand out alone; about walking tall on our convictions, and all the rest of them.'

The white man's jowl suddenly reddened. As if in search of a suitable response, he brushed back the few strands of grey hair which floated delicately atop his equally reddened scalp.

'I didn't mean to embarrass you, sir. But I am very much upset myself… even before I got here. I've been under great pressure all this time. I shared some of it with you when I returned from Lagos. Both times, I tried to explain to you how I got involved with the man, rather, how God brought us together. All you said was that I was psyching myself up for a fresh brainwave. But it's not so. I strongly believe it is a matter of destiny. Prof, I need your support! This is the opportunity I've been waiting for, to work on a manic-depressive of Dezmond's history alongside a traditional healer…'

Dr Gavel was gazing away from Shaban, with his hand under his jowl, his mind far away from the surroundings. His seemingly unreceptive posture frustrated Shaban all the more, as he stopped mid-sentence to test whether he was listening. The old man was indeed lost in his own concerns.

'Sir,' Shaban intoned in a loud manner. 'I had almost left your office when you ordered me back. Or so I thought.'

'Yes, Dr Mshelia. But we don't intend that you hoodoo us into committing the centre's scant resources to this hazy venture.'

'Well, supposing I'm able to raise some funds? Could you please, grant me one more week? That way, I'll—'

'I've already told you. You can do worse than take a weekend,' Prof. Gavel cut in. 'Good afternoon, Dr Mshelia!' he concluded, wheeling round his chair to continue with his more important work.

Shaban stomped away to his own office at the end of the same block. Turning the door handle, he went in, shut the door with a thunderous bang and locked it.

He sat at his desk, got out a plain sheet of paper, and furiously set his pen to work.

Two days later, he was again standing before Prof. Gavel.

'I will not let you do any such foolish thing,' the director said, as he tore the letter of resignation and dumped the shreds in the wastebasket. 'I think I'm fast approaching burn-out,' he commented, sighing. 'We oldies must begin to yield to the new order. I've decided to give you a free hand! A week's leave, funds, the combi bus; all into the bargain!'

'Thank you very much, sir!' responded Shaban, wide-eyed with surprise.

'Your blackmail worked!' muttered the old boss frothily.

The way was through at last!

Chapter Nineteen

The combi turned off the narrow, crocodile-teeth remains of tarmac, and nosed into a half-caked mound of laterite on the shoulder of the highway.

Dr Shaban Mshelia jumped down, muttered an instruction in Hausa to his driver, and hit the dirt road. It's faster on foot, on some of these so-called feeder roads, he ruminated. He was heading for Ampia Hill, the old retreat of colonial masters. Once upon a time, it was a kind of health farm, an enviable resort. But since the British had packed their bags, it had withered down to a ghost of itself, peeping pallidly through an expanse of irrepressible *ichicha* grass.

The combi backed off the sand dune, with adolescents and adults alike cursing at the billows of red dust being spurted up by its whirling tyres. The victims were among the early birds going to Ukwo market, trotting in with their head-carried wares from the many footpaths that lead out of the bush into the main market place of Aroji. Each of them had a greeting for the stranger they met going uphill. He could only nod, smile, or raise his hand in salaam.

Dr Shaban Mshelia strode on, lunging forward his body as he progressed, in order to more easily assail the increasingly steep gradient. There was no sign of suspicion or surprise at the sight of this stranger in a cream kaftan and knitted cap who only returned greetings by gestures.

For decades, this laterite road was trod upon mainly by white colonialists, and was maintained by a well-trained, well-paid road gang, right down to a team of sweepers who manually propelled a colossal contraption on which hundreds of brooms were rigged up. Those were also the days of the Holy Ghost Fathers, with their fire-spitting matchboxes securely thumbed down on their indispensable cigarette packs, carrying their missal in the other hand. They stalked Aroji land, reducing to smoke and ashes the old gods of the people in order to clear the ground for their own unknown god.

At other times, this same Ampia road was taken up by shaggy Bohemians bearing the name of archaeologists, who courted solitude amidst their rusty findings taken from the belly of the ageless hill. In recent years, it was more often the 'black-white men', as the people called them, who were to be seen ambling up the hill, which had been abandoned to menacing giant grass. Shortly after the final survey, several dragon-like bulldozers and earth movers arrived from the Benue Provincial Works Department at Makurdi, and set to work. Their roaring noise alone scared away the numberless types of animals and birds for which Ampia was famed and revered by the natives.

That time, most mornings, instead of proceeding to their farms, village folks would gather to watch with awe, the mighty hoe of the earth mover carving its spiral road up the hill. In a matter of days, the hilltop was levelled into a plateau, and to that new creation, young men of Aroji excitedly rushed to sign up for labour, assisting in the construction of chalets from stone bricks hewn at Otukpo divisional headquarters, by former Second World War soldiers. So keen were the labour gangers that, even in the peak of the farming year, they abandoned their old parents in the bush in order to earn the white man's copper pennies. Sadly enough, because of the perennial lack of water in Aroji, all the construction had to be done during the rainy season, which was also the time of weeding, nurturing of yam sprouts, and other farm chores.

Indeed, by their ancient unwritten statute, the five founding brothers of Aroji had dedicated Ampia Hill as a spiritual retreat where their priests would withdraw for cleansing and renewal of powers. They also had a provision there for those possessed of the gods to go into seclusion, in the same way that the man who was to be the beaded chief of Aroji was required to undergo secret rites on the hill, for fifteen days.

Then came the colonialists, whose eyes never miss the most pleasant of locations for their resorts. However, owing to years of neglect by the native authority, the once idyllic resort had since become the preserve of hermits, quarantine cases and deranged minds who were kept in custody, awaiting referral.

On the fringes of the plateau, buttressed up by concrete embankments, was a cluster of living quarters, the nucleus of which had been a thatched clubhouse. To enhance privacy, these quarters were screened off by a rolling mound covered with close-cropped green grass. Thickets of pine, elm and orange trees divided this section from the rest of the sundry concrete structures on the hilltop, ringed round by an exotic garden, assembled there from among the forests and rivulets of Aroji. In those luxuriant days, a borehole existed, from which the plateau was abundantly watered by the white man's gardeners.

On the approach to the hilltop stood a police post, one of the more recent necessities. Next to it was the old dispensary which ended up specialising in the eradication of yaws. On the departure of the white men, the two-room facility was converted into a maternity services facility, but Aroji women preferred Grandmother Nature to what they considered the abomination of opening themselves up to strangers with ghostly rubber hands.

Just opposite the old dispensary, and within earshot of it,

an earth house stood all alone, looking rather like a gigantic Chubb safe. It used to serve as a cell for hard cases, but thanks to long disuse, it had since been neo-colonised by spiders and reptiles. That was before the clamorous return of Dezmond Adama to his home town.

Shaban stood before the earth house, which was now cleaned out and freed of the invading grass, rodents and insects. Nobody in sight! Now that his muscles were resting, he began to sweat even more. He pulled out his damp handkerchief and mopped his face, taking a deep breath; rubbed his palms together; took another deep breath; and placed his hand on the doorknob.

Suddenly, glancing behind, he hesitated, then withdrew his hand. That was not how it was supposed to be! His brief was that he would meet some policemen guarding Dezmond. He decided to bide his time, and pace around the grounds until someone perhaps showed up.

The time was yet eight o'clock. He felt strong and fresh despite the long climb, having broken his arduous journey at Otukpo the previous night. The harmattan mist still overhung the hill as he wandered around this former haven of the colonial torch-bearers of Benue Province.

His waiting yielded no fruit. What next? he seemed to ask himself as he eased down on a smooth rock, weighing the whole situation over. No doubt Dezmond would be in there. And how eager he was to meet him again! But how could he be sure what now to expect? He had not set eyes on him a couple of weeks... Suddenly he felt estranged, perched all alone on the hill. His heart began to trouble him as he glanced nervously around. Surely, he had made a big mistake in hurrying straight uphill. How could he have allowed his feelings to so overshadow his right senses? He should have driven directly to the palace of the chief of the district, and sought his blessing for his mission! Was it any wonder he had already come to a dead end?

All by himself, Dr Mshelia felt embarrassed. Slowly he arose and made his way down the hill...

The combi driver, Mallam Dreba had found an enthusiastic gang of school pupils to help him heave the vehicle out of the soft sand which deeply overlaid the road. His marked forehead and red, kola nut-stained teeth gave him away as he showed off his expertise, artistically revving his engine a few times for the benefit of the curious group of watchers. Having rewarded his helpers with this display, he eased the combi into the cool shade of a low-hanging *ujuru* tree, then hunched over the steering wheel for a short nap. But word had gone round, and he was not to have any rest in a village where a bus with curtained windows was enough to excite the idle elements of the market place.

'*Salaam Alekwu!* Driva, I greet you!' A bare-chested man in threadbare khaki shorts was holding on to the wing mirror of the combi. His body was covered with reddish dust from a half-day's toil on dry-season earth.

'Aleikun Salaam!' responded the driver, pleased to hear a typical Muslim greeting in a remote Idoma-speaking village. 'Ka tashi?' he asked, seeing that the man was just returning from the day's work.

'Senu,' responded the man, exposing the many gaps in his dentition as he garbled a few more phrases in his own unique version of Mallam Dreba's language. He proudly announced his name: Audu Idoma. This was a sort of ethnic pigeon-hole into which he had been put the day he was recruited to fight the white man's war of thirty-odd years previously. The recruiting officer, an old Scot, could not pronounce 'Aud' Omamanya', so Audu instantly lost his real identity, and his canines alike, defending the Allied forces in North Africa. Many times on such market days, this ex-soldier was fortunate enough to run into itinerant comrades-in-arms who often stopped to regale themselves of the choice palm wine for which Aroji is reputed

throughout Nigeria. When he saw Mallam Dreba, he took him for one of those ex-combatants, and automatically warmed up to him.

For his part, Mallam smiled generously, and sometimes laughed as Audu struggled in a mixture of broken English and broken Hausa, to boast about his reminiscences of battles he had actually fought, and others he had only heard about. Unfortunately, the poor driver had no war experience whatsoever to flaunt in return.

'I only look big,' he tried to explain, to Audu's surprise. 'At that time you are saying, I was too young to carry a gun. I only heard that the eldest son of my father's eldest brother fought in Burma. The war ate him, though.'

'Eeyaa!' exclaimed Audu in sympathy. 'Was his body—'

'No, he may be alive,' Dreba clarified. 'Some say he got charmed by a woman of Burma. Others say the war got into his brain and turned him into a wanderer who could not find his way back home.'

Audu had not yet done with his probing. Next, he wanted to find out Mallam Dreba's mission to Aroji. After some chatting he drew closer to the driver's ear and whispered something, to which the stranger nodded vigorously with a look of great relish. Mallam hopped down, locked his door, and checked to ensure that all the rest were equally secure. Upon which, the ex-combatant wheeled round and stepped out in a slow-motion version of the good old forward march in quick time. Without doubt, the parade-ground bellowing of his erstwhile British drill 'Sarge-Major' was still ringing in his ears.

Meanwhile, a pack of schoolboys, clad in their all-purpose khaki shorts and grey shirts, engaged themselves around the combi, trying to unravel the unfamiliar abbreviation on it. They had recently been taught a lesson on common abbreviations but they doubted whether even their teacher could decipher this one. One boy proudly guessed that NMRC had to do with Nigeria Mining Coal. Indeed, it was a close shot, because at that time a mining company was mobilising towards exploiting the large deposit of high-grade coal at nearby Owukpa.

'You may be right,' commented a heady urchin, notorious for arguing with boys of a higher age group. 'But how about the letter R? What does that one stand for?'

'This motor is too clean for coal miners!' argued another. 'Has any of you ever seen a bus with curtains hanging in its window like our HM's office?'

During all the prattling and roundabout inspection of the combi, Akawo Adama stood aside listening, thinking and saying nothing. It had dawned on him that some men who recently visited his father's house had come in a car with this same abbreviation. They have surely come to take my brother away, he lamented quietly. A pall of familiar gloom fell over him. He remembered a triumphant day, two and a half years previously, when a car had arrived at the compound of his exalted father to take Dezmond the first leg of his trip to America.

Overcome with sadness, the boy sneaked behind a stall as tears began to fill his eyes. Thus, Akawo, who often took centre stage in peer group banter was forced to refrain from the babbling exchange of schoolboy speculation on the meaning of NMRC. What, indeed, could the combi be doing in Aroji? Unfortunately, as it was an issue of literacy, none of the curious adults around was qualified to arbitrate. Neither were the boys bold enough to approach the stranger who was watching their carrying-on from a safe distance. Perhaps this whole scene of lingering around his vehicle was beginning to annoy him; one could not tell. Not many owners of pleasure cars, for example, would treat kindly any boy who so much as attempted to see the reflection of his image on their car mirrors.

'You little things, get away from there!' Audu Idoma was

marching back now, whistling an old drill song. 'Why do you press your bellies on someone's motor? See how your little mouths are running just like those of your idle mothers! Have you never seen a small bus?' He stood straight as a ramrod, a keg of wine dangling from his clenched fist. 'You little house-rats! What is this noise all about?'

The boys chorused their answers at the old bully: they were practising their *abbrevashun* lesson. After all, Teacher had given them a simple guide for increasing their learning: scraps of paper picked up on the road are not to be read, as they could make one blind. Abbreviations and the legends written on lorries and taxies are for learning good and bad English alike!

Audu took more interest in the gang's curiosity as the boys boldly carried on despite his roaring rebuke. The combi truly looked more like a little cabin than a car, with a camp bed and refrigerator fitted in. Before he went to buy palm wine, he had not been told the driver's mission to Aroji. It was, perhaps, more sensible to find out from a neutral source. He therefore began to befriend one of the boys, in order to extract from the group, whatever they had gathered from their own snooping.

'Why don't you boys ask Akawo Adama?' he prompted, pouting his lips in the direction of Akawo who had wiped off his tears and was standing close by, to hear what his peers were saying. 'Is that not Akawo who writes and reads all sorts of letters? I hear he can even tell what is inside *telegra*. Ask him!'

Akawo stood aside, watching, saying nothing.

'It looks as if Akawo knows this thing,' volunteered one of the boys. 'Only he does not want to tell us.'

'I know why!' shot in another. 'He thinks that that *abbrevashun* may appear in our examination and nobody else will get it, only he.'

'If Akawo does not tell, who else can?' asked Audu, who was running out of patience, as the boys were becoming like a persistent swarm of bees. He wanted to get rid of them, even as he set down the keg. 'Now, go ask your teacher, all of you! Go now!'

Mallam Dreba was pleased to see his friend return to the stall. Audu took the string handle of the keg and placed it in Dreba's palm, like one awarding a trophy, saying, 'This is your drink! You never went to Burma, but your brother did. We are all one!' Laying two drinking gourds beside the keg, he added, 'The whole keg is your own. If you want, you can take it with you, but not the calabash itself. The wine seller must have it back. But if you like, we can finish the wine here,' he advised Mallam Dreba, who only smiled back in appreciation, not very sure as to the hidden agenda in Audu's rigmarole.

The men had a taste of the wine – one gourd each, for openers – and nodded together in approval of the foaming keg. To Audu Idoma, son of the soil of palm wine, this was pure, undiluted nature's brew. As the milky draught flowed down his gullet, it stirred up a little storm in his stomach. A ball of gas was kicked back up his throat, promptly exploding in a well-rounded belch of titanic volume. Another round followed; they chatted some more, and refilled the gourds, their gullets having been wetted, waiting for more. Yet another round…

'This wine, *kai*!' extolled Audu. 'It has power!'

Mallam Dreba was so titillated that he removed his cap and began to rub his scalp, baring his red teeth as he smiled. The sensation was so strong that he plunged his forefinger into his ear, wildly rolling it with his right eye shut tight.

'Akro wine!' continued Audu Idoma as the drink registered its effect all the more. 'This is the type Aroji men call *efru*! Gunpowder! The stuff of real men!'

'Allah!' responded Dreba. 'This one can knock down a

man, *walahi*!' he exclaimed, letting out a war yell.

'Give me a handshake! I never knew you Hausamen understand good palm wine! You are right. *Efru* throws a man up and knocks him down again. Like thunder!'

Another round of drinks ensued. With each serving, Mallam Dreba took pains to skim off the layer of debris, drowned bees, and floating pieces of palm fibre which sat on the brim of his gourd.

'Not like that!' Audu said, coaching him. 'That way, you waste the drink.' With a swipe of his little finger, he cleared off the unwelcome layer of murk atop his own gourd. He then laid the keg on its side to deceive any likely self-invited drinker into believing that its contents had been exhausted.

'That is how to clean your wine,' he explained, splattering the scum into the dust. 'Or, if you want, just dip your lip under the top and suck! The foam and the dead flies can only end up on your moustache! Everything has its own place. After all, our people say that the maggot inside of meat is meat!'

'Kai!' exclaimed the driver, squeezing his face in disgust, to Audu's amusement.

'But that's how we value our wine! It is only he who has had his fill of pounded yam who can afford to remove the yam pellets to throw away instead of chewing and cherishing them.'

By this time, conversation was overflowing between the men. This seemed the right opportunity to enquire into the purpose of Mallam Dreba's visit to Aroji. The driver said he did not know the details. His boss had only mentioned something about a friend of his who had just returned from America who was sick and needed his presence around him. That hint was enough for Audu to begin to pour out everything he knew about Dezmond and his family...

'The day he set foot on this ground, we were all there!' he went on... and on. 'I was at Ukwo market. I saw it happen myself!'

'*Kai!* You saw him with these two eyes?'

'*Walahi!* I saw him myself! He flew into the market like *Ak'takpa* masquerade.' he added, then rambled on. At last he began to conclude. 'What caused his madness is not from outside. It is right in his father's house. But I'm not the one to tell you! Tell your master that the person he should go to is Obochi Itete. That man was the only one who was able to cool down Adama's son. He will tell you people everything. When you are going there, take palm wine and kola nut for the old man. Nobody goes to Obochi empty-handed.'

'Audu Idoma, enough! You have spoken enough!' rang out a voice from nowhere.

'Ubu, what do I have with you?'

The three men charged into the stall, and picked up their main exhibits, the half-empty keg and two gourds.

'Why do you do this?' Audu challenged them. 'Did Och'Aroji send you to spill my drink?'

'Sit back on your buttocks, you knower-of-foreign-tongues!' shouted one of them, wearing a brown fez. 'You know that you have done wrong!'

'But I am trying to explain!' ventured Audu.

'Close your mouth!' ordered the second brown fez, lifting his baton.

'Why? Were you sent here to unsex Aud' Omamanya? Or do you forget? I have fought and beheaded even white men. I cannot fear your big stick. Look at this man! Do you know why government sent him and his master here?'

'Those are the questions you will answer. Since you are now the one who buys wine for strangers in the name of an old soldier, you can answer for yourself. Och'Aroji himself summons you!'

*

Och'Aroji stroked his whiskers pensively, his embroidered toga spread lavishly on a patchwork of animal skins. His Royal Highness was holding a court session. Finally, the last case...

'Audu, son of Omamanya! You do well to buy drink for a stranger. It is, therefore, not for your kindness that you are brought before our court. Kindness, especially to people from other lands, is wise, and to be encouraged. For if we ourselves do not receive the reward for it, our children scattered in foreign lands will.

'Idoga!' saluted Audu, bowing lower still, even in his squatting position.

'But,' continued Och'Aroji, raising his voice, 'what great conversation were you making with Mallam Dreba? His master should be our guest.'

After a nervous false start, Audu bowed again, and responded. '*Idoga!* I have no plea. I agree with whatever you say. Long live Och'Aroji!'

'That is good! Accepting guilt is the first step to peace. It is said that before a load is to be put on the head, it is first placed on the knee. Elders of Aroji, is that not so?'

'You speak wisely, *Idoga*!'

'This stranger that you want to entertain for us, do you know what brought him to Aroji?'

Audu sat mute.

'He who keeps silent, accepts fault. You made it look as if the man came to Aroji to drink wine. Or that it is a matter for the market place. You think it is wise to wag your tongue about something that is not your concern? Can a child roast a black pea?'

'No,' chorused the court. 'Because he knows not the difference between a black one and a burnt one,' they concluded in unison.

Och'Aroji took a long, hard look at the offender and went on to deliver judgement. 'If it were in those days before white men came and turned us into women, we know what we would have done to your sharp tongue. But these days are different. The world has changed! The new law has tied our hands. You catch a thief with all ten fingers in the oil and the white man's law says, evidence? The thief buys a lawyer, and before your eyes, black is turned into white… But, Aud' Omamanya, this is my own court! No other government will come here to tell me how to keep order in this land! This court now decides, and it is so decided, that for the next three moons, you will help me run the palace!'

'Idoga!' shouted the whole gathering and those standing around.

'*Idoga* has spoken,' pleaded Audu. 'But I do not understand what this penalty means. Who will help me?'

One of the court members came to his rescue. 'All the wine needed to entertain visitors to the palace for the next three months – you will be bringing it.'

Audu's jaw dropped in shock.

'*Idoga*!' repeated the court, moulding their fists in homage and as a sign of their desire that the chief may live long. 'You have spoken with wisdom! Long live *Idoga*!'

Chapter Twenty

The reverberation of the combi engine in the forest, coupled with Shaban's tiredness after his futile climb, began to lull his senses to sleep. Lying flat at the back of the bus, he found the rocking dance of its tyres less violent than he had previously experienced. The swooshing sound of the newly tuned-up engine added to the drowsing effect.

As the combi pulled up in front of Nnamdi Azikiwe Conference Centre, Mallam Dreba gave it a final, flushing rev and his passenger sprang up from his sleep, momentarily confused. The thirty-minute drive to Nsukka seemed to have taken only a wink of an eye.

Shaban sprawled on his settee purposely to take a nap. He was avoiding the fuller comfort of the bed in order not to sleep beyond the ninety minutes he allotted himself, having booked a wake-up call with reception.

The day had not been far spent although it had started off so early that much had already happened even before noon. Dr Mshelia was going over details of the day's happening in sequence, right from when he woke up at 6 a.m. at Otukpo to that moment he found himself slouching on the settee. He felt hollow and unfulfilled, as he could not lay a finger on any concrete achievement of the day; except perhaps the valuable tips his driver had got from the ex-combatant on how to get a cordial reception at the palace. He began to imagine Dezmond's condition in a dark hole on the hill, probably reduced to bare bones for want of care. He wondered if he went back to Ampia Hill immediately after getting Och'Aroji's blessing, whether the guards would be on their beat, to enable him get into Dezmond's cabin.

Sleep did not come, after all. Rather, as his belly rumbled continually, he suddenly realised how hungry he was. He looked at his watch. It was 1.30 p.m.! Time to stop courting sleep and go for lunch! By the time he would have had his lunch, Mallam Dreba would have done his *zuhur* prayer. They would then set out for the palace of Och'Aroji, seeing how near Aroji is to Nsukka.

It was just as well that Dr Mshelia had been unable to set eyes on Dezmond earlier on in the day. His offence would have been considered more serious. The proper protocol required that any visitor of rank and importance should visit Och'Aroji first, but in his anxiety the doctor had gone straight ahead to where he would quickly see his friend. Soon, however, his drunken driver told him all that Audu Idoma had revealed. It was then that Dr Shaban Mshelia realised how damaging his breach of decorum would have been. Despite the fact that he had with him a formal letter of introduction from both his own employers, and the Institute of Culture, he had unwittingly downplayed the role of the chief concerning Dezmond. From the details he gathered from his driver, he now saw that the chief's involvement went beyond mere protocol and fatherly blessing for a worthy mission. Thus, his early-morning embarrassment in not meeting with Dezmond or his police guards turned out to be a blessing in disguise.

The afternoon was a less busy period in the Chief's palace. Dr Mshelia drove in from his hotel room, refreshed enough from his short nap en route. He was hopeful that this was the appointed day of reunion with Dezmond Adama.

After a brief waiting in the visitors' lounge, he was ushered into the presence of Och'Aroji, this time, with only a few royal advisors present. To the visitor's surprise, after having acknowledged his greetings in Idoma-Aroji dialect, the chief opened up in superb English, delivered in a well-practised, dignified tone. The Och'Aroji set aside the letters which had been handed him through an aide, in order to first present the visitor the traditional welcome gesture of kola nuts and palm wine. After the first serving of drinks to wash down the bittersweet taste of the nut, it was time to broach the issue at hand. Och'Aroji cleared his throat. This time, having since finished with the pleasantries, the business of the court was to be conducted in the proper, official language of the land. The court interpreter had already taken up his usual position.

'Tell Dr Mshelia that we welcome him once again, to Aroji. His journey is for good reason and Och'Aroji thanks him. We also thank the people who sent him. They have taken our son to be somebody. If not, they would not have shown this concern…

'Dezmond only bears the name of Adama, but he belongs to all of Aroji… Our people say that your child is your own only while he is in the womb… once he is born, he belongs to all. The situation of our son has brought us great sorrow; we were all rejoicing when the news of his return came. But the way he finally landed, put us to great shame. You have heard that he is on the hill; that is so… but we did not just catch him and put *odo* locks on his legs.

'That first day when he scattered the market, it was some age-mates of his who pursued him and brought him here. Indeed, it was myself who ordered that he be taken to Obochi, our own great doctor here…' The few in the chamber applauded on hearing the name of the great Obochi Itete. The chief resumed his account. 'We did not know that Dezmond would agree to drink herb medicine from clay pots. He was cooled down at first… then it all came back. Every day, we were receiving reports. Doctor, whoever worked this madness on our son has gone for the worst of it.

'The time the harmattan reached its high point was the worst. You know that the season of harmattan puts fire into mad people. He managed to escape from Obochi's hand… Those who saw him said he was speaking out all the big, big things he went to learn in America… Obochi did not sleep; he nearly went mad himself when his government patient disappeared… After three days, we heard that Dezmond had joined a hand-clapping church… They said they were praying for him.

'They went about breaking people's shrines… That was when he set fire to the sacred forest of Aroji… We saw big trouble coming if we did nothing. We did not know what he would do next, or what harm somebody might do to him; because, in Aroji, if you break up someone's shrine, you have killed such a person. That is so. It was then we ordered them to put odo on his legs while being treated in Obochi's place. When his eyes came down, the lock was removed and he began to walk about. Not long after, something happened again… This time, I heard that government was sending people to take him. Then, for fear that he may again run away, I arranged for men with power to watch over him…'

'Idoga,' Dr Mshelia gently cut in, raising his hand to ask a question. 'Is it the police you mean?'

'Yes, my son. We were forced to hand him over for sake of safety. We had to protect the people, and the young man himself. Once you have heard the early sounds of an approaching war, that war should not catch you unprepared. We also had to protect our position. We heard that government was going to send an ambulance to take him to a big hospital at Kaduna. My fear was that if they came, the way you have now come, and did not find the young man, I will be in trouble…'

The chief concluded by giving a free hand to Dr Mshelia to visit Dezmond, his parents and Obochi, who had been treating him even under police custody on Ampia Hill. He appointed a guide for him and offered him a guest house within the palace.

As the usual refrain of *'Idoga!'* rent the air, Dr Mshelia stood up to respond to what he had heard. 'May Och'Aroji live long!' he said, saluting with both his fists. 'I feel honoured to be hearing this report directly from our father's mouth. I want to thank you very much for all that you did. After going round to see things for myself, I will be in good position to say more. I can assure you that the people who sent me here will leave no stone unturned in making sure that your son recovers and gets back to his work. As for your offer, I am most grateful... but I will not be able to sleep here.'

'Why not?' interjected the Och'Aroji, not waiting for any interpretation from English to Idoma.

'Idoga!' responded Dr Shaban Mshelia, fast getting in tune with the custom of addressing the chief. 'I will not be able to sleep well. I am too small to sleep in the palace. Of course. I am your guest but I ask that you permit your servant to be sleeping at Nsukka.'

'Well, as you want it.' conceded the chief, who instantly ordered his aides to remember to load Dr Mshelia's vehicle with yams, plantains and coconuts on the day of his departure from Aroji.

The court stood up in obeisance as Och'Aroji withdrew to his private quarters, accompanied only by a couple of senior court members and some personal aides.

*

It was well after two o'clock before two of the policemen swaggered back up the hill. They had been revelling in the market place, freeloading, when the story hit the air that the long-awaited government doctor had arrived at the palace.

Though unimpressed by them, Shaban was relieved to find them manning their beat this time. They greeted him with an exaggerated form of military salute intended to ingratiate them to him, but he paid little attention to their antics.

'You abandoned your post!' he said accusingly.

'Sorry sah! We carry our sitrep go Chief house, sah!'

'Which chief?' barked Dr Mshelia. 'And what sitrep?'

'Och'Aroji, sah!' thundered the sergeant. 'Situation Report, sah!'

'Liar! Maybe you don't know, but I am coming straight from the palace. Do you know how serious it is to abandon your post?'

'Sah, please, help us! We went on break. Please forgive and forget!' said the corporal, kneeling down.

'All three of you left the place at once, on break?'

'Sah, please, don't put sand in our garri, we beg you!' pleaded the sergeant on behalf of the team.

At this point, Shaban was certain that he had put sufficient fear into them to expect good conduct in their assignment henceforth.

'I want that door unlocked,' ordered Dr Mshelia, nodding towards the lone, bunker-type mud cabin. The corporal rushed forward, rummaged in his breast pocket and strode to the door.

Shaban's veins were bulging. This was not just another medical situation. Neither was his brain now operating as that of an empirical research scientist. A short reel of images rolled before his mind's eye. Now, right behind that door, he would find Dezmond, the man for whom he had spent two weeks searching!

The corporal held the door for Shaban and the sergeant. They stepped in. Nobody! At first, Shaban thought the dim room was playing a trick on his sight. But even after his eyes had got adjusted, all he could see was stark naked space! He turned speechlessly to the sergeant with the self-evident question. Confused, the operatives of what was called 'de madman cabin' stared back at him.

'Where's he?' asked Shaban, as calm as still water.

That moment, the corporal came to his boss's rescue. 'He is dere, sah!' he shouted, pointing straight over Shaban's shoulder. 'De cabin get two apartment, sah! Room and parlour, sah!'

What Shaban had mistaken for a back wall turned out to be a plywood partition in drab grey which blended easily with the overall dimness. Relief showed on the face of all three. Excited at this opportunity of a one-up advantage over his sergeant, the corporal went a step further. 'Dis very room we are standing, is like buffer zone for de man,' he explained. 'It was one big cell before carpenter divide it into two. De man say 'e no wan' surprise entry… 'e say he mus' get outer apartment to warn him when somebody is coming.'

Shaban heard sounds of brisk movements inside the next room. He waved off the policemen and knocked. He heard a creaking noise like that of a weak-jointed chair from which a heavy occupant is attempting to get up. Another tense moment.

'Who's this?' came the familiar big voice, only sounding more fatigued. 'Give the password!'

Shaban hesitated, not sure how to proceed. Nobody had told him about password. In all his imagined scenarios of this reunion, he had least expected to be thrown off-balance just at the threshold. He coughed, then cleared his throat.

'It's Shaban! Shaban Mshelia! Remember?' he shouted through the panel door, trying hard to play down the anxiety that came through, even in his voice.

A deliberate, slow shuffling and rustling of papers followed, which took several minutes. Dezmond then unbolted the door, and hesitantly opening it, lowered his gaunt frame to see who really it was.

The two stood on either side of their Rubicon, staring speechlessly at one another. At last, when it appeared to him that Dezmond was about to slam the door on his face. Shaban ventured, 'Remember me? Shaban...' He wasn't sure which of his several rehearsed openings to now cue into.

The other man kept staring at him, rather like a pugilist sizing up an opponent. The fear of that door being slammed on him still hung over Shaban. Not knowing what next to do, he simply uttered what occurred to him that very second. 'Frankly, I'm at a loss what to say.'

'Why?' Dezmond asked.

A difficult question, thought Shaban, but better than this stony silence! 'Well, you wrote me a note,' he continued. 'I wondered where to find you. You said not to bother searching, but it wasn't easy to just sit down and forget you. I was relieved... I am now relieved.'

'I don' want to remember that Island place,' Dezmond said quietly.

'Well, I am glad I've found you!' said Shaban, smiling to break the tense atmosphere. 'I'm glad we've reunited!'

'Come inside,' ordered Dezmond, stepping backward as Shaban bowed through the passage. 'Sit there,' he added, showing the one squeaky chair to his guest.

'No provision for guests here?' quipped Shaban as he sat down.

'This was a cell. Maximum security. One prisoner, one chair... but prison is a dunghill. Here the mushroom of fraternity thrives...' He stepped forward and shut the door, bolting it. 'As you can see, nobody else is here... except I, me, and myself. And air, which is almost everywhere. Like God...' As he spoke, he fumbled among the heap of papers under his whitewood table and struck a match. His faithful kerosene lantern was resting at a corner of the earthen floor. As light filled the cabin, Shaban got an opportunity to quickly survey the man and his abode.

Dezmond stood, feet astride, wearing a singlet and tennis shorts. He seemed to be deliberately posing to oblige his visitor. From Shaban's sitting position, he looked shorter than his natural height. His head was coated with a dry greenish paste which, in the near darkness before the lamp was lit, looked like a crop of new hair. Perhaps, reasoned Shaban, it is his close haircut that made the man look shorter. Plus, he had added more flesh to his lanky frame. His face looked rather plump for his build. It bore a menacing stamp, like that of a bulldog reared on soya bean. His beard was full and unkempt.

'You came to talk,' was Dezmond's curious remark as he hung on the edge of the table. He seemed to be addressing whatever he guessed was going on in Shaban's mind. His friend understood.

'To start with, I'm glad you're somewhere! How are you doing?' No response. 'I really got scared when I read your note!'

'Why?'

'I thought I would never catch up with you again. Now, where do we begin? Imagine all the drugs you had to take in Lagos, and now, the herbs... We must draw a line—'

'I have,' Dezmond cut in. 'The line's in me. Eternity this end is every twenty-four hours. No, that's not right! Eternity has to be circular. It has no end. But I know when the line was drawn. In any case, I've put Lagos behind me! Backward never, forward ever! If you've come to take me, that's your answer.'

'I've not come to take you. I've come to talk. How did you get here, after all?'

After another long bout of muteness and gazing, Dezmond resumed talking. 'I got here sick... very sick. I don't know, but I remember most things. I was at Offa. The train became a centipede. The ticketers wouldn't let me be. They chained me to a drunk. Dragged me all over. We looked weird. He said, "Let's jump train!" An' we did... oh! The man fell in pieces. Then I broke off him and ran... How I got back here, only God knows! Guess most scared kids run to their father's house. I said I wasn't coming back here. I don't know... must be a below-conscious thing, y'know. I just kept walking and hiking... trucks, bikes, anything. My neck was stiff, my head was like lead... no sleep for days... just shivering through day and night, unable to get a wink. No question of food! My tongue was dangling. Just dangling hopelessly, way out of place... couldn't say something. That's when the medicine man came in. He made my head look like a fetish stone!' He paused. 'Got my note?' he asked.

'Yes... and I've heard about the man.'

'Said I have brain fever. Can you figure that?' Dezmond chuckled. 'You talked to him yet?'

'Not yet. But I've asked the chief to make my wish known to the old man. It's a chance of a lifetime!'

'Yes,' remarked Dezmond, smiling. 'The old man's far out!'

Dr Shaban Mshelia looked round in between the dialogue. High up the thick unplastered wall, he could discern a narrow vent, stuffed with old rags.

'How d'you sleep here?'

'There.' Dezmond indicated the strip of earthen platform by the wall, stretching his lanky leg in that direction. 'Bare and cold. An essential balm in the old man's healing science.'

'How can a man breathe in this rat-hole?'

'Through the same old nostrils,' answered Dezmond. 'Air is spirit... mysterious and omnipresent... almost. I often play games in here, some hot days.'

'Like?'

'Simple! Pull out the rag up there, and let in oxygen... Then it's time for aerobics of the medulla oblongata!'

'How's that done?'

'Well, see that door?'

'Yes.'

'Guess its height?'

'Six feet?'

'Good shot! An' I'm six two. Or was!' He stood up.

'Yes,' nodded Shaban, amused, watching.

'Any time I can't breathe, or feel crampy, I walk back and forth, bending through that door to the other room... Done, I climb up and block the vent.' He sat back after demonstrating. 'You guys are only used to clean places,' Dezmond continued, loosening up all the more in speech. At last, here was a person of like mind, the type he had not been able to talk to since leaving Lagos. 'You've never been chained and left in a mud cabin, have you?'

'I've only been luckier, that's all!'

'Well, I know you're always different... how come?'

Another question that Shaban did not expect.

'Umm... I guess I try to be natural... nothing special!' he replied.

'Nobody else shows concern about this place. But I'm going to have the last laugh! I'll refuse to quit! No bull-dozer can move me from here! Unless they're moving Ampia altogether.'

'What would you be doing?'

'The things hermits do... I'll turn this hill into a new monument – to myself! Nobody will harass me while I stay here, listening to the soul of the village.'

'What's the soul of the village?'

'Once you've been up here this long, you've been with spirits. Back there in the valley, you can never really be at home again.'

'Dezmond, much depends on you... or whoever stays that long up here. Now, tell me about being a hermit.'

'But, you know, I'm not even sure where you're coming from. Why did you think I'd forgotten you? When two friends meet again, do they just stand and stare at each other? You know I had to run away. I would have died already... Know something? I hiked my way to Ile-Ife without one cent!'

'What for?'

'I went to bury a brother... shot dead in the US. I didn't let you know, but I had a piece of him all along. He'd asked to be buried where he said his ancestors come from.'

There was another long, unstrained pause as Shaban waited for more explanation. It never came, however.

'Listen, Dezmond, tell me more about that experience.'

'Never mind! You'll understand. You told me to try and recollect everything in order to forget them... something like that. Didn't you? Then don't ask what happened to Brother Wale-Jay! I've put him behind me. For ever!'

Shaban let it pass. As he sensed another long lull descending on them, threatening to freeze the flow of conversation, he found another wick on which to rekindle Dezmond's light.

'How d'you kill time here?'

'Time?' He laughed. 'It is timeless here. Irrelevant... Our people tell time by the sun, anyway. In here, there's no sun. So, nothing tells time. Except the sounds of rural life which filter through my wall vent now and then.'

'What sounds, for example?' teased Shaban, adjusting himself on the chair.

'I remember how you said it... gestation and delivery, packed into an hour, right? I tried some poems, y'know? That's one thing a hermit can do. Make poems and other things.'

'I'd love to study all of your creations,' responded Shaban enthusiastically. 'You call it exorcism, don't you?'

'You've got it!'

'I'd love to see some of your exorcism,' he said, urging Dezmond on, and they laughed. Shaban hardly realised when Dezmond began to recite his lines by heart, in a deceptively normal conversational tone.

The plaintive xylophone of pestles speaks of dusk;
These dying days, every household pounds cassava
Delivered of the year's produce.
The cycle of monotony! Men are already digging
To find where to hide seeds for the next harvest;
You sow, you reap… you reap, you sow
Meanwhile we eat tapioca flour with harmattan soot.
The difference is fine, finite, finito!

'Wow! This is surely coming from somewhere! Your note said you'd started writing. Is that bit from there? This can't just be coming out of your mouth!' Shaban could not hide his excitement.

'A blind man goes by aid of a stick. Every man has a crutch. Mine is the word. Left to them actin and aeroplanes alone, my brain would've burst by now. Have you seen our Big Wheel?'

'What's our big wheel?' asked Shaban with amusement.

'The chief… most things end with him. If they don't also begin with him!'

'Yes, I had to begin with him,' confirmed Shaban, laughing at Dezmond's rebellious perception of the chief of Arojiland.

'I told you… but I thought he'd be hunting palm squirrels, like his subjects. Witnessed any of our harmattan bushfires yet? At this time, the forests crackle with fire… I lit one myself! Just tied some dry grass to the tail of a lizard, lit it and let go! The result was a straight line of freedom!'

'Dezmond, was this for real?'

'When I was in Obochi's place… I needed to do something for the people, since I brought them nothing from America. You see, there's a big forest where nobody is allowed to hunt. It is reserved, so all the game that escape from everywhere else run in there. Once a year, the chief sends young men into that forest on a festival hunt for him. All the big game is shared by him and some of his elders. This year, I had great fun letting loose the poor creatures in that forest!'

Shaban recalled the chief's own account of the incident. 'The Och'Aroji told me that was a serious defilement.'

On hearing that, Dezmond burst into a guffaw. 'Well, I promise him more! Maybe, the first time, the ordinary folks were afraid to kill and eat. But I'll do another liberation for them! That's how to begin to snuff out the elders' witchcraft from this land…'

Dezmond and Shaban carried on their conversation until nightfall. Owing to the enclosed nature of the cabin, they were not aware of the time spent until Shaban took a look at his watch.

'Phew!' he whistled in surprise. 'It's 6.36 already!'

'Did you bring along a sleeping bag?' asked Dezmond.

'How d'you mean?'

'Gets quite cold up here at nights.'

'You'll be disappointed, Dez. I'm not sleeping here.'

'Oh, well!' gasped Dezmond as if he had just realised something. 'Of course… Where will you be sleeping?'

'I've already checked into a chalet.'

'Oh, someone must have built a hotel while I was away.'

'No, not here! At Nsukka University; the Zik Conference Motel. Man, Aroji could well have been Igbo country!'

'No, thanks! retorted Dezmond. 'Everyone belongs

where he belongs!'

As Shaban stood up, Dezmond also moved away from the table. A heap of papers suddenly collapsed underneath it. Seeing how nervously Dezmond hurried to shove back the stack of sheets, Shaban got very curious. The question on his mind was evident on his face as Dezmond looked up from his abortive effort at concealment.

'The garbage of hermitage!' explained Dezmond. 'I tried to hide it when you knocked, but…'

'Whatever you want is okay by me,' remarked Shaban, shrugging. 'But what goes up must come down!'

'Some things go up but don't come down,' retorted Dezmond. 'Like prices, for example.'

'You know something? We just got talking and went on without end.'

'That's right! What are you here for? It's by talking that things begin to happen.'

'Well, I want you to know I've come here only for our sakes. I believe you and I have been brought together for a purpose. I have come here to fulfil a destiny. We'll talk a lot more tomorrow. It's been a long day for me…'

Dezmond led him into the other room and offered him a handshake without a word more. He looked too sombre for the man who had been chatting so excitedly a short while previously.

Shaban took his hand and looking him straight in the eyes, added his parting shot. 'I have a mission to fulfil with you: to help you get back to full health. You're right on track already. I've promised myself that you're going to be the toast of my career. How that will be, we'll discuss tomorrow afternoon. Keep exorcising, friend!'

'I know! You are coming all the way just for those sheets! That's a lot of trusting, man! You think you'll achieve something?'

Dr Mshelia stood, his face brimming with great expectation. A snapshot of his shaky entrance into Dezmond's cabin and the moments of the staccato exchange of question and answer flashed before his eyes. If, in one day alone, he could elicit such a level of response from Dezmond, then he had good reason to feel so satisfied. His bold experiment would be well worth the adventure.

'Well,' responded Dr Mshelia, offering a handshake, 'we're off to a good start. I see things working out fine. Take care now!'

With these words, Dezmond's visitor strode into the dusk.

Chapter Twenty-One

The sun had barely risen by the time the combi bus took off from Nsukka, heading for kilometre 72 on the outskirts of Aroji. There stood a wooden signpost with the name 'OLEBO' scrawled in irregular letters. Below it an arrow was drawn, pointing to a wide, motorable path, bordered by a hedge of Bahama grass interspersed with assorted fruit trees. Only a few, perhaps, of the thousands who ply the trunk 'A' road ever gave thought to the meaning of this innocuous name among the jamboree of public and private signboards which assault your eyes as you drive through Aroji country; it means. 'Place of Peace.'

The Place of Peace, situated two kilometres into the hinterland of Aroji, was the best-known of the traditional medicine houses in the area, and was run by Baba Obochi. He hailed from the stock of Itete Eeta, known in folk history for its successive generations of powerful shamans and healers, particularly gifted in the treatment of mental illness and fractures.

Along the two-kilometre drive to the Olebo healing home, a settlement of farmers had grown over the years. On either side, Dr Shaban Mshelia saw groups of children waving greetings. The combi soon pulled up before a rectangular house with sheet metal roofing, around which were built two rows of thatched huts, whitewashed with fermented tapioca paste. More fruit trees dotted the premises at regular intervals. The grounds looked well tended and the loose beach-like sand was firmed with gravel. A teenage boy ran out to receive the visitor.

'Welcome, sir! My fada is greeting you,' he said pointing to the central building. 'He says for you to go dere.'

Baba Obochi was squatting beside a patient with a leg fracture from a pre-dawn motorcycle collision. Two cyclists without lights had crashed into each other on a narrow footpath. The man was screaming so loudly that all Obochi could do by way of welcoming his visitor was to signal him to sit down.

'If it is not *ibri*, the devil, how was it that two motorcycles without headlights happened to be passing that very way at that same time?' the old man wondered aloud to himself. Without taking his eyes off his patient, he signalled to his son, Ijoni, who promptly dashed off. He soon returned with a cockerel in his hand. Leaving the accident victim groaning on a mat, Baba got hold of the bird and began to press its leg at various points. Each time he pressed a particular spot on the cockerel's leg, the man would scream more, writhing on the mat. As his fingers kept stroking the cockerel's bone, so did he engage himself simultaneously in small talk.

'My son, thank you for coming,' he at last opened his mouth to greet his guest, with Ijoni translating. 'I received your message from Och'Aroji, and I am ready. I want to tell you, I like the ways of you black white men. See how you sent ahead to prepare me for your coming!' He left Ijoni talking with Dr Mshelia while he concentrated on the patient.

The visitor watched with rapt attention as Obochi continued pressing the cockerel's leg bone, with his eyes darting from time to time to his now groaning, now screaming patient, whose leg wriggled in pain.

'Ijoni, tell the visitor what I am doing,' Baba Obochi instructed his small boy. 'The one you don't understand, I will explain it to you, then you will interpret.'

'My fada is using de fowl's leg to find out where de man's bone is broken,' explained the boy.

'Yes, I can see that.'

'Tell him, there are many ways of getting to a stream,' Baba instructed without looking up. The old man was pre-empting a common question from people who had watched him perform orthopaedic wonders, using the art his ancestors had passed down to him.

Suddenly, the man on the mat screamed louder than ever, and went mute. Baba in turn left the cockerel while his son rubbed an oily substance on the man's leg. After that, he tied it with a string, having supported the fracture with two splints of wood. He then poured out a potion and handed it to the patient. That done, Ijoni brought him a calabash of water and held it up for him to wash his hands.

'I welcome you…' said Baba Obochi in greeting, for the hundredth time. Ijoni now put away the calabash and as usual, took his seat beside his father. Not new to the job of interpreting, he had developed proficiency in his own style of spontaneous translation. Sometimes, his father would speak directly to whoever it was; then his boy would run alongside with his translation even as the old man spoke. Sometimes a familiar question would be asked which had a stock answer already known to him, and the boy would go right ahead and address it.

'I will now take you round,' announced Baba. 'My people are already up. The harmattan cold doesn't worry us much here.' He led the way to the front of the house, closely followed by the boy. At the threshold, he stopped.

'This is my own office,' he said, pointing. 'The huts you see here are for the ones who stay back for long treatment.'

'What is the shortest time someone who is sick in the head has stayed here?' asked Dr Shaban.

'Five or six days,' answered the boy.

'Ask him if he saw some people on the road as he was

coming to this place.' The boy interpreted the question.

'Yes.'

'They are the ones who have stayed here longest. Their condition is no longer serious... but they have decided to stay and farm around here,' explained Baba Obochi. 'Follow me!' He led his guest to the back of the building and across the grounds, to the last row of huts. On sighting them approaching, a bare-chested man who had been grovelling on the sand sprang up and bolted off.

'That one has not agreed to drink his medicine for three days now,' observed the old man, turning to his visitor. 'He is almost well... only that every year when the cold harmattan comes, something enters his head, and then, they bring him back. This is their season...'

As they walked past the door of one of the huts, they heard a female voice screaming curses at another woman who had caused her madness in order to keep their joint husband to herself.

'How are you able to look after so many of them?' wondered Shaban. 'I wonder who else is helping you here?'

'Ah, it is the God in the sky who is doing this work... I am only helping him,' answered Baba through his ever-agile son. 'Also, among the ones who are healed, some of them help me to keep order... Even your man, in his last days, was helping in my office. You too! Even if it is only three days you will stay and watch, you will also help us. We need your own kind of doctor here too!'

Shaban laughed at the teaser and added, 'What do you need white man's medicine for? You are doing very well the way you are... I even hear that some of these sick people come from white man's hospital, after trying there and failing.'

'You are not lying. But we do not know some of the things you know in the white man's way of doing things; and some ways we know, you do not know,' explained Baba

Obochi.

'That is so,' responded Shaban, radiating with warm interest and anticipation.

'In this work, most sicknesses have their roots in the spirit,' went on the old man. 'Only the way of the spirits can cure those ones… For such, the injection you people give only works on the surface. Unless you extract the root of it, the madness will hide inside the person and come out whenever the spirit wants.'

'That is as you say,' agreed the guest.

At that point, Shaban heard someone laughing aloud from the top of a nearby tree. The contorted form of a human being was swinging recklessly around the crown of a palm tree, held on only by a strap of climbing gear.

'You see that one up there? We are allowing him to climb until he gets tired of climbing. When the sun comes overhead, we make him come down for some food and medicine. After that, he goes back again, until normal people are getting ready to go up for the evening wine tapping… then he comes down for the day.'

'It looks like he could fall down and break his neck,' observed Shaban, careful not to be judgmental of Obochi's mode of therapy.

'Leave him. He will not fall,' Obochi assured him. 'It is because you are watching him that he is doing *igwengwe* for you,' came the direct translation. John was not able to find an English equivalent for 'showing off', a problem he only occasionally encountered in translating from Idoma. 'When nobody is looking, he is idle,' he added.

As the boy was busy explaining it in many words, a half-naked, full-breasted girl emerged before Baba, muttering to herself with violent gesticulations.

The next minute, she stopped and abruptly raised her voice; and with her palm, she hit first the ground, then her bare bosom, and resumed her mutterings.

'How many of your patients have died, say, this year?' asked Dr Mshelia, ignoring the distraction.

'This year? None. Since ten years ago, when my father left me with this work, five people have died... one man, four women. I remember each of them very well.'

'Well, people die in every hospital,' observed Dr Mshelia. 'Five in ten years is not a bad loss.'

'It is so, but I want to say most of them died before they came here...' Shaban winced at that, but an explanation soon followed. 'The man had lost much blood in a motor accident... but his people only knew of his broken bone. When I was working on the bone, he died. We did not know this until after. As for the women, one killed herself by chewing devil's mushroom... the others, I could not understand why they died until I asked the oracle. One thing was that they all went mad immediately after giving birth to their first-born. I never saw something like that before!' exclaimed the old man.

'How many days after giving birth did they go mad?'

'A day or two, all of them. What surprised me was that they were all drinking the herbs I have used for many years. The others with the same kind of madness were taking the same treatment and getting well. When the third death happened, I went to dig to the root of it, and I found that they were killed in the spirit long ago.'

'How is that so? I mean, what was the reason?'

'They all had other husbands in the air; the spirits got angry when they delivered children for their husbands who are human beings.'

'That is one of the things I will learn about... when I return here to stay for some weeks.'

At that point the half-naked damsel screamed, as if to draw attention to herself. Baba Obochi approached her, held the front and back of her head, uttered some cold, hard words into her face, and let go. The trio watched until she completely calmed down and went back the way she had come. The inspection round continued.

'Her own case is among the easy ones… only she makes it difficult. She has something to confess, then she will be set free; but she is ashamed of people's faces, so she will not do it…'

'What has she done?' asked Dr Mshelia. 'And how did you know it?'

'A very bad thing,' translated the boy, the best way he could quickly muster English equivalents for his father's answer. The old man had actually used the word for 'abomination' but, in all his resourcefulness in spontaneous interpretation, the boy could not immediately find a better English word to correspondent to it.

'What she needs to do is face the gods of her fathers to confess, and beg for mercy. She abused her mother's bed…' explained Obochi, 'But she continues to deny, swearing false oaths. How can anyone hide such a bad thing from the gods who see and know all things? I cannot help her… It is only where the gods give me way that I can do something.'

'So was it the gods who told you she defiled – abused – her mother's bed?'

'Yes. In some hard cases, we must go and ask… I have a brother who is a fortune-teller. He is the one who helps me in such cases.'

As they made a turn round the farthest hut, they came upon a man whose ankles were locked in heavy fetters of wood. A thick, long chain coiled around his chest and jangled along as he dragged the weight in between the huts. A brawny man, he was sweating so profusely that beads of water cascaded down his bare head. Obochi noticed the expression of agony which came over Shaban's face.

'It has to be so,' he explained. 'Our people have a proverb which says, "He who won't let the small one drop, may find the big one falling out of his hand." This man has run away four times since he was brought here. We search everywhere, we find him… he runs again. And not only that he runs away. As he goes about, he destroys people's things any way he wants. Whenever that thing comes on him, he does terrible things. One time, the evil spirits took him to the place of burial, and commanded him to start digging up dead bodies with his hands…' The more he narrated about the man, the more horrified Shaban looked.

'I want to ask… what do you know about how he used to be, before he became sick?'

'You see him looking big like this,' answered Baba Obochi, 'but in years, he is a small boy. He has gone very far in the secret doing of our fathers. He grew up in the hand of his grandfather, a very powerful man in things of the spirits… Just as I am training my son, that is how his grandfather trained him. He gave some powers to him. We do not see much of that in our days. Elders like me are dying with their secrets…'

'Why is this so?' asked Shaban, not wanting to assume he knew the reason. He could not take his eyes away from the struggling man, who had only advanced a couple of metres. 'Why won't they pass down such secrets to their children and others?' he reiterated.

'You know, don't you? You young men of these days are not ready for it! If we show you some things, they may even end up killing you. Your ways are different. The things you should do to keep such secret powers, you won't do… the acts that are against them, those are the ones you will do… and bring harm on yourselves…'

The poor fellow in fetters continued tugging at his weight, seemingly oblivious of the movements and utterances around him.

'Plain brutal!' muttered Shaban under his breath.

'Ijoni, what did he say?' asked Obochi.

'I was wondering how this man's sickness started,' lied

Shaban, rightly guessing the old man's question.

'It is a sad story...' answered Obochi. 'As I told you, his grandfather gave him a load... which became too heavy for his neck. That man was married. The woman bore from her stomach, nine girls, one boy. In the whole of Idomaland, it is a great worry if you have only girls, girls, girls—'

'Same with my people,' chipped in Shaban. 'Our Bura people say that kind of man has only one child, not ten!'

'Mmm... it is so here, my son,' affirmed Baba. 'The only child who is your own, is the male child; the girls will all go by marriage. But that was not the only problem. The man's wife suddenly became sick in the last pregnancy, and died. The *bomboy* came out with his hand first... To tell it short, the man's grandfathers wanted to kill the woman. She did evil things... Before she stopped breathing, she herself confessed it, in order to be free in dying. She confessed that her husband's dead father and grandfather were standing near her bed. My son, it is said that after rain, it is easy to know which bird owns which footmarks...' Obochi let his son battle with the proverb a little while, then continued. 'The man's wife confessed something that ears should not hear: out of the ten children, none was her husband's own!'

'What?'

'She said she did not know what to do. Her husband was not a man... if he had penis, there was no child in it.'

'So, she went outside to have his children!' added Dr Mshelia.

'Not only that,' resumed Obochi. 'Her husband knew what she was doing; he wanted his shame to be covered by any way at all. Only the gods of his fathers know why they waited for such a long time. Maybe the gods are sometimes like people. When it was girls, girls only, there was no problem; girls grow up and go away to answer another person's name. As for the boy, he is the one to carry forward the family name; but because the boy is not the man's own, his ancestors went and made it known to everybody. Even the spirits do not joke with anything that concerns being a man...'

'Poor man – he didn't have to marry!' remarked Shaban, sighing.

'In which other way can a man hide such a thing?' asked Obochi. 'In Aroji, when you reach the age of being man, you must begin to show that you have man-ness; if not, people will start calling you names. So, the man's trouble started from the day that woman died... The first sign was when he attacked the gravediggers. You know, in Aroji, it is forbidden for a husband to watch when his wife is being buried; but the man escaped from his house and attacked the gravediggers. He said they should give him his wife... do you know why?'

'No!'

'In Aroji, anyone who dies such a death has no ceremony – no coffin, no crying of anybody, at least, not where there are people. In the olden days, such a dead body was thrown into the evil forest. Nowadays, they bury it in a small grave, naked...'

'Kai! Kai! Kai!' exclaimed Shaban, cringing in horror.

'The man said it is a must for him to bury his wife properly. So, at night, he went to find the grave. He just fell on the first fresh grave he saw and began to dig. That's how his madness started.'

'How many years ago?'

'Six years now. He has been here for six years. He has stayed the longest time here.'

'How about the children?'

'They are there. You need to see him together with his *bomboy* whenever he visits. He is a small boy; but where he is, nobody makes mouth about his father—'

'His father?'

'How should I say it? We do not know of another father.'

'The boy has a strong heart.'

'Yes,' agreed Obochi. 'He is the only person that man listens to. Everybody else is his enemy – and he can fight!'

'I see... Is that why he is in chains like that?'

'It is so,' confirmed Obochi. 'Six strong men put those things on him. Your friend, Dezmond Adama, was here at that time. He also used to ask me the kind of questions you are now asking. He did not want us to suffer the man like this... but how will I do?'

'I think my friend is correct, you know. You must have herbs he can drink and then sleep. That way—'

'But that is the problem!' Obochi interrupted, 'He will not open his teeth to drink! And he is not a child we can force to drink... it is by fight we wash his body! That is when he manages to sleep in many days.'

'I want to say something.'

'Say it.'

'Remember, I told you I am happy with how you helped Dezmond.'

'Yes, you said so!'

'I also opened my mind to you, that I came here also to watch how you people treat madness.'

'That is so,' replied Obochi, nodding.

'That means we can work together. See that man in chains? I can give him an injection that can make him sleep by force. That way, his power will come down and he will not be able to fight again. After some days, he can begin to drink your own medicine, if he still needs it.'

'Aha! If you can make his eyes come down, I will like it. Our work is to bring peace to sick people; is it not so, my son?'

'Thank you, Baba! Next time, I will come with my doctor's bag. As you are teaching me your own, I too, will show you some of our own things—'

'But wait-o!' interjected Baba Obochi. 'Is it the kind of injection they pumped into your friend, Dezmond, you are thinking of bringing here? The one that made him look *shukpe-shukpe* like a dying leaf? I don't want that one!' Caught between medical science and a unique learning opportunity to which he had looked forward many years, Dr Mshelia preferred to protect the latter.

'No, Baba. This one is different, just as there are different kinds of madness. My own is an injection that will make him sleep and make him calm; then we can talk with him, and find a way of digging into the root as you said before. When he is asleep, we will remove that big load from his legs… and the chain, of course.'

'What if he begins to fight people again, or even runs away?' asked the boy, on his own account.

'He won't. We will be watching him. If he shows such a sign, we give him another sleeping injection.'

'Ijoni, my son, I know the one you asked him; but what he said back to you, interpret it to me.'

When this was done, Baba Obochi replied, 'Tell him, I do not like many, many injections. That one can bring another sickness to the body. When he comes, he will first try his injection small and see how it works. As for the *odo* on the man's legs, let us leave that one and the chain yet.'

Shaban accepted Obochi's condition. He was building another plank towards attaining the trust he needed for a breakthrough with the old man. He could never have had a more viable opportunity for such a level of involvement, given that traditional healers generally resist what they perceive as the suspicious inroads of Western science. Here was one, at last, who confidently threw open the doors of his practice, having had similar exposures in past years, which in return enriched his own means and methods.

As Shaban mounted his seat in the combi, he gave the

old man a parting shot.

'One question before I go... Other great men like you do not welcome outsiders like me, and I come from a far place. How come your own reaction is different?'

The old man laughed when Ijoni completed the interpretation.

'Let me tell you, I know the benefit. I am learning something. Also, it is only what I want you to see that you will see! Not so?'

Shaban nodded in agreement as he waved Baba Obochi and his son goodbye.

Chapter Twenty-Two

Dr Shaban Mshelia literally glided downhill on his way from his next visit to Dezmond. He was in haste to meet a lunch appointment in the village. Courtesy aside, it was vital for his mission to befriend Dezmond's family and study them. Like Aroji itself, thought Shaban as he slid down the last slope to the foot of the hill, Adam' Ododo is part of the rooted realities with which Dezmond must reconcile, if he is to find peace. The genesis of the man's aggressive phobia is not in America, but right in his father's house…

Adama's household had an early lunch and assembled to see the doctor who brought them new hope from Zaria. A group of women and children arose in welcome as the combi headed down the path that led into Adama's compound. Though they cheered excitedly, the best you could see on the faces of the adults was subdued curiosity. The combi lurched to a sharp stop in the sand, thanks to the boisterous directions of a guide who had been all too willing to help when it had stopped at Ukwo to confirm the way to Adama's house.

'Na here! Na here-o!' yelled the guide, repeatedly banging the dashboard, more for the benefit of the onlookers who might not have noticed his exalted position.

Adama stood up from his hammock-like easy chair, retied his loincloth, and stepped forward to receive his visitor. 'Where is this boy?' he asked, looking all about him. 'Visitor, welcome!' he greeted in Idoma. 'But where has

Akawo disappeared to? I told him the dokto will come any time. Now, look, he is here, and there is nobody to speak for me!'

The exchange of greetings and handshakes were followed by the presentation of kola nuts. The visitor was expected in turn, to ask the older man to share out the nut lobes, according to Aroji custom, but innocently, he pocketed one whole nut, presented one to Mallam Dreba, and began to chew the third one, whole. The host, his household, and the other people gathered, watched with a mixture of amusement and awkwardness, exchanging glances in mute embarrassment. The unnatural stillness of the atmosphere was so obvious that Dr Mshelia sensed that he had done something funny. Must be the kola nut! he ruminated, as he slowed down his chewing. He remembered, now, how a similar reaction arose when he was presented with kola nuts in Baba Obochi's place. 'Now I must ask. The strange ways of these Aroji people!' he muttered. 'For them, this common *goro* is not just for chewing… so much ceremony, like their Igbo neighbours…'

At last, Akawo emerged with half a bowl of clean water. From the sweat beads on his face, he must have walked far for the sparkling clean water.

'Where have you been?' asked his father.

'Mama sent me to fetch drinking water from Teacher's house.'

'Uteriza!' roared Adama. 'Where were you when I was looking for this boy?'

'Oh, Pap'Akawo, forgive me,' pleaded Teriza from the kitchen. 'My mind was in this tomato I'm frying. I did not even know that our guests are already here. Sorry, I sent him to get drinking water to keep for them.'

Dr Mshelia decided it was time to speak, and so, cleared his throat to signal his intention. However, before he could start, Adama Ododo signalled him to wait. Food was on the way.

The rice and chicken stew was set on a low stool, in a separate hut, away from the hungry eyes of the onlookers. Akawo led Dr Mshelia to table but the guest had a different idea. He would be happy to share the meal with the family right where they were seating.

'Tell him we have eaten our own,' Teriza said to Akawo who, in turn, passed on the message.

'Even so,' responded Dr Mshelia, 'I want to eat here. I don't need to hide to eat, as if I am a new wife...'

Everybody laughed when Akawo, himself amused, translated the response.

'If that is how he wants it, take the whole tray and put it in front of him there... and you others whose work is to stand and look, I beg you, move to another place. Allow the visitor to eat freely!'

The crowd shifted away as spontaneously as they had gathered. Three metal bowls were brought in on a white tray, in a corner of which was sandwiched a stainless steel cup, filled with water. When Dr Mshelia uncovered the first, he found a steaming heap of gleaming white rice. The second bowl contained portions of chicken. True to Aroji hospitality custom, the whole chicken had been served, quartered up in huge chunks, leaving out only the entrails, the head, and feet. It was left to the good judgement of the visitor to return as much or as little of the meat as he wished. The third bowl contained palm oil tomato stew, spiced with locust bean, green pepper and the aromatic *ikp'eche*.

Shaban picked one of the bowl covers and helped himself to several spoonfuls. As he did that, he glanced at the chunks of chicken and made a remark to his companion, in Hausa.

'Akawo, tell dokto to please, accepted the food as it is...'

pleaded Mam'Uteriza. 'Rice and meat is what we village people know to be the white man's food… I hope the pepper is not too much.'

'*Haba*, Mama!' protested Shaban, even before Akawo had finished translating. 'This is wonderful food even for a king. What else does a man want?'

'Thank him for what he has said. I am very happy today that somebody like him has eaten food prepared by my hands!'

Shaban smiled in response. Having placed his own helping on the stool, he stuck his spoon in it, and handed his driver a plate cover. 'What are you waiting for, Mallam?… Let's eat together.' The man reluctantly held the plate cover but was not willing to take any food. Shaban, sensing his reason, ignored him. He turned to his host. 'Baba Adama, you eat with me. This is rich enough for six people. I beg, join me.'

'Tell him I've eaten my own. For me, food does not go into my body again. But I just chew and swallow to keep life going.'

As if to agree that life must go on despite their present predicament, Shaban went at the heap of rice with gusto. The sharpness of the spices helped to drive out the residue of harmattan cold in his body. The flavour of locust bean reminded him of *dadawa* sauce back in Zaria. The tangy taste was a savoury departure from the monotony of hotel meals. In front of Dr Mshelia, Akawo squatted. As an act of respect and for convenience, he held the brim of the guest's dish and, with the other hand, continually refilled his cup. The guest had politely objected to this rather cumbersome mode of respect, but to no effect. Mam'Uteriza watched from her kitchen, flattered by the visitor's show of appreciation, but she wondered why the driver was only holding an empty plate cover. The host asked his son why the other man was not participating. In fact, he had now dropped the plate cover altogether. Embarrassed, Shaban again muttered something to his driver. A subdued exchange of words ensued, then stopped as abruptly as it had started.

'If he doesn't want to dip hand in the same plate as his master, Akawo's mother can give him his own,' suggested Adama, who was observing the situation.

'Tell them not to worry about him,' responded Shaban, admiring the deep-fried chicken thigh which he was about to take to his mouth. *'Ina ruwa na?'* he mumbled. He couldn't be bothered!

'Master, why do you worry?' responded the driver. 'I am not eating because I do not know who cut the cock's neck.'

'Oho! Haka ne?' retorted Shaban in Hausa, laughing derisively. 'Is that it? Do you see any place of prostration or minaret around here?'

Mallam Dreba's face held sheer contempt for his *arna*, infidel boss. He seemed to be telling himself, Better to stay hungry but in the law, than touch meat slaughtered, or worse, strangled by the hand of an infidel!

'Look,' Shaban said, in between chewing, 'our work here has not even started, so you better make up your mind. Maybe, you found a Moslem *buka* at Nsukka where to eat, but next time we come, we will be staying here at Aroji... Even now, I can smell palm wine in your breathing. But you want to be sure whether perhaps an imam killed the chicken before you eat!'

Evidently, something had gone awry between the guests, but their hosts thought it wiser not to involve themselves in their cold fight.

Finally, the meal was over. After a reasonable period for allowing the food to settle down, the mother of the home, Mam'Uteriza, picked up her stool and joined the men in her husband's hut.

'My son, dokto,' she said, 'thank you for touching my cooking.'

'Indeed, Akawo, tell him that we are owing him much,' said Adama. 'The day of proper thanking will come... that he is here in Aroji gives us hope. Only the God in the sky can thank him for what he has done for us.'

'Dokto, thank you for helping to bring him home. Here, we can at least be seeing him with our eyes.' She knelt in front of the guest as a mark of gratitude.

'He will be all right,' replied Shaban. 'Almighty God will help us. Please, tell her to stand up.'

At this point, Akawo ran to his mother's hut and brought a fat keg of palm wine which he presented on behalf of his father – to wash down the rice, he explained. Shaban, however, declined the offer, saying he had no space left in his stomach.

'Tell him that this is the real Aroji welcome,' insisted Adama. 'He cannot refuse it. Instead, if his belly is too full now, let him take it with him. Tomorrow, he can bring back the calabash. What can we give him to show our thanks? Nothing! Tell dokto that I stopped climbing palm trees long ago, but I myself tapped this fresh *akro* for him this morning.'

'I do not refuse it, Baba,' replied Shaban, directly addressing Adama, though Akawo kept up the translation. 'We are still in Aroji for some days; there will be another day. For now, let me take a little of it, to show you that I have accepted it. The rest of it, you will please drink it for me.'

As Shaban tipped the keg to his cup, Mallam Dreba's eyes followed his every movement. Even as Akawo was taking back the drink, his eyes trailed him until he disappeared back into the hut.

Dr Mshelia then drew aside Dezmond's parents, with Akawo following, for an exclusive discussion which took over an hour. He concluded by admonishing them not to worry much or lose hope, because such a situation would delay their son's recovery. 'I will stay longer when I come next time,' Dr Mshelia assured Adama, as he rose. 'As I told you, I am satisfied. I am happy that Dezmond is getting better very quickly. This sickness will not come back again.'

Adama also stood up to see him off, with his son walking between him and Shaban.

'When next shall we see you here, dokto?'

'Maybe in two days. I will try... but I have only a week to stay for this first visit. So, if you don't see me, it will be when I return.'

Adama was still clutching the combi door, even when the visitor had settled into his seat and was ready to move off. The old cloud of anxiety reappeared on his aged face muscles as the gallant front of hospitality began to crumble. He was sweating, even in the gentle breeze of the harmattan afternoon. Shaban tapped the dashboard and the driver switched off the engine.

'Does he have a question in his mind?' he asked Akawo. 'We can still talk if he wants.' Akawo turned to his father and asked if he had a question.

'They do not allow us to see Deshimondu. Since they took him up, they allowed me to go in only one time, and it is fourteen days since my son was taken from Olebo to Ampia.'

'How does he get his food, then?'

'His mother's sister goes there with Akawo. But you know these are children; what an adult sees, sitting under a tree, a child cannot see, even from the top. I want to go and see Deshimondu for myself; that way, I myself will know all the things you have told me about how he is; and as his father, I want to tell him certain things. As you can see, my son, I am an old man. My breathing can finish at any time.'

'Well, that is true for all of us. Anyway, Akawo, what have you been telling your father about Dezmond?'

'He refuses to eat,' answered Akawo. 'Even water, he won't drink.'

'He won't touch even the *umu* which he liked drinking when he was small,' added Adama, guessing the question that Akawo was answering. 'And yet, they say he is growing fatter again. And his talking will not stop. He talks and talks.'

Shaban covered his impatience with a grin. 'Baba, just give it a little more time. He'll be okay soon. If you take everything you hear, your own mind will scatter. You know that Dezmond took some strong medicines to make him sleep; the medicine and much sleep can make someone grow fat. And he does nothing... maybe it is a matter of the time. Sometimes he feels like eating a lot. Believe me, he will be all right. Worrying like this will not help him or you. We must go now. When I come back we will talk some more. Until we meet again!'

The combi lurched backward, heaving as it were, and did a spinning U-turn with an exaggerated rattling from its tail.

He would have carried on to no end, if I had allowed him, Shaban ruminated as the Volkswagen engine roared through the vast Ogwugwu Forest and sped along the highway leading through Ukwo market towards the east. 'Poor father! How many broken dreams he must be nursing! How can he understand that he himself is an inducer of his son's aggression. How can he take a rebel such as Dezmond and want to turn him into an alter ego, a projection of his own self. The poor man loves his son so much he wants to pour his life into him What a pity!'

Past Ukwo, the nerve centre of Aroji, the combi bus approached the Aroji–Amra boundary, slowing down to half throttle. Mallam Dreba was manoeuvring round the rows of high ramps and small ditches, grim landmarks from an early phase of Nigeria's civil war.

Finally winding across the last bit of brutally bastardised macadam, the vehicle spurted onto a long stretch of regular tarred road, accelerating fully as if in revenge for lost time. The driver's taciturn concentration and the monotonous rattling of the combi seemed at one with Shaban's contemplations. The old man's afraid to face it, he told himself, recalling Adama's fears about his son's rejection. His sense of fatherhood is killing the poor guy!

The distant view of a valley and the sharp rise to the crest of a hill spurred the driver into charging downhill, and with the momentum, swinging through the valley, then up the other side. One more bend, and there emerged the sign, 'Ubol'Afor', a melting pot of travellers on the north–east axis, a refuelling den for machines and men alike. As always, the highway here was choked with vehicles ranging from taxicabs through ten-ton lorries and commuter buses, to hideous-looking long-haul trucks. A harassing hoard of hawkers weaved in and out of the incessant flood of travellers and yet more hawkers, ready to swarm round their next victim.

The driver meandered through the unmarked space left of the trunk 'A' highway, honking continuously until he got to the Ubol'Eke T-junction. He looked for that turn, and was making to swing over to the left, when Shaban tapped his arm. 'Not that way! Turn right to cut across to Nsukka!' he said. Mallam Dreba remained as dumb as he had been since the vehicle took off from Adama's house.

'There's the motor park! Look right... yes, right there! Turn right!' Shaban shouted, pointing to the obvious landmark.

'Haba!' exclaimed the driver. 'I do not remember this way. Is this the same one we took when we went?' asked the driver in Hausa.

'I don't know. You should know better,' retorted Shaban. 'Or aren't you the driver?'

'I can't understand this one,' Mallam said, throttling at top speed.

'A driver should have a sharper sense of places than you demonstrate,' Shaban snapped in rapid English – one of the rare occasions he spoke to his driver in a language other than Hausa.

'I no know Inglis, *Oga*,' said Mallam Dreba, not the least amused. He did not seem to enjoy the further distancing caused by what he took to be Shaban's sudden switch to a foreign language which he did not understand much.

'Well, if you no know Inglis, you better know your road at least,' continued Shaban in English. 'It's best to take any road one eye-stretch at a time, and ride it as it comes,' he carried on, hardly reckoning with the man he was seemingly addressing.

'*Haba*, masta, I do dreba long tam bipore dem born you!' protested the driver, invoking his many years of driving experience before Shaban was born. Shaban sat up.

'That's the problem with people like you and Adama—'

'Frobelem? Where ze frobelem?' asked Dreba in a shrill tone.

'You've been driving since Henry Ford, so?'

'Masta, no vex. But I know dis woke. You get am your own woke. Me I get am my own, *cikina*! Das all, I get licence. Any tin get tyre I pit drive am. If you sign letter sack me sef, I fit find food tomorrow.'

The combi bumped over the bulging edge of a crater across the dirt road. That welcome signpost again: 'Nnamdi Azikiwe Conference Hotel, 2 Miles'. Shaban heaved a deep sigh as he shifted his gaze to the blurred images of vehicles and people returning from another day's toil. My work here is only just beginning, he mused. We must operate in concrete terms. If words are all that Dezmond has to show for it, then we'll pile them up until something concrete results. We must prove something, something the ordinary Aroji man can reckon with. Otherwise, the man may indeed remain on the hill for ever…

*

Two days later, Ijoni had his ears tuned to the road all morning in eager expectation. As soon as he sighted the now familiar cream-coloured VW Combi bus approaching, he rallied himself to the welcome.

'Good morning, doctor! Welcome, driver!'

He opened the side door and rolled it back enough to squeeze his small frame through. Picking up Dr Mshelia's kit, he jumped out and stepped ahead, leaving Mallam Dreba to his routine chores. He led the guest towards the central block of Olebo, proudly arching the shoulder on which he was swinging the kit.

'Is the Thorazine medicine inside this bag?' asked the little boy, smiling at Dr Mshelia.

'Yes. And other medicines and instruments. You must be a clever boy! You still remember "thorazine". You'll make a good doctor!' Mshelia patted him on the back.

'As if you know!' Ijoni exclaimed, excitedly. 'But our teacher says it takes a very long time to become a doctor.'

'Takes a little longer than others. But if you enter secondary school next year, in eleven years, you can become a doctor, if you study hard. You are twelve now, aren't you?'

'Yes, sir! I know what you want to say!'

'What?' Dr Mshelia asked, smiling at the boy.

'That when I am twenty-three, I will be like you. I want to be curing mad people.'

'Well, yes,' responded Dr Mshelia, still beaming with an understanding smile. 'First, you become a general doctor. After that, you go back to take a special study such as fixing broken bones, or being a children's doctor, or curing mad people.'

'Are those ones still called doctors?'

'Yes. Or consultants in their special area. Don't worry. When the time comes, you will know all that. I think you'll be a good consultant. You'll mix what Baba is teaching you now with what you will learn in university.' Ijoni swung the kit lightly round his trunk and smiled.

'Doctor, thank you for telling me these things. You are giving me a strong heart to become a consultant.'

'Thanks, Johnny! I know you'll be a very good one too.'

Baba Obochi was on his toes, craning his neck to see why it was taking the two so long to get to the block. 'Is his bag so heavy that two of you cannot carry it?' he shouted jokingly to them.

'We're coming, Father!' responded Ijoni.

When Dr Mshelia entered the room, he sat down and brought out an ampule of chlopromazine while carefully explaining to Baba its expected effects. Satisfied, the old man then led him to the hut where his patient lay strapped in chains. With a little cajoling, he was administered the drug. Baba Obochi suggested he be observed for a while even as the man in turn, looked on curiously at his 'visitors'. Not long after, he began to get drowsy.

'I can see! It works like our snake-bite medicine!' observed Baba Obochi. 'It is quick and sharp as a knife. The man is already beginning to sleep!'

'You will see the change in his eyes after three days,' replied Dr Mshelia as he cleansed his hands with a methyl-soaked swab.

'Now, I will show you somebody who is lying down in that hut near my office…' offered Obochi. 'I kept her to be the last one you will see, because that is how your man was when he was brought here. I want you to see what too much injection can do a person.'

Inside the hut lay a lone human figure on a narrow length of mattress, face up, covered with a fine piece of cloth. Her age could not easily be guessed from her appearance. She looked so distended and still that she could have been mistaken for a corpse. Her joints were very tender, and her stomach wall was inflamed like an over-sunned drum membrane. For several minutes, Obochi squatted near her, calling her name repeatedly, without response.

'You can see for yourself…' he remarked, bending to check her eyes. 'This is what those Lagos doctors wanted to do to Dezmond. If he had stayed there for more injections, he would now be looking like this woman. She cannot move. When she tries to move, her whole body shakes like water in a basin.'

Shaban nodded and continued to observe the woman. He took hold of her wrist and checked her pulse. 'What's her name again?' he asked.

'Echeune,' answered Ijoni who was leaning on the door.

'Johnny, move from there so I can have some light,' Shaban instructed. Taking the patient's hand, he gently squeezed it, calling her name very close to her face. She did not even stir. Shaban continued to examine her, pressing her abdominal wall, her lower eyelids, and practically invoking her name as if to call back her spirit. Obochi got up, and, stretching to the edge of the thatched roof, removed a vial from which he poured out some oily paste which he rubbed into the patient's face, massaging it down from her forehead to the neck.

'Help me turn her round,' he said to Dr Mshelia with gestures, then poured out another bit and rubbed it on her bare scalp, on the nape of her neck, and her back. When he finished, he turned her round and laid her on her back.

'Her own problem started at Warri; her husband works with the people who dig petrol. One day, she got up, broke everything in the man's house, and began taking strong medicine into her body. After seven days, her husband brought her home to die. But she will not die again. What I am trying to do is to bring down the power of their Warri medicine.'

'So you think Dezmond also had too much strong medicine?'

'Think?' retorted Obochi, much amused. 'Our people have a saying that you do not ask after someone's family when you can see a corpse on the floor. I did not think,' Obochi continued with emphasis, 'I knew it! But that of Dezmond was different. I will try to explain it in a way that our *taprita* can tell you well. When he came, his skin was as hot as fire, and he was shaking as if cold built a house inside his chest. But he wanted to talk; only every time he opened his mouth, his teeth started knocking together... then all his tongue was drawing out like that of a thirsty dog. That first day, we did not give him any medicine. We said, "Let us watch him." The second day, we went to find out. The gods answered us quickly; they said that Dezmond knows the reason for his madness, and that we should ask him. Sometimes, the gods speak like men who are afraid to say what they know... or maybe, somebody covered their mouths against Dezmond. But Adama, his father, is also a strong man in the secret things of Aroji. He too was running up and down, but he only came back with a proverb: that a man who falls down because his toe hit a stick should not eye the ground where he fell, but the stick. That means the spirit of madness followed Dezmond from home.

'And so it was,' continued the old man, 'that his shivering stopped only after three days. His tongue went back, but it became heavy and he still was not talking. I saw that there was much medicine in his blood. You know, our people say the heart has no bone. His father and mother could not rest... they went about making sacrifices for their son.

'One day, Adama came to tell me a strange dream. In the dream, two groups were fighting a war. Dezmond was in their middle, but nothing touched him. Then Adama saw one man moving slowly to shoot his son. But before the man could shoot, another bigger gun scattered all the fighters and killed many people. In the end, he could not find Dezmond; but when the dead were being counted, they saw him on the ground, covered with blood. Something strange happened as they touched him. He jumped up and stood on his own feet! He had no scratch on his body; the blood was another person's blood. Till today, no seer can explain this strange dream.'

'Strange, indeed,' agreed Shaban, wondering why Dezmond's father had not told him of this dream if it was that important. He waited for Obochi for a while, and then a question came to his mind.

'How about his friends… the group found him in the bush? What happened to them?'

'They used to come, every Ukwo market day, two or three of them. Other young people used to come with Bible to read to him, and sing and clap hands in his hut…'

At that point, Dr Mshelia noticed that Echeune had moved her head somewhat. He stooped and tried to hear her faint muttering. The woman opened her eyes a little, gazed briefly at him, and shut them again, murmuring unintelligibly.

'That is a good sign,' Obochi commented. 'Soon, she is really going to sleep. Let us leave her for now. Next time you come, you will find her talking.' They came out and strolled towards the central block, as they resumed their discussion on Dezmond's condition.

'He began to get well,' continued Obochi, 'after seven days in that condition I told you about. He started becoming a person again; he began to eat normally, and sleep well. Darkness left his face; he became strong and began to walk like a person. But he now talked all the time, always looking for paper and pencil.'

'What things did he talk about?' enquired Shaban.

'I cannot say,' replied Obochi, shaking his head. 'Even Ijoni, with all his schooling, could not tell the head or tail of that kind of English. Myself, I wanted to know all those things he was speaking – I know the importance of that. But he was quarrelling in the white man's language. Some days, he will go into my office and lock himself there.'

'Writing, I believe?' Shaban chipped in.

'Yes. Has he shown you some of his writing?'

'No. But I know he writes a lot.'

'*Igrigi*, writing, to him is like eating food,' observed Obochi.

'When I saw that it was like that, I put plenty of paper for him. That made him busy and gave him peace.'

'I wish I could see what he's been writing,' Shaban thought aloud.

'But you are his friend, are you not? Why not tell him to give you what he is writing?'

'I know,' said Dr Mshelia, hardly addressing the two people before him. 'I've tried… and I'll keep trying. His secret is locked in there, but he does not want anybody to see whatever it is, let alone lay hands on it.'

'I know, even with my blind eyes, that something is there,' said the healer. 'It must be something he wants to hide. When I watch the man digging his head in his papers, I fear the power of those signs! He used to write and write for a long time… He did so every day until his ink dried up—'

'You said you will show me the herbs that you used to boil for him,' Shaban interrupted, in an attempt to change the conversation.

'Yes – when you come back to Aroji. We are just beginning. I will show you much, and tell you the things I am allowed to tell. Let me tell you the truth. I gave him very little medicine, only something to make his body strong. As I told you, too much white man's injection was already worrying him.'

'You said so.'

'To complete Dezmond's story,' concluded Baba Obochi as they returned to the main issue, 'after fourteen days, the man became another man completely! One morning after sunrise, he went to Enumoko stream, far away down there. When he returned, he became his clean, fine self again. I was not able to understand. Dezmond Adama walked to my office, sat down and greeted me by my title. He began to talk to me like anybody else. It was too much, I tell you! But it was not something which only one person saw. One of his age-mates was there that morning. It was he who ran to tell the good news to Adama – but what happened after that? Before his father reached here, the man changed again! This time, he escaped to the forest of the elders. That night, the whole bush was on fire! Nobody does that and goes free! Some people ran there and saw him calling everybody to come and kill animals for themselves. Och'Aroji sent police to catch him and all the other men who were there that were up to the age of sleeping with women. It was the same Dezmond who saved those ones; he told the chief everything.

'I used to go up there to give him medicine, but when they said they were taking him back to white man's hospital, I stopped… in order to give gap as I did when he came at first. That is how it happened.'

'Thank you very much, Baba. Now I have the full story from the time I saw him in Lagos. This is just the beginning of our working together. As I told you, this visit is just to come and see the ground, before I come for the proper long stay.'

'Let God agree,' replied Obochi, 'for that time to come.'

Shaban slouched on the seat as the combi cruised through the narrow avenue of fruit trees which led out of Olebo, across Aroji, to Ampia Hill. With the morning breeze soothing his face with its freshness, he found thoughts of Dezmond fleeting through his mind, even as the driver pressed harder on his accelerator pedal to get to his destination, which was just a teasing five miles away.

Madman – madness – how facile! he thought. The simple mind sees life in its naked form. Who's in position to say who's mad? The ones still wearing their clothes? These people insist that their son walked home a madman. He has been through the expert, Baba Obochi; then comes another doctor of madness. Or so they think... When the day comes, who will accept a clean bill of sanity? To them, it would be like saying a medical certificate clears a leper of the stigma of stubby hands and feet. His whole clan looked upon him as their deliverer from centuries of poverty and despair. Then he comes trekking home, empty-handed, only full of big words, even from the land of plenty. Their elders say that he who has no male dog uses a bitch for hunting. Who knows? His pages of *igrigi* may yet become the key to his locked-up dream.

The combi drew up at its usual parking lot at the foot of Ampia Hill. Dr Mshelia hopped down and began the now familiar climb to his friend's place of exile. With every footfall, his thoughts about Dezmond bore down on him as he propelled his weight up the incline.

Chapter Twenty-Three

'How was your night?' asked Dr Shaban Mshelia, with a boyish smile forming on his face.

'Slept like a soaked sponge,' answered Dezmond, eyeing him with suspicion. 'Did you drug my juice?'

'What juice?' asked Shaban. 'Now, confess where you got the Valium?'

'No big deal,' responded Dezmond. 'Bought some myself, way back. But, don't worry! I downed the last two last night. There's none to buy here.'

The two men were sitting on a rusty garden bench under a leafless orange tree just outside the earth cabin. The morning harmattan breeze blended with the sweet scent of the orange in early bloom.

'This place makes me think of the day you'll walk down from here,' remarked Shaban.

'Except for parole, that won't be. Once you've been up in this earth house, there's really no walking down,' explained Dezmond. 'Our folks have a saying that a stream may dry up, but its name sticks; madness may end, but its blank stare stays on.'

'I understand. It's like one man against all the rest.'

In the empty moment that followed, Shaban grabbed a branch of the tree and pulled himself up by his arms, as if to fill the gap in conversation. Several flowers flaked their way down. He dropped with a thud, clapping off the dust on his palms.

'Did you say something?' wondered Dezmond, like a

sleeper just awakened.

'I said when you leave a place like this, it's your word against everybody else's. That's how one gets isolated, but it's not always so. It depends on you. Depends on what you do, what people see.'

'Is it that simple?'

'Maybe. Maybe not,' explained Shaban. 'Depends on the person. The most important thing is oneself. If I have a hold on my mind, but every other person calls me nuts, what does it matter? I know I'm not. And if I have something to show for it, that makes all the difference!'

'Like what?'

'Listen, Dezmond, you're sitting on a book! Get published!'

'Where have you seen a book?'

'You know what I mean!'

'Even if you've seen something, can you imagine an unknown creature with no dime, paying a hungry publisher to be put on the shelves! How far can a man go to prove a point?'

'I don't know,' responded Shaban. 'But you must start somewhere. D'you think Wole Soyinka just woke up one morning and became a Nobel laureate? Look at Chinua Achebe! His *Things Fall Apart* has sold millions in the US alone. It's a prescribed text for many schools!'

'Shaban, you believe these sheets hold some promise, a key into my mind. So you put so much value on them! You may be wrong, you know? I need to warn you. Looks like you're getting insane! How can you come all the way just because you think there's a book in those leaves?'

'Plus, I'm supposed to be your psychiatrist, working with Obochi. I am supposed to take you back with me.'

'Where?'

'Your workplace, of course.'

'Who says?' demanded Dezmond in an aggressive tone.

'Everybody! The University, the Big Wheel, myself,' insisted Shaban. 'You can't stay here and rot away. Plus, you need the salary, man.'

'I'm through with salaries!' he declared with finality, folding his arms in resignation.

'Why d'you say that?'

'Don't patronise me, Shaban! I know it! Where would I be earning a salary now?'

'ABU, of course!' chided Shaban, his brows creasing. 'You know the rules. You were on study fellowship. You fell sick. You remain on your full pay for a half-year, then half-pay after that, for some time... But before it gets to that, you'll be well. You've put the worst of this whole experience behind you already. What remains—'

'Look!' shouted Dezmond, bracing his upper body. 'I go nowhere! I remain here until God knows what happens! This place is safe from hassles. And talking of ABU salary, I have no good reason now for touching their money! In fact, I'm owing them a doctorate certificate,' Dezmond went on in a deliberate, calculated tone.

Shaban saw how futile it was to argue with him or to press on with more persuasions. He became more cautious in order not to alienate him and perhaps unwittingly staunch his self-revelations. Still, one question needed to be put to him for further insight into his thinking.

'I still can't see you condemned to this cold place for... how long?'

Apparently forced out of the doldrums of his own thought, Dezmond came back. 'But I've answered that. It's all the same to me. Whether I remain in this mud bunker or live in the valley or in the north, it's all the same. It is one long parole for the rest of my days! Remember their proverb?'

There was another long hiatus of silence.

'Your parents...' resumed Shaban, changing the subject.

'My father, you mean? I know. Worries his arse off about his big boy, his pride, his hope, and all that. You heard that song when you visited him.'

'What song?'

'Song of aborted Messiahship!' exclaimed Dezmond. 'That's his pain. Invested all his dreams on one bleeding soul.' All tensed up, Dezmond turned his back and poured out his soul in great agitation. Shaban leaned on the tree and watched. On impulse, he was about to place his arm on Dezmond's shoulder but he resisted it. After some minutes of anguish, Dezmond turned round to face him again. 'You didn't say any of those ordinary things like, "Take it easy, Dez."'

'Of course, I didn't,' responded Shaban, who knew too well where Dezmond was heading. The man loathed being patronised.

'Why didn't you pat me on the back and tell me to cool down... "all will be fine", and stuff like that?'

'I don't know. I actually wanted to do so but, I decided not to, after all. What's the use stopping you from letting off steam?'

'Why?' asked Dezmond vaguely.

'Why?' echoed Shaban, trying to understand the direction of his question. 'Why should I have stopped you?' queried Shaban. 'You have the privilege to get as mad as you wish about your old man. Everyone does, once in a while.'

'Mine's a pain in the neck!'

'He's still your dad. Whatever you call him, you can't go somewhere and exchange him. So you've got to come to terms with him. There's no other way out. Nobody can teach the old man anything new about life. You should understand his problems better than he could ever begin to understand yours. I've given some thought to his situation in all this, and we're talking already. But just now, the more you express your anger, the better for your catharsis, or whatever you call it.'

'That makes sense,' conceded Dezmond. 'What are you up to, yourself?'

'Well, I'm working on the clues you gave me at Yaba. That's how come I told you I've started on your old man. And do I love to hear him unload his anxiety! Except that you say I often provoke much talking.'

'Some kind of word acupuncture, that is!' observed Dezmond, chuckling.

Shaban suddenly drew down the goatskin bag slung on his shoulder. 'Have a look at this,' he said, abruptly pulling out a full imperial cardboard sheet. Dezmond's face gradually smoothened into a smile as recognition dawned on him.

'Eh! How did you come by this portrait?' he asked.

'I studied the man and tried to reconstruct the person behind the mask. Since you can tell who, I guess I've succeeded.'

'Congrats! Now, I begin to understand,' said Dezmond slowly, his eyes fixed on the cardboard, like a child marvelling at his own image on a mirror. Shaban was watching him intently, to observe all the observable details of his reaction.

'You only told me about your poems. You didn't mention that you're also a graphic artist.'

'Not really. I got an unusual inspiration just for this.'

'Great fun! What's the title?' asked Dezmond.

'No title yet. Doesn't really need one. But if I have to give it one now, it would be: *Speaking for Itself.*'

Dezmond held the portrait an arm stretch away from his eyes, in order to view it from a different angle. The model must have sat erect, with his eyes fixed on the horizon. The broad chest indicated that he must have been a tall man. His head had been scraped clean like a farmland awaiting rain. His face looked quizzical, a situation which both exposed and mystified him at the same time. Gazing long at it, you would get the impression of an intense mind of great vision in a haste to come to grips with the foreground of the portrait. Yet, his level gaze did not exactly lose sight of the distant horizon.

'I read conflict in here,' remarked Dezmond, still studying it. 'Your man is abreast of his terrain. At the same time, his mind is in the distant unknown.'

'That's important for his therapy,' explained the artist. 'Conflict is basic to life. When disorder sets in, it's the conflict which determines the solution to that disorder. I'm glad you immediately picked that out,' observed Dr Mshelia, smiling at his friend's grasp of the portrait. 'Your understanding of what this is, is very important as to where we're going.'

Dezmond nodded. 'Yes, the present is inescapable if we're to link up with tomorrow,' he observed, meditatively. 'The portrait seems to suggest that until one confronts the present, the future may be hindered… But penumbra does lead from darkness to light, doesn't it?'

'Depends,' responded Dr Mshelia, smiling.

'On what?'

'On which direction you're looking at the situation. Whether from the side of light or from that of darkness,' explained Dr Mshelia, still smiling.

Dezmond sat still, examining his portrait, now stretched out on his lap, apparently weighing his friend's comments against his own observations. What an uncommon experience this Shaban is proving to be! he thought. He recalled how, from the very first day he met him in Lagos, he noticed how unusual and different he was from all the rest who had come to probe him. Even as he was escaping from the Island Neuro-Psychiatric Centre, he knew that Dr Mshelia would search him out. Here he was, with an unflinching faith in what his friend had in his hand. And with each visit, thought Dezmond, this equally crazy companion of his had a new trick to unfold.

*

The next day, in the afternoon, Shaban made his last call on the hill for this phase of his visit. He had now become so used to the climb that it seemed much shorter and less taxing on his muscles than the first few times.

The security man hurried to the earth house and unlocked the outer door. The middle door was agape, and through it, Shaban could see the hurricane lantern still burning. He cautiously stepped in and found the occupant deeply engaged in a strange-looking body exercise. He was sitting in the lotus position with his trunk turgidly erect, his face jutting high up in the air, and his index fingers pulling sideways at the corners of his lips. Strewn on the bare floor around his contorted legs were hundreds of foolscap sheets covered with bold writing.

'Yoga of the buccal cavity, or what?' asked Shaban at last, after having observed him for some minutes, expecting that he would suspend his weird exercise on seeing him. He did not look ready for any intruder, though having left the middle door ajar, he seemed to have been expecting a visitor. In the next move, Dezmond loosened his legs, stretched them far apart, and slowly bent his body from the waist, lowering his jaw as he strained himself, with his arms held closely parallel to the floor like the wings of a taxing aeroplane. Shaban wondered, is this an enactment of some gymnastic fantasy? Or is it a test of bodily endurance, as when Fulani youth lash each other as part of their manhood initiation? Or was it just an absurd drama of self-inflicted punishment?

For another ten minutes, the man kept this tortured

posture, at the end of which he began to slowly raise his chest, bringing his arms together by the same count, and finally letting them drop limply in front of him. Shaban felt relieved to see his friend unknotted to a normal person with whom he could better identify. Perhaps the long-awaited explanation would now come from the horse's mouth.

But not yet! Dezmond remained sitting, gazing ahead, utterly passive, his face one inscrutable, plastic mask. Shaban never had an inkling that he ever engaged in any form of yoga, which itself was sufficiently weird and repellent enough to his own sensitivities; but as the exercise went into yet another stage, the intruder apparently became drawn into it. Watching Dezmond so intently, he found himself subconsciously aping some of his movements. He seemed to be pulled by an immanent force which soon gave rise to a higher tempo in his involvement. The thick effluence of carbon dioxide from the lantern further darkened his mind, as there was little or no outlet for it.

Increasingly, Shaban's mind dimmed as asphyxiation set in, and in a fit of dizziness, he staggered and crashed to the floor. He lay there helplessly, oblivious of Dezmond, until his head cleared a little; then, groggily, he arose and groped his way out into the clear hilltop air. The sting of smoke was still lingering in his eyes when Dezmond emerged on the threshold of the outer door. Before Shaban was able to turn, on sensing his movement, Dezmond was into his final act for the day. This time it was a recitation in the well-modulated delivery of an accomplished stage actor.

> When the sun beats straight down, Adunga heads toward Adum-Oko... at high noon when the rays are strongest. A strange man with a secret axe, he mouths his quarrel, both walking and turning. His destination is the horizon as his hot eyes overshoot the

> tallest of palm trees. The women of the market places say Adunga treks beyond Adum... One day, he set out early at dawn, he confessed, to catch the moon! At sundown, he plodded back, empty-handed, a spent ghost of the noontime Adunga, his wild gesticulations and bloodshot eyes, tamed... sobered... Until his heady demons return when the new moon is full and the wheel again is made to spin...

He paused for breath. Shaban sat and listened as he continued.

> One evening, Big Wheel elected to parade his royal person. Any one-man parade causes laughter. More so if it is Big Wheel in person. What was more, he was dangling, naked to his bare buttocks. The lesser demigods followed, doing as their leader. 'An ill-omen!' cried an old man. Some women covered their eyes against this ancient exposure. 'Abomination!' they too screamed. 'A curse on our land! Call the oracle! Let the five elders bury salt of the covenant!' But the virgin priestess was too possessed with sacred wine... So Big Wheel kept running, his followers following... Downstream, the current drew everyone else into a stampede as nobody knew why everybody else was running...
>
> Uphill and down, the sun returned to bed. Aroji merged with the dusk. Silence descended on the land except for the tall voices of benighted wine tappers, the staccato derangement of pestles in mortars, and the great grunts of oil tankers on our hilly highway.

Like a stage player who slips behind the backdrop after delivering his lines, Dezmond eased out of his sudden performance, switching from the declamatory tone to his normal style as he approached his companion.

'Sorry, the place got you choking,' he said, apologising. 'I was occupied with my secret leisure when you invited in yourself.'

'Your signal door was half-open.'

'Yes. I'd told you of my exercises,' he explained.

'Was that a kind of yoga? You almost tore your mouth apart,' teased Dr Mshelia. 'What exactly were you experimenting at?'

'Well, can you ever imagine the strange pastimes of a prisoner? I've got hours to kill, so I try all manner of fantasies. Started as idle fun. Y'know, do a contortion or something, then laugh at yourself later on, when you think of it! Then it began to grow into a systematic routine. But it's perfectly valid, you know. Yesterday, I had to unwind when I heard those zombies jangling their keys.'

'Tell me, how do you unwind?'

Dezmond retraced his steps, opened the outer door wide, then strode inside and blew out the lantern. Shaban waited.

'Unwinding', explained Dezmond as he re-emerged from his earth cabin and sat beside Shaban, 'talks about the stages of flow: you have warm-up, fusing or engagement, then nothingness! You flow up, then settle back down. The second part is when you unwind. Of course, you should know that the ultimate state of flexibility is nirvana. Or what d'you call it – life after life?'

'I don't know. Let's worry about that when we get there! For now, let's try to do more good acts than bad.'

'When did you become a Moslem?' wondered Dezmond.

'No. I adopted "Chrislemism".'

'What? Sounds like one of these hybrid cults.'

Shaban would not be drawn into any spiritual ping-pong. 'Did I distract your exercise?' he asked.

'Not at all. You saw how it was! I'm sure you're aware that it's not really these eyes which see, but the mind's eyes. When you stepped in, I must have attained my target level of flexibility.'

'Dezmond, where's all this big stuff coming from? Did you do TM?'

'Let's forget about TM and guru stuff. I'm able to put my own thing together. Of course, I dabbled in TM and Transactional Analysis. That's the college vogue in the States right now. Have you heard of phrenology?'

Shaban looked blank.

'That was one of my last electives at LCU. We had a white weirdo who specialised in how skull structure correlates with intelligence. I had to bomb out of his crazy course when he came up with some racist bunkum he called "Sign Test Analysis of Lip Thickness as a Constant Variable of Ethnic Intelligence".'

Dr Mshelia was all at sea as Dezmond went on and on. When he finished his anecdotes of crazy happenings in LCU, a long pause followed. As if prompted by the animated chat of the police guards who where watching from a safe distance, the two friends resumed their conversation and stayed at it until the forenoon rays of the sun became too sharp for them to continue sitting outdoors.

⋆

Dezmond stood up from his earthen bed and set to picking up his strewn papers, arranging them by pages.

'D'you know, I was able to flash through one of them,' confessed Shaban, relieved that he now had an opportunity to draw Dezmond into the issue of his writings. 'Sounds like the very bit you recited is the page I skimmed through. You've done some memorising too, I can see!'

'Now there'll be no need to hide them,' lamented Dezmond, apparently to himself. 'I've always been able to protect the sheets each time I hear steps. There'll be no more hiding. The cat's out!'

'Know what, Dez? I don't usually tolerate cats, but I'd love this one! D'you have more of them hiding somewhere in this hole?' Shaban pressed on, taking full advantage of Dezmond's unusual receptivity, to anchor his point. This looked like the moment of epiphany he had desired for Dezmond. He stepped in front of him, toe to toe. 'Listen, friend,' he said emphatically, clasping him by his shoulders. 'I didn't plan to say these many things. But, it looks like today's a day of telling it like it is. You and I know from what point things began to fall apart—'

'No, you don't!' reacted Dezmond sharply, shaking off Shaban's hands. 'How could you have known?'

'Maybe I'm being presumptuous. I'm sorry. I guess I'm just excited. But you know what I'm trying to say.' Dezmond's brows were arched as he stood peering into Shaban's eyes. 'But *you* gave me the clue!' shouted Shaban. 'My main idea of where your vital link lies is in your manuscript and notes! That's where your healing is, and that's what inspires me! That's what drew me out for you! You know I haven't come here for sake of psychiatry or sociology! I'm here for you! Take my word for it. I'll give NAA no rest until your luggage is found. Meanwhile, make hay with what's in your hand!'

'Even then... even then,' intoned Dezmond, looking away from Shaban as he continued to arrange his mixed-up sheets. 'There'll be time. An unfinished work of art is a man naked in his closet. He can't come out like that, even to receive friends. Let the right time come.'

'That's fine by me!' responded Shaban. 'In fact, that's what I've been waiting to hear. I'm glad you're opening up like this on my last visit for now. Nobody else may know who I am to you, or indeed why I took on this project, so to speak. But we do, you and I. We know, don't we, that for all the chlopromazines and herbs and barks, your full recovery depends on how well you exorcise your tensions, as you rightly put it. You remember how this idea came to me first as a guess. And it grew stronger as I tried it out. Dez, I believe this moment is the right time to tell you this. My insight has developed into a vision that has driven me to get hooked to your complete recovery. Even Prof. Gavel does not know my hidden agenda. The Obochi experience is just on the side, an attractive cover, if you like...

'Dez, I have faith in you. I'm convinced the breakthrough you've been desiring is in your hand. I want you to open up and stretch it out! I've not spoken out all along because everything has its right time. I was waiting for an indication from you that you're ready to hear me and to accept the push. I know you are a very private person, plus, I don't like patronising people either, no matter who it is I'm dealing with. This project is so important, so exciting to me, I've been careful that it does not backfire on my face. This is the moment, Dezmond! The Creator has caused our paths to cross so that your destiny and mine will shine at this point. Every experience in this orbit has a purpose in the divine plan. That's how, for instance, I see the disappearance of your manuscript! We may or may never find it. But good a thing, you've since started writing again. And, look at the details of how we got to meet at INC, and how, in fact, our paths had crossed way back at ABU and so on! All these cannot be coincidental, I tell you!'

'You asked me to begin again, remember? It was on a last visit like this,' recalled Dezmond in a nostalgic tone.

'And the note you sent me said you started writing that very night! Looking at those sheets, you've done much work. If the zeal of writing one poem can sometimes drive me so much that I'm unable to concentrate on anything else, then your book will pursue you to the end! Dez, I've spoken much. My mission with you, no matter how it takes, is to catalyse your first book, to midwife your recovery; I have great faith in what's in your hand.'

'Maybe,' responded Dezmond non-committedly, shrugging his shoulders as he paced round and round. He had turned his back to Shaban even as the conversation unrolled. But he listened all the same, weighing every statement, every challenge. His thoughts seemed to traverse vast spaces and time zones which could not be impeded by the thick mud walls of his confinement. Shaban's words had scratched a mass of pain inside him which he had not had the right frame of mind to confront, having been long numbed by psychiatric drugs. For the first time since putting Lake City behind him, at least physically, some new realities of his situation began to simmer in his soul. Shaban's words had jolted him into a different level of sensitivity to his condition. His feeling about those words seemed to be both sweet and bitter, but having taken his time to consider them, he seemed to appreciate Shaban's spirited prompting.

'Maybe I should say this,' Dezmond continued, having paused to rearrange his thoughts. 'You're overrating something which is scattered and incoherent, y'know?' He punctuated his statement with wild, long-armed gestures which seemed to encompass the whole floor. 'You may have a dream. But it could turn out to be just another dream. You may just end up with nothing but the garbage of idleness. Don't misunderstand me, please! I've heard you. But let's caution ourselves all the same.'

He broke his pacing as abruptly as his train of thought, and resumed his harvest of papers as his tired eyes scanned all around the edges of the floor. 'You woke me from a trance. I wasn't shocked. Your words were gentle in my ears. But, before we part, let me ask you to clarify something.'

'Surely!' Shaban responded with enthusiasm.

'Now you're talking of a dead past... reviving a dead past. Will one's dream be fulfilled if one joins back one's broken pieces? The future maybe there but this present haunts me. Do you notice how it provokes me even in speech. My mind is agitated so much, I speak differently nowadays. Maybe, like the books I should be writing...' He punctuated his thought with a quiet laugh.

'Friend, we've been through this before. What I've always said is this: the best way to get over your whole setback is to face it squarely, then forget it! If you really want, you're now well able to undertake that personal therapy all by yourself. Of course, life is a linked chain of past, present and future. That link breaks and a man becomes a box of loose nuts and bolts! Each person must keep account of his own linkages as he or she moves along. As for your fears as to what I'm expecting from all this, I see a solid book, not just a describe-yourself composition for a fortune-telling psychiatrist. I dream of a book that makes a point, a work which will mend the past and blend your present with a solid future. That's the vision which, as you rightly said yesterday, is turning me crazy myself! But it's well worth it!'

Dezmond stood at attention, clutching his sheaves to his chest. Those words again, which cut rather deep, unlike the overprotective spirit in which everybody else had been relating to him since he was first hospitalised in Lake City! Maybe this is a sign, he thought, that I am again about to grow out of the sequestered cocoon of a vegetating pupa, into the real world of rugged challenges and victories!

The rarified breeze of the hill had since dispersed the lantern smoke, soothingly swathing Dezmond's abode with a freshness he had not enjoyed since the spring days.

The man yawned. The very manner in which he was now sprawling on his earthen bed showed how exhausted he was. Judging from the lantern that had been left burning all day, he seemed to have worked through the night. He gave another raucous, braying yawn, then he stretched and yielded himself to slumber, placing his head securely on his neatly stacked sheaf of papers.

Dr Shaban Mshelia got up as noiselessly as he could from the squeaky chair and tip-toed his way out. He had a brief chat with the police guards, handed them a slim wad of naira notes, and hurried downhill.

Dezmond Adama was so deeply asleep that when he finally opened his eyes, Ampia Hill was wrapped up in pitch darkness. His awakening unfolded in stages, from the moment in half-sleep when he became conscious of his whereabouts, to the point when he fully came to himself. After three hours of slumber, he experienced that wholesome, refreshing feeling of a well-rested body and soul. His spirit also was alert even as he lay on his back, eyes still closed, with a vague expectation continually bubbling in his heart. He could not immediately identify what was causing him such a ripple of excitement. His thoughts drifted backward to the point when he first lay spreadeagled on his earthen bed. He was not able to identify a cause for this generally good feeling. Could it be the mere satisfaction of a sound rest?

He groped around his table for his ever-faithful matchbox and struck a light. As the lantern's rays dispelled the thick darkness, his eyes immediately caught the heap of papers which had served as his pillow. At that moment it dawned on him that he had been discussing something with Dr Shaban Mshelia when sleep overtook his senses. He opened the nearer door and strode to the exit. The guards had locked up for the night. As he slowly walked back from the door, his very movement triggered his mind into recalling portions of the long, intimate discussion between him and his friend. He began to feel somewhat lonely at the thought that that was Dr Mshelia's last visit for weeks to come. Yet those pleasurable bubbles persisted. Whatever good tidings did he give me, which so sweetly tickle my soul? Dezmond wondered.

He moved to his table, and placed a sheet of paper before him. When he tried to write, his chest began to pound so heavily that he dropped the pen and sat back. Gradually, his memory began to open up. He vividly pictured the sudden entrance of Shaban when he was midstream in his exercise, and the conversation which had ensued, even the sequence of their open-hearted talk, plus the small hard core of their sharing. It suddenly dawned on him that his friend had caused some time-worn scales to drop from his eyes, and led him to a new realisation of himself and his situation. He went on to recall how the evening's encounter had ended with Shaban putting a charge on him. In response, he recalled that he had quietly made a commitment...

That very night, he sat up scribbling until the crack of dawn when the police janitor came to let him out for his new routine of watching the sunrise. Thereafter, he found a system of sleeping for four hours in the day, and writing through the night. Some days, the zeal of his work would be so overwhelming that, for three days in a row, he would turn back even family members who had brought him food. At such times, he depended on fruits, fresh palm wine and the hilltop brooks for sustenance, thanks to the paid assistance of a guard.

Within days of his night-long lantern-burning, even the policemen testified that Dezmond's condition had stabilised and his countenance had become more sober. The rare times he sat amidst them to chat, they discovered how very warm and humorous he could be. Nothing in his utterances pointed to insanity. What baffled them, however, was how he could stay without food for several days and yet remain alive.

Grapevine news about Dezmond's condition floated around Aroji, getting embellished and garnished at each stop as it spread all over the district. The mainstream story was that he had recovered as a result of the visit of the black white man from Zaria, but that he had grown so accustomed to his hill dwelling that he had been permitted to sojourn there. Others said he had refused to leave Ampia for his place of referral, so his visiting expert had abandoned him in frustration. Only the Och'Aroji had a fairly authentic account of the situation, having been briefed by Dr Mshelia before his departure. He had been informed that, with the progress Dezmond had made during the week of his management, referral to Kaduna might no longer be required. However, he had placed him on three weeks of convalescence until he returned to review his condition, and finally take him back to Zaria. Baba Obochi had been mandated to visit him every three days to monitor his progress.

In Dezmond's reasoning, however, his continued incarceration was for no other purpose than to provide him with an opportunity to complete his project. Indeed, he progressively visualised it as a practical test of his stability, a second chance to salvage his name. His morale now became so high that nothing else mattered except the pursuit of his work which gradually expanded and filled up his whole being as the days went by.

Day after day, he was able to sustain this frenzied tempo of action, being forced to lay off only when his bones and flesh could no longer stand the pressure. Even then, he would only permit himself a little respite to recoup enough strength to power him through a renewed assault on a challenge which towered like a colossus before his mind's eye.

Physical fatigue aside, some distractions soon set in,

despite the impregnable outlook of his cast-iron determination and of his place of seclusion. After working at his peak for seven days, a very strange phenomenon occurred. According to Dezmond's own account to Baba Obochi on one of his periodic visits, some impish creatures twice appeared in his cabin. The first time they mounted his desk, squealing with laughter, then hopped and flapped around his ears. Before he could raise an alarm, they had disappeared. The second time, he clearly heard them mocking him in a shrill chorus concerning the countless midnight candles he had burnt at No. 19, Pine Avenue, which had only ended up in thin air. The only measure which could be taken against a recurrence was for the police guards to shift their night post to the entrance of Dezmond's quarters, planting one armed constable right inside the anteroom. For his part, Dezmond resorted to leaving on his lamp even while sleeping. And to improve the ventilation, he unblocked the air-hole of his cabin, burning up the old rag stuffing. These readjustments, coupled with the re-assuring voices of the guards, very much reduced the other-worldly eeriness of his surroundings which curiously enough, he had never noticed until the ugly goblins visited his room.

Another entirely different kind of presence had been assailing Ampia Hill almost daily, before sunrise. However, this did not affect Dezmond, shut off as he was by thick, windowless walls of mud.

Every morning before dawn, Oy'otona would shout his way round the hamlets, streams and groves of Aroji village, all alone. Often, he was sent climbing Ampia Hill, and the message was always the same. His voice would ring out with great vigour and authority, echoed by the thick foliage of palm trees. He marched like an infantry soldier, his eyes fixed ahead, proclaiming his bidding with a command that was beyond his physical age and frame. His movement, even the bulging veins of his neck, portrayed his sense of urgency regarding the business at hand. Sometimes, some village mischief maker would pelt him with clods of earth, or hurl insults at his back. Nothing deterred him. In the face of such provocation, he would often burst into song, marching to its rhythm as he did his rounds.

Since removing the rags from his ventilation hole, Dezmond often heard the plaintive voice of the youngster. At first, he was curious to know who would so regularly climb up the chilly hill, shouting so enthusiastically to the trees and empty old buildings. Within days, he got himself accustomed to this voice as part of the unorchestrated background noises of the dawn hours. The chatter and occasional laughter of the policemen aside, that voice was at least another human presence with which he could identify, unlike the little scrawny gnomes who once sprang upon him out of thin air. Besides, the regular, clockwork timing of Oy'otona's visitations became for Dezmond a means of knowing the hour. He no longer had to wait for the jangling of keys to know that another dawn was creeping by. As a result, whenever Oy'otona stopped going up the hill for two or three days at a time, Dezmond was bound to feel a sense of loss, a vague notion of a missing something. Then suddenly the lad would reappear, belting out his proclamations and challenges well within earshot of the mud house.

One morning, Dezmond decided that he might as well use the time of the lad's distraction as a break period from his work. On hearing Oy'otona's voice, he would immediately leave his table, stretch his body, and walk around his room. As the plaintive cry rang stridently over the hill, Dezmond would sometimes indulge himself by sitting on his bed and straining his ears to capture the lyric of the teenager's oft-repeated chorus:

The blood prevails,
The blood of the Blessed Lamb!
Power to save and heal
As in the olden days
The blood prevails!
No matter what men may say.
The blood of the Lamb prevails!

After singing, Oy'otona would fire his usual salvo for the day and return downhill as free and fulfilled as a newly delivered mother. But, in the night the Spirit was sure to load him yet again.

This stripling of seventeen was to become a thorn in Dezmond's flesh, swayed as he was by the youth's zeal and resilience. Without knowing Oy'otona, he pictured him as a close reflection of the commitment and diligence of his own teenage years. He began to desire to meet this lad some day, that he may behold an image of his own younger days. For a man who had fashioned the art of killing time with weird contortion exercises and long monologues with spiders, it would be a more rewarding treat, perhaps, to hide and sight this curious youth from a closer range, and find out what he was made of.

Oy'otona knew the story of Dezmond Adama, as did anyone who had ears in Aroji. For over a year, he had been engaged in early morning cries all over the village, convinced that he had a divine calling to that kind of evangelism. Even when there was nobody staying on Ampia Hill, he had faithfully kept up his beat in obedience to his explicit command that the good news be preached to *all* creation. To his age-mates who ridiculed him for his manner of shouting at trees, hills and bushes, he would quote Scripture to them, declaring, "'We know that the whole creation has been groaning as in the pains of childbirth... as we, God's children, also are groaning, waiting eagerly for the final redemption of our bodies."'

So, for days with only an occasional break, he would rise from his knees and march out with his message ringing through the pathways of Aroji. Whenever he got to a village square or a market place, he would stop and preach a sermon to an imaginary gathering of souls, which, in his believing eyes, were really present. To those who challenged him and accused him of fanaticism, he would explain that God had warned him against observing the clouds or gauging the wind before sowing. He would then add some of the very words of his Master, '"The wind blows wherever it pleases. You hear its sound but you cannot tell where it comes from, or where it is going..."' He would also add that he was compelled to call his townsmen to repentance, so that God would not hold him responsible, should any of them end up in hell.

Often, on his knees at night, taking stock of the day, Oy'otona would marvel at the boldness with which he always carried out his errands, addressing all kinds of questions and situations. He would then lift up his voice in praise of God whose Spirit alone could have so empowered him in undertaking such daring ventures.

At one point, Dezmond decided that he had had enough of distractions from Oy'otona's visits. His mind reverted fully to the work at hand, as he had purposed to present his first five chapters to Dr Mshelia on his return in nine days' time. He, therefore, switched back to working at full blast, having pushed Oy'otona's persistent distraction to the background. Yet whenever he did not hear the lad for two days, that same sense of vacuum, of something missing, would again sneak back into his spirit.

One such morning, Dezmond found himself poring over some snatches of statements he had scribbled in his jotter. Those snippets had been gathered from a few days of

Oy'otona's messages, for no apparent reason than for idle fun. But this one page of pithy statements and incomplete portions of Bible quotations soon turned into a worrisome whetstone of a kind. For a man who had decided not to read any other thing since he disposed of the newspaper he had bought in the airport, having resolved to write his own book, he felt rather awkward, even glossing over the page of gleanings from a shouting voice. As he dwelled upon them, questions began to build up in his mind. His thoughts went to Bro. Maazi. How he wished he could pick up a phone that moment and talk with him!

Day by day, Dezmond's questions grew in size and this rendered him all the more restless as he strived in vain to push them aside. His pet project now progressed only in spurts and jerks being caught up in unusual false starts and countless blocks every time he attempted to return to it.

The first face-to-face encounter between Dezmond and Oy'otona happened like a comic skit. Having just completed the day's errands, Oy'otona was marching home when, to his surprise, a tall, lanky adult suddenly dropped from a vantage spot on a tree, and accosted him.

'You must stop coming here!'

Startled, the lad starred at him briefly then, regaining his composure, asked him, 'Why, sir?'

'Why not?' he fired back, blocking his path. 'Why d'you keep coming here to worry my soul?'

'"All souls belong to God,"' he quoted. 'That's why Jesus died for all men, including you and myself.'

Dezmond hesitated as the boy watched him intently. 'Why am I here, then,' he asked aggressively, 'if I too belong to God?'

Oy'otona had since learnt that every person to whom the Spirit sent him had his or her own unique manner of handling. He had come with divine insight that Dezmond's kind of thirst would be shown by way of the many questions he would be asking. As the lad gazed at him with compassion, he remembered Gideon, son of Joash, and how he had boldly challenged his Lord in the Book of Judges. Then he immediately saw the wide difference between Gideon and Dezmond and began to think about it.

'I asked you a question,' insisted Dezmond, seeing how the young boy was taking his time.

'Yes. I was thinking of Gideon. Your question reminded me of him. Sir, have you come across him?'

'I like Gideon. Prof. Alvin told me about him. Maazi said he was a bold guy. He challenged God, and all that.'

'He asked the kind of question you have just asked. But then, there is a big difference between you and Gideon. He was a son of God. God was his father. He had a right to ask him any question.'

'I am no less a son of God!' retorted Dezmond. 'After all, God is the father of all men!'

'Sir, I'm sorry, that is not actually so. What most people think is often far from what God has clearly spoken. A man can give birth to a child and he grows up to deny him, cut himself off completely from him, and answer another man's name. Haven't you heard of such a thing before?' Dezmond made no response. 'That's how most people have stayed cut off from God, the way of Adam and Eve. They are sons and daughters of Satan, the opposer. Upon their heads there is a law of sin and destruction. Only the mysterious blood of Jesus has the power to quash that law and free them from Satan's slavery. Sir, you have been here and there because Satan wants it like that. His own occupation and recreation is to kill, to steal and to destroy. But there is a standing offer of redemption to all who choose to come to God through the wonderful blood of our Lord, Jesus. This moment, he says to you, "Come, all you who labour and are weighed down, and I will give you rest!" That rest—'

Dezmond brushed past Oy'otona and headed for his cabin, with the guards trailing a few steps behind. He then stopped abruptly and turned to the youngster, who had also turned his head to watch him beat his brusque retreat.

'I'm sorry, young prophet! You're all too smooth! Too simple! I've heard similar things before. They're all the same! They can't address my need!'

'Sir, the blood of Jesus is the most powerful power in the universe!'

'You make me uncomfortable talking so much about blood. Maazi only prescribed "born again".'

'That is correct, sir,' explained Oy'otona, very gently. 'It is only by the blood of Jesus you get purified and transformed into God's son: born again. After that, you are qualified to call the blood of Jesus into action, provided you are not back into sin. You must first be born again.'

Dezmond turned again, but hesitated, muttering to himself, his face all puckered up.

'Sir, I believe you want to ask another question,' Oy'otona prompted him.

'It's all coming back to me!' he exclaimed. 'Why does this thing keep following me, even to this remote hill in a little village?'

'The hill is nearer heaven where God's help comes from!' quipped the lad, smiling. 'The Lord loves you so much that you have nowhere to hide. Adam and Eve couldn't hide! David could not imagine where anyone could hide from the God with seven eyes! The questions you just asked have been beautifully asked for you by that great servant of the Almighty. He asked God,

> *Where can I go from your Spirit?*
> *Where can I flee from your presence?*
> *If I go up to the heavens, you are there.*

If I make my bed in the depths, you are there.
If I rise on the far side of the sea,
even there your hand will guide me.

But as you can see, David is speaking here again as a son of God, as a friend of God. But, as for you now—'

Dezmond rushed off, shaking his head ruefully. Oy'otona watched him knowingly, satisfied that he had spoken as directed. Only the Spirit of God knows how and when any man gets convinced of his need to turn his life over to God. His heart went out to this long-suffering kinsman of his. And the Spirit seemed to whisper in a still, small voice, 'Not by power, not by might, but by my Spirit.'

Just before Dezmond reached the entrance of his cabin, Oy'otona again shouted to him, this time in Idoma, 'I believe you have other questions you want to ask!'

'How d'you know?' he shouted back in English, interrupting him.

'God told me! It is good you ask them. Our elders say that he who asks about the road will not miss his destination. My brother, do not look down on my age. I have an old friend who teaches me these things. I will come back again day after tomorrow, if you want me to do so.'

Dezmond dived into his cabin and banged the heavy, oak door with a resounding bang which echoed over the hill.

Chapter Twenty-Four

He flung his body at his table, almost crushing it under his weight. He was angry with himself for having wasted quality creative time in what sounded to him as mystic talk. His only consolation was that his curiosity had been satisfied concerning the voice that was daily shattering his morning peace. He resolved that the lad and his antics would no longer divert his mind from the work he had in hand. Moreover, he reasoned, there was this all too familiar ring in the young man's utterances which reminded him of a recent past he wanted to have buried.

Dezmond encouraged himself with the thought that a much older evangelist, Brother Maazi, used to burden his life with similar religious talk until he got tired and copped out. What chance then, did this adventurous teenager think he had? He decided to put aside the morning's encounter. Rearranging his table, he spread out his memory notes and fell upon a virgin sheet of paper. The only time he budged from his crouching position was when his police courier came to deliver a fresh keg of palm wine. That was the beginning of another three days of marathon work, feeding only on wine and water.

The last image that flashed across his mind's eye, before he fell asleep at sunset, was that of himself being led away like a ritual ram, seemingly to a destination unknown. He heard faint echoes of his very last request to an onlooking friend, to continue praying for him. His friend had promised to do so, knowing indeed that there was nothing better he could do for him. This friend had since proved for himself the word which says that the fervent prayer of a man in God's righteousness truly achieves much in every way.

Dezmond woke up, kicking and punching the air, his forehead crowded with beads of sweat. He sprang up, startled. But he was at once relieved to discover that he had only been dreaming...

In the dream, he was standing on a podium in the middle of a magnificent banquet hall, which was beautifully furnished and crammed full with formally attired men and women. It was not clear to him what function it was, or where exactly it was taking place, but his reaction was perhaps one of excitement at being so visible in a gathering like this of the glitterati of some great city. As he turned round in admiration of the scene, he saw a massed orchestra at the far corner of the hall, tuning up or taking position. To his left side on a still higher platform was a long table, decorated with flowers, at which the crème de la crème of the day sat in full array.

Suddenly, from the speakers, a booming voice was heard, apparently concluding a session of questions and answers. After that, as if by some signal, all eyes turned to Dezmond. He looked down at his feet, then lifted his eyes to find a microphone being passed to him by a hand he could not see. Gripped with fear, he hesitated, looking down again at his feet, which were now suddenly bare. As if this was not strange enough, he found himself suddenly clothed in a tuxedo. When, a moment later, he again looked up, the microphone had disappeared and the crowd had melted into nothingness. The whole surrounding turned into a barren landscape of charred tree stumps in the middle of which he saw himself turning round and round like a child lost in the woods. The booming baritone came on again, shaking him out of his confused state. He attempted to run off, only to find his legs tangled up. He was still struggling to get free when he woke up…

He sat up, wiping his sweat with his palm as he tried to survey his surroundings. The dream was so real that he found it hard to believe his eyes. He tried to recollect its details but the more he strained the more futile it proved to be. He drew his lantern closer, turned down the wick, and lay back very gently as if afraid that any emergent memory of the dream might be shaken off by his slightest movement. He closed his eyes in order to cut off every other stimulus, only searching for an anchor to this dream he desperately wanted to reconstruct. Suddenly, he saw a glimpse of the waste land, and some words of the encounter began to come back faintly to him. Among them was one which sounded distinctly like a place name. As he repeated it over and over to himself, it sounded like one of those phrases he used to hear in his favourite Lingala song of the Congo. But he could not establish a definite link.

Malinga… wondered Dezmond, lying still in his mood of recollection. Must be a place name. But where on earth would that be? He kept repeating that sound until something clicked. Now it suddenly dawned on him that he knew an English word that sounded like that. His old headmaster in St Joseph's had the habit of rebuking him and his mates with a similar-sounding word. He remembered that the word had something to do with loitering or lingering about. But he was yet not satisfied. Of all words, why should it be such an obscure one from the days of his childhood pranks that would now crop up? There may be more to this word than I know, reasoned Dezmond. But there was no lexicon within reach except for his old elementary school companion, the *Michael West Dictionary*, which Akawo had since inherited but had recently loaned back to him. Dezmond knew better than to go searching in *Michael West* for such a word.

One thing, however, now stood out clearly in his mind concerning the dream. He felt strongly that he was under some kind of rebuke for not taking up a role that had been reserved for him – a role of honour, obviously, judging by all those men and women of calibre and esteem. He fretted in his effort to rebuild the details of the dream but it was fruitless. He gave up and just lazed away on his bed, feeling empty and hollow.

Not long after he fell asleep, he drifted off back into dreamland. The microphone reappeared, this time, with its head covered in a blood-red foam damper. On looking up, he beheld the microphone cord being lowered from a mountain precipice to a bare valley below. Someone stood astride gesticulating with his hands lifted up. Dezmond saw that it was none other than himself who was in that valley, straining toward the high floating microphone. In a moment, he froze, hearing many voices that sounded like waterfalls breaking over him and over the surrounding waste land of the valley. As the voices went on, numberless trumpets backed them up with a grand flourish, followed by a thunderous ovation which filled the sky. He scanned the firmament in order to see the source of this sound. Then appeared an astounding spectacle. At first a colossal banner streamed across the sky all round him; then it rolled over and became a massive wall of reddish waters swooshing down to overwhelm the entire valley. Yet as those mysterious waters rained on him, he did not feel their contact on his body. He was so dumbstruck that he collapsed in awe, even as an ethereal brilliance flooded the whole environment, transforming the man and everything around him beyond recognition.

As dawn was approaching – Dezmond's normal waking time – his body began to gear up in its accustomed clockwork manner. Between his mind-racking dream and waking, he'd had only three hours' sleep. He arose like a phoenix, doused his face in a bowl of harmattan-chilled water, and turned up the lantern. As soon as he sat down at his work table, something flashed across his face, and he saw himself as if transported back to his study desk in the attic of No. 19, Pine Avenue, Lake City. He sat there transfixed, reviewing, as it were, a reel-to-reel playback of his whole life as far as it could unwind...

All his labour, with the frustrations and futility of decades, uncoiled upon him like a vicious cobra. Suddenly, he sprang up in an attempt to escape from the monster, shouting as he shoved away his table and everything he had heaped on top of it. 'Once is enough! Once is enough!' he screamed. 'One abortion, pain enough!' he screamed repeatedly, as he trampled all over his earthen floor. From among his debris of things, he suddenly picked up a large cardboard sheet, tucked under his arm, and lifted the table back on its feet. When he placed the cardboard on the table, he noticed that it was the portrait which Dr Mshelia had recently presented to him. He gazed at it for some moments and turned it face down on the table. Shaking his head, he grabbed a felt pen and drew a big circle on the sheet. He then searched for his bottle of black Quink and dipping each finger of his right hand in the inkpot, hurriedly shaded the space within the circle. 'This is the biggest "full, final, stop" anybody ever made!' he exclaimed, laughing heartily as he held it up for his own admiration. Having satisfied himself, he fished out a roll of Sellotape from his drawer, stuck the giant sign on the wall over his table, and slouched back to soak in his latest piece of self-expression...

*

Oy'otona ended his normal three-day fast bodily deflated and faint. But in spirit, he was sharp, with his face set like a diamond. The unmistakably still, small, voice that had separated him into the ancient chalk caves of the Enumabia River now led him to the hilly trail of Ampia. From the foot of the hill, he began to extol in song after song the perfect finished work of the blood of Jesus. He would then pause to command the ageless spirits of mountain places, that their ancient gates be lifted up for the King of Kings to enter. He seemed drunk with the spirit of a latter-day Elijah as he raised his voice under an unusual inspiration.

The voice that cries in the wilderness of Aroji!
Prepare the way of the Lord!
Make straight in the forest, a highway for our God!
Every valley shall be lifted up... and every mountain and hill be made low!
The crooked ground shall be made straight and the rough places made plain!
And the glory of the Lord shall be revealed... and all flesh shall see it together, for the mouth of the Lord has spoken...
All flesh is grass!
The grass withers, the flower fades, but the word of our God stands for ever!

It was the same old clarion call, but it went out with a fresh decisiveness and even greater power and urgency. Dezmond shook off his state of inertia as the words ricocheted over the hill, bouncing into his thick-walled cabin. He sprang to his feet and dashed to a spot below his vent, listening intently as Oy'otona bellowed his declarations and prophetic utterances into the wind.

Thus says the Lord to his anointed, whose right hand he holds... to subdue nations before him and loose the loins of kings, to open gates before him...
'I will go before you and level the mountains!

I will break in pieces the doors of bronze and cut asunder the bars of iron!
I will give you the treasure of darkness and hidden riches of secret places, that you may know that it is I, the Lord, the God of Israel, who calls you by your name.
I surnamed you, though you do not know me.
I am the Lord, and there is no other.
There is no God beside me…
I girded you though you do not know me…'

As Oy'otona paused for breath, Dezmond rushed towards the door, but on hearing him resume with a song, he darted back to his listening post and strained his ears in order to catch the lyrics. The more he gleaned from the air, the more he thirsted to hear. Then followed another song about the saving fountain of blood. As Dezmond absorbed it, his whole dream began to unfold to him and gradually, its details began to fit together. He inclined on the wall directly below the vent as Oy'otona launched into yet another song.

How lovely on the mountains are the feet of him who brings good news!
Proclaiming peace, announcing news of gladness,
Proclaiming salvation, and saying to Zion,
'Your God reigns! Your God reigns! Your God reigns!'

He sustained the refrain, triumphantly declaiming it as if to underscore God's sovereignty over the very firmament. The song faded off and he resumed his spirited proclamations as if now propelled by a different kind of inspiration:

Break forth with singing, you waste places of Aroji, for the Lord has comforted his people!
Thus says the Lord to his servant:

'This day have I appointed you, a Jerubbaal.
The mountains shall be made plain before your face, and all the high places of the land!
Before your eyes which I have anointed, their witches and mediums shall flee!
Therefore, set your forehead against them!
Be strong and of good courage!
Speak only the word I have put in your mouth!
Not by power, not by might, but by my Spirit,' says the Lord!

While he was yet listening, Dezmond found himself sliding down the wall. He crumbled on all fours and was thrown prostrate on the floor. Floods of water streamed out of his eyes as if from a broken cistern. The words he had just imbibed now took on the form of lightning flashes which prevailed until he saw himself transparently in its flood of light. Even as he lay sobbing, he sensed that a powerful, yet friendly presence had saturated his room. He finally reached a stage where he completely surrendered himself, flat on the ground, ensconced in an internal dialogue that was broken only by heavy-laden silences.

That night, Dezmond later discovered, he had unwittingly copied down a strange dialogue between himself and the Spirit that had filled his room.

'I know you are a living God... I now accept that you have been speaking to me,' he reported.

'Gideon heard when I spoke. What about you?'

'I have come... Where can I hide? You are omnipresent. Here I am, prostrate...'

'Have you become just a slave, without a will of your own?'

'Joyfully, by my own choice. A free slave! Ransomed by precious blood...'

An altar of ancient stones and totems plastered with caked blood appeared, then rapidly faded into oblivion.

'Not the blood of numberless goats but that of the lamb. This is the choice I have made.'

'Choice... It is very precious in my sight that you speak of choice. I desire all men to get this wisdom, and make the right choice.'

'Maazi said I would eat and drink with you once I open my heart to you.'

'Yes. New bread I give you from this day. New wine I give you. Drink it to overflowing. As for water, the real mountain spring I give, which cannot be fetched by paid hands.'

'That I understand. But God, why did you not finish off Satan so he could not be wreaking all this havoc?'

'My ways are not your ways. Neither are my thoughts. I am the All-in-all. Every situation that comes about gets fitted into my eternal purposes concerning all things. So it is with Satan. He is left to be prince of the earth only for a season. And for a reason. Even then, Jesus got rid of him! On the Cross of Calvary. Satan's purpose is to make your choice free and, therefore, valuable to me, not forced and cheap.'

'Thank you, Father!'

'Receive witness in your heart this day that you are my son... The spirit, the water, and the blood bear witness on earth, and the trinity agrees in one. My anointing is upon you, to proclaim the willing day of the Lord, and his hour of vengeance; to comfort all that mourn; to give them beauty for ashes; the oil of joy for sorrow; the garment of praise for the spirit of heaviness, that they might be called trees of righteousness; the planting of the Lord, that he might be glorified. Arise, shine! For thy light is come, and the glory of the Lord is risen upon you! From this day, I name you a new-covenant Jerubbaal...'

There seemed to be no end to this sweet encounter which lasted so long that Dezmond needed two days of recollection to capture elements of it in his burgeoning jotter. So rapturous was it that, when he considered it days and months later, he was not sure whether it had all happened in his room or in a rarefied heavenly domain. He only found himself awake in the same old mud cabin, bogged further down by a creeping sense of loss and emptiness. But soon there was a deep-seated, unspeakable joy in him as he went over that incredible dialogue and then remembered what had happened up to that point.

He sprang to his feet, so charged with zest and joy that his immediate impulse was to burst through the door and run round the hill and down the valley, shouting out the epiphany he had experienced. As he made for the first door, he stopped abruptly, and after a moment's consideration, turned and paced to his table in slow, measured steps. His face bore the serene stamp of a man lowering a pail into a deep well. Pensively, he pulled out a brand new jotter and slowly began to scribble and scribble. The more he scribbled, the more his thoughts flowed. Within days, he reached a crescendo, at which stage the writing began to run away with itself. The currents of his new-found inspiration swept him along in full strength, and he unleashed himself like a possessed man. It was not long before he found himself sitting on the crest of a wave.

Any moment Dezmond was not writing, he would hunger for the young crier, as if for his necessary food. At last, on the third day, around noon, Oy'otona reappeared on the hilltop, heralded, as always, by a song on the wonder-working power of the holy blood. He had hardly completed his gatecrashing anthem when Dezmond sprang up from his knees, burst through the outer door, and rushed past the unsuspecting guards in the direction of the wind-borne voice of the young prophet.

'Here I am!' he shouted in great relief as he fell on his knees in front of Oy'otona, his arms thrown up in the air. 'I have come! Take Dezmond to the water of burial!'

'Yes, to the water of burial! Then resurrection!' shouted Oy'otona, equally lifting up his eyes and hands. 'For, if anyone is in Christ, he is a new creation! The old is gone; the new has come! Who can be compared to you, Lord, on earth or in heaven? Even among the gods, there is none like you! Your works cannot be compared with any other! For you are great and you do wondrous things! You alone are God, greatly to be feared and worshipped in the assembly of the saints! Justice and judgement inhabit your throne. Mercy and truth go in front of you. Blessed are those who know the sound of your voice, for they shall walk, O Lord, in the light of your countenance! In your name they shall rejoice all their life, and in your righteousness, they shall be exalted.'

Dezmond remained on his knees, silent, his head bowed. Oy'otona laid a hand on his head with the other lifted high, as he sang in worship, *'I ascribe all the greatness to you, God, my Rock. Your work is perfect, and all your ways are just. O God of faithfulness, without injustice, good and upright you are…'*

Pausing for some moments, he brought a second hand to bear on Dezmond's head, and loudly spoke out the words that were bubbling out of the living waters of his bowels. 'The hand of the Lord God is mighty upon you for great exploits… For he has anointed you as his battleaxe, a sharp weapon of war, to break apart many iron bars of bondage, and open blind eyes by preaching the gospel with power from on high… defending the fatherless. The Lord has separated you from birth to be a Nazarene of the new covenant. Therefore, he has bathed you in the precious blood of his son, and healed you of all your diseases! He has ordained you a royal priest and set you over the nations to uproot, to pull down, and to destroy… to build and to plant. His word has he put in your mouth, and thus says he unto you: "Is my word in your mouth not like fire? And so, every one that opposes it shall be as wood before fire! The day of your showing forth draws near when you shall arise and go forth!'"

Oy'otona led Dezmond to the Enumoko stream, made tepid by the noon sun. As they waded through the shallows, he narrated to Dezmond the baptism of Jesus by the hand of his own lowly servant, and how the Holy Spirit, the one whose chief mission is to glorify Jesus, bore witness as to how pleased God was, with the life of the son of man. When they reached the point where the water was waist-high, the young man read some verses from Matthew, chapter three, tucked his slim Bible into his back pocket, then solemnly lowered Dezmond's body into the water. As he lifted him back up, he declared, 'I baptise you, Dezmond Adama…' when Dezmond signalled him to stop.

'No. Not Dezmond. Gideon Adama!' he corrected. 'Dezmond's gone,' he explained further.

'I baptise you, Gideon Adama,' continued Oy'otona, joyfully picking up the prompting, 'in the name of the Father, and of the Son, and of the Holy Spirit. Amen.'

News of the sudden transformation of the incarcerated madman of Ampia spread like a harmattan fire. Yet nobody except the new man, Gideon Adama himself, could really have told the story beyond the physical changes which were evident in and all around him. And his jotter bore ample witness to it.

For days after his death-and-resurrection initiation, he floated in an exclusive new world of excitement and joy beyond description. He would lie down, sit up and kneel down in turns, meditating on his life; and many times, he would melt into tears when he tried to pray a prayer of thanks to God who alone could turn around a life and fill it with such joy and peace that he had never imagined.

Gideon's transformation was so total that he instantly lost interest in all engagements except to study the Bible and other spiritual books which Oy'otona took to him. He would devour them for hours without end, take a meditative walk around the plateau, and return to more study with copious note-making. Now and then, he would sit down with his police guards and steer their conversation towards the serious issues of life which he was discovering by the day. He felt so free that whether by day or by night, he took liberty to now leave his doors unlocked, having given the guards licence to call on him, should any of them desire to enquire on any matter he had shared with them.

After days of visiting him alone, Oy'otona contacted two brethren of Gideon's age with whom he regularly visited Ampia, and they spent many hours studying the Bible, discussing and praying together. Gideon would listen with his every breath and scribble notes as the brethren answered his numerous questions on the rudiments of prayer; the meaning of worship; the ways in which God speaks; being baptised by Jesus in the Holy Spirit; how to handle revelations from his private study; and other such enquiries. Once he had confirmed by direct experiences that God does speak back to his children in prayer, he desired to do nothing else but pray each day and night for long hours which, to him, were not even adequate, as he testified in his notes. However, having discovered that he could deal so directly with the highest heaven, he began to grow in leaps and bounds. He listened all the more in the midst of the brethren, and took his many questions and discoveries to God in a daily interaction which grew into a face-to-face kind of friendly conversation.

Gideon was certain that he had found fulfilment in a life of monastic study, prayer and writing. The prophetic pronouncements upon him were to manifest years later when he had almost forgotten them, except for his diligently kept record, which he occasionally reviewed to keep track of his walk with God.

Meanwhile, word had reached Mam'Uteriza Adama that her son had started a strange, crying church on the mountain. Both her husband and Obochi had brought home the cheering confirmation of her son's miraculous recovery, but it was marred by the now common knowledge that Dezmond had started a hand-clapping and wailing church on the hill.

One day, suddenly, Mam'Uteriza presented her tearful, pitiful self before her son.

'Mama, I'm happy to see your face again,' he said cheerfully, although he encountered a sorrow-filled, stony countenance at the door. 'Come inside!'

'What am I hearing, my son?'

'What are you hearing, Mama?'

'They say you have left our church for a strange group of people! I want to hear it from your own mouth, then I will believe. That's why I'm here this morning. Is it true?'

'Mama, I have not left any church,' explained Gideon as he drew closer to his mother. 'It is only now that I have actually *entered* the church—'

'You mean, all these years,' she interrupted, 'you did not know which side you were facing? How can a man's eyes meet something that belongs to him, and he says he has seen a ghost? I who carried you in this stomach for nine months, have I led you to the bush then? Since when did your mother become blind?'

'I have not said so, Mama. Why not sit down?' pleaded Gideon. 'I thought you came here to ask how I am. Mama, sit down. I have many things to tell you.' He plonked himself down on his earthen bed as if to prompt his mother into taking the chair. She made a move, hesitated, and stood there, eyeing him with much suspicion.

'I have heard how the only talk from your mouth these days is the blood, the blood, and nothing else! What is all this talk about blood? I was rejoicing that my son's illness is finished, only for me to start hearing strange things about you. Dezmond, have you joined the blood drinkers?'

'Please, call me Gideon,' interjected her son, watching her intently. 'The old me is gone. From today, call me Gideon. As for blood drink—'

'Eeeh!' exclaimed Mam'Uteriza. 'So, it is true? You even changed your name from Dezmond to another one! But that is the name *Sen Josef* gave you when you did baptism. What have you done to yourself, Dezmond, my son? You have wiped your name from the church register!'

'Mama, Dezmond is dead and buried!' He smiled broadly even as his mother placed her palms on her gaping mouth in bewilderment. 'That is what I want to explain, but you refuse to sit down. The Lord has done a great work—'

'Which lord? Which work?' she screamed at him. 'This old me standing here is the very one who brought you out from between my thighs! I have not shown you any other lord than the one in *Sen Josef!* I do not need to hear more. I now see that truly, you have put your finger in my eye!'

She burst into violent tears, and as Gideon moved closer to comfort her, she broke off and stormed her way out of the room. On seeing one of the guards approaching, Gideon strode to the door, bolted it, and went down on his knees...

Chapter Twenty-Five

Dr Shaban Mshelia set out a whole fortnight behind his scheduled time of return to Aroji. Days before the date of travel, he had mentally made that journey several times over. As he settled into his usual front seat in the combi bus, his mind's eye surveyed the whole seven-hundred-kilometre space between Zaria and Aroji. What a long haul! How he wished he could find himself suddenly swept off the ground and dropped at Aroji! But he soon reconciled with the familiar rattling of the VW engine.

Almost every half-hour, he urged his driver to press on harder. In order to save on time, enough snacks had been packed for the trip. Except for refuelling at Lafia, and for the two times the driver asked to refresh himself by stepping out for a short leg-stretch, there was no break in the journey. Still, for all the haste, Aroji did not come within radar until it began to get dark, too late to even stop at the palace, let alone attempt to climb Ampia Hill. Dr Mshelia, therefore, decided to head straight for Nsukka, secure a good rest at The Zik Conference Motel, and return to his mission the next morning, refreshed.

The front office clerk gazed at the completed check-in form and welcomed the guest yet again, only more intently this time. 'Sir, are you Dr Mshelia?' he asked.

'Yes, of course. Why?'

'Well, you know, sometimes the big men send somebody to check in for them,' explained the clerk.

'I'm not that big yet!' quipped the guest.

The clerk laughed as he searched in his drawer. 'Your room key, sir. And a note from Dr Otonti.'

Dr Mshelia gazed at the personal card of Dr Otonti, wondering who this stranger could be, and what tidings could have been awaiting him at Nsukka. On the back of the card a message had been hurriedly scrawled saying,

Colleague Mshelia, ask for me at the Psychiatric Section when you return to town. Any time from 8 a.m. After five, catch me at the UNN Staff Klob.
Otonti.

*

Shaban rolled over on his bed, turned, and reluctantly opened his eyes. He glanced at the door, gazing at it as if to conjure up the determination to jump out and get going. The sharp strip of light across the bottom of the door indicated that the sun had been up long before he awoke. The time was 8.40. As soon as he set eyes on his watch, he remembered Dr Otonti's note. He immediately sprang up and dashed to the bathroom, driven by a certain sense of curiosity.

At the Psychiatric Section, Dr Mshelia met a large, shirtsleeved faculty member panting his way up the stairs. Somehow, he was sure that he had got his man, even as the stranger turned and smiled questioningly at him.

'Dr Otonti?' asked Shaban, smiling back as the stranger hesitated.

'Wrong number, ol' boy!' gasped the large man, heaving himself up the next rung of stairs.

'Sorry, please,' muttered Shaban.

'It's okay. Only, I cannot be Otonti. Point one, he's a bloody Ikwerre fellow. And two, he's never as punctual as I am.'

'Thanks. I've never met him in person so when I saw you, I just thought you might—'

'No matter!' interrupted the man. 'You can wait in his office. Who are you, though?'

'Shaban. Dr Shaban Mshelia, from Zaria.' They stopped to shake each other's hands. 'And, may I have the pleasure?' Shaban added.

'Idika! Professor Idika Ezeka. A freeborn son of Ohafia autonomous kingdom! You are surely a new quantum in this Wawa countryside!' Shaban nodded, amused. 'I guess by the sound of your name you're a Hausaman. Incidentally, during the Biafran War, your people used to be called "Northern vandals"!'

'Well, Mr—'

'Professor!' interrupted the man. 'Prof. Idika, for short. I'm not to be taken for granted. Everybody insists on his proper title these days. Even the chiefs and princes are being upstaged by the high chiefs. Mine is a hard-earned one, never mind these shirtsleeves! This barrel standing before you is a Rhodes Scholar! I took my doctorate at the MIT in Boston, USA! I was chief consultant to the BWBT!'

Shaban smiled sympathetically. He recognised his new acquaintance as one of those deranged geniuses of the war of secession.

'Prof. Idika,' Shaban called.

'My very title! Thank you!'

'What's BWBT?'

'Biafra War Brains Trust,' he announced enthusiastically. 'And, to give you privileged info, I'm writing the definitive book on the civil war. Wait for it! Don't waste your naira on the booklets being hawked about by some chaps who are claiming to be war heroes. Most of them never saw one bit of battle!'

'Prof, what exactly are you writing about?'

'The motivation behind the war machine! As far as Biafran technology is concerned, if our Igbo ingenuity is properly harnessed, Nigeria could jump a whole century in industrial advancement. That's if your people will allow the men with the brains to venture!'

'Well, sir, I wish you the best,' responded Dr Mshelia a trifle impatiently, as they inched down the corridor. The professor carried on about his book until he heard the unmistakably quick, short steps of Dr Otonti on the last flight of the stairs behind them.

'Now, there comes your Otonti!' remarked Prof Idika, turning in the direction of the steps. 'Ol' boy, come and take your guest! Dr Mshelia from our great University of Zauzau! He's been waiting for you. Next time you fail to keep your appointment, I will charge money for taking care of your visitor.'

'Thank you, *dede* Prof! I am late because my old banger ran out of petrol. Besides, I wasn't sure which particular day my guest would show up. I appreciate it, Prof!'

'Thanks for your company, sir. I'll look out for your book!' Shaban shouted to him as he trundled away to his own office.

'Sorry, I'm so late!' said Dr Otonti apologetically. 'But no doubt our tireless humorist here has been good company!'

'Indeed so! I've enjoyed him. But I'm more glad you're here!' Shaban chuckled. 'I've been rather anxious since I got your note. I could hardly sleep!'

'Well, you'll soon know what. My office is just two more doors ahead. Actually, I've expected you since last week. I've kept the parcel for a week but I have no idea what's in it.'

'Oh, thanks!' answered Shaban, still wondering what parcel had been sent to him through a man he had never known. Soon, they swept into the office.

Dr Otonti handed Shaban a large tightly-wrapped package which bore the seal of the Nigeria Airports Authority, Ikeja-Lagos. Shaban's eyes flashed with excitement as he nervously tore it open. Enclosed was a fattish file of typed sheets and a thick jotter on which was pasted a note bearing the name 'Dr Mishelia'. No doubt, this was the long-lost manuscript of Dezmond Adama in which by Shaban's own reckoning, was hidden the key to Dezmond's recovery and breakthrough! He browsed through the forwarding note, and pulled out the big jotter, flipping through its pages, which were all crammed full with writing. Carefully rearranging the contents of the envelope, he hurriedly bid Dr Otonti farewell, and rushed out to the staircase.

*

On entering his room, Dr Mshelia first fell upon the typed sheets, then the handwritten pages, seeking to get a quick snapshot of the mind behind the writings. For the next three hours, he devoured as much of the contents as he could, only occasionally lifting up his eyes to savour an image here or a phrase there, which he considered a significant reflection on the author's subconscious. It was only with Mallam Dreba's persistent rapping at the door that he realised how far advanced the day was. Reluctantly, he broke off his furtive research and came out for the trip back to Aroji. He was bouncing with excitement as he breezed into the waiting combi.

As the bus approached Aroji, Shaban wrapped up the prized parcel and shoved it under his seat. He would have enough trouble containing his own excitement about the recovered writings of Dezmond, without complicating the situation by presenting it in a manner that might shock its owner.

On arrival at the hill, he found his friend with three

policemen. One of them was crouching over a small copy of the Gideons' Bible. When he had recovered from the boisterous drama of two friends reuniting after a long separation, Shaban noticed to his surprise that the doors to both Dez's rooms were wide open. The place was well ordered and all cleaned out; it was full of light and clean air, smelling fresh and wholesome.

The familiar jumbled-up atmosphere, which had been the constant feature of the inner room, was gone; every item was now neatly in its proper place. On the table, he noticed that all the books, magazines and writing materials were neatly stacked up against the wall. He, however, did not recognise his portrait gift, now turned upside down, and serving a different purpose on the wall above the books. He had also expected to see a huge pile of recently written up sheets of paper, but he saw none as his eyes searched carefully all around the room.

The few clothes which Gideon possessed had been washed, folded up, and placed at the head of the earth platform. And at a corner of the wall, plates from his last meal had been washed and arranged face down on a tray. The final impression conveyed by this uncharacteristic orderliness was that the occupant of the earth house was all set to move habitation, or at least to take a long, long trip. So engrossed was Shaban in the transformed setting that he hardly noticed how radiant his friend looked in a dazzling white kaftan, thanks to the vent through which sun rays penetrated the old earth house.

'I've been waiting for you,' explained Gideon.

'You've got tired of the place, no doubt,' observed Shaban.

'I'm free now!' replied Gideon as he reclined at the foot of his bed, utterly relaxed and casual in attitude. 'It's all over, Shaban! I'm going home! I tell you, I'm free indeed.'

As Shaban sat opposite him, studying his every utterance, his every movement, he saw a different Dezmond. He saw a changed man, imbued with deep peace and assurance, a far cry from the much harassed, much twisted, spirit which had ruled him only weeks before. Surely, a dramatic turnaround had taken place in this man which he urgently needed to investigate.

'Something has happened!' prompted Shaban. 'I've missed something!'

'Something happened, yes! A great, wonderful something!' affirmed Gideon, for once, raising his voice in excitement. 'But I wouldn't say you've missed it. Depends on you,' he added thoughtfully. 'It really depends on you.'

'Dezmond, what are you up to?' wondered Shaban, peering at him. 'What's going on?'

'Much! Just let's take it one bit at a time. Then you might share in my secret.'

Even as Gideon was speaking, Shaban noticed that his words flowed from a deep-seated well of confidence and peace which he could not fathom. Has the good news of the parcel perhaps got to him? Shaban wondered.

'To tell the truth,' resumed Gideon, 'I have something to share with you. But how would you begin to understand it?'

'Try me!' responded Shaban. 'I know you have a surprise package up sleeve. I too have one for you! That balances up, fifty–fifty, okay?'

'To confess the truth, I sympathise with you', continued Gideon. Shaban looked somewhat embarrassed. 'You have great charm. And you've been a really committed friend. But I now know that's not what counts. D'you understand?'

'What are you talking about?' asked Shaban, wondering whether he had not been too hasty in assessing his friend as having already recovered.

'Something marvellous has happened which I must get

across to you. After all the psychoanalysis and loads of drugs, I began to wonder, what's his own bag of tricks? But you turned out to be a real encouragement. More than the old man's spiced herbs! You showed great interest in my writing, so much that to you, my recovery was locked in there. You actually made me believe I'd be fully restored only if I knocked up a book. And I really got down to it – only to discover that the book that actually makes great waves in life is not the one I was trying to write!'

'That is, however, a step in the right direction,' remarked Shaban, glancing at the door as if in regret that he had not brought along the parcel. This seemed to him the right moment to pull out his trump card. He could not wait to see the reaction of his friend on sighting his lost and found treasure. That would surely change the direction of the present conversation, thought Shaban.

'Not that,' observed Gideon, noticing Shaban's distraction. His face lit up with eagerness. 'I've made a great, new discovery that's simply out of this world! When it gels, boy, it will publish itself!'

'I'd love to hear about it,' Shaban told Gideon, convinced all the more that the man had suffered a relapse during the weeks of his absence.

'You surely will! I owe it to you, before every other person who must share in it. I myself, I'm just beginning to understand it. But I can't wait to hint you. We've come a long way together. You want me to talk, but can you figure out what I'm trying to tell you? I've not even started.'

'I wish you had! Then, when you finish, I'll give you my own surprise. What's this marvellous thing that's happened to you?'

'Well, God sent one teenage boy up here who turned me the right way up. A miracle happened to me! My life is now transformed! I can't begin to describe it. I'm discovering new things about me, about life, and everything. Each time

I dig into the book, I mean, the Bible…'

Shaban froze on his seat like a garden statue. When he recovered, he felt numb with embarrassment, not knowing how to handle what Gideon was trying to unload on his mind. The most charitable consideration he ever conceded to those in the university's Christian flock who spoke in like manner was to call them lunatic freaks. He now feared that, after all the apparent progress that had been made, this man had only ended up with a different presentation of psychosis, albeit tolerable in kindred circles and concealable under the cloak of pentecostal manifestations.

'Who's this teenager who works wonders?' enquired Shaban, not knowing what next to say. Gideon smiled.

'He's called Oy'otona, the evangelist. When the appointed hour comes, you will meet him. He's left me on my own for three days now. But he'll come.'

'Okay!' exclaimed Shaban, springing impulsively up from his chair with an awkward clap of his hands. 'Time to show you my own package!'

As he stepped towards the door, Gideon called him back in a grave tone, urgently beckoning to him. Rising to meet the confused Shaban halfway, Gideon placed his hands on his shoulders, looking him straight in the eyes. 'Shaban, I already know about your surprise package. The Holy Spirit showed me that you would bring along my missing scroll. He even revealed how you were hiding the parcel under your seat…' Shaban's mouth fell in utter shock. 'Part of the new gifts I'm discovering! It is a thrilling new life I've found!' continued Gideon. 'I'm sorry but I've finished with all the old scripts of my history.'

'What?' shouted Shaban in shock. 'You mean we're going to junk—'

'My friend, it's all over now! I've got the old era buried. That includes every leaf I ever wrote before. I am now a new creature. Old things are become new! I know this, deep in my heart. Every blessed day, He makes me newer as I turn to the Bible with a fresh expectation as to what this God can do! I find that my life has only just begun. What could I have been writing about anyway, except trash?'

'Listen, Dezmond—' Shaban began.

'I'm now *Gideon,*' he announced to Shaban who was still visibly in a state of shock. 'Dezmond is dead and buried! My resurrection name is Gideon... Why don't we sit down so I can begin to tell you my new story? If I owe anybody an explanation, it's you first of all. The Lord will give you understanding.'

Slowly and reluctantly, Shaban stepped back and sat, this time, on the mud platform, beside his friend. With his elbows dug into his thighs, he rested his jaws on his palms and listened pensively to Gideon's testimony, intermittently peering into his eyes...

Chapter Twenty-Six

Gideon's expected final departure from Ampia Hill was postponed for four days on the initiative of Dr Shaban Mshelia. At first, the change in his life, which Gideon himself had described as a radical transformation, was taken by Dr Mshelia as 'a fresh challenge in empirical enquiry into the dynamics of a recuperating mind', as he described it in his diary. The more he heard from his evidently changed friend, the more he questioned, and the more convinced he became that he would revisit the case for onward research and documentation.

For his own part, Gideon welcomed the extension of his date of discharge because it gave him an opportunity to discourse at length about his new birth experience. He recalled with excitement one of the earliest truths he had memorised from his daily scripture study, that 'faith comes by hearing, and hearing, by the word of God'. He therefore made up his mind to remain on the hill for as long as Dr Mshelia had questions to ask. If that is my only sacrifice for the seed of life to get planted in the seeker's heart, so be it, he had told himself.

Each morning, just after Gideon's pre-dawn study and prayers, Shaban would arrive to continue his round of probings. He would watch intently as Gideon spoke with unaccustomed authority and zeal. It was very apparent that in thought, expression and comportment, this was a different Dezmond from the one he had known for almost four months. Shaban regretted that a cassette recorder was not available for him to tape the discussions verbatim. He, therefore, resorted to writing longhand in his diary, filling many pages of the two foregoing months of 1977 with copious notes and scripture quotations from Gideon's mouth. Some days, alone in his hotel room, he would go back to those notes to bring up previously discussed issues which he had found difficult to reason out.

At last, the fourth and penultimate day of Gideon's seclusion dawned. It was time for Shaban to shelve spiritual matters and visit the more mundane concerns of his friend's imminent discharge.

'Well, to be frank, I'm not yet clear about how a living man can become instantly saved,' remarked Shaban that morning. 'But for now, let's try and sort out your rehab.'

'What rehab?' wondered Gideon. 'Who needs rehab? I'm doing just fine, if I get your point.'

'Okay. So, you'll now return to your Institute, won't you?'

'Why? I already told you! Now more than ever I won't return there. Except to go and fulfil all my rightful obligations for bureaucracy's sake.'

'What?'

'I mean, complete their forms for withdrawal of service and things.'

'Are you settling for full-time preaching then?' wondered Shaban. 'What church can support you in this place?'

'The way I understand it, Shaban, looks like God's business has got to be full time. Always... No matter what other thing I'm going to be doing, my Father's work will be full time. I don't know if that makes sense. Yet, we've not even started. Nobody's talking of preaching just yet. I have a long way to go even to get prepared for whatever it pleases the Lord to do with me.'

'Which Bible college are you thinking about, then?'

'If there's any college I need it's first and foremost the

one I call the Quarry Institute of the Holy Spirit.'

'Where's that? Sounds very strange.'

Gideon chuckled as Shaban waited for an answer. 'The Lord is yet to shape me up, deal with my life, and fit me in,' he explained. 'The quarry is about a divine shaping to make me fit into the Master Builder's pattern.'

'I see...' conceded Shaban, rather reluctantly. 'My question remains, who will feed you? When you finally decide to remarry, how will you manage? How would you run a family?'

'My friend, these are genuine concerns. But you need not trouble your heart. Talk of feeding the same one who's been feeding me all my life, will provide. As for your other questions, the Lord is well able to meet my needs according to his will for my life. I shall not fret. In any case, why d'you want me to attempt crossing the river before I get there?'

'Listen, Gideon! Even for all your being born again, you didn't exactly get back into your mother's womb!' exclaimed Shaban, his voice tinged with irritation. 'Nobody will believe you, if you go on talking like this. That's my problem with you right now.'

'I'm not after proving anything to anybody,' retorted Gideon very calmly. 'My healing will publish itself any way the Lord wants. That's okay by me. Whatever people think, I guess, it's left to them. I can't do much about what people may think, can I?' Gideon arched his eyebrows at Shaban as if to drive home his question.

'As far as your folks are concerned, they'll never agree that you're okay... until you go back to putting corn and cassava on their table. Even if you're going to preach down thunder, they'll only say another stage of madness has seized your head.'

Gideon chuckled again, resting his eyes benignly on Shaban's face. 'I understand,' he said, 'and so I don't blame you. When you try reasoning it out, it seems crazy to trust God all the way. But I know what I know. I believe the verse that says, "He that comes to God must believe that he is, and is a rewarder of they who diligently seek him." Well, let me put it like this: I'll engage myself in whatever the Lord directs until He gets me to the stage where we can no longer combine any other work with His. Even then, He will continue to provide.'

Shaban sat, resigned to his friend's well-expressed intention, lost for words to articulate his deep-felt fears. Gideon's confidence still baffled him, despite the barrage of soul-searching questions which had arisen from his many sleepless nights of battling with Gideon's claims on his new birth.

Thinking that Shaban had withdrawn into one of his recent throes of inwardness, Gideon left him alone. Having learnt that spiritual things are foolishness to natural, earth-bound men, he felt rather sympathetic and patient towards his embattled friend. Still, as his mind ranged over their discussions of the previous three days, he began to nurture a hope that these deep, well-reasoned questions of Shaban could not have been for intellectual curiosity alone. He well recalled how unresponsive he used to be to Bro. Maazi's efforts at convincing him about salvation through the blood of Jesus. He concluded that, compared to Dezmond, Shaban had shown a far more receptive attitude to what he had so far heard.

'Well,' gasped Shaban, suddenly breaking the long stretch of silence. 'The other aspect—' He stopped short, glancing at Gideon who lay prone on his bed of earth. 'Is the man asleep?'

'You said, "The other aspect",' responded Gideon, not opening his eyes or shifting his body.

'Okay... Let's now talk about our preparation for taking you back to your people. How about that?'

'Yeah!' he exclaimed springing up to a sitting position.

'Isn't that exciting?'

'Yeah! Going back down the valley!' shouted Gideon. 'I've caught the mountain spirit, I know, but I love my valley folks.'

'I guess, you can say that. I like the poetic sound of it at least.'

'It's more than you can tell,' remarked Gideon, standing up and stepping towards the spot below the air vent. 'I'm the guy who's going down there. I've tasted the rare oxygen of the mountain; I've breathed the freedom in freedom. The valley suggests a depression. Is that what you're trying to appreciate?'

'Something like that, yes.'

'Don't be afraid for me, man! I've gained enough mountain experience that will overcome the valley. The mountain breath remains with me wherever I go.'

'Fair enough,' replied Shaban, as he watched Gideon gazing up at the vent.

'Besides,' continued Gideon, now looking at Shaban, 'I believe you've caught that same spirit. You know, something like a rub-off effect. You should expect it... Now,' he added abruptly after a pause, 'what's the game plan for going back home?'

Shaban then took his time to give Gideon the details of the arrangements for his reabsorption back into regular life, beginning with his immediate community. Part of the plan was that a private audience would be held with Och'Aroji, much to the relief of the royal father and custodian of community peace. Here, Gideon was required to acquit himself to the whole court by speaking impromptu in Idoma language on any given topic. Obochi was to be in attendance alongside Dr Mshelia, being the experts that were believed to have jointly nursed him to sound health. Finally, a royal proclamation would go forth, to confirm and legitimise Gideon's full restoration to normalcy.

The news of their son's second homecoming sent the whole of Odod'ojo clan agog with excitement. Each house rallied round its members in order to ensure that a bumper reception was held for him. The gods of their forefathers had at last opened the way, and in so doing, removed reproach from their faces!

Shaban now took his leave of Ampia, clutching his much prized diary to his chest. He would hurry down, he explained, to complete his final round of consultations and confirmation visits, and be able to return to Nsukka before nightfall.

'Well, Brother Gideon,' he called, offering him a handshake. 'We've come a long, long way!'

'Yes, indeed,' said Gideon, smiling and gripping his hand. 'The Bible says, "The end of a thing is better than its beginning."'

'Makes sense to me… where is that in the book?'

'Ecclesiastes, chapter seven. I believe, verse eight or eighteen.'

'I buy that, indeed,' reasoned Shaban. 'This day is surely better than the day you were brought up and shut in here. Wow! Gideon, this is your last of many nights in this prison! This time tomorrow, you'll be saying goodbye to your earth house!'

'I already did! Except that it's not been a prison, after all. You know, I met my redemption in here. Isn't that what we've been trying to talk about for days? A whole lifetime is not enough to partake of that wonderful eye-opening.'

'Yes. We'll get back to it again soon… I must get cracking now,' Shaban replied, loosening his palm from Gideon's grip. 'No more new writing tonight, okay? Now that you're packed up!' he said as he gave Gideon his final pat on the shoulder.

'No way!' Gideon responded. 'The Holy Spirit would

have us pray all night… And I saw that Jesus often went up the mountain to pray through the night. It is my honour to follow in his footsteps!'

'Right on!' Shaban affirmed as he turned and strode towards the door.

Gideon finally laid down his head in the early twilight. Drained of energy but full of inward quietness and divine assurance regarding his intercessions and petitions, he slept like a well-suckled, well-cuddled baby. His peace was such that makes a young man see a sound vision. And he did…

In that vision, it was as if Shaban had not left after all, but had rather tarried with him. Their vigil over, the two friends were seemingly walking downhill, side by side, discussing an imminent rally. Now they could see a large gathering of human beings, spread over a vast space, as vast as the sea, stretching from the mountainside right down to the belly of the valley:

'You need a fitting mansion,' came the unconnected remark from Gideon's companion.

'What for?' demanded Gideon. 'Is that the thing to talk about right now?'

'"Even foxes have holes,"' he quoted, looking straight ahead. 'Where would you be entertaining the important ones among that crowd yonder?'

'My boyhood hut is intact and made ready. It is enough shelter for a pilgrim. Tell me, rather, about the great rally.'

'Aroji Square is set!' continued Gideon's companion. 'Not one dead leaf! Your age-grade masqueraders are dusting up their masks. A white horse—'

'I can't stomach it!' protested Gideon vehemently.

'What can't you stomach?' asked his companion.

'The horse,' explained Gideon, his face puckered up. 'Who gave them such a bogus idea? Me, mount their horse? What on earth for?'

'But, isn't it going to be your own durbar?' he asked. 'It would be good fun for your people to watch you parade on a white stallion! After all, you're now a prince, nay, a king! You yourself said you

are now reborn a king! Allow your lowly folk to have good fun…'

'What fun?'

'Why?' wondered the companion scowling in mock surprise. 'They'd love to hail their homecoming king on a white stallion!'

'Hail me for what? Not me!' Gideon intoned emphatically, taking another short step as they glided carefully down the rocky slope. 'Do you know what you're saying?'

'What am I saying?' he retorted, freezing his movement but looking straight downhill, as if avoiding the eyes of Gideon. 'I only mean well.'

'A stallion speaks of power, victory, pride. Mounting any horse speaks of one who has made it, a man who has arrived—' argued Gideon.

'But this is your triumphant re-entry into the land of your ancestors,' retorted the other man, interrupting him. 'Or, do you prefer to ride on an ass? An ass speaks of humility, you might agree?' he pressed on.

'That would be sacrilege!' insisted Gideon, resisting the notion. 'Get thee behind me, Satan!'

Gideon turned almost right round himself to see how his friend would take this famous rebuke. But he could not catch his eyes. Not even his face. He then turned his feet back on the stony trail and took another slow step downhill.

He looked far down, and to his shock, the vast sea of heads had suddenly disappeared, leaving a yawning void all the way down to the dark valley. So confused was he that he kept mute, taking one slow step after another, as his companion now stepped along in a strangely eerie, weightless motion. Yet the voice was clearly that of Shaban, even as he pressed home his argument.

'But then, you talked of following in the Master's footsteps,' he continued, giving a deaf ear to Gideon's borrowed rebuke. 'Surely it's okay to ride on a donkey, like your lowly Master.'

'No! I wouldn't even have allowed the rally. Except that the Holy Spirit hinted me He'd reveal the Lord, even glorify him, to those of them who would believe in Him. That's why I'm going.

Otherwise, I'm not for any show—'

'Consider!' interrupted his companion. 'Do you really care for your people's feelings?'

'Go tell them! If their gathering is about a white stallion, they'd better forget it! I don't want any horse or donkey business. And no masks or masquerades, either!'

'How about akro palm wine, fresh and undiluted?' he asked, cocking his head in a taunting manner. 'That one's not brewed by man's hands!'

'No old wine for them, if I had my way,' retorted Gideon. 'But that day is coming. It takes miracle blood for a leopard to have its spots cleansed off. That's the blood of Jesus!' he exclaimed excitedly as he again glanced back at his supposed companion. But to his confusion, he saw him suddenly scurrying away, his cloven feet lifted off the ground, as it were, and his hideously menacing eyes turning for a last stare. That vile-looking, impish face could only have belonged to a fiend, not a human being! Gideon froze in his tracks, shuddering, as he watched the figure disappear into the clouds over Ampia. A chill fell over him as he immediately recalled a similar ugly creature which once broke into his room.

Turning briskly back to his path, his eyes beheld afresh a teeming mass of human beings, swelling by the minute. They had reappeared in the wink of an eye! Gideon stood still, filled with awe, his head bowed in thought. Suddenly, he found himself again lifting up his eyes, and surveying the scene. Before him stretched again an endless sea of heads, standing so close that they looked like still brush spots on a colossal canvas. But then they started moving, somewhat. He could hear their continuous rumblings sweeping across as when the mighty waves of the ocean come roaring in rolls, breaking on the shore line. In the distant background, a huge banner floated gently in the breeze. Gideon strained his eyes, and was able to decipher an inscription in his native Idoma orthography, proclaiming, 'O'jila gi Jisos' – *'Gathered unto Jesus!'*

Instantly filled with boldness, he threw his hands into the air, and in a thunderous voice, began to call out to the massive gathering in his native tongue:

'My people of Aroji! I have glad tidings for you! News of peace and joy have I brought to you, sons and daughters of our red earth! You who have toiled for mere palm kernels all your lives! But God Almighty has sent you today the answer to the curse that seems to lie upon this land and upon your children... You all know about the sacrifice of blood already. For we and our forefathers have been sacrificing animal blood to our gods – ejebi, ima'achi, otugrafu, enyanwu, ojete, ichekpa, ineji, *and all the rest of them. Blood sacrifices, yes! But there is another sacrifice of blood which is perfect and all-powerful! It is the only one that God accepts! It is sacrificed once and for all! And it talks to every situation in this life and in the spirit world. Men and women of my fatherland, listen to my word!'*

An unearthly silence fell upon the mammoth gathering as Gideon seized upon the moment. Standing like an iroko tree, larger than life, he scanned the numberless faces that were lifted up to him. His voice was mysteriously amplified, encompassing the whole surrounding area, echoing in waves over the valley, and far across the distant plains...

On hearing his own voice booming all around, he suddenly leapt up. To his chagrin, he woke up, still belting out the rest of his message as he stood on top of his bed, his fists kicking the calm, silent air of his earth house...

Epilogue

The Sonshyne Voices struck up their recessional song, *a cappella*, to signal the end of the function. The singers clustered around the microphone stands, with a giant banner as a backdrop. Though exquisite in its artwork, and printed in triumphant colours of gold, red and emerald, only in part did the banner depict the glory and charming character of the evening's event.

BENUE HOTEL AUDITORIUM
Saturday, 31st December, 1977
MAIDEN BOOK LAUNCH:
Footprints in the Storm
by Gideon Adama
Shalom!

The festive atmosphere of the hall was heightened by the splash of coloured balloons; potted plants and several vases of fresh flowers; scripture posters; banners of felicitation; and multicoloured bunting. The guests were mostly the friends; old schoolmates and university colleagues; brethren; and members of the author's larger family. On the VIP dais were the Och'Aroji in ceremonial attire; the author's parents, looking mostly bewildered, even in their joy; an executive representative of the publishers; Brother Shaban Mshelia; and Brother Gideon Adama, himself, looking uncharacteristically in tune with the prevailing euphoria of the day. Beside him sat the gospel messenger of the hour, as the MC had introduced him. He conducted the book dedication proper, shortly after a fiery thirty-minute sermon which sent tremors of mixed emotions and reactions through the auditorium. If tearful eyes and trembling knees were to be considered a visible proof of spiritual sorrow, then many a soul must have been thoroughly primed unto lasting repentance. Indeed, one of the elders was so enraptured that he had no words to describe the evening's experience than to call it an earnest of heavenly fellowship.

The guests arose in unison to savour the final benediction song as the soothing balm of its lyric poured forth:

The Lord bless you.
The Lord make his face
To shine upon you.
And be gracious unto you
And be gracious unto you.
The lord lift up his countenance
on you, and give you peace.

But even after the sharing of the valedictory grace, many of the guests seemed reluctant to leave the venue. Apart from those clamouring around the book sales table, there were groups here and there, greeting one another with hugs and kisses and backslappings amidst the righteous *joie de vivre* of a united family of God's people. Now free of straitjacket imposed by public gaze, even the high table was agog, straining and elbowing towards the man of the moment. Gideon stood tall and serene, drinking in the unending stream of excitement. Not to be outdone, a pack of schoolboys burrowed their own way up the dais to receive their own share of new celebrity handshakes. A zealous team of autograph hunters followed suit, jostling their way into the outpouring of people. Gideon Adama had become an instant human lodestone, drawing men, women, the youth, and hordes of inquisitive children up to the high table!

The seemingly unending flood of admirers gradually thinned out, leaving behind a straggling team of four who were waiting patiently for their own turn. A man, woman and two teenagers stood out distinctly, being the only whites remaining behind. Though a trifle uneasy at the typical effusions of African fellow feeling, they could not exactly shut their tamer instincts against the dominant spirit of celebration.

The man and woman were beaming with smiles as they watched the boisterous carryings-on all around them. However, the teenagers could no longer contain themselves, and they began to jump up and down, waving frantically in the air. On sighting white hands flailing over the sea of heads, Gideon became curious. He craned his neck and saw the foursome. He could not believe his eyes! Suddenly he became fidgety and confused, with cold beads of sweat emerging on his disconcerted face. Now perching on the edge of his chair, he shook his head repeatedly and began flicking his eyelids. He wondered if this was some waking dream. Perhaps he had sighted a family of ghosts! Or had he come under a sudden bout of hallucination? He abruptly stopped winking, rubbed his eyes, and sat frozen for a few minutes.

By the time he recovered and arose to take a second look, the first in the advancing train of four had rushed right up to him. Gideon found himself spontaneously opening his arms and sweeping the heavy lad from his feet.

'Incredible! Just can't believe this! Just marvellous!' he kept shouting, lost for breath as he repeatedly hugged and embraced him. 'Junior, of course! This is miraculous! Praise the Lord, Jesus Christ!' The four clustered in front of him, aglow with joy, with Gideon scanning their faces in turns, overflowing with excitement. Within a few seconds, he burst into a fresh round of huggings, backslappings, and the good, old AfroAmerican handshake that Junior had learnt from his old friend and playmate.

'Dear Laura! What a really lovely lady you've grown to be!' exclaimed Gideon, pecking her on the cheek. Penny then stepped forward, hugged him staidly and stepped aside for her husband. 'I'm so overwhelmed, it all feels like a dream!' he commented excitedly. 'But it has to be Jesus! Only he can work such a miracle,' he said, his voice beginning to tremble.

'You're right, Dezmond, er... Gideon,' agreed Prof. David Gordon, as the two men shook hands, then broke into a lingering bear hug after a frigid, clumsy start. 'Your testimony's just wonderful!'

'Professor Gordon is it, in flesh and bone!' exclaimed Gideon excitedly.

'Yes, it's me all right!' he responded, repeatedly patting Gideon on the shoulder.

'Thanks be to God for his wonderful works! His mercies endure for ever! How could I ever have imagined that y'all were sitting right here in this hall?'

'Sure we were!' remarked Penny, looking rejuvenated and even more sprightly than she ever was. She wore a warm, kind smile as she watched Gideon and her husband slapping their palms together several times over. 'We saw it all! It's been simply wonderful! Great!' she added.

'And we enjoyed it all!' added Prof. Gordon. 'Especially the wonderful flow of your Nigerian worship. Never seen such warmth and liberty of expression in God's presence! Penny dear, looks like we're gonna get our local assembly over here to learn one or two things about worship. What d'you guys think?' He chuckled with unusual bonhomie, looking from his wife to Laura, then to Junior.

'Well, Dave, now we've caught the spirit of worship in

Nigeria, I'd say, why don't we just take it along and transfuse it into our own assembly back home?'

'Yes, Dad,' chorused the two teenagers. 'Let's do that!'

'Hey, listen!' Gideon burst in. 'Just what are we standing here doing? It's time to celebrate!' he declared, grabbing the hands of Laura and Junior. Then, as if he suddenly remembered something, he stopped short. 'Wait a minute... I'm so excited, my senses aren't working right. You didn't just drop in straight from the airport, did you?'

'Oh, I know what y'mean,' Penny volunteered, smiling. 'We're checked into this hotel, if that's your problem. Plateau Suite.'

'You mean you're lodged right here in Benue Hotel? And I had no idea?'

'Sure!' answered Junior. 'But it was only this afternoon. They had no room left. I insisted they had to fix us up so, we got their big suite. You can ask Dad. I did the hustling!'

'Righ',' confirmed Prof. Gordon, laughing. 'This young Turk wouldn't take a "no" for an answer! Paid off well, this time! To everyone's benefit!'

They all laughed along as they held hands, bustling and jubilating away to Plateau Suite.

*

'Prof, you pray, please,' prompted Gideon, as the trolley rolled into the suite, stacked up with a dinner which he had covertly ordered.

'You pray, Gideon,' retorted Gordon. 'You're our senior partner in this business, you know. And host, besides.'

'Sure!' exclaimed Mrs Penny Gordon, laughing at the apt joke and smiling expectantly at the host. Laura and Junior had since gone ahead to bow piously over their warm but empty china plates.

'Shall we pray...' Gideon solemnly intoned, stretching

his palms over the trolley. 'Father Almighty, my heart is overfilled with joy...' He paused to swallow a lump in the throat. 'Thank you for this great treat... five of us sitting together at one table, united in love as one family of your kingdom. Thank you, Father, for our miracles of salvation through the precious blood of our redeemer, Jesus Christ! You, indeed, are the only wise God... Your ways are truly past finding out! We praise you for this package of marvellous surprises this day... Lord, my heart is just filled with your wonder! Who can understand your ways, O Lord? For it is you who works within us, both to will and to do your good pleasure! Thank you, Jehovah Jireh, our God who provides, even for this dinner of reunion. We declare that it is blessed and sanctified of you. It will, therefore, be for us, a blessing of continued fellowship with one another, and with you. Lord, let this dinner be a token of the glorious banquet we hope to partake in heaven with you for all eternity. We pray in Jesus's name.'

'Amen!'

A chef and a waiter were at hand to explain the two-choice menu of pounded yam with fresh *giwan ruwa* from the Benue river, or braised *Gembu* steak, garnished with side salad and assorted vegetables, with chilled *zobo rodo* red for the reunion celebration. The Gordon family opted for the shredded chicken pepper soup aperitif, which was so hot that it instantly became the centre of spirited table talk. Everyone had something witty to share. The flow of conversation was such that, several times, three or four persons would find themselves simultaneously launching out, only to get entangled upstream.

'I know what!' Laura shot out when a rare opening cropped up. 'This is a round-table dinner. There's no head. We're all leaders here!'

'I beg to object!' shouted Junior in mock seriousness, thanks probably to some phony board meetings he had watched on television. 'Professor David Gordon is recognised to speak. Any counter-move? Unanimously carried!'

'Then who next, Mr Chairman?' asked Laura when the laughter had subsided.

'Once Daddy gets going,' Junior explained, 'everything will work itself out.'

'Thank you, Junior, for bringing some order into this business luncheon,' commended Prof. Gordon, smiling from one face to the next.

'Now, Dave, what was it you were trying to say when these two leaders started blabbing all at once?' asked Penny.

'Now, what was it, I wonder...' echoed Prof. Gordon, ruminating in his memory, as it were. 'Yes! I was trying to tell you how an old favourite hymn of ours began to make real sense to me only a coupla hours ago.'

'What hymn, then?' asked Penny. 'We had quite a few songs you and I used to croak through in our younger days together, remember?'

'"God works in mysterious ways!"' Dave Gordon began to sing, his face lit up with excitement... '"His wonders to perform",' he added.

'"He plants his footsteps in the sea",' his wife joined in, '"and rides upon the storm"!'

'Wonderful! How very true!' exclaimed Gideon as he and the children began to cheer the duet. 'Did you notice? The Sonshyne's *pièce d'occasion* is similar in spirit to the words you just sang.'

'Now, Dez – beg your pardon, Gideon, what's the French you just wasted?' queried Mrs Gordon, playfully scowling at him.

'Oh, another bit of the old man we're still working on! Forgive my showing off. I mean, the very spirit of those words you guys just sang, was this evening's theme song of The Sonshyne Voices,' explained Gideon.

'"God works in mysterious ways",' re-echoed Prof.

Gordon, this time in a meditative tone. 'I can't figure out now who composed those lines.'

'William Cowper, of course,' answered Penny promptly. 'English poet and letter-writer. Died, I believe, at the turn of the nineteenth century.'

'Mummy's right,' added Laura. 'Hey, Dad, would you like to know something else about Cowper?'

'Sure? What d'you know?' urged her father.

'I read about him. Can't remember exactly where. But at one time, he faced so many terrible hassles, he decided to take his life. First, he took poison. Didn't work! He then wen' over to the Thames and tried jumping in. Somehow, he couldn't dare jump! Next day, he threw himself on a sharp knife and it was the knife that got broken! At last, he tried hanging himself. Still he didn't die! He was found unconscious up there, and brought down. Later, he read the Bible... I guess, the Book of Romans... then he turned his life over to Jesus. Now you know how your favourite song came about!'

'No wonder, then!' exclaimed Prof. Gordon. 'That's a far-out testimony of God's kindness.'

'Great, Laura! To think we've been singing that song before you were born, yet we never knew all that! Thank God! From now on, we'll be singing it with more heart.'

They had almost all put aside their soup bowls and were by now relishing their choices of the main course. Except Junior.

'Tell you what, er... Gideon,' said Prof. Gordon, resuming the small talk after a while. 'Here's why we all agreed with Junior to come on this surprise visit... Well, the credit goes to him, really.'

'Daddy, remember? First thing you said about it was, "Crazy idea!"' teased Laura. Junior was quietly filtering chicken shreds out of his hotpot.

'Yeah, I thought, what a dumb idea for a winter holiday!

Plus, New Year's Day was around the corner. Y'know, it was gonna be our first New Year's day together after those several years the devil was cheating on us. But then, the Holy Spirit went to work! Thank God, he's accomplishing his purposes in all of this... Brother Gideon, I wan'ed that we meet so we'd share our incredible testimonies face to face, to the glory of our great God. Y'know, people of the world talk of burying the hatchet? But for us, the blood of Jesus is perfectly okay. We've got no hatchet or whatever else to bury, do we?'

'No, we don't,' agreed Gideon, thoughtfully shaking his head. 'His blood has cleansed away all our sins, bitterness, guilt... and his grace is indeed sufficient to keep us even to the end.'

'Amen!' responded Laura and Mrs Gordon, in Afro-American tones, clapping their hands.

'Better believe it, Gideon! Your letters started it all,' explained Mrs Gordon. 'The first one you mailed after your miraculous deliverance set me thinking and asking many questions. I asked myself so many searching questions I became restless. It was then I began to confront my old emptiness. I knew way back, I had this haunting feeling of a big hole in my heart. But then, I reckoned it was on account of our broken home I felt so hollow and unfulfilled all those years. Didn't know it was worse than just heart-break syndrome. Didn't know I'd been condemned and was dead in the sight of God! Thank you for those inspired letters! Remember, I'd raise issues in my replies? And you'd take all the trouble to explain everything patiently? That's how, gradually my eyes began to open. My heart began to grasp the truth. Sometimes, Dave, remember I shared this with you sometime... I wept when I meditated on some of those wonderful verses you quoted for me. My God, I never believed such great stuff existed in the Bible or anywhere! Glory be to God!' she concluded in a voice broken with emotion.

'Glory!' echoed her husband as Gideon listened, his hands arched over his plate, with his head resting pensively on his knuckles. Laura and her brother chewed on silently. 'I came across a coupla those letters,' he added. 'They sure were inspiring. Very encouraging, and full of insight! Over time, we began to share them as family treasure, with our Bibles opened alongside.'

'Prof, I know you'll get there, but I can't wait to hear from you how you experienced the new birth,' Gideon prodded him.

'To tell you, when I first heard our kids talk about the incredible changes in their Mum's life, I pooh-poohed it outright. I said to myself, here they come again with this old hassle. But our God is to be feared, I tell you! Next thing I knew, He arranged for my Penny and me to bump into each other on a shuttle flight between LC and – wait for this – Philadelphia!'

'Heh! City of brotherly love!' exclaimed Gideon.

'Yeah!' responded Prof. Gordon. 'Never heard of any man who ever escaped from a determined lioness way up inside a 727!'

'No chance!' growled Penny, assuming the fearsome look of a she-cat. Gideon watched, with a pleasant smile playing on his benign face.

'Well, I encountered a completely transformed Penny,' continued Prof. Gordon. 'She was more beautiful than the day I fell in love with her! Nobody needed to tell me more. It was pretty evident something wonderful had happened to her, right from the inside.'

'Praise God!' gasped Gideon. 'We all now understand.'

'An' y'know what, Dez? Oh, sorry, Gideon,' added Laura. 'It was right there, in the Philadelphia Holiday Inn, Mummy led Daddy into Christ's hand. God answered our prayers during that trip! What's left for Daddy is to completely let go of his ego, so Jesus'll baptise him in the Holy Spirit. Looks like he first wants to read all about it, then listen to all the cassette tapes on it, before he gathers enough faith to submit himself. As for Junior, it's like—'

'Like father, like son!' Penny cut in, laughing to herself.

'How about you and Mummy?' Gideon asked Laura, as his eyes flashed from her to Junior, who seemed all the more preoccupied with his soup bowl. 'You both baptised in the Holy Ghost yet?'

'Well, as Daddy told you, we all read your letters, sometimes, like a Bible study exercise! Then we'd discuss and all that. I didn't have to wait, seeing how real the word of God had got to Mum. The good thing was, she didn't fuss about it. She didn't hassle us or anything. Junior and I saw for ourselves. Then we just decided it was best we joined in the prayer, Bible study, neighbourhood fellowships, and stuff. Both of us made the decision, same day in church! I'm baptised in the Holy Spirit, same as Mummy. But I try to control speaking in other tongues 'cos I don't wanna discourage somebody, or make them think, oh, look, how holy she sounds!'

'I quite understand you,' remarked Gideon, and turned to Dave Junior. 'Junior,' he called, but the lad did not heed. 'Don't you worry, okay?' he said to him all the same. 'All of God's purposes in our lives shall be accomplished, Holy Spirit baptism included.'

'You're right, Gideon,' affirmed Mrs Gordon. 'There's no doubt about that,' she added, yawning covertly. 'We'll share more of the Lord's dealings. Y'know, what we've heard is just a little of the icing on the cake. We've got all of two weeks to enjoy your beautiful country. We hope you'll be able to show us round. We'd like to visit Arojee for the real feel of an African village. And, of course, look in on your mountain-top retreat! We'd like to meet with the new convert groomers, Christ's Fish Smokers, you called them?

Makes sense! Guess fish lasts best when smoked! We hope to also be able to get a general feel of the gospel work around here. If you're free, we plan to have a day's family shut-in with you, maybe on Ampia mountain? And we must visit the place called, Yankaree Game Reserve?'

'Sufficient unto the day…' said Gideon. 'We'll discuss all of that tomorrow after Sunday service. I think we should now thank God for all this, then I'll leave you to rest. It's been a long, long day! Prof?'

'Yeah.'

'Your turn!' prompted Gideon.

Suddenly, all attention shifted to Junior. Bowed over his bowl, he had been sobbing unnoticed. Now he was all but choking. Gideon got up quietly and stepped over to his side, bending down to help him.

'Listen, Junior,' Gideon began, placing his hand gently upon his shoulder. But before he could find the next word, the lad dropped on his knees. Holding unto Gideon's leg he gave full rein to his pent-up remorse, trying not to choke even as he struggled to unburden his heart.

'I'm awfully sorry… I've been that way ever since… for what I did to you. I know the Lord's forgiven me, but I wan' you to know I really am sorry. I've been… I'm glad you didn't die… thank God you pulled through! To think, what would've happened! You'd have ended up in hell-fire… And I too, for being the one who sent you in there…'

As the tension melted down Junior's face in rapid streams, amidst gasps and groans, his old friend stooped to his knees and closely cuddled him, not uttering a word. Dave Gordon, his wife and daughter, rose up as one, and formed a ring around the two, holding each other's hands and praying silently.

Thus did they remain, enmeshed in a bond, having since yielded themselves as living immolations unto loving service. Their solemn heart-whisperings and wordless tears

gradually swelled up, blooming into a kind of ethereal orchestration. Gideon finally pulled up Junior to his feet. The circle opened up, and they too joined in.

Instantaneously, the room was caught up in diverse, heavenly utterances, mingled with songs of angelic quintessence. They stood there hand in hand, with one heart and as one body worshipping together. The angelic euphony finally began to recede. Then, in a clear, modulated voice, Mrs Gordon began to translate the words that had just come out of her husband's mouth.

> 'Thus says the Lord,
> who sees the end from the beginning;
> *"The blood of the lamb has entered your temple*
> *and reconciled you all*
> *before he who sits in the holy throne,*
> *to whose sonship Christ Jesus has delivered you*
> *by his perfect, precious blood.*
> *He is your peace, your only mediator,*
> *having made peace by his priceless blood,*
> *having slain the enemy of peace and love.*
> *Now are you truly brothers and friends,*
> *having been reconciled to God,*
> *and with one another, through him,*
> *to reconcile all people, and all, with him.*
> *I have my ways in your whirlwinds*
> *and in your storms..."*
> Thus says the Lord.'

They stood, bonded in one body and spirit, together absorbing the extraordinary word of comfort just prophesised by the mouth of husband and wife; then spontaneously they broke into a criss-cross of embraces and greetings.

> 'The peace of the Lord be with you!' said one to another.
> 'And with you too!' came the joyful response.
> 'Shalom!' said the other, preferring the Jewish version of the peace salutation.
> 'Shalom!'

'Thank God, tomorrow is another day!' Prof. Gordon reminded everyone, releasing Laura's hand, and to his left, tenderly squeezing his wife's palm. Following the cue, Gideon stepped ahead to the door, his arm resting assuredly on Junior's shoulder.

Quietly they strolled to the lobby of Plateau suite where, one by one, they again hugged Gideon.

'Prof, Penny, Laura, Junior,' Gideon called in one breath, 'have a good night's rest!'

'Goodnight, Gideon!' responded the Gordons in unison.